Think of Earth as [...]
shaped well whose w[...]
climb away from Earth.

Paint the walls of the funnel in zones of different colors to represent the various space traffic control center jurisdictions. The ones nearest Earth are controlled from national centers. The ones further out are watched by seven other centers located in GEO. And the ones in the nearly flat upper part of the funnel are four in number centered on L-4, the Moon, L-5, and a huge "uncontrolled sector". . . Now spin the funnel . . .

Located on the walls of this madly turning multi-colored funnel are marbles spinning around its surface. Some of them are deadly marbles; come close and you'll burn. Others are big and fragile, but massive enough to destroy your ship if you hit one. Still others are ships like your own . . .

Your mission: without coming afoul of any of this, get to the flat tableland on top, then locate and dock to a group of fly-specks called L-5.

Try it on your computer. Good luck.

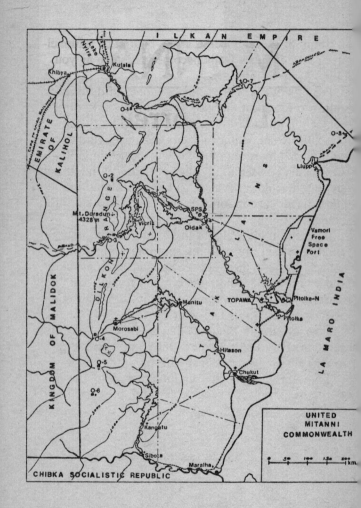

MANNA

Lee Correy

DAW BOOKS, INC.
DONALD A. WOLLHEIM, PUBLISHER

1633 Broadway, New York, NY 10019

To Ellie and Dave

First Printing, January 1984

1 2 3 4 5 6 7 8 9

DAW TRADEMARK REGISTERED
U.S. PAT. OFF. MARCA
REGISTRADA. HECHO EN U.S.A.

PRINTED IN U.S.A.

Contents

CHAPTER 1

Warrior in a Strange Land

Soldiers were marching in the streets. Flags were flying. The schools were closed. Shops and offices were shut.

I hadn't paid enough attention to what I'd read about the United Mitanni Commonwealth. Everyone was taking a week off to celebrate both the fiftieth anniversary of the Battle of Oidak on Christmas Day, 2000, and the forty-ninth anniversary of the founding of the Commonwealth on January first, 2001.

Holiday or not, there I was, and there was no returning.

I walked down the almost empty esplanade of Topawa International Airport with my documents clutched in my hand, looking for customs officers or security police who were common fixtures in every other international airport. But no one was interested in seeing passports. Not wanting to be detained later as an illegal immigrant, I approached a Commonwealth Aerospace Lines employee, recognizable by his uniform.

Unlike his counterparts in New York and Paris, he wore a 25-centimeter dirk on his hip. "Excuse me," I asked deferentially, not wishing to offend an armed citizen in an unknown land, "could you direct me to Passport Control and Customs, please?"

The man noted the bag I carried, and replied, "This is a free country, sir. We don't use such things."

Well, I'd never used a passport to go from California to Arizona . . . or from the United States to Canada, either. If these people wanted to chance terrorists, revolutionaries, and criminals slipping in and out of their successful little country, that was their business. I was here to work for them if they wanted me to.

I found a place to sit down in relative privacy and took the hard copy of the classified ad from "Help Wanted, Aerospace" comm/info net bulletin board. I read it again.

"PILOT, atmosphere and orbit ratings, recent professional military background. Immediate employment. Call collect 144-203-794-1171."

I'd made the call and discovered that Landlimo Corporation headquartered in Topawa, the capital city of the United Mitanni

Commonwealth, was interested enough to foot the bill for airlift to Topawa for an interview. The man called Wahak Teaq who'd interviewed me seemed interested but not sanguine. Personnel types are usually trained to appear that way. I'd agreed to come, but when I tried to learn about Landlimo Corporation, I struck out. It wasn't listed in Standard & Poor's International or any other corporate registry I could get my hands on in the United States.

Folded behind the hard copy of the want ad was the hard copy of Landlimo Corporation's letter of interest informing me to pick up my prepaid ticket at the nearest Commonwealth Aerospace Lines office and to call a specific telecomm number when I reached Topawa.

I punched the number into my wrist phone, hoping somebody would be in the offices of the Landlimo Corporation. A phone robot answered with voice-over the video image of a stylized logo. "This is the office of the Landlimo Corporation. Because of the Unification Holiday, we're closed until Monday, three January, twenty-fifty. Please call us then. The Vamori Free Space Port office is answering the emergency code. Thank you."

The letter of interest didn't give an emergency number.

I asked myself what I was going to do for two days in a strange land where I don't know anyone.

Answer: Find a hotel in Topawa, do some sightseeing, and wait.

I'd rather be in Topawa anyway. Under the circumstances that caused the U.S. Aerospace Force to retire me, I hadn't wanted to spend the holiday season at home in Santa Barbara locked in intellectual combat with my pacifistic, professorial father. He knew more history and always won our arguments between his commitment to non-violence and my own commitment to service in the military forces of my country. He couldn't understand my ulterior motive: going into space in the most advanced equipment available. The fact that I might have to fight didn't bother me.

My mother couldn't care less. If she couldn't manipulate it in a bio-engineering lab, it wasn't part of her world. She never understood the philosophical barriers between my father and me. To a large extent, she never understood me, either, and therefore adopted a detached attitude. *Never* pick a scientist for a mother!

I went looking for a bank or currency exchange booth and discovered there wasn't any. In every country in which I'd travelled, even as a USAF officer, the first thing I did after clearing customs was to exchange whatever type of money I was carrying for the local currency minus an exchange fee for the bank.

But the United Mitanni Commonwealth seemed to care about currency in the same fashion they cared about passports. "We'll accept any money," the ticket seller for the railway into Topawa remarked when I purchased my ducat at his window.

The Terrestrial Almanac and Book of Facts had said nothing about this sort of thing. Neither had Sloane's definitive book on the UMC. In fact, neither reference source mentioned the holidays. I decided books couldn't describe or report on all facets of any nation, much less one as new and developing as this one.

I found the rest room clean and the plumbing working. Eric Hoffer had observed that one could determine the general state of affairs in a country by how well the plumbing worked.

The signs directing me to the railway to downtown Topawa some 20 kilometers west led me to a covered platform. I was a few seconds too late. The train was already moving. The lighted board announced the next train in thirty minutes.

As I watched the train leave, I sensed something I hadn't known since my cadet days in the energy labs of the Academy: the smell of burning coal from the locomotive.

I had trouble believing anyone would *burn* coal. Why not alky-electric or even FotoFuel, I wondered? Then I remembered what Sloane said about the huge bituminous coal fields in the Dilkon Range.

This was like stepping back a hundred years into the twentieth century but without the problems that twenty-first century technology had solved in the meantime. The photos and video of the last century were reflected in the sights that had assaulted me since stepping off the otherwise modern aerospace liner.

I didn't remain alone on the platform for long. Other people gathered to await the next train.

An attractive couple accompanied by a small, stocky barrel of a man with dark hair and a huge, bushy mustache waited about five meters from me. The young woman was armed with the usual short dirk hanging from the girdle resting lightly on her hips, and the mustached man wore a small curved scimitar. But the other young man bore no visible arms. Since everyone in this country seemed to go about armed with those short daggers, he must have just arrived via air.

I couldn't help overhearing their conversation in English, which was the common language of this country, albeit spoken with a different accent, rhythm, and inflection and with vowel shifts that were quite unique.

"Ali, *why* did you do it that way?" the beautiful young woman was saying.

"Vaivan, what recourse did I have?" the young man replied doggedly. "It wouldn't have made any difference anyway. I wasn't dealing with mere governments. All of us knew I'd be facing power groups out to get us. That was the only reason for the meeting."

"I'm pleased that you did not take any nonsense from them! They looked and acted like barbarians moving in for the kill. *Nyeh Kuhltoornee!*"

"Omer, you're a great pilot and a good friend, but I'm glad you weren't the one who was in Santa Fe," was the quiet reply from the beautiful woman.

"*Da!* Russians are good at playing diplomatic games, but I am no Russian."

I'd seen the unarmed man somewhere recently. The couple looked related. Brother and sister perhaps. But Commonwealthers looked alike to me then in spite of the fact that this country had been a melting pot of Africans, Arabs, Europeans, Indians, Chinese, and Malays for centuries. In fact, there was no real national racial phenotype. Some high-tech bigots called them mongrels.

The comm/info network produced so much news, so much data, and so much information that most people were over-communicated. They recalled only what directly concerned them when they heard or saw it. There wasn't time to absorb the details of the entire world system.

But I could recall them when necessary, thanks to my Aero-space Force Academy training. A military officer had to assimilate, evaluate, store and recall a great deal of information rapidly and accurately. Some day, the fortunes of the service might demand some scrap of information without an opportunity to consult the comm/info library.

The mention of Santa Fe triggered my memory. I'd seen the young man on telenews. There was no mistaking his square face, piercing dark eyes, curly black hair, broad but determined mouth, and proud bearing. It had to be Alichin Vamori, the UMC delegate to the First International Space Commerce Convention, the Santa Fe conference.

In the Chaveney-Villepreux Airport during the plane change, I'd caught the thirty-second telenews scene showing Alichin Vamori walking out of that conference in protest. I didn't hear why he'd done it.

I grew concerned. The Commonwealth's open borders were

conducive to the easy movement of terrorists and assassins. These three had to be important people and therefore targets for terrorists. Why were they standing openly on a railway platform waiting for public transportation? Other national leaders, corporate executives, and powerful people rarely exposed themselves in public without security cover which wasn't evident here.

I was a stranger and it wasn't my job to protect them. But if there were trouble, I might find my anatomy uncovered. I began to glance around the platform at the others gathered there. My Aerospace Force training had included security precautions and visual personality profile evaluations. I'd never used them, and I didn't like hand-to-hand. But I scanned for tell-tale signs of potential trouble.

The wail of a three-tone steam whistle announced the arrival of the next train. It slipped into the station with a screaming whine as the locomotive swept past.

The noise and sight drew the attention of everyone on the platform—except two people.

My peripheral vision didn't see the details, only the motion involved in the sudden sweeping aside of a kaftan. My eyes shifted, and I recognized the distinctive black shape of a Zastava pocket autocarbine.

It took a fraction of a second for the gunman to slip the muzzle strap over his left hand so the light composite plastic weapon could be fired with accuracy.

In that fraction of a second, I had to act because a Zastava has a cyclic rate of 1200 rounds per minute.

I covered the six meters between us in two strides and a leap. I caught the gunman waist-high with my left shoulder with the only body check I'd thrown since personal defense sessions in the Academy gym many years ago.

The assassin fired a clip of forty rounds. The noise of the Zastava sounded like a giant tearing a box. Everyone heard it, even over the noise of the halting train. But I'd hit him first and the bullets went into the roof of the platform shed where they exploded on impact.

I hit the platform atop the gunman. His body broke my fall. I rolled clear and was on my feet.

A scimitar appeared from nowhere and slashed the fallen gunman's throat.

I discovered the tip of a short dirk at my throat, too.

I didn't move. The young woman accompanying Alichin Vamori was holding the hilt of that blade which didn't waver or tremble. She radiated her exotic beauty in the manner of women who know they have it, know what it's for, and are unabashedly unashamed of it. Sexual assault in the Commonwealth had to be rare if all women were as armed and willing to use their weapons as she appeared to be.

Looking directly into the dark eyes of this gorgeous woman, I said slowly, "Is this the way you show gratitude for saving your life?"

"Are you sure that's what you were doing?" she replied with equal coolness.

"Why else would I have gotten myself mussed? Or should I have let you handle it in your local fashion, whatever that might be?"

"Let the outlander be, Vaivan. I saw what happened," the mustached man put in, wiping the blood from the scimitar with the gunman's kaftan. He replaced the weapon in the scabbard at his waist and reached down to pick up the now-useless pocket autocarbine. He looked it over and remarked with a slavic accent, "Assassin's weapon, Zastava Vee-zee ninety-five. Zbrojovka manufacture, from the proof marks. Good only for one clip of forty, then throw it away. Nothing like this in Commonwealth service."

Alichin Vamori was kneeling over the dead body of the gunman. "There's an Ilkan i-d tattoo on his arm, Vaivan."

The woman called Vaivan withdrew the tip of the weapon from my throat and returned the dagger to her waist. She offered both hands, palms up. I took them in mine because they were beautiful hands. "My apologies, sir. I didn't see the action. I heard only the sound of the Zastava. We're indebted to you. I'm Vaivan Vamoru Teaq, and this is my brother, Alichin Nogal Vamori." She indicated the other young man who looked so much like her.

I reached out with my right hand and grasped Vamori's. "I saw you on the telenews coverage of Santa Fe," I said to him.

"And you are . . . ?"

"Alexander Sandhurst Baldwin, Captain, United States Aerospace Force, retired."

"I know of you," Vaivan Teaq said. "You're in the Commonwealth because of Landlimo Corporation?"

I nodded.

"I'm the security manager of Landlimo Corporation. My apologies, Captain. This isn't the usual way we welcome visitors to the Commonwealth," she said.

"I'm no longer a Captain," I told her. "And I'm sorry we had to meet under these circumstances, Madame Teaq . . ."

"Please," she pleaded, "there are so many Teaqs and Vamoris that several of us would answer to 'Madame Teaq.' Since you'll be working with us, please call me Vaivan."

She could make any request of me any time she wanted to, but I replied, "Only if you'll promise never to call me Alexander or Alex. My friends know me as Sandy. And I haven't been interviewed yet, much less accepted whatever job you have in mind."

"You've just been interviewed," Alichin Vamori pointed out, looking down at the dead Ilkan gunman.

"If you can fly as well as you can fight, no problem," Vaivan added. "That is, if you want the job . . ."

"We'll talk," I promised, "elsewhere than on a railway platform with a dead gunman at our feet."

"Such things don't bother us. Twenty-first century civilized we may be, but we aren't many generations removed from somewhat violent ancestors."

The man with the mustache and scimitar was introduced to me as Omer Kolil Astrabadi, the "Mad Russian Space Jockey."

"Russian?" I asked. "Your name sounds vaguely Arabic."

Astrabadi grinned toothily under his mustache. "I am not Russian. There was a time when my ancestors came westward over the steppes and ruled all the Russias. Now Russians rule us as part of the Soviet empire . . . but that will not last forever. I am called Russian only because I was born in Tyuratam. I am Kazakh, or Cossack, by blood, but I have taken a Common-wealth name."

"Omer's one of the Soviet cosmonauts who defected to us," Alichin added.

"Ali, you're acting like a Russian. You confuse history to suit yourself. I defected to Gran Bahia and then came here," Astrabadi reminded him. "I will like flying with you, Sandy. It is good to fly without stupid politics in the way."

The police showed up to study, photograph, and remove the body of the gunman who was, according to his tattoo, a citizen of the Ilkan Empire located on the northern borders of the Commonwealth. The police asked questions of us and others on the platform and otherwise conducted police activities in connec-tion with the disturbance. I had to produce my passport for a quick inspection, but they merely noted I wasn't a Common-wealth citizen. Statements were taken on video and audio recorders. They wrapped the body in a plastic sheet and stuffed it into the trunk of a ground car. After about an hour, they finished their work and went away. It seemed to be a closed case insofar as I could determine.

"There'll be an inquest to clear the matter for the record," Vaivan explained.

"But Omer killed him," I reminded her.

"Before he killed us," Vaivan said. "There were many witnesses."

"A police investigation is nothing more than this?"

"What more do they need? And why should we waste time and money to investigate a hired gunman who's already dead?"

In the meantime, two trains had departed.

The Commonwealth trains run on time with great regularity. I found myself accepting with pleasure Vaivan Teaq's invitation to board the next one with the trio.

Looking back on my first hours in the Commonwealth, they seemed filled with fortuitous circumstances that were almost improbable. But remembered later in the context of the Commonwealth culture I didn't understand then, these almost coincidental happenings were no more accidental or lucky than other occurrences which shape our lives.

Once aboard and in the comfortable compartment, I was asked by Vaivan, "What were your plans in Topawa, Sandy?"

"Your phone robot told me the offices were closed until Monday. So I was on my way into Topawa to find a hotel and wait."

"That won't be necessary. You'll be staying at Karederu," she said.

"Pardon?"

"The Vamori family compound," Vaivan explained. "We have an obligation to you. And I'll have two days to interview you and explain your job. As our advert said, we need a skilled pilot with military background . . ."

"You presume I've accepted," I observed cautiously, inwardly excited that I'd have the opportunity to be a guest in her home for the next two days. I really wanted to see a lot more of Vaivan Vamoru Teaq.

"If you want to dicker, I'll turn you over to my dickering brother, Alichin."

"I'm sorry. It just seems you're being a bit presumptuous," I admitted.

She sighed. "I keep forgetting about Americans. You could be offered the best job in the world, one you've always dreamed about, and yet you'd want to investigate and discuss all the perks and fringes. The old employment game."

"You seem to have us all figured out," I remarked.

The Topawa-bound train was rolling smoothly and swiftly past irrigated farmlands that came right up to the right-of-way, and the coach was rocking just slightly at speed. Alichin Vamori hunched over and put his elbows on his knees, folding his hands before him. "Sandy, I know your ways, but I keep forgetting you don't know ours. What do you know about our Commonwealth corporations?"

"I hear Commonwealth firms are somewhat paternalistic. Seems you learned a few things from the Japanese."

"Some. We don't own our companies outright any more than President Nogal owns the Commonwealth's government corporation. We're part-owners along with everyone else who works for the companies. We believe in a participative meritocracy. I like my position as Ell-Five manager for Comspat and Landlimo. It's to my advantage to do my work well. If I don't, I'm hurting only myself because I'm working for myself as well as for the company. This goes all the way up the line. Vaivan's husband Wahak Teaq will remain Landlimo CEO only as long as he does his job. Otherwise, the stockholders will replace him," Alichin Vamori explained over the quiet sounds of the speeding train.

That's why Vaivan had the Vamori family name plus the additional "Teaq." I was decimated. Vaivan Vamoru Teaq was already married to the man who'd be my boss if I came to work for them.

Alichin Vamori continued, "The world goes around only because people turn the crank on the industrial machine that makes it a place of plenty. Fifty years ago, we decided we'd do some cranking ourselves because it was the only way to make things better for everybody in this part of the world."

"Too bad the Ilkans and the Emirate don't think so, too," Omer Astrabadi pointed out.

"When they get tired trying to take it from us," Vaivan said, "they'll discover it's easier to trade than raid."

"Most of the rest of the world still has to learn that one!" Alichin put in savagely. "I found it out the hard way in Santa Fe!"

"So I hear," I said.

"What do you know about the International Space Commerce Conference?"

"Only what I saw on the telenews."

"That was distorted. The telenews networks are run by members of the Tripartite Coalition."

"Whoever runs them, they slant the news to suit their purposes.

I learned always to look behind the headlines to find out who's doing what to who and who's getting paid for it," I observed. "And if I've figured Santa Fe correctly, you're going to need my military background more than my skill as a pilot."

"We don't need any more military pilots," Omer observed. "The Outland Brigade is at full manned strength—land, sea, air, and space."

"And we're not at war," Vaivan added.

"You will be," I told them flatly.

CHAPTER 2

The Killer at Karederu

"I agree with you," Vaivan Teaq replied, "and we may not have much time left to prepare for it, either."

Alichin Vamori looked quizzically at his sister. "Vaivan, who'd want to fight us except our neighbors? We can handle them."

Vaivan motioned to her twin brother to be silent, arose, and began to inspect the inside of the railway carriage compartment with a small plastic box.

"Vaivan, you're getting paranoid," Alichin told her. "How could anyone bug this compartment? We selected it at random when we boarded."

"Ali, people get into trouble when they believe something's impossible." Vaivan completed her check, resumed her seat, then asked me pointedly, "All right, Sandy, what do you know about what's going on?"

I was riding in a private compartment with two armed people, both of whom I knew from recent experience were not loathe to use their weapons. I decided I'd better play it straight arrow if I wanted to leave the compartment alive. "I only know what I see and hear on the telenews. It seemed to me somebody was setting you up for a simple looting by economic pressure. Such measures often lead to armed conflict."

"I agree it's the sort of stage they seem to be setting," Alichin observed. "But that's a long way from war."

"Armed conflict is among the consequences of failure of economic conflict. I can give you several historical examples where failed economic pressures resulted in armed conflict fought on the adversary's terms by their puppets."

Vaivan inclined her exquisite head, crowned as it was by her mass of dark hair kept up off her neck and shoulders in the dry heat by jeweled clips of local design and motif. "It's unusual for a warrior to have the sort of historical depth you seem to possess."

I sat back and folded my arms. "I'm United States Aerospace Force Academy Class of Forty-one."

"So? You're an educated professional warrior."

"And something a bit more," I tried to explain. It was obvious that the different culture of the Commonwealth would consider a soldier differently as well, so I wanted to clarify what I meant. "The primary purpose of a military education in the United States isn't the production of officers who can fight, although we're taught to do that, too. It's an education in the art of armed conflict—what causes one, how it starts, how to spot one that's about to start, how to win it in a decisive manner if that's the political goal, or how to prevail in a stand-off, Korean-type truce. From my education, I know that economic pressure is a classic precursor to armed conflict."

"Not always. Our Founders' War didn't start that way," Alichin said. He paused, then went on, "We know what war is."

"Pardon me, I don't think you do. You still call it 'war.' "

"What else is it?" Omer Astrabadi wanted to know.

"There hasn't been a war since the last one stopped in 1945 and everyone decided they weren't going to fight wars any more. Since then it's been called 'armed conflict,' " I said.

"You Americans play with words like Russians," Omer observed distastefully.

"I think we've considered all the consequences," Alichin Vamori said. "I knew what I was doing when I walked out of the Space Commerce Conference. You'll get the full story when I report tonight. Sandy, I'll be interested in learning whether the facts cause you revise your conclusions."

I hadn't accepted a position in any of the corporations run by these people, and yet they appeared willing to let me sit in on an internal briefing. "I don't believe I'm working formally with you yet, and I haven't taken a security oath."

"I did some checking before we invited you to the Commonwealth," Vaivan said. "Most people are aware of military intelligence activities, but few know of the commercial intelligence networks. It would be impossible to do business without them. But whether you accept a position with Landlimo or not, you're our personal guest at Karederu."

"You don't have to accept our hospitality," Alichin explained. "If you decide this isn't for you, you can be on your way home this evening."

In spite of the fact that I was getting all the wrong signals because of a cultural gap, I was growing to like these people.

They had audacity. They were certain to get into trouble with the rest of the world. I tried to apologize. "Please pardon me. I'm still an American in my world view."

"I know that," Alichin Vamori said.

"You seem insecure and defensive," Vaivan remarked in an offhanded manner and then asked politely, "Perhaps you might like to tell me about the situation leading to your retirement from the United States Aerospace Force."

I shrugged. "The official documents say one thing, but what happened was something else. I was there; the investigating officers weren't. And they never told me it was classified. So what have I got to lose? I was on routine proficiency flight in a Space Hawk, flight plan and beacon code all tickety-boo with both Cheyenne Mountain and Wichita Space Traffic Control Center. Nothing for anyone to get suspicious about, but the Soviets probably had some bad intelligence. A Black Bear space cruiser began tailing me. When he stopped tracking and pinned targeting lidar on me, my gut reaction told me I'd better do unto him what he was about to do unto me. I zanged and shot . . . and watched him burn-in over Kergulen Island."

"Good for you, Sandy! The Black Bear was provoking you! Standard procedure in the *Kosmonautika*," Omer said with a grin, his white teeth showing under his mustache that stood straight out on both sides of his face.

"No, it wasn't good for me. It made the State Department unhappy, and they made the Aerospace Force *very* unhappy. Seems I'd violated Standing Order Romeo prohibiting aggressive action without provocation. The current U.S. foreign policy is conciliatory towards the Soviet Empire. Live and let live . . . if you don't get shot first. So to placate the Soviets, I was permitted to resign/retire."

"*Bojemoi!*" Omer muttered in disgust.

Alichin Vamori put in after a moment of silence, "Sounds like a flimsy excuse for dismissing an officer they'd spent a lot of time and money educating and training."

"The United States is extremely sensitive about military space activities," I explained. "Both nations have enough stuff stashed in Earth orbit to wipe out the other's space facilities. If that happened, the door would be open for the earth-launched thermonuclear strikes that are prevented by space laser facilities. And everyone's worried about the Chinese who've elected to retain their inscrutability. Look at it this way: What's cheaper, one man, or an armed conflict? Or haven't you been aware of American foreign policy for most of this century?"

"I'm aware of it," Alichin said. "But why didn't you fight in defense of what you did? The Aerospace Force might have backed off because of the publicity."

"My career was finished anyway. I won't fly a keypad at Boondock Aerospace Force Base, Alaska . . . or be a 'professor of military science and tactics' at Alcatraz Military Academy for young hellions. The Aerospace Force doesn't really want tigers. They allowed me to 'voluntarily resign with honor.' You can't fight Headquarters."

Except for the well-muffled sounds of the wheels rolling on the rails, there was silence in the compartment for a moment before Alichin Vamori said, "You'll be working for us Monday morning."

The quiet, swaying coach ride changed. The train began to slow as it pulled into the Topawa yards. "He's already on the payroll," Vaivan remarked. "If he doesn't want the position, he'll be paid for today in any event."

"But I haven't done any work!" I objected.

"I recall a recent incident on a railway platform," Ali said.

"Debts are always paid," Vaivan added.

I liked the dry heat of the Commonwealth, but I was wearing the blue slacks and blue shirt of my old uniform along with an ancient blazer that was too heavy for this weather. Having just returned from a colder part of the world, Ali wore American business garb. Vaivan, on the other hand, was attired in an open-weave loose cotton tunic in light colors. I'd have to buy suitable clothes, but I didn't yet know what kind because the Commonwealth's climate was so varied.

The intertropical convergence zone kept the storm tracks north in January, leading to a warm and dry winter season in Topawa and the coastal plains. But it was quite different in the Dilkon Range whose resorts offered some of the best all-year skiing to be found anywhere. Many people carried skis in the hot Topawa railway station.

A large alky van met us, driven by a man whom I envied greatly: Vaivan's husband Wahak Vaya Teaq. He gave an initial impression of being a nice guy, but he seemed introverted. Maybe he was just a quiet person. Certainly he must have something on the ball to snare a prize like Vaivan. He wore a Commonwealth pig-sticker at his waist, but he didn't look like he'd use it.

I wasn't eager to find out. These people's apparent acceptance of personal combat wasn't my cup of tea. I preferred technological fighting: man and machine against man and machine at a distance, and may the best systems manager win.

There was only family small talk among them as we drove through the streets of Topawa. It was a fascinating capital city. It didn't *look* or *feel* like any low-tech city I'd ever seen.

In the first place, Topawa was clean, bright, and a mixture of old and new.

There were a lot of people walking. They were a mixture of racial and subracial types—Hindus, turbaned Sikhs, Arabs with and without their traditional kaftans and haiks, Mediterranean types, Negroes, Orientals, and Caucasians. Some women, probably Muslim, were veiled. It was obvious that the people of the United Mitanni Commonwealth were a mixture of nearly every humanoid type on Earth.

The same hybridization was evident in the architecture of the buildings. Some showed the influence of past European colonizers— the Portuguese, French, Germans, and British, although not in that order and for varying amounts of time dependent upon the spoils of European warfare. Some were built of an interesting intermix of native red sandstone and the abundant steel and glass produced in the UMC. A few looked new with lacy and airy structures made from space-produced composite materials.

The streets were laid out square with the world as in most western American cities, the work of a surveying crew rather than a herd of cattle. Various vehicles ran in the wide, straight streets—alcars, fotofuellers, and electric trolley cars. The vehicular traffic was disciplined; the Commonwealthers actually did lane driving. I saw no human- or animal-drawn vehicles. There were a few automated traffic signals but most traffic was directed by a human policeman in the middle of the intersection.

Some of the Commonwealth's factories were probably highly automated in order to produce competitive goods in the world market. But in other nooks and crannies of the culture, people were used instead of machines. The Commonwealth had a population of about three million, and one of the national problems would be finding work for everyone because of the Commonwealth rule: Everybody works at something because there is a lot of work to be done.

I'd been told that in the Commonwealth you worked unless you were a tourist, visitor, or guest. The Commonwealthers were known for taking good care of their sick and infirm by family means if possible and by charities otherwise. They'd deliberately eshewed most of the trappings of the welfare states. I began to understand their emphasis on family ties.

Karederu was situated on the low bluff on the south side of the Topawa River valley in which the city nestled. It didn't have a wall, but any unwanted visitor would have to get through the thick vegetation around it.

Inside, the spread of about a hundred hectares seemed more like the suburban subdivisions of the old American metroplexes.

There was a brief discussion between Ali and Vaivan spiced with terms in their old Gallo language concerning familial relationships. It was finally settled that Ali would be my host since he was yet unmarried and had a spare room.

"Seems like a rather large estate," I said, looking around at the open land with small cottages located so they were private dwellings.

"That's the wrong word," Ali told me. He picked up his bag and began to walk toward the nearest cottage. "Karederu is a concession to the old life style. Each family unit has its own dwelling. We'll go over to the Center about sunset for dinner."

Alichin's place was a small, self-contained home. He tossed his bag into a room, told me to pick a room for myself and toss my bag there, then switched on the cottage electronics.

I was suddenly tired, exhausted, fatigued, and somewhat nauseated. "I feel lousy, Ali. Probably my circadian."

"I was on the same flight from Denver and Paris, so my circadian rhythm's in sad shape, too," Ali admitted. "A short nap with subliminal circadian reprogramming will take care of it."

I had the mental discipline to handle the disoriented semi-confusion of circadian asynchronization because of my space experience. But this was different.

Through the nausea that was beginning to wipe out everything else in my mind, I suddenly knew what was happening.

"Ali! Turn off your electric power! Grab the main switch! Hurry!"

He took three steps and fell on his face.

I stumbled and finally crawled toward an electrical distribution and switching box on the far wall of the kitchen . . . and got to it just before the nausea overwhelmed me completely. With practically my last bit of strength and will, I pulled the main switch.

The nausea disappeared immediately.

When I opened the panel, I found what I'd suspected. I pulled the little plastic box out, ripping loose the two wires that connected it to the mains. When I staggered back to the main room, Ali was sitting up and holding his head.

"You okay?" I wanted to know.

"Yes. What was it?"

I held up the little black box. "Somebody planted a Killer ERG here."

"What's that?"

"Earth resonance generator. I don't know where this one came from. There're no markings on it. It's top secret in America. The Aerospace Force uses them to protect sensitive facilities. It modulates the terrestrial magnetic field in the vicinity. I don't know how since I didn't have a 'need to know.' It can kill in minutes by disrupting neural activity."

Ali held out his hand. "Vaivan's technicians will want to have a look at it."

I gave it to him. In America, it was classified. But this wasn't America.

"That's twice in one day," Ali said.

"Put it on the tab," I told him. "It would have killed me, too."

"As far as I'm concerned, you're one of us," Ali said with finality. He went to the kitchen, put the black box away in a cabinet, and brought back a bottle and two glasses. "*Supaku*," he said and poured a glass of the clear liquid. "Recycled rocket propellant. Free choice!" He raised his glass in a toast and downed it in one gulp in the same manner as Russians drink vodka.

It had high ethanol content and indeed could have been used for propellant. It burned all the way down, hit bottom, then spread its warmth outward from my belly. I began to feel better.

"I want to see what telenews is saying about Santa Fe. I've been out of touch for about twelve hours. Got any particular choice of telenews nets?" Ali asked.

I wanted to find out, too. "No. They're all biased."

"Which one do you think is the least biased?"

"Try Weltfenster."

"Why?"

"It's Swiss."

"Oh? Are they non-biased on world affairs?"

Ali might be testing me, so I told him, "They've been a neutral porcupine for centuries."

"Ah, yes! The North American mammal covered with spiny quills! Well, so's the Commonwealth. But what makes you believe their reportage is any less biased?"

"With Hong Kong and Bahrain, they're bankers to the world. They've everything to gain and nothing to lose because everybody does business with them. Most politicians are either in hock to them or stash their loot with them. They don't have to toady to anybody," I observed.

"You've got a lot to learn, Sandy!"

"You know something different?"

"Let's see what the unbiased 'World Window' telenews people have to say."

Alichin instructed the receiver to interrogate the Weltfenster net, search for all news records of the International Space Commerce Conference for the last 12-hour period, record the subsequent data dump, and present the menu on the screen. There was a lot. Ali found a video report of interest and punched it up.

The segment opened with a long shot of the Santa Fe conference center. Ali suppressed the subtitle ribbon when the receiver queried language preference.

It was the usual talking head opener. "Good evening from Santa Fe," the reporter's image began. "The agenda of the International Space Commerce Conference here was altered today by the walk-out of the delegate from the United Mitanni Commonwealth, Alichin Vamori." The screen cut to tape showing Ali striding out of the meeting. "Vamori, a leading member of one of the ruling families of the Commonwealth who control the Vamori Free Space Port, lashed out at the Conference, claiming the proposed space commerce levy was nothing more than, in his words, 'a twenty-first century version of the old protection racket.' According to the Conference organizers, the purpose of the space import-export levy is not only to reduce the citizen tax burden in those nations who've subsidized space utilization for the past fifty years, but also to aid the world's non-space nations who don't benefit yet from space industry and power." The scene cut to a view of the chairman of the Conference making a speech, but the reporter continued voice-over, "The reaction of other Conference delegates was swift. Not only did Vamori's walk-out precipitate an early acceptance vote of the proposal, thereby short-cutting what might have been prolonged debate over minor points of difference, but also resulted in the acceptance of an amendment which imposes a boycott against non-signatory parties. Thus, Vamori's own actions have backfired on the United Mitanni Commonwealth and the profitable Vamori Free Space Port. The success of the boycott remains to be seen. It cannot help but reduce the activity at Vamori Free Space Port which now handles more than forty percent of the world's space commerce. Gran Bahia, the world's other free space port, obviously stands to gain, but Bahian spokesmen had no comment when Weltfenster queried . . ."

Ali switched it off and sat there. He said nothing.

I broke the silence. "They set you up."

"We knew that was going to happen," Ali replied with apparent calm.

"I hope you're prepared for the consequences."

"We think we are."

"Militarily?"

"That, too."

"Is that why you wanted a military pilot?"

"No. Landlimo Corporation placed the advert before the Santa Fe Conference. We've always needed all the help we can get."

"How do you know you won't get into another Chase situation?" I asked.

"One Colonel Joseph T. Chase is enough for any country," Ali remarked, referring to the man who'd been defeated by Ali's grandfather that Christmas Day fifty years ago. Ali looked directly at me, his piercing dark eyes almost boring right through me. "We've never turned down help, but we're careful these days to see to it that history doesn't repeat itself. We can use your help, Sandy. But it will require your total commitment."

"I want to know a lot more about the job," I told him flatly, looking back at him with equal intensity.

"You'll get what you want." Ali got up, stretched both arms out to his sides, and flexed his fingers as though he were releasing great tension within him. When he looked at me again, he was the pleasant, controlled Alichin Vamori I'd gotten to know on the train. "Until dinnertime, why fret? I'm going to take a nap. I suggest you do the same. We've got a very intense evening ahead of us. Do you want to use subliminal programs for circadian readjustment?"

I didn't need them.

When Ali shook me awake, the light of day was fading.

"What's the dress for dinner?" I wondered aloud.

Ali was attired informally in khaki shirt, shorts, and knee socks. His dagger hung at his side; he shrugged. "Clothing used to be a badge of rank to signify relative position in a group. But today we have other, more subtle badges. We don't dress special except for diplomatic meetings or business conferences where we dress in the manner of those we're conferring with to make them feel more secure and more pliable in negotiations. Wear what you want; everyone else in Karederu does."

I wore another blue shirt and blue slacks out of my single bag. I shaved because the 24-hour stubble on my face wasn't enough to qualify as a beard and because I noted that this culture favored clean-shaven men except in the case of Omer Astrabadi who was following his outland custom.

We walked together through the open compound in the evening light. "You've got what amounts to a private park in the Commonwealth's biggest city," I observed and wanted to know, "Is this typical of the life style, or just of the ruling families?"

"The former. And forget the shibboleths of the telenews. 'Ruling families' is a semantically-loaded term. 'Rule' is a null-word. Ergo, so is the word 'ruling.' You've obviously seen the wealthy and powerful in America. Notice anything different about the way we behave?"

"Yes. Why do you use public transportation? You can surely afford better if for no other reason than security. I can't figure out why someone as important and wealthy as you doesn't have his own aerospaceplane and limousine."

Ali replied quietly in matter-of-fact tones, "We were ordinary people once and still are. All we wanted was to eat regularly, raise a family, run our own lives, and make and trade things. When we saw that the world wasn't going to pieces and when we got access to the comm/info satellite networks, there were enough people like The General who'd had enough of bemedalled, strutting tyrant leaders and corrupt politicians. Why don't I have my own aerospace plane and limousine? Why don't I live in a great castle? Why aren't there a lot of servants around? Sandy, even in your culture the ostentatious display of those things isn't necessary in order to live well and do business successfully. And they create envy and covetous desires among those who'd rather take them away instead of make them by their own efforts. Why should I alienate my own people and my customers? Most successful businessmen found this out. This is a world of plenty if people would only realize it."

"You mean, all Commonwealth families live like this?" My initial contact with the Commonwealth was causing culture shock.

"No, some families are bigger and have more land. Some prefer urban living in blocks of condos. Many Vamoris are either out of the country or in space enough that we savor the feeling of Earth when we're here." Alichin Vamori paused, then added, "Besides, The General likes it. Most of his generation worked hard to gain this security."

I missed the implied meaning and noted, "I didn't see any security fences or gates when we came in. Look, you were the target of terrorism twice this afternoon. Seems to me you need a compound with very tight security.''

Ali grinned and said, ''It's secure.''

''Without fences and guards?''

''Does the U.S. Aerospace Force still use physical barriers and human guards around its sensitive military installations?''

''I can't talk about that, Ali.''

Ali walked along briskly. ''Don't try to get into Karederu except through the gates where the security screen will recognize you and not make a fuss.''

''Then how did the Killer ERG get into your cottage?'' I wanted to know.

Ali looked puzzled. ''I don't know. My twin sister Vaivan is the security expert. The only way it could have gotten in is if someone familiar to the security computer brought it in.''

Karederu Center was a large building with a gently sloping roof and overhangs coupled with open-wall construction that let the tropical breeze through. It had kitchens and other rooms, but I only saw the big hall full of people.

There were more than two dozen people there. I still don't recall everyone I met. For some reason, some of the most important people in my life don't start out being important; I can only vaguely remember meeting them, yet I come to know them better and better as time goes by. People grow on me.

Alichin first introduced me to the most important man there, the patriarch of the Vamori family and the near-legendary founder of the United Mitanni Commonwealth.

General Anegam Dati Vamori had to be over 70 years old, but he didn't look his age. I wouldn't have been surprised at this in any hi-tech country where apparent age is a consequence of biotechnology and biocosmetics. General Vamori, Victor of Oidak and First President of the Commonwealth, was older than the country he'd helped found, yet he was still strong and mentally sharp. He took my hand in both of his and told me, ''Welcome, and thank you.''

I thought he was referring to the railway station incident; aides must have told him. ''I did what was necessary, General.''

General Vamori smiled and shook my hand gently. ''A properly trained warrior always does—within the proscribed bounds of his culture. I'm sure the Black Bear pilot was doing the same. In any event, thank you for bringing your audacity into our camp. It's not often appreciated in high-tech, but we'll always welcome new infusions of it.''

"I'm sorry. I thought you were referring to the incident this afternoon," I said.

"That, too. It would have been a disaster if you hadn't been as honorably motivated as you are."

"Your perception is interesting," I told him. "I'm a military man, but I don't like to brawl."

"I'm sure you don't. But it's impossible to perceive of you as other than an honorable, duty-bound person in the way you look, act, move, and speak."

"Pardon me, but I wasn't aware of it."

"Perhaps I can make you understand by a negative example," General Vamori said. "If one acts like a slave, one will be treated like a slave."

I suddenly understood why this mixed bag of people hadn't gone the way of former colonials in other low-tech nations, but had instead pulled themselves up in fifty years of bootstrapping in a way most people in high-tech couldn't understand.

"But the obverse is also true, sir."

"And that is . . .?"

"If you act like you have something of value, somebody will try to take it away from you."

"We can prevent that if we've done our planning correctly."

"Pardon me, but what can a business corporation do that your military forces cannot?"

"Wage energy warfare."

CHAPTER 3

With No Recourse

"We haven't briefed Sandy yet," Ali told The General.

"It's time you did," I said.

"Patience," The General replied smoothly. "You'll learn more tonight, Sandy."

"And if I don't like it?"

"You'll like it. It involves a fight, and you're a fighter," The General wasn't totally correct. "Ali, make Sandy feel at home. And tell Vaivan I applaud her selection."

This old man may have had extraordinary insight, but I doubted it. Or he may have gotten a thorough background investigation made—which I also doubted because there hadn't been time since the Black Bear incident.

But I did admire him for his openness. He was an old tiger, but far from a toothless one.

I knew why everybody addressed him as though his rank was capitalized.

I liked The General.

But I wasn't quite ready yet to fully trust him or any of his family.

The first reaction of anyone to a new place—even if one only relocates to a new city—is feeling like an outsider and therefore not trusted or trusting.

Maybe I was getting the wrong signals. Maybe this was the way these people operated.

I was surprised to discover that *all* Commonwealth women were attractive. Even Alichin's mother, Canela Nogalu Vamori, who was old enough to be my mother, exuded an exotic attraction that I was unable to put my finger on. The younger women—cousins Sila Tatri Vamori, Komel Tatri Vamori, and Emika Nogal Kokat—seemed deeply involved in the Vamori enterprises, yet they didn't let business matters interfere with the obvious fact that they were women.

The only one who seemed vaguely and strangely uninterested in me was Tsaya Vamoru Stoak who wasn't in the least unattractive. She seemed cool and detached. I couldn't figure her out. As a result, she fascinated me.

I began to wonder how these armed women made love. Fearlessly, I suspected, and on their own terms. Women who go about armed are *not* second-class citizens capable of being coerced against their will.

Would I be offered the guest privilege here? Would I be allowed to choose, or would one choose me instead? It could be an interesting evening.

I recalled The General's admonition about acting like a slave. These people didn't act like slaves. They were in control of their lives. Male or female, they were no people to fool around with.

The children present reflected this, too. If the Commonwealth had second-class citizens, they were the children. I didn't really understand children because my life had been one of cloistered living in dorms and BOQ's. These children were far from the service brats who were the only children I'd had even remote contact with. They were obviously under the control of their parents with no nonsense being tolerated, yet they didn't seem to be suppressed or traumatized. They knew their place and appeared to be proud to occupy it. They seemed to know that someday they'd join the ranks of the adults, and they looked forward to that.

These were proud people, and they inculcated it in their young at an early age.

Until I learned more about this culture and its people, I decided I'd act as politely and inoffensively as I could. I wasn't precisely certain of all the niceties of Commonwealth custom, but I rather suspected from my brief encounter with it on the railway platform that it was a matter of "well deserved" if someone got it while carrying out an act of perfidy or violence. Maybe it wasn't justice in the Anglo-American style, but it apparently worked here.

What would happen if they let me in on their secrets and I decided not to join them? Could I get out of the country alive?

On the other hand, they'd taken me into their trust, and I had to reciprocate.

Not everyone I met had a Commonwealth name. A short, stocky, bald-headed man walked up and introduced himself as Heinrich von Undine. His grasp was small but firm, and he bowed slightly from the waist as we shook hands. He wore a business suit whose white shirt collar looked like it was two sizes too small for his thick neck and little round metal-framed eyeglasses, even in this day of advanced biotechnology. He explained he was with the Chiawuli International Exchange and Factoring Company and handled most of the outland financial transactions of the Vamori enterprises.

"Haven't I seen something recently on the telenews about an American named Baldwin? Would you be related to him?" von Undine asked. I'd fully expected a thick Teutonic accent, but he had none. His speech was Commonwealth English with its musical inflections and altered vowel sounds.

"I shot down the Black Bear."

"Then your presence makes sense," von Undine said.

Ali and Vaivan came over to us and steered me away from von Undine. Ali asked his sister. "Vaivan, *why* is von Undine here tonight? Who invited him? This is strictly internal Commonwealth business!"

"Kariander Dok and Tonol Kokat were very insistent," Vaivan explained quietly. "I don't see anything wrong with it. Heinrich's our agent with Frankfurt and Basel."

"I don't like him," Ali said, "but I don't know why."

"We've been dealing with him for a long time," Vaivan reminded him.

"I don't mind if The General trusts him as long as we have strong controls on him." Ali turned to me. "Sandy, sorry to burden you with these internal problems."

"I'd find out about them sooner or later," I told him.

Ali, Vaivan, and Wahak took me in tow for dinner. It had been a long time since I'd been to a pot-luck faculty supper with my parents in Santa Barbara, but that's what this dinner amounted to. Each part of the family brought something. The result was a trencherman's paradise.

"Everyone loves my guacamole and refried beans," Ali remarked. "If I hadn't been outcountry, I'd have been told to bring some. Personally, I think my Texas chili is better, but . . ."

"Where did you learn to make that?" I wanted to know.

"In school," Ali replied. "We've all brought back favorite recipes from places we've been."

"Tell me," I asked my host as we proceeded through the line past the loaded table covered with dishes from around the world, "are there any native foods here?"

Ali shook his head. "No, but you wouldn't like them anyway."

"Why?"

"We don't like the last native specialty people such as The General had to eat to during the war. Canine meat's too tough, gamy, and strong flavored. And occasionally you'll hear the old insult." He spoke something in the Gallo language, full of clicks and glottals.

"Which means?" I wanted to know.

" 'Some day I'll eat you.' "

I didn't bring up the subject of local food again.

We ate at tables for eight. It was nothing I wouldn't expect anywhere in the world.

Karederu Center was equipped with fully automatic kitchen equipment, so no one had to do the dishes or take out the garbage. That meant everyone could get right down to business afterwards.

The General didn't preside. The meeting was called to order by Ali's father, Rayo Sabinos Vamori, eldest son of The General. The conference extended beyond Karederu Center common via interactive voxvideo display screens revealing other Commonwealth people gathered in their own centers plus people located all over the world and in space.

I thought of a dozen ways someone could tap the net.

Vaivan guessed I was thinking about it because she remarked, "The subcarriers on our leased transponders don't use standard encoding, Sandy. In spite of the fact that I handle security matters for both Landlimo Corporation and Commonwealth Space Transport or ComSpat, I don't know how it's done. It's something like pseudo-random noise coding with frequency shifts and jumps combined with multichannel switching. Aunt Roseiada—the older lady sitting over there—is the only one who knew the software program."

"Past tense?"

"It's so complex that only the master computers remember it."

"Difficult to crack."

"Impossible, Sandy."

"Didn't you tell me about the dangers of believing something to be impossible?"

"Seven levels of serial encryption coding would require more attoseconds to scan than remain in the life of the universe."

"Everybody on?" Rayo Vamori wanted to know as he stood before the assembled group and the banks of the video display screens.

Other members of the Vamori family were on the net, as well as some other families I hadn't heard of yet—Stoak, Tatri, Abiku, Teaq, Tehat, Delkot, Kom, Dati, and Chiuili. Commonwealth given and family names sounded vaguely familiar. I didn't know whether their sounds were distorted slightly by the Commonwealth accent or whether they were indeed altered.

Some of the participants were definitely outlanders. Each of them identified themselves as part of the meeting protocol, although it was apparent they were known in the group—the Chungs from Hong Kong, the Wangs of Singapore, Nissamaghadi Phalonagri of the Madras Bank Phalonagris, Hudayadha-ben-Mukhalla of Dhahran, Captain Kevin Graham of the League of Free Traders at the Vamori Free Space Port, the round-faced Skinner "Trip" Sinclair in Houston, and two who were obviously in the weightlessness of a space facility, Jeri Hospah and Ursila Peri whose attractiveness was apparent in spite of the effects of zero-gee on her face.

I was asked to stand for introduction. "Sandy Baldwin, former Captain, United States Aerospace Force, now of Landlimo," was the introduction Rayo Vamori intoned . . . and I hadn't even formally joined the company yet! But now everyone involved in the operation knew me, and this meeting would certainly bring me up to speed on what was going on and *why* they needed a military aerospace pilot.

"I still haven't said yes," I mentioned aside to Ali. "How do you know I won't snitch to my former employers?"

Ali shook his head almost imperceptably. "As an Academy graduate, you hold personal honor high on your list of priorities. You won't twig to anyone for the simple reason that I ask you not to, whether you come with us or not . . . which you will, I'm sure."

He was right. I was already in and swimming with them . . . against the tide, perhaps. And even if I didn't go along in whatever they were planning to do, I wouldn't run back to the Aerospace organization, not after the way I'd been treated for doing my job.

"Alichin Vamori is back from the Santa Fe conference," Rayo Vamori began. "We knew what was likely to happen, so now we weren't caught totally unprepared. Some, but . . ."

"Did you believe they wouldn't move as they did, Vamori?" Phalonagri of Madras remarked.

"We were surprised."

"But we had adequate advance intelligence data," Wen-ling Chung of Hong Kong pointed out.

Rayo looked at Vaivan who said, "We had good data, but some didn't believe the Tripartite would really go through with it."

Trip Sinclair in Houston broke in with, "I've got to agree with

Vaivan. Most of my colleagues here didn't think the Tripartite had the guts . . .''

"They did," The General interrupted. "Never mind recriminations. Perhaps someday there will be time to analyze everything that led up to this. But we can't afford that luxury now. Let's get on with what we must do."

"We'd best start with Alichin's report," Rayo Vamori said.

Ali stood and walked to the center of the group where he had the best view of the gathering at Karederu Center and the screens showing the other people participating in the telecon. He inclined his head toward one of the video screens. "President Nogal, you'll get my formal report as soon as I draft it and put it in your computer. I'll be happy to make an informal verbal report to the Executive Commission . . ."

The image of a middle-aged man on one of the screens inclined his head and said, "Most of the Commission is on the net as well as the Chairs of the House of Trustees and the House of Directors. Time is of the essence."

Ali took a deep breath and said to everyone, "I didn't relish representing the Commonwealth in Santa Fe. I didn't trust the people who set up the Conference, and I didn't trust the people who participated. They're puppets of their respective power groups. But since all of you believed I knew more than anyone else in the Commonwealth about the overall space activities of interest to us, I accepted the appointment reluctantly. However, once appointed I tried to act in the best interests of all of us. If anyone has a serious complaint of a personal nature concerning the way I handled things in Santa Fe, arrange to meet me and wear your iklawa."

Ali was a good speaker with an excellent command of the English language. When he addressed a group like this, he shifted out of his Commonwealth accent into one that was universally heard on the comm/info net telenews and educational programming. People in high-tech countries tend to forget the comm/info net is used more in the low-tech world than anywhere else because information is vital to their existence in low-tech. I found myself wishing that more people had taken advantage of it as the Commonwealthers had.

"We knew in advance the Conference was rigged," Ali went on. "But none of us anticipated that one hundred and eighty-six nations would support the tariff agreement. We thought we'd find *some* support for the Commonwealth amendment."

There'd been nothing on telenews about any Commonwealth amendment to the Santa Fe space tariff agreements.

"We should have realized that the Conference was held on the home ground of the Tripartite Coalition," Ali continued. "They knew where everyone was quartered in Santa Fe. They could establish communications easily any time they wanted, whereas I had difficulty reaching reps from other countries who'd given us indications of supporting our free trade amendment. The Tripartite obviously made a prior arrangement with the PetroFed and probably also the Socialist Hegonomy. They had *everything* worked out long in advance. The Conference was intended only to put official approval on the tariff agreement by the governments involved."

"They don't really believe the Commonwealth legislature is going to change the basic laws of this nation and install tax collectors at Vamori Free Space Port, do they?" the Commonwealth President wanted to know. "Even if the legislature managed to do it, the Board of Jurisprudence would rule it unconstitutional the first time somebody brought it before them."

"We'd bring suit immediately," Captain Kevin Graham of the League of Free Traders put in from his space port office. "Vamori-Free is absolutely essential to the continued operation of free traders in space. In fact, the League itself—to say nothing of other traders—wouldn't exist without Vamori-Free and the free-ports in space."

"Was the Conference made aware of the internal problem of the Commonwealth in implementing the Santa Fe tariffs?" asked Vaya Volkatu Delkot, manager of the Vamori Free Space Port who would have looked more at home in the high fashion studios of Paris, Beverly Hills, or Tokyo.

"Very few people in high-tech understand the Commonwealth," General Vamori said. "The Tripartite and other power groups probably didn't believe their own evaluations, projections, and intelligence sources. That's been their history. They've lost a lot of conflicts because of it, but they've won more over the long haul because they control capital. They don't control ours and never have. Fifty years ago, we made sure they couldn't. It didn't bother them then; they wrote us off as an impractical experiment that couldn't succeed in the light of the history of this continent. We were an impossible institution; therefore, we wouldn't continue to exist. We did. And, as we anticipated, our success threatens the foundations of their power."

"South Africa," Wen-Ling Chung of Hong Kong observed, "was a highly successful experiment, too. But they nipped it before it became a threat."

"It took longer there because only small power groups were

involved," Trip Sinclair in Houston corrected him. "The Diamond Trust and the Gold Debasers have been in bed with the Eurobanks for centuries."

The General broke in, "We've all been taught history. We must now write some history of our own. We must modify Phase Two because of the boycott amendment they adopted after Alichin left the Conference. Does anyone have a copy of that yet?"

"I do," Vaivan told him.

"So do I," Trip Sinclair added. "You're getting pretty fast, Vaivan."

"Or you're slowing down, Trip. I've got much the same channels as you do."

"Perhaps. But mine work through several Old Boy and Good Old Boy networks here in the States."

"What's the difference between them?" Ali wanted to know.

"One's New England and New York based, and the other extends from Atlanta to Dallas. Both have extensions all over the Western Hemisphere."

"How do we know we aren't being penetrated by Tripartite intelligence agents right now?" Ali asked.

"We're penetrated," Vaivan admitted. "I'm reasonably certain their agents are on this net."

"Our only defense is their own historic inclination to disbelieve the reports of their intelligence operatives and analysts because the reports don't agree with their world picture. The world's run with very little real knowledge—mostly by hunches, emotion, and sheer wishful thinking," The General said and admonished Ali, "Let's get back on track."

"Trip, give us a run-down on that amendment. All I know is what I heard on Weltfenster telenews a few hours ago," Ali said.

The Houston attorney looked to one side and punched his office keypad. We couldn't see what came up on his VDT, but he told us, "To summarize the main points, signatories to the Conference tariff document agree to boycott non-signatory organizations. Note that I used the world 'organizations' because that's the way they phrased the amendment."

"Apparently they know enough about us to realize that Commonwealth space commerce activities have no political regulation," Vaya Delkot said.

"Yes, the wording is such that the boycott will affect *all* space commerce activities carried on by the Commonwealth and its registered space facilities," Trip Sinclair observed, "even the League of Free Traders, Kevin."

"How about our Lagrangian operations?" Ursila Peri's video image wanted to know. "How can they boycott trade operations off-planet?"

"Is your air bill current, Ursila?" Trip asked her.

"Yes, but even if it wasn't, nobody out here would cut off another person's life support. If the credit line got over-extended by too much for too long, we'd put the debtor on a ship home. We work together because there's a lot of nothing waiting for everybody beyond the bulkhead," she said. "They're going to have trouble enforcing tariff arrangements and trade boycotts out here. That agreement sounds exactly like something written up by a bunch of people who always have pressure around them and gravity to keep their feet on the floor. Earthworms!" She made it sound like an insult.

"That's what I mean about changing the planning for Phase Two," The General said, but with more insistence this time. "We didn't consider a boycott as a viable option for them. They made the mistake of believing it to be workable here and in space. Therefore, we're ahead of them in several respects. And we've got to revise our programs to take advantage of this. Look at the elements of our situation."

He didn't have to move into voxvideo pickup range; the pickups moved to him instead. He began ticking off his points on his fingers.

"One: they don't understand us, but we understand them, even though we don't have them as thoroughly compromised by espionage as we'd like. However, what advantage we may have in their lack of understanding may not last because the Japanese members of the Tripartite can tell them all about this sort of thing from both sides of the fence. I'm referring to Tsushima, Pearl Harbor, and Space War One.

"Two: They're big and we're small. Therefore, we can move faster and in novel directions. We can put them off balance and keep them that way if we're innovative.

"Three: They're certain to squabble over the spoils as these begin to come in from signatories to the tariff agreement. This will slow them down and consume some of the time and effort they'd otherwise direct toward us. Greed born of scarcity plays a big part in their lives. On the other hand, all of us know there's more than enough for everyone.

"Four: The tariff agreement and the boycott amendment are unworkable off-planet. We can certainly take advantage of that because it meshes with existing plans for Phase Two. It will take them some time to discover how unworkable it really is. That's time we can use to our advantage.

"Five: We can further distract them by purporting to go along with their game but being forced by our own internal politics to change our national laws. This is a stalling tactic to allow us to get our own programs set up. That gives us more time.

"Time is on our side if we use it wisely. We must not squander it because, unlike the rest of the universe, it isn't plentiful."

I was fascinated by his grasp of what seemed to me to be an incredibly complex worldwide activity. And when The General spoke, *everyone* there and on the net listened. The apparent leadership power of this man was uncanny. I felt as though I were listening to a modern messiah.

"There's always some common ground for negotiation in anything, including this situation." It was Heinrich von Undine who spoke up. Some people present looked at him with severely sharp expressions. "Ali, perhaps your actions in Santa Fe were a bit precipitous—although I intend that only as an observation after the fact. The Commonwealth has existed for fifty years and there's a great deal of foreign investment here. The aid and assistance of foreign corporations and consultants have been hallmarks of Commonwealth progress. In short, the people you believe are out to despoil the Commonwealth by destroying our free trade activities may simply be acting in their own self interest. Try to see it from their point of view. The watchword of *weltpolitik* for a century now has been co-operation, not physical coercion."

"I cannot agree with your assessment, Heinrich," The General countered with unexpected grace. "Once we became big enough to threaten the major world power groups and therefore worthy of their attention, they chose not to co-operate with us but to bring us under their control. When they discover they can't do it, they'll try to destroy us. We'll have no recourse but to fight. However, we'll fight on our terms, not theirs."

General Vamori looked around, then continued, "We can win if we change the game. We can utilize the new element in the world power game: space. It's a game element they don't realize exists. We do. If we carry out all the proper actions at the proper time, we can defuse this international situation and create a new world power game based on the reality that we live in a system of plenty, not scarcity."

His resonant voice suddenly dropped to a level where we

could barely hear what he said with great sadness, "But if it indeed comes to armed conflict, we will have no recourse but to defend the Commonwealth proper and perhaps participate in what may become, God forbid, Space War Two."

CHAPTER 4

The Play of Power and Flame

Alichin Vamori broke the silence that followed his grandfather's words. "The first action in the revised Phase Two program lies in your hands, President Nogal. May I suggest that you make a public announcement on telenews dismissing me for poor judgement because I walked out of the Santa Fe conference and damaged the position of the Commonwealth in the community of nations? Then banish me to space where I can't cause any more damage."

Wen-Ling Chung from Hong Kong spoke up, "But, Alichin, that would dishonor you and you would lose face."

"Not really, although anyone outside this circle would react as you have, Wen-Ling," Ali replied. "A banishment for poor judgement provides President Nogal with logical justification for getting me out of the picture and gives him an excuse for making apologetic sounds to various governments about my behavior while promising to rectify things."

"An interesting suggestion, Alichin. It deserves serious consideration," President Nogal's image replied.

"You're becoming extremely devious, Alichin. May I compliment you?" Wen-Ling Chung said with a slight bow of his head.

"It's a perfect cover story for sending him back into space," Vaivan said. "Ali's being watched now. In fact, he's targeted."

"There's no question about it. I don't like it, but . . ." Ali didn't mention the railway platform attempt or the Killer ERG in his cottage. He looked around and said levelly, "I'm leaving for Ell-Five as soon as possible."

"Let me have your itinerary when you know it," Ursila Peri said from L-5.

"I will." Ali said this with a tone of voice and inflection that revealed his dislike for the political connivings of Earth people.

"Is your report completed, Alichin?" Rayo Vamori asked his son.

"It is. Any questions?"

"Yes." It was Kariander Kokat Dok of Topawa Finance &

Investment Bankers, Ltd. He got heavily to his feet. He was a large and pudgy man with soft features and a mode of attire that was extravagant in this group. Ali had introduced him as an uncle on his mother's side—not his mother's brother but the husband of his mother's sister. The English language doesn't have the proper terms to express the relationships within such large families. My first impression was that Kariander Dok enjoyed to excess a profligate life style quite unlike the people around him. The earring in his left ear lobe would have marked him as a sado in America, but I didn't know if the custom held in the Commonwealth. His wife, Tanyo Nogala Dok, showed none of the traits of the opposite side of what was usually a pair. I rather doubted that any psychological deviation of that sort could exist in Ali's family, so I was probably getting the wrong signals again.

Kariander Dok continued with a pleasant smile, "Alichin, are we facing the possibility of invasion? Surely you must have some thoughts on this."

Ali replied thoughtfully. "Santa Fe caused me to re-evaluate our adversaries. They're more dangerous than we originally thought. Their careful and complete casting and orchestration of the Santa Fe conference tells me they didn't want us to go along with it in the first place. They don't want co-operation. They don't want to negotiate. They intend to eliminate us as competition. It's a common practice in the business world. But I don't believe we face a military threat. Why? Because they can't control every aspect of world opinion, and it wouldn't be in their best interests to invade and conquer a small nation like the Commonwealth."

I got to my feet and called out, "Ali, as an outlander, may I make an observation?"

Ali looked at me and remarked, "You're an outlander only if you think you are, Sandy. We always appreciate hearing the viewpoint of a newcomer who may not be enamored by the prevailing logic. What do you see here that I don't?"

"First, I agree you've been brought under economic pressure, but it isn't intended to eliminate you as competition," I remarked.

"Is an armed conflict scenario more probable?"

"Yes. Consider a historic analog. When the Meiji put Japan on the road to industrialism, they found themselves without native raw materials necessary for an industrial state. They could have obtained those by negotiation, but they didn't know how to negotiate because they were still a feudal culture accustomed to using military force instead. Europeans and Americans had developed and were dependent upon the same resources the Japanese needed and threatened to take. Europe and America reacted by denying those materials. The final blow came when the United States embargoed trade and cut off eighty percent of Japan's petroleum. The Japanese then believed they had no recourse but military action, which they took.''

"What has ancient history got to do with what's happening now?" Kariander Dok broke in.

"If history doesn't repeat itself, at least the *patterns* of history do! I've heard the Commonwealth referred to as 'the Japan of the tropics,' '' I told him.

"Are you implying we'd go to war with the Tripartite and the PetroFed?"

"No, my analogy was intended to point out that the economic pressures being applied to the Commonwealth aren't necessarily a prelude to elimination of the Commonwealth as competition, but to actually destroy what presently exists here as a perceived threat. This will probably be done in a way we least expect. The United States, Japan, Bahia, or the Saudis won't attack you. You aren't a military threat to them. What your adversaries really want is to carve up the Commonwealth among your covetous neighbors who may be called upon to carry out the military actions. I know nothing about what you're doing except what I've heard here tonight, but that's the way I see it. What more can I tell you than what I've observed? It's free advice that's cost you nothing, and it may be worth just that," I told them and sat down.

The General spoke up, "Rayo, he may be right. Abiku, it would be wise to put the LandImpy and AirImpy on a higher level of readiness, but don't activate the CitImpy yet because it would reveal we're anticipating someone to move against us. Let things develop first. Implement Phase Two and accelerate it. Alichin, proceed with the space aspect at once. Kevin, your captains should be alerted to expect SMAT."

Rayo Vamori nodded at each recommendation his father made. If I was watching a "kitchen cabinet" of Commonwealth politics at work, it was obvious who the leader was.

"Should we sit tight and see how well their boycott works?" Vaya Delkot of Vamori Free Space Port wanted to know. "Or should we embargo *them*?"

"Let's get some feedback on that," General Vamori suggested. "Trip, what about it?"

Trip Sinclair thought for a moment before he answered. "I'd recommend business as usual, General. Except for goods already in the pipeline, the Tripartite may be able to make the boycott stick if not by financial pressures then certainly by political moves. However, a certain amount of trade will go on because not all large companies have Tripartite connections and can work around the restraints. According to my preliminary estimate, we can expect an initial sixty percent reduction in activity from North and South America and perhaps as much as seventy-five percent from Japan. I can't estimate Europe at this time, but maybe Heinrich can.''

Von Undine got to his feet so the video sensors could zero on him better. ''I would anticipate an almost complete embargo of European activity through Vamori Free Space Port.''

Hudyadha-ben-Mukhalla put in from Dhahran, ''Not all European commerce is under Tripartite control. The Spanish and Scandinavians will continue to send their trade through you. My best estimate for Europe is about sixty percent reduction, in line with Skinner Sinclair's estimate of the Americas.''

''You forget the leverage possessed by the Tripartite in nations such as mine,'' Missamaghadi Phalonagri in Madras remarked. ''Powersats owned by Tripartite-controlled firms provide India with a large percentage of its electrical power.''

''We know that, Missam, but I'll cover India's critical baseload.'' That came quietly from Shaiko Stoak, CEO of Commonwealth Glaser Space Power, Inc.. He was there in Karederu Center with his wife, Nyala Nogalu Stoak. I began to realize the extent to which this megafamily was interlinked.

Wen-ling Chung added from Hong Kong, ''We have the capital required for Phase Three. Trip, will Babson & Bowles or Rogers-Gates be willing to bid?''

''Babson & Bowles won't; Lyle Babson's a member of the Tripartite energy subcouncil. Neither will Rogers-Gates or Bozly Engineering in Seattle because of Tripartite-backed engineering projects in-house,'' Trip Sinclair replied.

''I'm worried about RIO's reaction,'' Captain Kevin Graham remarked from the space port. ''Our captains are concerned that PowerSat, InPowSat, and InSolSat powersats could have their power beams diverted to the American beam weapon stations on orbit . . . and we know where *every* one of them is stationed even though the Aerospace Force tried to hide them in inclined Clarke orbits.''

That was Top Secret information! How had the League of Free Traders found these battle stations, shrouded as they were with hard stealth technology?

Ursila Peri reported from L-5, ''I don't know if the powersat crews would carry out an order to redirect power beams to military battle stations. Whether the Aerospace Force has plans for a military takeover of the powersats is another matter, but such an attempt would put them in confrontation with the RIO teams on the powersats.''

I knew something about that. It was covered by the highest possible security classification, and it was difficult for me then to even consider revealing it, so thorough had been my Aerospace Force indoctrination over the years.

"*That* remains the big unknown in Phase Three," The General pointed out. "Alichin, it will hinge on how well you perform in Phase Two."

"I know."

"Anything else?" Rayo Vamori asked.

"Be on guard," Vaivan repeated her warning.

"We will," Rayo promised for the assembled group. "The Commonwealth Commerce Congress will meet on telenet at thirteen hundred hours Zulu time tomorrow. Any conflicts?"

"You always get me up at the crack of dawn," Trip Sinclair complained with a broad American grin.

"And it is late at night for us," Wen-ling Chung told him.

"Someday everyone but the farmers will operate on Universal Time regardless of the position of the sun in the sky," The General observed.

"We do that already," Ursila Peri remarked from L-5.

As the meeting broke up, family members with children in Karederu Center collected offspring from various rooms where they were either asleep or playing. Others moved to put away equipment and check the kitchen to be sure that the robots had cleaned and stored the eating equipment.

"Sit down," Ali told me, indicating a group of chairs gathered around a low table. "Heinrich, can you join us?"

"I'd like to, Alichin, but I have an urgent appointment with Muller. He's to call me at twenty-one hundred hours from Ottowa, and I can't keep him waiting." Von Undine seemed anxious to leave and did so without further ado.

The General and Vaivan joined the circle around the table. Tsaya offered me a tall-stemmed glass of a very dry white wine. I thanked her, and she replied softly with lowered eyes. I surmised she was shy, but with her natural beauty she didn't need to be retiring.

"Well, Sandy?" Alichin asked as I sipped the wine. "Do you understand what we're doing now and why we need a person like you?"

The wine was smooth and its modest ethanol content would

certainly relax me. "Frankly, no," I admitted. "I haven't the benefit of the background you take for granted."

"What don't you understand?"

I set the wine glass down on the low table. "The whole set-up. What's this Tripartite you talk about? The PetroFed? You talk as though they're countries. I know geography, and I don't recognize them. So who are they? Who's our opponent?"

"Who do you think?"

"Bahia maybe, since they've got the other free space port. The United States perhaps or maybe even Japan because both nations have strong interests in space commerce. They want a piece of your action that they don't have because you're stiff competition for them. Too stiff, probably."

General Vamori finished the wine in his glass and set it on the low table too. His put his fingertips together in front of him and said, "As one who's been militarily educated, Sandy, you naturally think of conflicts as occurring between governments. That may have been true three hundred years ago when the world was run by kings and emperors. But they lost their grip in the nineteenth century when it got expensive to run the world. Do you recall a family named Rothschild?"

"Didn't they control the European banking system until the French nationalized the last Rothschild bank in about 1980?"

"The French government really didn't do that, but that's what everyone was supposed to believe," The General observed. "Do you remember what Anselm Rothschild once said?"

"I've never studied financial history."

"Too bad. It's made the world go round in the past several centuries and it's the modern reason for the existence of military forces. Anselm Rothschild once stated, 'Give me the power to issue a nation's money, and I care not who makes the laws.' "

"How did he rationalize that?"

"The Rothschilds started out financing local princes," The General explained. "After about 1800, they started lending money to European governments. Then they saw to it that national affairs occurred so the loans were always paid with interest. In a very short time, the Rothschilds controlled the money supply of Europe. They owned the banks that exchanged various national money tokens."

"But how does control of a nation's money give any political leverage?" I wanted to know.

"You have a folk-saying in America that I learned in a Phoenix management school: 'He who has the gold makes the rules,' " Ali put in. "When you control a nation's money, you can tell kings what to do, depose prime ministers, get your friends and supporters elected to office, get wars started against competing financial organizations headquartered elsewhere, and control trade just like an ancient ruler with a castle and warriors commanding a critical point along a trade route."

"You've got it backwards," I said. "Military forces exist to protect commerce along trade routes."

"You've been to Europe?" The General asked.

I nodded.

"Remember the Rheinpfalz, the castle built on the island in the middle of the Rhine River by Ludwig von Bayer?"

"Yes, a very pretty place to build a castle."

"Ludwig wouldn't let a boat go by in either direction unless the captain paid a toll for the privilege of getting past Rheinpfalz without being destroyed."

"Well, that's a special case," I tried to point out.

"Oh? Nearly every city in Europe was built at a critical node along a trade route. At the heart of every city is one or more castles controlling a river, a river crossing, or a natural terrain feature. Paris, Luxembourg, Cologne, Geneva, Basel, Vienna, Prague, Berlin—the list includes almost every big city in Europe. American cities are located for the same reasons . . ."

"Hold on!" I objected, shaking my head. "Most American cities were built on trade routes, that's true. But they don't have fortifications at their centers."

"How many American city names begin with the word 'fort'? The forts are no longer there because they're no longer needed. Commercial buildings have been built atop the ruins."

"You win," I said. "But you're now talking about physical control over trade, and we started by discussing non-government control organizations. What are you leading up to?"

"The Rheinpfalz and Fort McHenry and Île de la Cité are no longer functioning military installations," Ali observed, "because governments no longer control the trade routes *or* the trade that goes on over them."

The General quietly tapped his fingers together. "A hundred years ago, control of trade was taken *completely* out of the hands of politicians and governments by the bankers and financiers because they had the money to make things happen. These financiers learned from the Rothchilds and became the power groups who elected the officials, provided the money when the Treasury went into the money markets for loans, placed their own people in positions of political and commercial power, and remained in the quiet background because it wasn't to their advantage to take the limelight. Today these power groups have better organization, communications, control, and police power than most national governments."

"General, with all due respect, sir," I remarked carefully, "that sounds like something from Radio Moskva. If the capitalists have indeed taken over, we'd know it from their excesses. There'd have been more wars in the last hundred years."

"No, Sandy," The General said, "I didn't say there was one big, monolithic power group. There isn't. There are a *lot* of different power groups. There's been continual competition between them to see who'd be in control at any given time. The competition between these power groups is the only thing that's kept the world from being destroyed in thermonuclear general war because such a holocaust is unprofitable to *every* power group. Small local brush-fire wars can often be to the advantage of one power group in its struggle against another, but any war like the two World Wars of the last century is now counterproductive to the purposes of modern power groups."

"Those are our adversaries," Vaivan Teaq said, "not national governments who are only front organizations to maintain obscurity and anonymity for those with the real power. Since the Founders' War, we've been careful *not* to ally ourselves closely with any major world power group for reasons that should be obvious."

"Who are these people?" I wanted to know. I also wanted to believe them because it made some sense although it didn't track with *anything* I'd been taught.

"You never hear of them," The General replied. "Their credo says their names should appear in the news when they're born, when they're married, and when they die. They don't need and don't want publicity or recognition. That dilutes power."

"Yes, but you've hung names on some of the power groups," I pointed out. "Who are they?"

"Here in the middle of the twenty-first century there are four major ones," Vaivan said, ticking them off on her long fingers. "One's the Tripartite Coalition that consists of people from the Americas, Europa, and Japan. Then there's the Socialist Hegonomy, a collection of political power groups who aren't socialists but state capitalists; they're large enough to be viable even if their lack of economic efficiency will never permit them to be on top. The Petroleum Confederation of PetroFed is the remnant of OPEC that still possesses of an enormous amount of well-invested capital generated by the defunct petroleum cartel of seventy years ago."

Her brother added, "The biggest unknown is the so-called 'Yellow Peril' in mainland China. They lost Space War One, and they've spent the decades since developing their technology base. They may now be in control of their population and food situations. That means they might be a candidate for future top group, although they don't have the energy resources right now to do it."

"Then there's the Commonwealth," I observed, "on the way up."

"We'll never be the top group." Wahak shook his head. "We're like the Dutch: too few people."

"But you're using high technology in a low-profile manner," I continued. "That gives you leverage you couldn't otherwise possess in spite of your small size."

Vaivan said, "The only leverage we have is alliances with other small power groups who don't threaten each other."

"Which you appear to have," I observed, "if my analysis of the people who were on the telenet tonight is correct."

"You're learning," Alichin replied.

Vaivan suddenly held up her hand for silence. "Did you hear it?"

"Hear what?" I asked.

"Listen!"

There came a muffled "thunk" followed shortly by another one. A pause, then a quiet rattle like a brief rain shower falling on the roof.

"Out!" Vaivan suddenly shouted in a voice much louder than I thought she was capable of. "Everybody out of the Center! Now! Move!"

She was on her feet, had her brother by the arm, and was on her way toward the porch surrounding the Center.

I followed without asking questions. There's a time for talk and a time for action. Talk time was over. I didn't know what the small noises were. Vaivan apparently did.

Once outside, Ali and Vaivan put distance between them and the building. Again, I followed suit. I got the fleeting impression that lots of other people were also fleeing the building.

Karederu Center blew up in a strange explosion.

There was a blast of heat and a muffled, low-order boom. I knew there'd be a shock wave, so I hit the grass.

One of the Vamori women was running beside me. As I went down, I took her with me, shielding her with my body against the heat, the blast, and the flying debris.

I felt the sharp point of a small knife low on my torso in a place where I don't like knives to be sticking me because I hoped to have children some day.

"Let me go, or you'll lose them!" the quiet feminine voice came in my ear.

She meant it, so I rolled onto the lawn.

I'd pulled down and landed atop Tsaya Stoak, the shy young thing who'd served wine. She wasn't a bit shy with that little dirk in her hand!

"Sorry, I was just trying to shield you," I attempted to explain.

"Oh, no!" It was both an expletive and a moan of disbelief as she looked behind us. I turned my head.

Karederu Center was fully engulfed in flames that towered in a huge column toward the night sky, thundering with a roar like a waterfall. The center of the building collapsed on itself.

It had happened fast. It *had* to have been arson. Although there'd been some wood in Karederu Center, a lot of Commonwealth structural plastic such as glasfiber had been used in its construction as well. Modern resins won't normally burn, but they'll melt and serve as a binder to other fuels if the fire gets hot enough fast enough. This one had.

Alichin and Vaivan sat together on the grass not two meters from us. Vaivan had a shocked look on her face that stripped away her beauty and replaced it with a mask of horror. The intelligence expert was appalled at the extent and ruthlessness of the violence that could accompany the intrigue of her area of expertise.

Ali's expression was hard and determined, and it was he who recovered his wits first. "Everyone! Head count! And let's get in as close as we can to see if anybody's caught inside!" he yelled above the roar of the flames.

A cry came, "Where's The General?"

"Oh, no! He's got an arthritic hip!" Tsaya Stoak exclaimed. "He can't move as fast as we did!" She leaped to her feet, but Alichin was up before she was and moving cautiously toward the engulfed Karederu Center, his arm held before his face to help shield him from the intense heat.

A short, stocky form suddenly raced through the group of people on the lawn. He had a blanket or shawl over one arm and he'd pulled his white shirt up from his back to cover his head.

"Omer! Stay out of there!" It was Vaivan who recognized the Kazakh.

"I see The General!" came the muffled shout in reply. And Omer Astrabadi threw himself into the inferno.

Ali was right behind him.

I watched transfixed until Vaivan shouted, "Get water hoses! Get water on them and around them!"

Nobody could exist long in or close to that holocaust. But both Ali and Omer were out in seconds. They carried and dragged a form between them. Ali's shirt was on fire.

I got to them first and pulled Ali away from The General's body. He resisted, but I tore him loose and rolled him on the ground. Others rushed up to help Omer.

I got Ali's fires extinguished. He was grimacing in pain but didn't cry out or whimper. Someone had turned on the lawn sprinklers so that a mist of water covered us. Somebody else had found water hoses and was playing them over those of us who were close to the flaming building.

Ali was badly burned over his shoulders and torso where his shirt had caught afire. Luckily, it had been made of Commonwealth cotton which just burned. If it had been made of artificial fibers, it would have melted to his skin.

"Easy, easy!" I told Ali. "We've got The General."

"How is he? He looked bad," Ali managed to grunt between short gasps.

I got under his right arm and picked him up. "We're too close. Let's get back where it's cooler."

Five people had carried The General across the water-sprayed lawn to a spot under a walkway floodlight. I followed with Ali who was in great pain from his burns by now.

Tsaya Stoak stepped up to Ali, tore away the remains of his burned shirt, and began to look him over.

"Don't touch him!" I tried to tell her. "You could infect those burned areas! Get a doctor!"

"I am a doctor!" Tsaya yelled back. "I'm both an M.D. and a witch doctor!"

In spite of what Tsaya said, I was tremendously relieved.

"Only first degree burns," Tsaya remarked. "About twenty percent of your body, Ali." She ran her hands over his neck and shoulders, then placed her fingertips on both sides of Ali's neck. I didn't see what she did, but for an instant she seemed to be intensely concentrating on Ali. "Better?" she asked.

"Yes. I'm all right if nothing touches those burns."

"I'll start therapy as soon as I take care of The General," Tsaya told him and turned to where the old man lay on a collection of cloths and blankets.

"How is he? He looked bad to Omer and me," Ali said.

There was no mistaking the gravity of Tsaya Stoak's tone. "The General has second and third degree burns over about eighty percent of his body. If we don't act fast, he'll die."

CHAPTER 5

Special Solution

"Where's the nearest burn trauma hospital?" I asked. General Vamori was an old man, I didn't know how good his heart was and it was obvious that his extensive burns would require the finest biotech facilities. I didn't think the Commonwealth had them.

"Vamori Free Space Port," Omer replied.

Of course! A space port would have facilities to handle very complex burn cases.

But it was Tsaya Stoak who broke in, "No, I want him in the Haeberle Clinic at Ell-Five. Easier on his cardiovascular system and easier to rejuvenate the burned areas without keloid tissue."

"Besides," Vaivan said, "he's going to be safer there if we're the target of terrorism."

"This isn't real terrorism," I pointed out. "Everything that happened today was harassment—fortunate if it worked but inconsequential if it didn't."

Fire control aerodynes were circling the area discharging suppressant gases through their vaporizers. Other aerodynes bearing the blue hex-kreutz of medevac began settling to the ground.

In spite of his burns, Ali seemed to be suffering little pain. He began to organize things. "Wahak, get medics to bring a pyro trauma tank here! Omer, get on the comm and alert Vamori-Free so that *Tuito* or the *Tonolia*, whichever's on dirt, can lift for Ell-Five ass-ap. Four . . . No, make that five aboard. Omer, you fly. Vaivan, you and Wahak will have to pull things together here and get our comm center back in operation."

"We'll switch to Vershatets," Vaivan noted. "More secure."

Ali looked up at me from where he was kneeling beside his grandfather. "Sandy, are you with us? Make up your mind *now*!"

"Do I have any choice?" I fired back. I didn't know who'd been responsible for the three incidents today, but I liked these people. I liked their openness and their unwillingness to knuckle under to coercion. Pacifists they weren't. Traders, merchants, and creators they were. In some ways, they resembled other peoples who'd refused to bow down to threats from bigger groups—my own ancestors in Philadelphia in 1776, the French Maquis, the Afghans, the Poles, the Afrikaans, the Mongolians, some of whom had won and some of whom had lost but had fought to the end nonetheless.

They could use me.

But they badly needed the leadership of the man who lay mortally burned on the ground beside Ali.

Time to fish or cut bait. Choose your partners and form squares.

"I'm in. We'll discuss details later."

It was the quickest and simplest decision I'd ever made. In the long run, it bound me more than any formal oath I'd ever taken.

"Can you find your way back to my cottage?" Ali wanted to know.

I ran the memory recall. "Yes."

"Get the aerodyne parked out back and get it over here. Start code is one-one-two-zero-zero-one. Mnemonic: the founding date of the Commonwealth. All our vehicles, including spacecraft, will respond to that start code, even overriding their everyday start codes."

"I'm not sure I can fly it. What kind is it?"

"Mitsubishi Victoria six-three-hundred."

That aerodyne was the Flying Ford of the world, about as universal as an air hauler could be.

I found it where Ali said it would be. The alky-fuel tanks were full. While the turbine was coming up to heat, I ran the preflight checks. It was important to make sure that the slot valves—especially the attitude system—operated properly because they controlled the lift generated by Coanda Effect on the directly blown surfaces. Most people have never seen an aerodyne except in the Smithsonian or the Deutchesmuzeum, but they were all we had for vee-stoll flight before lift drives existed.

The inferno of Karederu Center had been extinguished by the time I got back. I set down without even stirring the grass about ten meters from where The General was surrounded by Tsaya, Ali, and the rest.

The General was now totally immersed in the liquid of the pyro trauma tank with tubes, hoses, and connections coming out to provide his life support. Ali had liquid compresses and synflesh dressings over his burns. I tried to be helpful, but it was Ali who supervised the loading of the aerodyne.

As four medtechs put The General's tank aboard, Vaivan walked up to Ali and me. She was carrying a familiar object.

"Crossbow," I identified it.

"That's what I thought," Ali added.

"We got the team of two," Vaivan said. "They're Ilkans."

"The crossbow came from Kalihol," Ali remarked as he looked it over.

"And some of their equipment is Chibka," Vaivan added.

"Nice neighbors you've got," I said.

Vaivan looked at the crossbow. "Everything they used is perfectly legal to possess in the Commonwealth. Pyroaerosols using cee-oh-two capsules for misting a hundred milliliter of alky. Incense punk for an ignition source. Both capable of being strapped to a crossbow bolt, and the crossbows powerful enough to launch the loads a hundred meters from the road over the barrier and onto the roof of the Center."

Damned simple! Almost any flammable liquid could be aerosoled easily. Dispersed aerosols would lay right down on the roof surface within seconds. Then all it took was the arrival of the bolts carrying the punk. Vapor explosives are nasty.

"Who sent them?" Ali asked his sister.

Vaivan looked grim. "Probably never find out."

"Vaivan, send what's left back to the respective countries," Omer Astrabadi suggested. "Do it so it is not known how the remains got there but so there is no question about who they were."

"I'm quite capable of conducting counter-terrorist operations, Omer." Beneath the beautiful and cultured exterior of Vaivan Teaq lay something quite different. And I wouldn't put it past Commonwealth women, either. My brief contact with them convinced me the females were the vicious ones. Controlled, yes, but capable of powerful and effective action if required. Alichin Vamori seemed considerably less capable of deliberate violence than his sister. Maybe it was a sex-linked genetic characteristic. I understood why Vaivan Vamori Teaq was in charge of the security of Landlimo Corporation . . . and who knows what other organizations in this tightly interwoven operation.

I didn't ask questions at that point. I'd find out soon enough. I was with them, and I was glad to be. I didn't want to be considered an opponent.

The Tripartite Coalition and whatever other power groups had decided to crack the whip over these people were certain to learn the hard way that they'd enraged a tiger. It was either going to be long and bloody . . . or short and even bloodier.

"Omer, are you all right?" Ali wanted to know.

"*Da*," the Mad Russian Space Jockey replied. "I went into the fire with my white shirt pulled over me to protect me—is called a Baikonur Fire Safety Suit."

"Sandy, fly the aerodyne. Omer, navigate because you know the route and the Vamori-Free layout," Ali directed. "Tsaya's already aboard with The General. Let's go! Vaivan, Wahak, see you on the net!"

The aerodyne acted a lot differently with four more people aboard. In spite of the fact that I was hyped-up with adrenalin, I could tell I was getting fatigued because some of my reflexes weren't as fast as they should have been. With an additional load of almost 400 kilograms, the aerodyne took a lot more slot flow to break ground, and, once out of ground effect and clearing the trees, it frisbeed as its stability computer felt out the correct control responses and altered the control program accordingly. I managed to keep it right side up.

"Climb to a hundred meters. Come to a magnetic heading of zero-four-seven," Omer instructed me. "That's high enough to clear towers and buildings. Press to maximum cruise."

I queried the computer concerning maximum permissible air-speed with the present load. The answer came to 209 klicks per hour and told me what power settings and slot openings would enable that.

The lights of Topawa slid underneath us.

"Get a course line set up on the computer and presented on my HUD," I told him. "I'm not going to fly with my head in the cockpit through the traffic we're sure to have around the Space Port."

"You'll get what you ask for," Omer promised. Within three seconds, the data flashed on the windscreen head-up display in front of me.

"Topawa Track, Mitsubishi seven-one-four, medical emergency, over Topawa at one-zero-zero, heading zero-four-seven, going to Area Seven-three, Vamori-Free," Omer spoke on the comm to air traffic control.

"Seven-one-four, contact and track. Seven-one-four is cleared to Area Seven-three, Vamori Free Space Port, present heading. Maintain one hundred meters. We're clearing your corridor now."

"Seven-one-four, acknowledged."

"Traffic one o'clock going to twelve o'clock, two clicks, altitude confirmed at five zero zero."

"Tally ho!"

This was a time when I thanked the system for working

properly because I was fatigued, flying an unfamiliar vehicle, and under pressure.

As we cleared the urban area of Topawa and headed out over the darkened countryside toward the far glow that had to be the lights of Vamori Free Sport Port, Omer advised me, "Follow the road." The lights of the vehicles on the highway formed a necklace of brightness that pointed along our course.

Alichin leaned forward between our front seats. "Omer, Wahak couldn't get a crew for the *Tonolia* on short notice. The crews are on holiday leave. Can you handle it?"

"With some help," Omer Astrabadi replied curtly.

"I'm in no condition to help you tonight. Tsaya's pain block won't last much longer, and I'll have to let her use chemical pain suppression. That'll destroy my mental alertness. You'll have to pilot."

"I say again: I need help. The *Toreva* Class packets can't be flown easily with only one pilot."

"Sandy, you'll have to co-pilot the *Tonolia*."

"I'm not certificated for that class, Ali," I told him.

"Certification be damned! The ship's registered in the Commonwealth, and the Commonwealth will *ex post facto* certificate you."

"I'll need a check-out."

"How much?"

"I don't know. I've never been in the *Toreva* Class."

"Yankee," Omer said to me with a grin under his huge mustache, "I thought you were a hot jock from the U.S. Aerospace Force who says its pilots can fly anything that'll get off the ground."

"When you put it that way, I'll manage, Russkie. Just show me where the *Tonolia's* panic abort switch is. I'll figure the rest of it out."

"With my help, Sandy, you can hack it. We'll smoke that can to Ell-Five as fast as its delta-vee capability will permit," Omer Astrabadi assured me.

I really didn't need Omer navigating the aerodyne. ATC kept feeding me vectors to keep us clear of Vamori-Free traffic. And I couldn't have missed Vamori-Free unless I'd been blind or on the gauges. The place covered 7500 square kilometers and stretched out along the coastline for 150 kilometers. It lit up the night sky as its ramp, pad, and runway lights caught the haze of the ocean and created a corona effect above it.

"Seven-one-four, Vamori Air Track. Pad at twelve o'clock, two kilometers. Report it in sight," the comm barked.

Omer stretched out his arm and pointed ahead. "Vamori Track, seven-one-four has visual on the pad."

"Seven-one-four, the pad is yellow. I repeat: the pad is yellow."

"Roger, Track. We acknowledge that," Omer told him. "Seven-one-four requests a clear."

"Seven-one-four is clear to leave frequency."

Omer directed me to set the aerodyne down about a kilometer to the left of the pad. I had my hands full of an unfamiliar aerodyne, so I didn't get the chance then to see more than a launch runway with a hulking grey shape sitting on the start end.

The transition from aerodyne to space ship was fast. The pad crews had been alerted for our arrival with the critically injured General. There was a van waiting to transfer us. Six men wrestled the pyro tank aboard, and we clambered in behind.

"How is he?" Ali asked Tsaya.

The doctor was checking the readouts of the portable biodata pack. "I've got him stabilized," she replied briefly and then promised in that soft voice of hers, "I won't let him die."

I was concerned about the effects of lift acceleration on The General and told her so.

"Pyro tank immersion is not only beneficial to his burned tissue and prevents massive fluid loss, but he'll also be capable of withstanding many more gees," Tsaya said. In my excited and fatigued condition I'd forgotten the obvious consequences of putting The General in a pyro tank. That was the sort of shape I was in. Tsaya knew what she was doing, and she went about doing it in a quiet and totally competent manner that was belied by her quiet shyness. She was a pro.

The *Tonolia* looked familiar as we got out of the van at the pad, and I remarked as much to Omer. "She should," he said. "The *Toreva* Class packets were built at Vamori North Yards. They took the best features of your Arguello Yards' *Tribal* Class packets and mixed in some characteristics of the Osakhi *Hiko* ships."

"I can smoke her," I told him. "The Aerospace Force *Hopi* Class ships were the military versions of the commercial *Tribal* Class, and we used to bounce those birds all over on training and proficiency missions as well as liaison sorties. Is she as insensitive to payload as the *Tribal* Class?"

Omer nodded as we all walked over to the access stairs to enter her fuselage. "I make rough calculation. We mass three-eighty kilos all together. She'll lift a metric ton to lunar orbit, so we really move now. What gee limit, Doctor?" Omer asked Tsaya.

"No limit," Tsaya told him. "The General could be boosted more than ten gees in the tank."

Ali spread his arms to reveal the pseudoskin bandages over the burns on his arms and chest. "These won't gee-limit me, either. I'll be on my back."

"Then we boost at whatever STC approves for limiting acceleration," Omer remarked as we followed the men carrying the pyro tank into the open hatch of the *Tonolia's* fuselage.

The *Tonolia* was familiar yet slightly different from the *Hopis* I'd flown. Front to rear, she was the same—nose equipment bay, forward impulse bay, electronics bay, flight deck, passenger deck, cargo hold (empty on this flight), propellant bay and wet wings, aeroturbine bay, and engine and aft impulse bay. The difference lay in the fact that a lot of American-type redundant technological frills were missing. The *Tonolia* was a plain-vanilla high-performance high-efficiency Earth-to-space commercial hot rod, a Commonwealth copy of a Japanese version of a highly successful American design.

I settled myself in the right seat, fastened the harness, and reached down to pick up the flight manual and check list. The panel before me was strange at first. As I looked it over and began to locate the basic enablement switches, controls, and readbacks, the patterns of habit I'd learned in the *Hopi* utility corvettes began to be reformed into patterns for the *Tonolia*.

But I had some hesitation going through the power-up check list with Omer. The Mad Russian Space Jockey he might be, but he was amazingly patient with me that night. Never once did he reach out to touch a switch or control whose location he knew while I fumbled over the panels trying to find it. Never once did he tell me where to look; he let me find things myself so I'd know where they were if I had to find them again. He was in no rush.

Having powered-up, we ran through the pre-clearance checks, and I found myself getting better at it. It had been over a month since I'd logged time in the similar Aerospace Force ships.

"Ready to lift. Inform STC and get our clearance," Omer finally told me.

"Vamori Departure Clearance, this is *Tonolia*. Ready for launch, Area Seven-three, clearance request on file," I communicated with the local element of Vamori Space Traffic Control. "I hope Wahak or Vaivan or somebody filed for us as they were supposed to," I added, but only to Omer.

"They said they would, so they did," Omer replied flatly.

"*Tonolia*, Departure Clearance. Stand by on up-link for computer flight plan load. Five minutes and running."

I got the indication that the STC computer had fed the clearance to our on-board computer, so I punched up the display to check the clearance. So did Omer.

"Cleared for only two-point-four gees," Omer noted with disgust. "Withhold acceptance. Ask for a three gee boost. Tell them med emergency."

I did, but neither of us liked the answer. "*Tonolia*, unable your request for higher boost. AmSpace Command informs Wichita Center high boost will breach the engagement zone of critical American space facilities in GEO with a closure rate that's too great. Sorry about that."

"Can we get full boost if we delay launch?" I wanted to know.

"Stand by." There was comm silence for a moment while Vamori Space Traffic Control center queried their North American counterpart, then replied to us, "*Tonolia*, if you want to hold for three-point-five hours, Wichita will clear high boost."

Omer shook his head. "*Nyet!* Look at cleared flight plan data, Sandy."

"Vamori Clearance, *Tonolia* acknowledges computer load of cleared flight plan and accepts," I told them when I saw that our lower-boost clearance would give us an arrival time 2.3 hours earlier than waiting for a high boost clearance.

"Roger, *Tonolia*, two minutes and running. Stand by for transfer to auto."

"We've got it, Clearance."

"Contact Departure."

It was standard procedure from then on. At one minute, the floodlights came on, illuminating the kilometer of takeoff lane ahead of us that stretched eastward toward the shoreline and the Maro India beyond.

"Rails? Sled launch?" I asked.

"Easier on tires," Omer observed. "Rail slippers are cheaper."

What else should I expect from a free enterprise operation? The *Tonolia* had retractable wheeled landing gear like an aerodyne, but only for Earth landing. For launch, the ship with its landing gear retracted was perched atop a simple rail-mounted framework.

The launch procedure was *slightly* different from military practice. The main aeroturbines didn't initiate start-up at minus-five; the sequencer put them into start mode when the sled's linear motor was energized.

The *Tonolia* made a standard one-gee launch run. Her

aeroturbines were full-thrust by the time we rotated and were airborne at 100 meters per second a little over ten seconds after the sled began accelerating down the track at one-gee.

"Lift off!" Omer called as the ship began to climb out.

"Gear up!" I called out of habit, reaching for where the control was. But it was up already. I'd acted without thinking. "Correction!"

"You were right," Omer observed. "Gear *is* up! Keep cool stool, Sandy! Call two gees and sonic when passed.

The mains throttled up as we ascended, and acceleration rose to flight plan level. Two gees came on schedule. So did sonic velocity. The *Tonolia* wanted to do more, running light as she was. We could have packed as much as four gees without straining her, but we didn't have clearance for it.

I found myself thinking it must have been fun in the old days before traffic got so heavy and vulnerable Earth orbit facilities so numerous that space vehicles required flight clearances to make sure there were no collisions or engagement zone intrusions. Now it was computer-controlled and human-monitored according to the international rules of the road for space.

Our flight plan called for a direct ascent—no climb into parking orbit and apogee boost from there to lunar orbit. *Tonolia* was a hot rod; she didn't need those minimum-energy trajectories. I liked her. She jumped when booted in the tail.

We passed through four different Space Traffic Control Center jurisdictions on the way out, requiring us to confirm our beacon codes on each hand-off. Other than keeping tabs on our computers and verbally communicating with STC for security, Omer and I didn't have much to do during the hours it took to get to Lagrange-Five in lunar orbit. But we couldn't leave our posts. In spite of computers and automation, humans were still required to supervise and monitor the computer and autosystems. Things had gone wrong in the past. In fact, Space War I would never have happened if people had been in space and monitoring the automatic systems the day the sky burned.

I didn't get the chance to go aft to check The General's condition, but we got a report when Ali came up to the flight deck. "He's stable. The tank saved him. We've had a bit of trouble, however. The gasket on the upper membrane started to leak when we hit zero gee. Can't get it stopped."

"Bad leak or a seep?" I asked.

"Just a seep, but it creates liquid globs back there."

"Forget it. Gaskets are designed to leak; I've never seen one that didn't,'' I said. "Use the relief tube to suck up the big globs.''

Omer indicated the X-, Y-, and Z-plane displays to Ali. "*Moy preeyahtyel*, there is more than normal movement of traffic out here today.''

Ali peered at the displays. "Which ones are military vessels?'' he asked.

"Let's look at four-zero-zero-zero through four-five-nine-nine,'' I said. "Those codes cover Aerospace Force, the rest of the Americas, Bahia, Japan, and Europa. Your Tripartite boys, Ali.'' I told the computer to kill all blips except those transmitting the restricted codes and to display the codes.

Although slightly less than half of the Earth-Moon system was blocked by the mass of the Earth, the display showed a freckling of targets nonetheless.

"Tape that,'' Ali told me. "And do it again every fifteen minutes. When we get to Ell-Five, I want our people there to start taping all military activity. We'll want some computer analysis of the most active facilities.''

"You think the Tripartite is moving things around?''

"Yes. Sandy, I'd like you to confirm our data on the locations of the inclined geosynch Aerospace Force facilities when we get to Ell-Five.''

"Will do, Ali.''

It was a good time and place to chat because the *Tonolia* was free-falling out to L-5. It didn't take much to monitor displays in this mode, and things were quiet for the first time in a long time. Things *had* been a bit hectic since I landed in Topawa those long hours ago. Although I hadn't slept except for a nap at Karederu, I felt pretty good. I had my second wind, and I knew I was effective for at least another 12 hours.

"Was I hired because of what I know about American space facilities and operations?'' I asked.

"No, mostly for what you know about the law of modern armed conflict. The Commonwealth is signatory to all the various Geneva and Manila conventions,'' Ali told me, "Some people don't follow them, and we know it. But we're going to.''

"I find that strange in view of the rather strong and forceful ways of Commonwealth justice I witnessed,'' I said.

"Well, we're rather strong and forceful people . . .'' Ali began.

"You've never dealt with Khazakh internal law,'' Omer told him. "The way my people take care of their own internal matters makes Commonwealth law seem liberal, to say nothing of Soviet law which we don't even bother with.''

"There's a wide variation in the degrees to which *lex talionis* is used," I observed.

"Lex who?" Omer asked.

"The sort of law that requires an eye for an eye and a tooth for a tooth," I explained. "Some people think it's barbaric and savage; but properly administered, it's very effective.''

"Other nations have the same opinion of the Commonwealth," Ali remarked. "That's why we've had to develop some innovative methods of handling foreign policy.''

"Uh, Ali, the Commonwealth's not known for having a very strong government, much less a strong foreign policy," I observed. "In fact, the Commonwealth's a very low profile operation. I'm sure you can protect yourselves internally. But your capability to handle external threats such as the one we're now facing seems very weak.''

"That's exactly how we want to be perceived. A cat is a furry, purring piece of lap fur unless you anger it. Then it has claws.''

"What are the claws of the Commonwealth? They're not obvious or evident.''

"We've developed a special solution because of our need to keep a low profile until we were big enough to survive," Ali told me, gazing out the forward windows at the blackness of space. "Others tend to look to our foreign office, which isn't very potent *by design*. They don't look elsewhere because they don't understand our free market philosophy. Sandy, we have a very powerful foreign service. It's capable of diplomacy or conducting a decisive economic war. You're part of it now. It's the Landlimo Corporation.''

CHAPTER 6

The Top of The Hill

Lagrange-Five wasn't a big unified space facility but a collection of habitats, factories, power plants, and military complexes in lunar orbit. Everything's there because the region's the easiest place in the system to get to or from; it has no gravity well and sits atop the gravity wells of both Earth and the Moon.

There's an identical region called *El-chetteereh*—or L-Four in English—60-degrees ahead of the Moon where the Soviets have a facility that includes, among other things, a military complex. They don't talk about it, but the U.S. Aerospace Force knows about it.

The Aerospace Force has military facilities at L-5, and they don't talk about it, either.

It was a "balance of space power" affair.

The Aerospace Force permitted other organizations and nations who were members of the Ottawa Pact to use L-5, provided specific rules regarding the Space Defense and Identification Zones were scrupulously followed. Nations belonging to SocDef called at L-5 only occasionally and then with thorough pre-clearance.

If the United States and other "free nations" were indeed under the control of power groups as The General believed, it was probably a good thing that the Soviets had *El-chetteereh* to counterbalance things.

Or was it the other way around?

It made little difference to me now. I'd cast my lot with the Commonwealth.

Omer piloted the *Tonolia* during approach. In my fatigued condition, I might have botched it.

A docking crew from Commonwealth Space Transport and Forwarding Corporation—ComSpat, for short—was waiting in the portlock.

So was Ursila Peri whose enthusiasm for seeing Ali again was evident even though she was very careful how she hugged him.

"It's *so* good to have you back!" Ursila said as they embraced with a fervor I hadn't seen him exhibit thus far.

"Let Tsaya treat these burns first, *moapa*," he replied.

"Then we've got some catching up to do," she promised him. She had a slight accent, almost British except for a tendency to round her "o's" and clip her consonants. On her it sounded good. "How's The General?" she asked anxiously with the concern and respect evident on the part of everyone connected with the Commonwealth.

"I'll know more when I get him to the Haeberle Clinic," Tsaya told her, helping guide the tube-festooned pyro tank out the hatch.

Although it wasn't necessary because we'd met by video during the previous evening's telecon, Ali re-introduced me to Dr. Ursila Peri who seemed much more vital and animated than on voxvideo. I could well understand Ali's feelings toward her because she possessed a classic female attractiveness which provoked and excited. Like a veil that reveals yet hides, Ursila seemed to have *something* she wasn't showing. That excites men.

"Glad you're with us, Sandy," she told me as we touched hands. "We want you."

Ali put in, "Ursila, Sandy's one outstanding pilot. He'd been checked out only in the Aerospace Force version of the *Tonolia*, yet he flew right seat for Omer."

"I'll fly with him any time," Omer said curtly.

"Come, Ali," Tsaya reminded him in her cool, professional fashion. "I must see your burns under treatment, too."

"I'll tag along," Ursila said. "You can bring me up to date."

Ali turned to me and said, "Sandy, I'll be out of action for a day or so. In the meantime . . . Jeri, come over here, please," he called out to someone supervising the transport of The General's pyro tank.

A long-faced, long-limbed, almost skinny man broke away from the group of people and floated over to us. He grinned, "You bellowed, sir?" he said with mock obsequiousness.

"Sandy, this is Jeri Hospah. Don't let his attempts at humor put you off; sometimes he means what he says. Jeri, find a sack for Sandy and issue him some chits. Then fake up some paperwork that will keep the Ell-Five people happy," Ali instructed us.

"We saw one another on the tube last night," I told Jeri as we touched hands.

"Right-o! Your wish is my command, oh glorious leader." Jeri had a slight accent, perhaps British Londoner, perhaps lower down-east American—I couldn't place it. "I'll take care of him."

Jeri chatted with Omer as he led us through the station and through a secure airlock and transfer tunnel into the Commonwealth facility. Omer obviously knew where we were going but I was so bushed I didn't care. It was all sort of blurry and confused. I was relieved when Jeri showed me a cubicle with a sleep sack. I didn't even bother taking off my dirty blue slacks and shirt, the only remnants I now possessed of my Aerospace Force days.

Uncountable hours later, I awoke in the wan sleeping light of the personal compartment and was momentarily confused until I remembered where I was. I felt physically refreshed but still mentally fatigued. That's a dangerous condition in space because little things can kill a careless person.

Somebody had left a flight suit and a Remain-Over-Night kit. Jeri Hospah was either thoughtful or had a well-trained station crew. I took a sponge bath, put on the flight suit and slippers, and decided I might live if I could find breakfast.

The RON kit had a pack of chits—air, meal, water, airlock cycles—as well as an L-5 facilities directory and a visitor's card for the Free Traders' Lounge.

A note was in the kit. "Call me at 96-69-54 and I'll chit you breakfast—Jeri."

"I'll take you up on your offer," I told him when he answered his page.

"Be there momentarily."

It took only a few minutes before the hatch beeped. "Did you just get holed, or were you back-shopped that way?" Jeri said with his infectious grin as I opened the hatch and floated out.

"After almost getting killed three times in one day and making an emergency boost to Ell-Five, it's probably too late for maintenance. You'll have to scrap me," I told him. "Is my head still on? Feels like it went somewhere at Vee-sub-ee."

"Spoken like a space jock. We'll pick up Doctor Tsaya and get some calories into you down at the libration point libation joint," Jeri promised. "If breakfast doesn't change the lead in your ass to iron in your blood, maybe Doc Tsaya has something for tired space jocks."

"Jeri, I'm sure she has, but I don't think I'll ever get it," I remarked. "I accidentally fell on her at Karederu Center when the place blew, and she was within a millimeter of excising my family jewels."

"You make it sound so interesting when you use those big

scientific terms," Jeri said as we floated down the corridor together.

Things were still nagging at me, and I carefully opened the matter with this lanky spaceman. "Jeri, you've apparently been with these people for some time now. How'd you get involved?"

Jeri Hospah didn't answer for a moment, then said, "I came to work with Ali because he asked me to. I have a job description to satisfy the Ell-Five Habitation Committee, but I staked my future on a handshake."

"Same here," I admitted as we cycled through a hatch. "Can these people be trusted?"

"Explicitly. They have a high sense of personal honor and they'll back up their behavior with their lives if necessary."

"Why'd you come here in the first place?"

"It got me off Earth. I like frontiers. I'm originally an Aussie, raised in Perth. When I was a youngster, Perth was still a frontier; now it isn't."

"What's it like to work for Ali and his family?"

"I don't work *for* them; I work *with* them because they made me one of them. So I work far harder than I must. I think they know what it's like to work *for* somebody else from their colonial days and they've decided it's better to have people working *with* them instead. Regardless of what makes them to do it, they're successful at it."

I had to agree. They'd tacitly accepted me into their ranks without formalities. I was trusting the word of one man. In America, I couldn't do that. I must have come from a distrustful culture.

"By the way, Jeri, what are we in?"

"The ComSpat module leased onto Ell-Five. That lets us use their power and life support systems at a lower cost than running our standbys as primes. And we don't have to step outside to go to town."

As an Aerospace Force officer, I hadn't been encouraged to mingle with the feather merchants. There'd been little need to do so anyway, because the Aerospace Force was Big Daddy and took care of me well while in space.

The L-5 complex was a big space station, but when you've seen one space station you've seen them all, military or civilian. Is there much difference between a military office building and a civilian office building?

On the main hatch of the ComSpat module was a secure lock with screening. I was used to security in military facilities, but it surprised me to find it in a private one. But why not? Most businesses on Earth require a check-in screening in the lobby. "Free Space!" might be the clarion call of the private enterprise people, but that didn't include license to barge into their business facilities.

Ali was with Tsaya in the lounge. "My cousin's a good doctor," he said, anticipating my question as we joined them by tucking our legs under the table. He spread his arms which were now covered with an open-mesh dressing. "Zero-gee makes this a lot easier."

"You have only first-degree and a few second-degree burns," Tsaya Stoak remarked in her quiet way. "There's no need to hospitalize you. In fact, it's better for you to move around."

"How's The General?" I asked and I discovered I had the same sort of concern in my voice as any Commonwealth citizen.

"I got him stabilized at Karederu," Tsaya said. "Preventing initial shock is the most important factor in burn therapy. So I never gave him the chance to go into shock. He's resting comfortably now with glucose and water I-V and maintaining proper urinary output. He'll be on an oral diet tomorrow and capable of having visitors. I'll be able to start skin grafts from cloning as soon as the third-degree burn areas become granulated."

Ali remarked, "You like to work out here, don't you, Tsaya?"

"Yes. It allows me to do things I couldn't on Earth. For example, I can keep The General's weight off his burned areas, and I can get total asepsis. That's why I wanted him in the Haeberle Clinic."

I noticed that one member of our welcoming committee wasn't there. "Is Ursila joining us?"

"Unfortunately not." Ali's voice held a tone of disappointment. He explained, "Until you get current in our vehicles, we're short-handed. Both Ursila and Omer are out-base right now. Pulling the *Tonolia* out of Vamori-Free screwed up our ship scheduling and sequencing," Ali said.

"Ali, it took that old computer program ten seconds to work out the new schedule," Jeri complained. "It isn't the computer, but the old Holerith cards are wearing out and I can't get replacements except in an antique shoppe. Can't we get some better software?" The man had to be kidding, and he was.

Ali caught it and fielded it. "For shifting only twenty-three ships around ten runs? Ten seconds is fast enough. Sometimes old technology is perfectly suitable if it works. We don't want to fall victim to the New Technology Syndrome and end up like the Aerospace Force. No personal insult intended, Sandy."

"No offense taken, Ali. I know what you mean, and I don't work for them anymore."

We ordered from the menu console, and Jeri delivered our orders from the dispenser when they were ready a few minutes later. I knew I was all right because I was hungry.

As we ate, I remarked to Tsaya, "I apologize for frightening you at Karederu Center. I was trying to protect you from flying debris. I really didn't have anything else in mind. Your reaction, uh, rather surprised me."

Tsaya inclined her head and replied with the characteristic shyness she exhibited when discussing anything but her profession, "I, too, apologize, Sandy. I was rude to you. But I wasn't sure you understood our ways yet."

"I don't, but I'm learning. Out of curiosity, why did you threaten me?"

"We're taught to defend ourselves so we can enjoy an equality and freedom not available to many women in our part of the world," she said, then added, "Most outlanders and tourists don't realize what that means. In the confusion, I'm afraid my cultural indoctrination came to the fore."

"Does it always?"

She smiled shyly and replied, "No, not always. Haven't you noticed something else about Commonwealth women that's unusual for our part of the world?"

"Lots of things. What did you specifically have in mind?"

"Ours is the only continent where women deliberately make themselves unattractive as a defense measure. We've broken with that tradition."

"I've noticed."

"Good, because I wouldn't want our accidental confrontation at Karederu to give you the wrong impression." She didn't say anything more on the subject, but she'd given me a lot of encouragement not only for herself but also for others such as the exotically beautiful Vaivan.

"Well, what's our next move in the great chess game in the sky, Boss?" Jeri Hospah asked Ali.

Ali gave him a brief run-down of what had occurred since the teleconference. "When we've finished here, I want to get my sister on the comm. I need an up-date on what's happened since we left Topawa."

"And everyone at Vershatets will want to know about The General," Jeri said and sighed. "It's been like a recording; 'How's The General? How's The General?' In the Top Twenty and gaining hourly. Going gold this week for sure."

"I've already reported on The General's condition to Vaivan," Tsaya put in. "She told me the Karederu fire was the biggest news in the Commonwealth. It even made the international net because of The General. A lot of people wanted to know the extent of The General's injuries."

"I'll bet!" Ali growled. "Well, it's difficult for terrorists to get to him here with all the security laid on by Landlimo Corporation."

I'd wondered about the strange name of the company since I'd first heard it, so I asked, "What's the name mean? Is it an old Commonwealth word?"

Ali shook his head. "No, that would be too easy to decipher. Do you remember a language called Esperanto?"

"Lingual history wasn't a strong subject at the Academy."

"No matter. It's an artificial language created as an international tongue in the nineteenth century," Ali explained. "Two things kept it from being accepted. First off, it was based on Romance languages because Europeans were running the world then, but most people don't speak languages with Graeco-Latin roots. Secondly, like it or not, the comm/info revolution of the last hundred years made English the internatonal language of education, business, commerce, and transportation, poor at as it may be semantically and difficult as it is for people to learn. That's always been true of the languages of conquerors and conquered."

"Hold on!" I objected. "We haven't conquered anyone since World War Two."

"English was the language of those who conquered the world technologically."

"If that's the case, it should be a combination of English and Japanese," I told him.

Ali shook his head. "The Japanese are like us: take the best from others, do a better job with it, and sell it by speaking the customer's language."

"Point well made," I said. "So what's 'landlimo' mean?"

"It's an Esperanto word for 'frontier.' "

On the scrambled Landlimo Corporation conference net, Vaivan asked Tsaya when The General could come back to the Commonwealth.

"I won't move him for at least another forty-five days," Tsaya maintained gently. "It's going to take twenty days to get good cloning of his dermal and epidermal tissue, and I must do that here. Some of his burns are on joints. At his age I can't afford to take the chance of keloid tissue stiffening them. I'm also doing a great deal of reconstructive surgery."

Vaivan looked vexed. "Tsaya, we need him here as soon as possible. You know the hospital here is outstanding. And Vershatets is secure so we don't have to worry about any more assassination attempts."

"Any indication of who's responsible for the other three attempts, Vaivan?" Ali asked his sister. "Did you get anything out of the crossbowmen?"

"Unfortunately not. They were Ilkan fanatics loaded with psychodrugs. They didn't have anything left in their minds. So we sent them back to Ilkan in a suitable manner," Vaivan said without emotion or further elaboration. "But Abiku put the impys on alert at President's Nogal's suggestion because of the Karederu fire. We've spotted some minor troop movement in the vicinity of Khibya, but the Cape-to-Cairo Railway activity has been normal through Kulala, and there's nothing happening on the Lipuputa or Liupp river lines."

I tried to follow her report by referring to the Commonwealth map on the bulkhead. It was the first time I'd had the opportunity to really study the geography of my new land.

The Commonwealth was a typical creation of absentee rule. Its artificial borders had been determined in some long-ago and far-off conference where diplomats drew lines on maps. The southern border was the Lipuputa River which separated it from the Chibka Socialist Republic and was the only Commonwealth boundary based on a natural feature. To some extent the Dilkon Range formed the western boundary, but the summits were anywhere from 50 to 100 kilometers east of the border. The northern border with the Ilkan Empire was totally artificial, merely surveyors' lines across the Dilkons and the barren Ilkan Desert north of the Liupp River.

The state of affairs in the Ilkan Empire and the Kingdom of Malidok was evident by the abandoned railways. Colonials had left the area with an extensive and well-run railway system. Only the Commonwealth had maintained and expanded it to transport the natural resources they'd exploited to build the country.

"Vaivan, we may be wasting time considering a military attack on our borders," I said, indicating the map as I spoke. "The Commonwealth's wide open for about a hundred kilometers between the northern border and the Liupp River, but the Ilkan Empire probably can't mount an attack there because they don't have the road or rail networks to provide logistic support for such an operation. They'd have to use air, which means they'd need aerospace superiority."

"They haven't got it."

"I didn't think so. On the other hand, the Malidoks have a rudimentary road and rail system, but the only place they could really press us is through the Dilkon passes; so don't worry about them," I said, indicating the map as I spoke. "And the Chibkas won't force a crossing of the Lipupta River on the south because the south bank is swampy. So our critical border segment is in the northwest where the Rhodes Cape-to-Cairo Railway goes through Kulala. Either the Emirate or the Ilkans would fight there because we're at a disadvantage; we'd have to conduct logistic support over the Dilkons even though there's a railway through the pass."

Vaivan raised her eyebrows, then remarked to her brother. "Ali, since The General's incapacitated for a few weeks, Sandy should take over as our military liaison to both the Commerce Congress and the Defense Commission."

"Good idea."

"But I don't know a thing about the Commonwealth's military plans!"

"You just outlined them for us."

"Then what's this proposed job about?"

"As Landlimo deputy military director, you'll interface with Commissioner Abiku and his induno staff who handle the nuts and bolts. This is necessary because they've got to defend a free-market system without interfering with it," Vaivan said. "Unlike the American military, ours is subservient not only to civilian control but also to the needs of commerce."

I sighed. I was getting in deeper and deeper. "Let me think about it. There's a lot of time because we're not going to be attacked immediately. Our neighbors don't have any excuse other than territorial greed. They're weak or they'd have invaded long before this," I went on. "You may know commercial history, but I know the military history of this region."

"Very well, we won't worry about invasion," Ali concluded. "But we're fighting an economic war. Wahak, is there any indication the boycott's effective yet?"

Wahak Teaq looked at hard copy in front of him. "Not thus far. Vaya reports activity at the Free Space Port has been normal and expects this to be the case for a week or so because it's not economical or practical for shippers to divert cargo en route. Trip Sinclair has refined his estimates to sixty-two percent once the system has a chance to react. That's the worst we can expect in terms of economic pressure."

I noticed on the map a symbol located northwest of the city of Oidak with electric transmission line symbols leading from it to other parts of the country. "Are you sure? Who owns the powersat that feeds the Oidak rectenna?"

"Commonwealth Glaser," Vaivan replied.

"Who owns that company?"

"About a hundred stockholders here, in Madras, and in Hong Kong."

"That's a critical facility. What happens to our reserve if someone disables the powersat?"

"It provides less than ten percent of our baseload," Wahak said and went on to explain that Commonwealth Glaser's primary business was building and operating powersats for outland customers, and there were customers cued-up for increased output as it was built. ComGlaser had twelve ten-gig units on line and was selling power to other low-tech nations. There were three more units going on line in the near future. The Commonwealth was using powersat energy internally to keep Commonwealth technology current. Commonwealth Glaser's operating profits were retained earnings used to build more units. Until ComGlaser could satisfy all customers, the abundant Commonwealth coal reserves would be used to generate internal baseload. "We're bootstrapping, Sandy."

"Makes sense," I had to admit, "but how are you going to fight an energy war?"

"By supplying powersat electricity to countries the Tripartite cuts off their powersat system for ignoring the Santa Fe boycott," Wahak said.

"We're energy-independent, Sandy," Ali pointed out.

"That's obvious. But if things go toes-up, are we food-independent?"

"Yes," Vaivan replied. "The irrigation systems on the Toak Plains give us three growing seasons a year. We won't starve."

"And we'll make it insofar as international trade and foreign exchange go, too," Wahak Teaq added to his wife's statement, anticipating what would have been my next question. But he admitted, "It might hurt us a little if the Tripartite had a tight land, sea, and air embargo, but I don't think it would last very long. We export grain to brokers in Madras and Hong Kong, and they deal with the Indian subcontinent, southeast Asia, and China as drop-shippers. When those people got hungry, an embargo would be expensive to maintain. The Yellow Peril would certainly ignore it. A space commerce boycott won't hold, either, because Vamori Free Space Port is a true free port. We don't collect taxes or duties on any input or throughput because they create secondary spending. Space commerce may drop thirty-eight percent, but our tourist trade won't suffer even if the Tripartite countries invalidate passports."

"Your lack of passport control was one of the first surprises I had in the Commonwealth," I said. "But I didn't know the tourist trade was that big."

"The world needs places to play. We're an open society of working people anxious to give value received. We offer outstanding service and a variety of excellent resorts to people who want them. You never had the chance to get over to the Sun Coasts, Sandy. Pity. Later perhaps. Beautiful places. Same for the Dilkon resorts." If that was an invitation from Vaivan, I was tempted to accept even though her husband was on the net.

"Look, I'm sorry this telecon degenerated into a school because of my ignorance," I apologized. "There's time for me to do my homework now . . ."

"It's no imposition. Sometimes such educational sessions help us get our own thinking straight. And you can't understand what we're doing unless you understand how the Commonwealth functions," Vaivan said.

"How long does it usually take for an outlander to figure it out?"

"Sandy," Vaivan said, "you're not an outlander any more. I tendered your citizenship papers in Topawa today. Since the United States has some quaint policies regarding dual citizenship, I'll notify the embassy for you. Or do you have second thoughts?"

"No, no." I waved both hands. "I don't understand you yet. But you don't waffle and you're ready to fight for what you've got. I won't back out." The U.S. government was different. Once I was no longer trusted to follow their policies, what the hell had the U.S. government done for me and to me?

Vaivan went on, "Sandy, energy war isn't difficult to understand. Most low-tech countries will continue to do business with us in spite of any embargo or boycott. We provide value received and take very little off the top. The Tripartite may try to invoke sanctions against our customers by pulling their powersat plugs, but we'll be there with another plug. And we have a space port, space lift capability, primary metals and plastics industries, and the lunar mine and smelter at Criswell Center. You haven't see that yet, but it's just a lunar mine and smelter. Commonwealth Glaser's capable of supplying powersat electricity to anyone the Tripartite cuts off because they're now building powersats with lunar materials at a much faster rate than the Tripartite companies.''

''They'll react,'' I warned.

''How?''

''They'll go after your powersats.''

''In the face of international law and the Resident Inspection Organization? The insurance trusts won't stand for it,'' Wahak maintained. ''Those trusts are controlled by the Tripartite, but not even a consortium of all the Tripartite banks could possibly cover the insurance losses. And there won't be any because the insurance trusts will place a rather strong damper on any military powersat takeovers. Then RIO will drive in the bung.''

''RIO teams are un-armed,'' I reminded him.

''We'll see what happens when everybody shows their cards. RIO will have to become the first Space Patrol whether they want to or not because circumstances will force it . . . and so will we.''

CHAPTER 7

Tiger on a Leash

To me, a machine was something to be mistrusted, checked before use, operated within the limits set forth in an operating manual, and coddled. Omer Astrabadi, the Mad Russian Space Jockey, lived up to his sobriquet. He approached machinery differently. I never saw him run a pre-flight inspection; he strapped into the seat, powered up, and went. I never saw him consult an operating manual; but he knew the limits of the machine. There was no question whatsoever that he was the master of it. He wasn't gentle with it, either. If it didn't do what he wanted, he wasn't afraid to coerce it with violence.

Coming home on a flight with him to Dianaport to familiarize me with the *Bacobi* class deep space couriers, an APU power processor quit. Another APU assumed the load, so we didn't lose platform alignment or real-time course line computer tracking.

"I show you how to fix bad processors," Omer told me and took me to the equipment bay. There he grabbed two protrusions on the bulkhead, braced himself, and directed a solid kick at a panel bearing the label, "CAUTION! Only qualified personnel can repair this unit!"

"When it stops, kick it," Omer told me. "This model stops regularly. I told Ali not to buy from the lowest bidder . . ."

"Omer, you might have busted something!" I complained. "We'd play hell getting back without a computer and autopilot!"

He pointed to the read-outs. The unit had picked up its load. "I must train you for commercial operations, Sandy. For years you believe what the Aerospace Force told you."

"I'm still alive because of it."

"In spite of it," Omer corrected me. "I was in *Frontovaia Aviatsiya* before becoming cosmonaut. We kept aircraft flying under conditions you would not believe. I was taught to *make* a machine do what I wanted; if it couldn't, it would tell me."

"And kill you in the process."

"Only if I let it." Omer indicated the now-working APU processor. "What would you do?"

"Shut it down and go back to Ell-Five on the other. Maintenance would fix it after I got back."

Omer shook his head. "We're short of maintenance people. Sandy, some day your life may depend on fixing something. Now, tell me what would happen if we lost all APU power."

"We'd lose the computer and autopilot."

"Consequences?"

"We might not get back to Ell-Five."

"Aerospace Force thinking." Omer pointed to his eyes. "You have two eyes, good guidance system." He tapped his ear. "You have two ears. And you have optical instruments and a working comm unit. Three tracking stations follow us. 'Mayday' call would bring help, but we don't need it. We can astrogate by reference to Earth, Moon, and Sun. Do it." He reached out and shut down both APUs.

I'd been spoiled by high technology. But I made it back to L-5 without having to yell Mayday.

Space flight is mostly waiting. The old aviator's saying is also true for space: "Hours of boredom punctuated by moments of sheer terror." As Omer showed me the ins and outs of commercial space operations and got me current in Commonwealth space vehicles, it began to dawn on me exactly what had happened to me in the past few months. My life had been vented to vacuum. The more I thought about it, the more doubtful I became.

I'd always thought of myself as a tiger. I'd been one ever since Don Carlson, the class bully, beat me up in Second Grade. That led my pacifist father to proclaim from his ivory tower that fighting was a sign of barbarism and didn't settle anything. I was told that if I fought back the matter would only escalate to greater violence. After the second time Carlson beat me, I began to doubt my father's wisdom. The third time, I fought back and lost, but I became a less attractive sissy and Carlson began to harass easier targets. By the time Carlson got bored beating up everybody else and jumped me again, I'd learned enough to beat hell out of him. I was punished by my father, but no school bully picked on me after that. I became a bully in my own right until little Jamie Tagfield stood up to me. After that, I gave up brawling and got along fine with everyone except my father.

Over the years, society put more restraints on me. But when my life was threatened, they vanished. Maybe I was one mean sonofabitch underneath but that still didn't eliminate the doubts that had welled up in my mind following the Black Bear incident. *Was I really a military man capable of measured violence in service to a non-military boss?* Had my tiger leash been tightened so thoroughly that I wasn't really any good as a military person any longer?

Or was it the other way around? Was I now so committed to the commission of physical violence that I was no longer worthwhile as an educated military person?

Coming out of Vamori Free Space Port in the *Tybo,* sister ship to the *Tonolia,* I broached the subject with Omer after main engine shutdown occurred and STC confirmed our track to clearance tolerances.

"No, Sandy. You are slipping your leash."

"What do you mean?"

"You're a leashed tiger," he said. "When the leash comes off, you're as crazy as you think I am."

"Oh, really, Russkie?"

"*Da,* Yankee dog. That Black Bear pilot was trained as I was. Yet you slipped your leash and got him first. But your service did not want tigers who slip their leashes."

"I can drive aerospace ships okay, but that's not what I meant. I came to the Commonwealth in response to an ad for a military aerospace pilot. I expected to learn new things in converting to commercial operations. But I didn't expect I'd be asked to be a military advisor. You're more qualified for it than I am."

"No, Sandy, you have something I do not," Omer told me. "You have a military education. I will be happy to lead any attack squadron, air or space. That I can do. But I have not been educated in strategic doctrine, logistics, and tactical operations." I knew what he meant. Although we'd both served in our respective national military forces, I'd been taught the art of war whereas he'd been trained as an empirical astronautical engineer-pilot with little knowledge of how or why people fought. "You would be a good staff officer if you had stayed on the tiger leash." Omer added.

"No, I'd be dead now."

"Probably. Black Bears have very accurate tracking and targeting equipment. You are one hot jock, Yankee. And you will also be a good *aide de camp* to The General."

It made me feel better that someone had confidence in my abilities.

I'd willingly follow Omer into battle. He was a tiger-type who let it hang way out to see if he could get away with it. He was crazy with machinery, but he wouldn't waste the people who followed him.

When we docked at L-5, there was a message waiting for me.

Tsaya wanted me to call her. I wasted no time once I got back to the Commonwealth module. Tsaya fascinated me; I wanted to learn what was under that shy facade.

But she was strictly business. "The General is doing well," she told me in her professional manner. "He's wants to see you. It'll do him good to talk to someone other than me and the people in the Clinic."

I didn't want to visit The General in the hospital because I don't like hospitals. Even the antiseptic smell bothers me. I don't like to be around people suffering pain and illness. I especially don't like the appearance of badly-burned people. I saw enough of that in the Aerospace Force. My wingman had become a ball of fire in his T-99 at Sierra Vista when its landing gear collapsed. My academy classmate couldn't get out of his Space Hawk when it blew its tail off on liftoff ignition. Those two were enough.

Tsaya must have sensed my reluctance because she told me she'd come along.

The Haeberle Clinic was in the Canadian L-5 module. I was pleasantly surprised to find it had no antiseptic smell. And I was even more surprised at The General's appearance. His face and hands were apparently untouched by the Karederu fire. Between pseudoflesh dressings covering areas where cloned skin grafts were healing, areas of skin of slightly different color showed where first degree burns were already healing. The septic membrane that surrounded his floating body separated us but didn't prevent us from talking.

And it didn't keep The General from reaching out with both hands to the membrane. We touched with the septic barrier between us. The General was smiling.

"Thank you for coming, Sandy." The General's voice was as strong as it had been in Topawa and his eyes were bright and sharp. "How are you getting on with our people?"

"Very well, sir," I told him, "but the real question is: How are you getting on?"

"As well as can be expected, according to Tsaya, but much slower than I like. However, my doctor's beauty refreshes my day when she makes her rounds. I suspect you've noticed as well?"

"She brightens up the day for many people, including me," I admitted.

I thought Tsaya would blush, but she didn't. She smiled instead. When she was in her professional element, her shyness disappeared. "Sandy, The General's well known throughout the

Commonwealth for his flattery," she said. "You'll grow used to it."

"Tsaya, you've never grown used to it. Neither has any other woman I've known," The General remarked. "And, Sandy, I'm not a baby-kissing politician."

"Not many generals are."

"Sometimes I wish my military title hadn't become my symbol. But I chanced to be in the right place at the right time to take military command and do something worthwhile with it."

"That's the story of most successful military leaders," I pointed out. "What would you rather be, General?"

"My father wanted me to be a trader like my ancestors for generations before me," The General admitted. "I wanted to be an anthropologist and learn the history of human beings and their social institutions. But I am what I have become, and if people would rather look to me in a leadership position as The General, there's little I can do about it. I must be what I am publicly; I can be whom I want privately." He paused for a moment, rearranged a kaftan-like robe around him, and went on, "Sandy, I'm extremely pleased you accepted the position as my deputy for military affairs in Landlimo Corporation."

"I haven't accepted, General. I'm not certain I can do the job."

"I am. You should be, too."

"General, I know little about the Commonwealth and what you've already decided to do."

"With your background, you can learn easily and quickly from Alichin, Omer, Vaivan . . ."

"But that will take time we don't have."

"I have lots of time in my present situation. And I'll enjoy teaching you, Sandy. It's boring to watch TV or read all day. I'm glad to have a deputy to talk to. Samuel Clemens said it better."

"Mark Twain? I don't follow you, General."

" 'War talk by men who have been in a war is always interesting; whereas moon talk by a poet who has not been in the moon is likely to be dull.' We can talk of both. Sandy, I've seen and learned a lot in over a century . . ."

"General, you can't be more than seventy," I objected.

"The General is one hundred and fifteen years old," Tsaya broke in.

That brought me up short. "I didn't think high-tech gerontology had . . ."

"Had reached a low-tech place like the Commonwealth?" The

General finished for me. "Don't underestimate us, Sandy. We've taken what we've needed from your high-tech world—and paid for it, I might add, because we're not looters and never have been."

"This is what I mean about my ignorance of your ways," I told him. "I had no idea Commonwealth doctors possessed expertise in biotechnology."

"It's not the sort of high-tech biotechnology you know," Tsaya put in. "We've combined it with our own, although American biotechnologists have yet to accept what we've known and used for generations. They will eventually, but by that time we're likely to be far ahead of them. Right now, they call it witchcraft. It will be integrated into medicine in this century just as acupuncture and other low-tech medicine were in the last century."

"You used acupuncture on Ali at Karederu Center."

Tsaya shook her head. "That's Chinese. I used something else. We have a great legacy of folk medicine." She paused, then asked, "Sandy, what do you think about magic and witchcraft?"

"Hard to say," I had to admit. "The universe is full of strange things. I certainly don't know everything there is to know. Why do you ask?"

"I want to learn what you think about things unexplained by science."

I shrugged. "I'm neutral. Magic may be a meaningless word when all the data are in. If something works even though we don't understand it, we'll manage to understand it some day. If it doesn't work, why worry about it?"

Tsaya looked relieved. "Sandy, in high-tech they'd either ridicule or destroy me because I'm a witch, a respected profession in our culture; so I stand back from high-tech people until I learn their prejudices and if they understand I'm really a healer. But then, who isn't? Anybody can do it. I can teach even you, Sandy." There wasn't a bit of recalcitrance in her attitude now. She hadn't been shy after all, just frightened. Doctor Tsaya Stoak became fathomable.

"Some day, Tsaya, after we manage to keep the jackals at bay," I promised.

"I like your analogy," The General remarked. "We've got to keep them at bay until we're too strong for them."

"Then what, General?" I wanted to know. This was a critical question that had been nagging at me ever since I'd become exposed to the free-wheeling free market culture of the Commonwealth. "Once the Commonwealth becomes powerful, what restrains it? What keeps it from trying to conquer the world? What damps greed in this free-market state?"

The General replied simply. "A philosophy we all know and follow."

"What can that do if I wanted to take over as absolute dictator and set out to conquer the world?"

The General sighed. "Sandy, your namesake Alexander the Great—who wasn't so great after all—lived in a world of scarcity where there wasn't quite enough to go around. In my lifetime, that's changed. But people's perceptions and thinking haven't. We no longer live in a marginal survival system of shortages. There's no reason for anyone to starve now . . ."

"A lot of people in the world *are* starving right now," I remarked.

"They don't have to. We didn't."

"You were different."

"How?"

"Uh, well, I can't explain it yet," I admitted.

"What did I tell you at Karederu about acting like a slave?"

"But a starving free person is just like a starving slave."

"To a free person, starvation is a temporary condition to be suffered until game can be killed or crops harvested," The General stated, then went on, "We made ourselves free to make better lives for ourselves. But unlike most of the others, we knew we had to do it ourselves. No one was going to step in and save us. We bootstrapped ourselves over several centuries of slow and painful development by using our heads instead of our fists."

"So what's going to restrain the Commonwealth when we win?"

"You've heard of metalaw?" The General asked.

"I was exposed to it in case we ran into ETs."

"But you weren't encouraged to apply metalaw in contacts with intelligent terrestrial life?"

"That's hard to do, General."

"It is if you're dealing with the classical peasant economy."

"What's that?"

"Didn't they teach you any sociology and anthropology?"

"Only what we'd need as officers."

"Pity, Sandy, the human race has evolved in a peasant economy where, if things were the best they could possibly be, everyone had a little of everything but no one had very much of anything." General Vamori paused, then said with great emphasis,

"Now it isn't necessary to live that way! *There's plenty for everyone!* There will always be plenty for everyone from now on! By using our minds and applying technology wisely, we're using the Earth and, at last, the Solar System. What happens to greed when manna falls from the sky in such great abundance that it becomes senseless to hoard it?"

"Somebody will corner the market on manna and create an artificial shortage," I told him.

"Not if there's competition," The General contended. "Universal abundance makes monopolies, cartels, price-fixing, and other non-competitive activities ineffective and too costly."

"General, with all due respect," I told him with some exasperation, "it can't stop greed. That's part of human nature we'll never eliminate, just as we'll never get rid of the desire to fight."

"Sandy, you're not looking at the systems properly. It's bigger than you think. It's not just the Earth with all its untapped potential, although that's enough for some people. The system now includes the Moon, the planetoids, and the Galilean satellites." The General looked thoughtful for a moment, started to say something, stopped, then finally remarked carefully, "Americans almost had it. *Almost.* They came agonizingly close. Your forefathers began to understand there was plenty for everyone. But they panicked when they just started to be successful. It was different. It was new. It had no track record, as they once said. It seemed too good to be true, so something *had* to be wrong."

The old man relaxed in weightlessness, slipping into an open foetal position impossible on Earth—legs bent, back slightly arched, limbs floating, all muscles totally unstressed. "When everybody can have as much as they want without exhausting physical labor, greed goes away. Hoard if you want. Stash it away by the ton if you wish. Pile it up in the streets until you have no place left to put it. What good it is then?"

"It's valuable when you've cornered the total supply," I said.

"But you *can't*! There's *always* more and more and more!"

"Well, I wouldn't give it away. Sooner or later, I'd be the only one supporting a lot of moochers."

"What's a moocher in a system where there's plenty of everything?"

"Somebody that sponges off the system and doesn't earn his keep. 'There's no free lunch.' "

"Very well, Sandy, suppose you have a system with plenty of everything for everyone but with the 'no free lunch' principle. What do you do with all you've managed to get hold of? You can use just so much of it. What are you going to do with the rest?''

"I'd swap it for something I don't have, that I want or need, and that somebody else has.''

"That's greed?''

"No, that's trade.''

"That's what the Commonwealth's doing. It operates that way because we're probably the first people in history to understand there's no free lunch but so much of everything that it can't be controlled by monopolies, cartels, politics, police, or state capitalism. And it can't be taken away from armed traders without trading for something of equal value.''

"Seems to me you're talking a super-sophisticated form of socialism,'' I remarked. "If you're basing the system on abundance and free trade, you won't need money, for example . . .''

"Oh, but we do and will. It's one of the greatest of all human inventions. With it, we can trade with or for something in the future that doesn't exist yet. And since it's only score-keeping, we can use the comm/info net to do it.''

I was out of my element, and I knew it. Money was something that was fairly easy to come by if I worked for it, and it was primarily useful for buying bread and butter. I didn't try to fathom the "Free-and-Twenty-One'' economics where the actual value of money slipped and slid around, depending upon buying power. My standard of exchange was breakfast. Anywhere in the U.S., a good breakfast cost about ten dollars, and I used that yardstick to figure the value of currency when I was in other countries. I considered my primitive method of determining monetary value to be basic economics.

But I had to admit something to the old man. "General, you do a good job of explaining how the Commonwealth operates. It doesn't make sense to me yet. In the meantime, I can live with it. But tell me something: How does the son of a merchant become a general and evolve into a social philosopher?''

It was a moment before The General answered. "I was once befriended by an anthropologist who came to the old land of Mitanni to dig. He got me interested in where the human race had been and where it could go if it wanted to. I took my doctorate at the University of Pennsylvania and started the Department of Anthropology at the University of Topawa.'' The General explained. "When Colonel Joseph T. Chase set himself up as 'maximum ruler' and started looting the people who'd hired him to get rid of bandits, I happened to be in Topawa—it was just a village then. Chase decided he wanted power as well as immunity from the responsibility that must accompany power. I accidentally found myself in his path. The rest is history.''

''The history books say you're a man with a mission who took command of the native military groups to save your people and your country from a dictator.''

''The history books lie,'' The General replied gently. ''They always do. But history happened in spite of the historians. I stepped in to save myself and my family. Perhaps the historians will re-evaluate their conjectures in a century or so when our experiment is completed. We're still in the midst of it, and the crucial stage is about to begin. And I'm incapacitated in Ell-Five! So you may have to fit temporarily into my 'jack boots' and lead in my stead, Sandy.''

I was totally taken aback by this. ''General, I came to the Commonwealth as an aerospace pilot with military experience, not to assume a role in your government. I couldn't be a leader for your people! What makes you think they'd follow me?''

''If you show you're a leader, they'll follow.''

''How do you know I'm not another Colonel Joseph T. Chase?''

''You aren't. I knew him and I know you.''

''How long have you 'known' me, General? A couple of days? How could you really know me?''

Again, a long pause before The General said, ''I'm not immortal. Someone must fill my place. That person mustn't be exactly like me because conditions aren't as they were fifty years ago. For a quarter of a century I've studied information that's come in from a growing intelligence network. I've seen many promising young people come along only to destroy themselves with poor judgement and wishful thinking. I've kept tabs on you, Sandy, from the day you graduated from the Academy. But you aren't unique because I've tracked your colleagues and others as well throughout the world. And you weren't selected. Like me in Topawa fifty years ago, you've turned out to be in the right place at the right time. I really hope you'll make the grade, Sandy, because you haven't destroyed your potential yet.''

''Again I ask, how can you be sure I'm not another Chase?''

''I can't. But I'm willing to risk it. We must always be ready to take calculated risks. Even if I were wrong about you, however, the Commonwealth now has the proper checks and balances to prevent another Chase incident. And Commonwealth people know they live in a universe of abundance.''

''But this should be a job for one of your family—Alichin, for example.''

The General shook his head. ''They're fighters but not tigers.

Alichin is a good planner, a rebellious frontiersman, a businessman, a merchant, and a trader. He knows this and of my feeling toward you.''

''General, you're laying a hell of a big burden on me. I'm not sure I'll accept it.''

The old man tried to reach out to touch me, but the septic membrane halted his hand. He smiled broadly. ''Sandy, in spite of my age, I'm likely to be around for another twenty years. Doctor Tsaya here tells me in so many words that I'm too mean to die. Be that as it may, you're not faced with the possibility immediately. There's no vacuum that will draw you in quickly. It just seems that way because the leadership vacuum apparently produced by the Karederu fire is only partial and temporary until I heal. It gives you an opportunity as my deputy to learn what's going on.'' He smiled and withdrew his hand. ''It sounds like a big responsibility, but for a long time I may use you only as a go-fer, Sandy.''

I hoped he was right.

CHAPTER 8

The Weapon
of the Commonwealth

"The General enjoyed your visit," Doctor Tsaya Stoak said as we left the Haeberle Clinic.

"I did, too," I admitted. We cycled through the Clinic's hatch into the main gallery of L-5. "But he scares me."

"Don't be over-awed by General Vamori. He's just a human being."

Closing the hatch behind us, I replied, "To me there's no such thing as 'just a human being.' "

"I didn't mean it that way," Tsaya tried to explain. "A lot of people in the Commonwealth think he's a god. It's a hold-over from the past that's not easy to get out of people's minds."

"He isn't a god to me," I told her as we moved down the corridor. "The General's the Grand Old Man of the Commonwealth, the father image."

"Of course. It's going to be a long time before we shed the need for a father image, if we ever do. It's such a deep part of the human psyche that medical and mental lore is full of the symbolism of it."

We were moving along the gallery toward the League of Free Traders' Lounge. "Hungry?" I asked.

"Yes, but not for a full meal. Just a snack," she replied and went on to explain, "I have to watch my weight. I don't want to end up like those fat, jolly old mama types in the Topawa marketplace."

I gave Tsaya an admiring once-over. Gone were the loose cotton pull-overs and tunics worn in the tropical Commonwealth. Tsaya wore a white body stocking with slippers on her feet plus a white tailored tunic. Her long hair was held above her head in a net.

"I can't picture you as a fat old mama," I remarked with admiration. "You know too much about biotechnology to let that happen. At any rate, you're certainly in a position to take advantage of the biocosmetic centers in Europe and America."

"I don't intend to have to," she said as we sat at a table. She

punched-up fruit cocktail and electrolyte-balanced hot *chai*. Out
of old habit, I ordered the usual duty drink of an Aerospace
Force officer: milk. She went on, "But I'll begin to exhibit the
Rensch Snydrome if I'm not careful."

"Another medical term?" I asked her.

"You're a big man from a cold climate," she observed.

"Santa Barbara wasn't exactly cold, but you're right. My
ancestors came from jolly olde England."

"You owe more to your English ancestors than to Santa
Barbara's climate. You could survive where the temperature
drops below five degrees Celsius because you store insulating fat
everywhere on your body," she pointed out. She was right. I
was starting to get a little heavy from lack of exercise. She went
on, "My ancestors came from the Toak Plains near Manitu,
from the Arabian penninsula, and from the Iranian desert. Hot
places, all of them. For me, extra calories turn into fatty tissue
located where it interferes least with body movement and
cooling—my buttocks and breasts. I'm genetically equipped to
survive in a climate where the temperature exceeds twenty-eight
Celsius."

"I thought Commonwealth people were well hybridized by
now."

Tsaya shook her head. "Three to five generations aren't enough.
It may take ten. It took far longer than that in America because
you had social barriers. We don't. But on the other hand we
don't know what we're hybridizing for."

"Pardon?"

"Our future and our frontier is in space. What kind of human
being is optimal for that? Today the Japanese are good at living
in cramped tin cans in space. They're adaptable and have a
social system that's eminently suited to it."

"But cramped tin cans won't last," I argued. "We're creating
environments to our liking now. *Homo spatial* ought to be
non-specialized, able to function without life support gadgetry
anywhere there's oxygen partial pressure from a hundred to
five-hundred millibars, temperature from zero to fifty Celsius,
and gravity from three gees down to weightlessness."

Our orders came up on the call board; I picked them up,
parted with food chits, and returned to the table. Tsaya had
thought about what I'd said because she told me as I tucked my
legs under the table, "I can't argue that from the physiological
standpoint. Almost any normal human being in good health can
meet those criteria. But how about the intersocial aspects?"

"As you pointed out, the Japanese do well out here."

She squeezed *chai* out of the tube and smiled. I liked her smile. "But we're going to do better."

"How?"

"Where's your iklawa?" she asked with sudden coolness.

"Is that the word for the daggers you all wear?"

"That's right."

"Strange word."

"It comes from the sound of the blade being pulled from the body of an enemy." Tsaya lowered her right hand to her waist. The knife was in plain sight, but she was wearing it so naturally that I hadn't noticed it. "Arm yourself, citizen. Or are you ashamed of living?"

"Uh, sorry," I apologized. "I didn't think I'd be permitted to wear a weapon in a space facility."

"Others expect us to be armed. It's the mark of a citizen of the Commonwealth." She put both hands on the table and went on in a pleasant voice, "Do you have an iklawa, or would you like to borrow one of mine?"

"Can I, uh, borrow one, Tsaya?"

"Of course. I've noticed you unarmed and thought you might need the loan of one." She produced another small ornamental knife and its scabbard from under the flap of her body tunic and handed it to me. "I drew this at Karederu. Consider it a gift of welcome. You're a citizen of the Commonwealth. You must bear arms openly."

"I'll do that, and thank you very much, Tsaya. But what does this have to do with hybridization and the social aspects of space living?" I wanted to know.

"Everything. The Japanese are polite because of centuries of cultural training. You're not. I'm not. We're polite to one another now because there's no conflict between us; we wouldn't be polite if one of us had something the other wanted and thought it could be taken by force without suffering any immediate physical consequences. When you're openly armed and apparently capable of defending yourself, you'll be politely treated with good manners."

"Uh, okay, maybe, but that could lead to a lot of violence. If you can draw an iklawa and slip it into anybody you don't like, it seems to me it encourages murder."

"Quite the contrary. There have been no murders in the Japanese or Commonwealth space facilities. Yes, there've been deaths in our module, but they were outlanders who didn't believe our willingness to protect ourselves. Elsewhere in space, there've been the usual per capita ratio of fights, injuries, and murders.''

"So you think we're going to be the best space people because of both hybridization and personal weaponry?''

"It worked very well in your country before it got messed up,'' Tsaya reminded me.

"Messed up? The General said something like that, too!''

"We learned a lot from Americans. They were a dynamic, forceful, successful people. They made mistakes and we're not going to make the same ones. And it did get messed up. Look at what happened to you, Sandy.''

I found I couldn't really argue with her, so I didn't try. I already respected her and now I was beginning to like her. "Tsaya, I had you figured all wrong,'' I told her.

"Oh? What did you formerly think of me and what caused you to change your mind?''

"You emerged that night at Karederu Center as a shy, introverted wallflower, then faded into the background until the place went up in flames,'' I reminded her. "You were frightened of me to the extent you had your iklawa pricking me.''

"But I didn't know you then.''

"Obviously, neither did I.''

"I'm getting to know you better.''

"So am I.''

"I like you, Sandy.''

"The feeling's mutual, *moapa*.''

Tsaya bristled. "Don't you dare use that word! Do you know what it means?''

I was taken aback. "It's a term of affection and friendship. That's the way I've heard it used.''

"You know *nothing* of the implications of that word! You're just a boorish, barbaric, well-intentioned but ignorant American outlander! It'll be a long time before you're privileged to use that term with me! The fact that we happen to like one another well enough to eat together does *not* mean you have my trust and confidence as a *moapa*!''

"Look, look, I apologize! No insult or hurt intended, Tsaya!''

Tsaya sighed deeply and brought herself under control. "My apologies, too. I forget you're still a stranger among us. I'll try to compensate for it. But be careful; others might not.''

I'd made an etiquette blunder of major proportions and it aborted our tete-a-tete. I was going to have to learn it was not proper to eat with my knife, wipe my hands on the table linen, and make messes on the living room carpet. I was going to have to become civilized according to *them*.

And I was going to have to damned careful about using terms I didn't understand as well as misinterpreting Commonwealth customs I was just beginning to learn. I kept fitting these Commonwealth people in the molds of American stereotypes, and they wouldn't and didn't fit.

I would have been a lousy embassy aerospace attache. Probably would have ended up *persona non grata*. But if I wasn't careful among these people, I might end up *persona non vita*.

Over the next few weeks, *nothing* happened that Landlimo Corporation hadn't anticipated.

Real life never proceeds the way it does in fiction. "Cut to the chase!" may be a dictum for writers, but living is a lot like flying: long periods in which nothing happens separated by moments of frenetic activity. Most people relish the periods of inactivity and then hit the panic switch when everything turns to slime. A survival type uses inactive periods to prepare for the next time it hits the impeller. I'm a survival type.

Part of my training was taken over by Ursila Peri. A strong-willed young woman, she was different from Omar Astrabadi in ways other than physical. She drilled into me the procedures and techniques of deep space intra-orbital commercial piloting. This is mostly procedural, doing the right things at the right time to keep the various military forces in space from getting antsy. Sometimes it involved rather complex trajectories that needed a lot of computer power.

It helps to have computers to take over the details of making a ship go where you want, but software can get screwed-up even when it's debugged. In spite of their large array of gates far exceeding the number of neuronal connections in the human brain and their speeds many orders of magnitude faster than the human nervous system, the human pilot still had the upper hand. Computers might have been able to do it all, but nobody in his right mind wanted to trust human life in space exclusively to computers.

Besides, a computer doesn't have the human concept of "fun."

The fun of space travel was more than just getting from A to B successfully. Any computer could do that. "Fun" being an alogical emotion, it was strictly a human activity. It was hanging things out a little bit, daring the universe, and taking a risk.

Omer tended to ignore the computers and take great, big, juicy risks of the sort that scared hell out of me.

On the other hand, Ursila used computers as tools. She monitored them and let them do things she could have done just as well.

I fell somewhere in between Ursila and Omer. I used computers, but I never trusted them.

As far as I was concerned, there's always the possibility of the so-called "three-sigma deviation," the occurrence that falls outside the 3-sigma limit of probability computers were designed to handle. It kept sports from becoming cut-and-dried exhibitions of physical prowess. There's always the guy who isn't where he's supposed to be when he's supposed to be there, and there's always someone who fumbles the ball. This same principle kept human space pilots from becoming obsolete.

It also kept cyborgs from taking over because, being highly specialized, their use rate had to be kept high. Cyborgs, being partly human, needed rest, too. They couldn't perform 24 hours a day, 365 days a year like a machine. They were, to put it bluntly, technologically possible but economically unprofitable.

I liked Ursila. She was an attractive, provocative, highly competent woman who had the strange ability to shift from being cooly all business to warmly sociable like Tsaya. In some ways, she was very British and in other ways American.

During a flight with her, I remarked, "Ursila, you needle me about my American ways. Not that I mind; I probably deserve it because I'm provincial and naive. Were you once an American?"

"If we weren't both North Americans whose families have lived alongside each other for more than two hundred years, I'd feel insulted," Ursila replied without rancor. "I'm Canadian."

"Sorry, I should have known. I've worked alongside a lot of RCAF types," I said and observed, "There seem to be a lot of Canadians in space in ratio to the Canadian population. I'm curious why."

Ursila leaned back, checked a display, and looked levelly at me. "You Yanks aren't the only ones with a frontier heritage. Ever been on the Canadian Shield?"

I hadn't. I'd been instructed *not* to punch out over the Shield because there was little chance of survival.

"That's still our frontier. We've had a constant coming and going from the wilds to the settled areas. It's almost a rhythm in Canadian life," Ursila explained. "Does that answer your question?"

It did. And it gave me another important clue to the deep relationship between Ursila and Ali. If Ali hadn't gotten there first . . . But it was too late to think about that. If she and Ali hadn't had it going 100% between them, I would have become extremely interested because I wasn't having much success with Tsaya Stoak.

Tsaya and I became close friends . . . period. To be sure, our friendship grew and expanded as I spent time with her talking to The General and taking our few moments of free time together. But our relationship didn't progress to the physical point. Perhaps Tsaya was truly an introverted person who was working hard to overcome it. Since we didn't share the same background, it was impossible for me to make any sort of reasonable assessment of the situation.

Otherwise, I was very busy. The Commonwealth had extensive facilities and operations in the Earth-Moon system. At that point in the development of space industrialization, most of the risk capital still came from Earth. It was the early period of this frontier, but activities of a space-to-space nature were gaining momentum and importance.

The big multinationals were still involved—Exxo-Krupp, Atoshi & Kalidasha, CanIntel, AmArab General, and Embra Punto, among others. The various Commonwealth corporations dealt with them all and usually supplied essential services including drayage, factoring, exchange, arbitrage, proctoring, brokering, and the many commercial activities that go on below the surface of trade and exchange. Although some Commonwealth firms were involved directly in space industry, they were careful not to become competition to the biggies.

The Commonwealth seemed to be happy to hold a small percentage of a market or take just a smidgen off the top, nothing more than a minor business expense that wouldn't justify the time and effort to bypass the percentage or to eliminate the minor competition.

The Commonwealth space entrepeneurs were following their classical earthside policies: maintain a low profile, don't present a target worthy of justifiable attack, keep the percentages low enough to make it uneconomical to cheat, and build economic and financial strength quietly. The free market Commonwealth was doing well by doing good, following The General's philosophy that this was a system of plenty with enough to go around.

I began to understand The General's strategy.

A century or so ago, the legendary South Sea Islands were a tropical paradise where there was so much for everyone that all they had to do was reach up and pick it off the trees. Now the whole Earth was trending in that direction. It was the turning point between a system of scarcity and a system of plenty. The General had the Commonwealth already working with the system of plenty while at the same time preparing itself to handle those who still operated with the well-understood world of scarcity.

That was the true weapon of the Commonwealth.

But there were others, too.

Omer wanted me to see the latest "toy." He took me to a remote hangar bay at the far end of the ComSpat module where maintenance and repair of ships was done—inside pressurized bays if possible but outside in vacuum if the ship was big. Inside the bay rested a small black ship. Ursila was inspecting it when we arrived.

"The latest toy" was about the same size as the Aerospace Force SF-16 "Viper" but had six-degree-of-freedom maneuvering engines in addition to a reasonably large main engine. It had thick arrow wings and both radar and lidar stealth shape. Mounted in a forward location aligned with the ship's longitudinal axis was a 25-millimeter Rota-Rock.

"Looks like a highly modified Embrastrel Preto Passaro," I said as I viewed its fascinating lines. "But that ship wasn't designed for deep space work and was obsolete ten years ago."

Omer smiled. "It is what you think it is. We bought a dozen at a very good price from the Forca Estrella Natalia. Sriharikota reengined them to our specs. Then the Pitoika Drydock and Ship Company put in the finishing touches. Now we have a squadron of twelve operational skalavans," he said proudly.

"Plus spares," Ursila added.

"So? What's a skalavan?" I asked.

"Sandy, what did they teach you about space tactics at Colorado Springs?" Omer replied. "Tell me how you think this ship might be used."

I looked it over for a few more minutes, then ventured, "It's a small single-pilot craft with tremendous delta-vee reserve. It could be flown across the atmospheric interface. But the aerodynamics and structures are archaic! Okay, it's got tuck-wings to improve the ell-over-dee, but its skin will never withstand an entry at more than Vee-sub-ee. These little spikes on the leading surfaces would go bye-bye right away!"

"I didn't suspect you'd notice," Ursila remarked, fingering one of the blunted spikes that were arrayed on the front of the fuselage and wings. "I discovered data that had initially been buried under security wraps at the old Wright-Patterson Aerospace Base since 1965 and then forgotten in the U.S. National Archives. These are electroaerodynamic ionodes."

"Electroaerodynamic *what*?"

"Ionodes," Ursula repeated. "By putting an electrostatic charge on the space craft body and creating a charge sheath around it, the air flow can be tailored even at hypersonic speeds." When I looked dubious, she went on, "Want to see the equations? We can use this excellent subsonic and supersonic airframe in the hypersonic regime: Mach fifteen at sea level."

I thought about all this for a moment, then asked them, "You're not really serious about using this as a good old science-fiction space fighter, are you?"

"Why not? Nobody else has one. If we get into a shooting war, a skalavan squadron can raise hell in space and earthside. It's a predator," Ursila stated.

Omer grinned. "It's fun to drive this at Mach fifteen only a hundred meters off the deck! The shock wave carpet uproots trees! And I've got the Roto-Rock Twenty-five if I want to shoot."

"Know why the Aerospace Force opted out of these little birds?" I asked. "Space laser battle stations can burn them out of the sky, that's why. Space fighters and even space cruisers are scouts, and scouts are expendable. And expensive when they're manned."

"You're missing something," Ursila pointed out. "These are knobby with verniers."

"So?"

"What're the biggest problems faced by space laser battle stations?"

"That's a simple·question, Ursila. Detection and targeting. Then it takes a second or two to slew, aim, and fire."

"A skalavan can survive in the directed energy weapon environment because it has tracking sensors and can zang out of the way before the laser can be fired. It has the ultimate defense against a hell beam: Be where it ain't."

"Nice theory," I told her.

"Want proof? Omer, help me strap him in, then I'll take the *Shontu* and you strap on the *Taibu*. Time to have a little fun! Sandy, just *try* to hit either of us with boresight laser!"

The next hour of hard maneuvering trying to pin my practice laser on either ship and trying to shake both of them off my tail was enough to convince me. The Commonwealth indeed had the first effective space fighter which they'd named after the old fast and maneuverable Malagasay sailing vessel. It was such a hot item that I knew Omer was right when he told me I wouldn't qualify to fly it in combat. "You and Ursila do not have fast reflexes," he told me. "I do. I flew with *Frontovaia Aviatsiya* Mach five on the deck."

But it worried me that Omer had scattered the squadron—four at Ell-Five, four at Vamori Free Space Port, and four more in deep hangars at Criswell Station in the walls of the lunar crater Ley. "We're rather quiet about them," Ursila told me. "They're a weapon of last resort, so to speak. If things get really dicey, we'll use them for couriers and emergency packets to get people and limited equipment through any blockade. Each of them will take another hundred kilos without degrading performance too badly . . ."

I was glad to know the skalavans were available but I hoped we'd never need them.

But then again, we might. We watched and waited, and a strange thing began to happen:

The activity at Vamori Free Sport Port went down to 64% of the pre-embargo level, then began to increase.

During our daily staff telecon, I questioned this data. "Why?"

Wahak went through his usual ritual of checking the hard copy data on the table in front of him, then reported, "Kevin Graham at the League says it's because of the imposed duties at the other space ports. All ships belonging to members of the League of Free Traders are registered in the Commonwealth because our fees are low to cover only the computer time for logging, and nearly all the League ships are now using Vamori-Free. We're starting to handle ships registered in countries such as Annam, Sri Lanka, Liberia, Echebar, and Surinam. Even some Chinese manifests have gone through Vamori-Free. As long as we keep it open to space, we'll get tonnage, especially from those who want to avoid the Santa Fe tariffs."

"This can't go on," I pointed out.

"Why, Sandy?" Vaivan asked.

"Someone will try to plug the leak before it gets worse. Wahak, run a projection forecast. How long before we can expect one-hundred percent at Vamori-Free again, based on the trend of the data you now have?" I asked him.

He turned to his keypad. The answer didn't take long. "At present rate, sixty-two days."

"The traffic's going to increase on a cubic curve," I advised him.

"That can't be justified," Wahak replied.

"Yes it can," Alichin put in beside me. "The cubic curve's a standard projection, Wahak."

"It's outrageous."

"So's the rest of the universe that operates with it," Ali fired back. He called up Wahak's computer display on our own VDT, then punched in a correction on our keypad. "Let's see what the cubic forecast says . . . Well!"

"Twenty-two days to reach a hundred-percent level at Vamori-Free," Vaivan observed.

"I don't believe it," Wahak stated flatly.

"Tell me that in three weeks," Ali said.

"That will probably be too late," I added.

"Too late?"

"Wahak, look," I told him, "we aren't the only ones with access to this data. Tripartite comptrollers and planners have it, too. There's some delay in their system because they'll have to convince their superiors. I'll give them three days to do that, plus four days for Tripartite leaders to make up their minds what to do, and two days for them to act. Be ready for something to happen in a week or so, just to be on the safe side."

"Any ideas what it might be?" Ali asked us all.

There was silence among the Landlimo Corporation's executive planning group and its military advisor.

"Blockade?" Wahak suggested.

"Too many treaties and trade agreements prevent it, and it's an act of war," Alichin reminded him.

"Expect traffic delays from STC," Vaivan said. "There might even be some clearance refusals on the pretext of military necessity."

"Can't do that. No military emergency," Ali objected.

"They'll make one," I said.

Ali didn't agree. "There may be some delays in Space Traffic Control centers, but they'll cite equipment breakdowns or traffic overloads due to the activity shift caused by the Santa Fe tariffs at various hubs. They can't shut down space operations any more than they can stop air commerce."

"We're secure," Vaivan reported. "Short of open warfare, Vamori Free Space Port can't be shut down. Traffic originating or terminating at Commonwealth facilities can't be touched. Insofar as open warfare goes, the Commonwealth impys are on alert, and there's been no military build-ups or activity beyond our borders."

We kicked it around for another thirty minutes without coming up with anything that seemed reasonable or within the capabilities or intentions of possible antagonists.

"Be prepared for something to happen in about a week," I

finally told them. "We don't know what it will be, but they dropped the first shoe in Santa Fe. When they'll drop the other shoe remains to be seen, but drop it they will."

I had to explain what I meant about dropping shoes.

And we didn't have to wait long for the Tripartite to do it.

CHAPTER 9

Flying Down to RIO

"PowerSat Corporation, InPowSat, and InSolSat just cut SPS power beams to eleven rectennas in small countries."

It was the middle of the night in L-5, so the telecon was obviously an emergency. The Landlimo Corporation people ensconced in Vershatets were accompanied by Captain Kevin Graham, and the level of concern was evidenced by the fact that Rayo Sabinos Vamori was on the net along with Shaiko Stoak, CEO of Commonwealth Glaser, and Donalo Jon Tomason from the engineering firm, Rose & Mariyama, Inc. Corner montages showed Heinrich von Undine in Topawa and Trip Sinclair in Houston.

"We expected something like that," Ali spoke up from where he sat next to me.

"Why, Ali?" his uncle asked.

"It's the quickest way to exert leverage on countries who haven't gone along with the Santa Fe Tariffs and the Commonwealth embargo. I think I know who PowerSat pulled the plug on, but tell me anyway."

Shaiko Stoak named them: "Rectennas are cold at Echebar, Negri Sembilan, Selangor, Tongan, Hanian, Dragona, Natalia, Ugarit, Mazara, and Ghanzhi. Notice to expect cessation of service has been tendered at Alderney, Nireg, Atacama, Sorat, Annom, and Tregganu, plus nine rectennas in mainland China."

"Any reasons given?" Ali asked curtly.

"Default on power bill payment in some cases. Others were told their credit lines had been re-evaluated," Sinclair reported.

Shaiko Stoak—I could see Tsaya's resemblance to her father—remarked, "We wouldn't reduce a credit line without consultation. That's an excuse!"

"Of course, Shaiko," Rayo Vamori told him. "Vaivan, what's our trading status with each of those countries?"

"The eleven cut off the powersat net have either diverted their space traffic to the Commonwealth or have ignored the Santa Fe embargo."

"We've been diverting manifests destined for those countries," Kevin Graham put in. "In some cases, captains of inbound ships got instructions in mid-flight from their contractors to divert to Vamori-Free. Some League captains have ignored their nation-of-registry directives declaring their registry invalid for use in Commonwealth facilities and claim registry is only a factor of convenience."

Trip Sinclair said. "Not under old United Nations' treaties that were never revised. The nation of registry has liability and accountability for space vehicles operating under its flag."

"The General should be here," Vaivan insisted.

"Tsaya won't move him out of the sterile environment for two more days," I put in. "I'm his deputy."

"With no offense intended, Sandy," Rayo said, "we need The General's advice."

"You'll have to learn how to get along without it. You're doing fine so far."

"How much capacity has been dropped off the powersat net?" Ali tried to get back on track.

"Fourteen gigawatts," Shaiko reported. "The cut-offs involved split beams, so no powersat is totally off-line, but One-Zero-Five-East and Six-Zero-East have near-zero loads."

I didn't like that. "Which powersats will have near-zero if they pull the plug on Annom, Nireg, and Sorat?" I asked.

Shaiko consulted a nearby display before replying, "Two-Zero-East and One-Zero-Five-East."

"That drops One-Zero-Five-East down to zilch, doesn't it?" I observed.

"Pardon?"

"Any load left on One-Zero-Five-East if Annom and Sorat go off?"

"No."

"What are you worried about, Sandy?" It was Vaivan who caught my concern.

"A ten gigawatt powersat can pump a *big* laser, Viavan," I explained. "A high-energy laser—they're called hell beamers from their acronym, H-E-L—is limited in beam power density and range only by its energy source. If it's a self-contained unit, the space facility is large and vulnerable. But if a hell-beamer's energized remotely, it's small and hard to identify. Powersat One-Zero-Five-East could put its ten gigawatts into a hydrogen-fluoride hell-beam station to punch a beam right down to surface from GEO!"

This was obviously news to them. Rayo Vamori broke the silence, "Is there a battle station over us?"

"The Aerospace Force has them over *all* parts of the world in sixty-degree inclined geosynchronous orbits. Kevin Graham's captains have spotted them."

Ali said slowly, "I'd better pay Peter Rutledge a visit."

I went with Ali to the Resident Inspection Organization's headquarters, GEO Base Zero. Ali needed a pilot, and he wanted me to meet those upon whom the delicate stability of space power depended.

I'd never known any RIO people. They kept to themselves as an anational paramilitary organization with a tradition of non-involvement. They had to be aloof. Thanks to RIO, there hadn't been a conflict in space since the Sino-Soviet Incident.

Ali wanted to make certain that RIO knew what was happening with the powersats. He was also covering his anatomy by insuring that Powersat One-Zero-Five-East or any other powersat didn't get its power beam redirected to a hell-beamer.

The approach to RIO Headquarters was a two-man job. The first challenge from RIO came at a thousand kilometers. We answered with the proper transponder code. Then we had to close at no more than ten meters per second, matching orbits and station-keeping ten klicks behind at zero closure rate. There we were thoroughly scanned. Once we proved we were sweet, pure, and unrefined as well as incapable of swatting a bee in revenge for being stung, they put a RIO pilot aboard. She strapped into the jump seat between Ali and me and flew the ship. It was rather disturbing to sit next to someone wearing about twenty kilos of Comp-X around her waist. From her accent as she reported on her comm set to RIO Approach, she was Japanese. I knew she wouldn't hesitate to self-destruct and take the ship and the two of us with her if we tried to ram GEO Base Zero.

The portlock guard was polite but firm: We had to leave our iklawas with him. Nobody was armed in GEO Base Zero and RIO members were deliberately unarmed at all times. An escort led us to the quarters of Inspector Peter Rogers Rutledge.

Peter Rutledge turned out to be veddy British even to his gingery mustache which matched his red hair. Even in the non-uniform of RIO, Inspector Rutledge would have looked at home in the Officer's Mess of any Royal Aerospace Force station. RIO policies tried to eliminate all national tags, but they weren't successful. Knowing the Britishers as I did, I doubted that RIO would ever be able to strip Rutledge of his quintessential English appearance, attitudes, and mannerisms; they were as deeply rooted in him as my own American traits were in me.

Rutledge spotted it immediately we were introduced by Ali. "I say, another Yank for your cause! Good show, Ali! You Commonwealth blighters are building quite an international cadre. I dare say you might become as multinational as we like to believe we are in RIO."

"We'll take all the help we can get, Peter . . ."

"On your terms, of course."

"One Colonel Chase is enough for anybody."

"Right-o. Never caught the bloody mercenary, have you? Pity Interpol isn't what it used to be. Can't understand why the French have stubbornly refused to computerize it. Well, I can't offer you civilized hospitality of a drink or even tea. Policy." As we slipped into stools around his conference table, Inspector Rutledge went on, "Best get on with business, then. What was so bloody important that you couldn't ring me up about it, Ali?"

"You know about PowerSat Corporation cutting back output to eleven rectennas and possibly cutting ten to fourteen more?" Ali asked.

"Of course, old boy. Resident teams are on every powersat, you know. And we have rather secure signals systems . . ."

"This leaves some powersats with excess capacity," Ali pointed out.

Rutledge nodded. "We don't anticipate that to last. PowerSat Corporation can't afford to have idle capacity. Their stockholders will begin to complain a bit on the next quarterly report. Rather, they'll make more nuisance if the declining quantity of delivered power is reflected in the stock markets."

"It already is," Ali pointed out. "PowerSat stock dropped five points today in Houston, three in New York, and seven in London and Hong Kong."

"Fascinating! We don't track such things, of course."

"You should. Economic factors have a bearing on potential military activities, Peter."

"Quite true," Rutledge admitted, stroking his mustache. "I was quoting Commandant Otasek's official policy. On the Q-T, one must keep up with what's happening in the world to be most effective in this job, as I'm sure you realize since we've discussed it. But PowerSat's financial situation wasn't the reason you came to chat."

"You understand why PowerSat is pulling the plug?"

"Something do to with a meeting in Santa Fe, wasn't it? I seem to recall you were present for a time."

Ali nodded. "Peter, I'd appreciate it if you'd keep an eye on Powersat One-Zero-Five-East."

"Oh?" There was an entire question encased in the former Britisher's word.

"If PowerSat carries through its threat to cut space power to Annom and Sorat, One-Zero-Five-East won't have any customers on the ground," Ali explained.

"And we have a tendency to get a bit nervous with ten gigs sitting idle above our horizon," I added.

"Oh?" Again the complete question in a single word.

"The United States Aerospace Force has a number of stealthed objects in a sixty-degree-inclination geosynch orbit." I didn't know how much Rutledge knew, but I didn't tell him everything.

"We know of them."

"Some of them are hell-beamers."

"Really?"

"Do you know something about them?"

"Something."

"Well, Inspector," I said with a sigh, "I just wanted to make sure you realized that the power beam of One-Zero-Five-East could be redirected to one or more of those . . . uh, objects, which would certainly power a large hell-beamer."

"We're rather well aware of a number of things going on, old chap," Rutledge replied in an off-handed manner. "But, Ali, I'm rather glad you thought to call One-Zero-Five-East to my attention. It confirms some information we've come onto. I suspect we'll lay on some additional surveillance and stand ready to take whatever steps we can to keep the balloon from going up."

"Peter," Ali put in quietly, "you should also be aware that we're ready, willing, and able to help . . ."

"And perhaps engage in a bit of action yourself if RIO doesn't?" Rutledge interrupted with a slight smile.

Ali nodded. "If we have to."

"That's probably down the road yet," I added. "Redirection of a power beam to a hell-beamer would be an act of war, and things haven't escalated that far yet."

"RIO isn't charged with the responsibility for taking action," Inspector Rutledge reminded us, "because we're only sentries. We'll sound the alarm should we detect something awry. However, as I'm certain you're well aware, Ali, sentries are often capable of defending themselves."

"Yes, and you can count on us if you need us."

"If the situation escalates that far, old chap, your Landlimo

Corporation will also find itself rather actively occupied. Oh, don't raise your eyebrows, Ali! What makes you think I wouldn't know what you're doing?"

"You and who else?"

"Come, now! We wouldn't enjoy one another's trust if either of us were to run hither and yon snitching like school boys, would we? I need to know these things as vitally as you do should RIO have to take appropriate action."

"What sort of action would RIO take, Peter? I know your Commandant. He's a righteous, principled, peace-loving man who hates to fight," Ali fired back, "the modern incarnation of his national hero, Good Soldier Shweik."

Rutledge said nothing for a moment but pulled at the ends of his ginger mustache. "Sometimes one needs a Good Soldier Shweik, old chap. After all, it's not RIO's responsibility to fight. We're just supposed to give the warning."

"Then stand aside and let the blokes go at it?" Ali mimicked our host and added, "Peter, I don't think you're going to be able to step aside. You'll be right in the middle of it."

"Hah! Yas! There is that, isn't there? But don't be so certain it will get that far, Ali. RIO must defend itself, mustn't it, especially after it's done its job and things get a bit sticky, what?" Rutledge paused, then disengaged himself from the table, indicating he considered the meeting over. "If it does come to trading swats, we'll all be in the thicket, chaps. Jolly good that you're siding with the Commonwealth, Baldwin. As for One-Zero-Five-East, we'll pop over and see whether or not they appear to be getting ready to cook something."

Neither Ali nor I said anything until after we'd returned to our ship, undocked, threaded the needle of clearances and vectors, and dropped the RIO pilot. Alone together in trajectory back to L-5, I asked Ali, "What did you make of that, chum?"

His answer surprised me. "Peter Rutledge is on our side."

"Really? He was as non-committal as a loan officer."

"He had to be. How much do you know about RIO and how it's run, Sandy?"

"Only what I've read, which was reasonably extensive because the Academy wanted future officers to understand RIO not as an adversary, but as a potential obstacle."

The Resident Inspection Organization had been the factor which permitted the powersat network. Without non-national or international inspection, who was to know whether or not a powersat also contained a hell-beamer? Who could have ascertained whether or not an attack satellite was hidden in the structures of the photovoltaic panels? And who'd be sure that the power beam wouldn't be diverted—as Ali and I now feared—from the ground rectenna to an otherwise passive and silent hell-beamer satellite? Could someone really pirate the pilot beam that kept the power beam phased on the rectenna and then concentrate several power beams on an Earth or space target, even though the power density of a single powersat beam is only one-fifteenth that of a microwave oven?

These questions left unanswered posed a military threat which in turn made a powersat a military target because nobody could take chances if an armed conflict appeared imminent.

A powersat is a terribly vulnerable thing—square kilometers of solar panels and bus bars carrying megawatts of power. No businessman, entrepreneur, financier, banker, or investor would have risked a worn penny on a powersat that was a certain target in the opening moments of any future war. Neither Lloyd's nor Macao's would or could have underwritten the insurance required for the long-term financing.

Obviously, a non-political international inspection organization was required. But how could it be organized, financed, and operated to insure that it remained non-national? That had been an enormous problem.

But technology always creates the new social organizations necessary to finance, manage, and control it.

People hacked away at the problem until RIO was organized at the Hartford Convention. RIO was formed with the funding from the groups who'd lose the most if a powersat were attacked as a military target, whether it was an actual threat or not. The damage or destruction of a multi-billion dollar powersat would be an expensive loss to the insurance underwriters.

The world needed space power and the insurance consortiums were the critical bottleneck. Whether or not there were economic pressures applied is a moot point today because the fraction of a percent that was tagged onto the kilowatt-hour consumer electric bill amounted to billions of dollars in insurance premiums which in turn more than paid for the 2,000 RIO inspectors and specialists with their independent communications and transportation systems.

Rutledge had been accurate in using the sentry as the analogy for RIO.

A lot of people didn't understand that an unarmed RIO was considered to be very effective. If a resident team or one of the ubiquitous spot inspection teams under the command of Rutledge found something unusual, there were two options open to the team leader: (a) report it covertly to RIO Headquarters for evaluation there; or (b) in a real emergency communicate the military activity to *everybody*. In the latter case, it was then important for RIO to get out of the line of fire.

Because of its unique anational character and novel operational methods, RIO often acted in strange and unfathomable ways. Unarmed as they were, they posed no military threat to anyone. But the threat of their capability to saturate the comm/info network with the danger cry of the watch dog was a sure and certain restraint on military space activities.

I suspected—and knew in some cases—that RIO had intelligence operations which penetrated deeply into nearly every military organization in the world. It wouldn't have surprised me, either, if their intelligence activities also embraced the world of commerce.

A lot of military planners had spent a lot of time and effort drafting plans and programs for circumventing RIO. The Aerospace Force—whose job was ostensibly to keep and guard the peace, too—had a continual highly-classified think-tank activity going on "should it be necessary to activate such plans and programs." But the job of *any* military service is to ensure the security of its nation. It was said a long time ago that "all's fair in love and war." Sad, but only partly true.

"If Peter Rutledge is on our side," I told Ali, "then he's violating his RIO oath. And he certainly didn't act like he's taking sides."

"Sandy, he was in his office," Ali reminded me. "You've heard the old saw about *quis custodiet . . .*"

I thought about that one for several minutes. Finally, I said, "I guess Rutledge went as far as he could under the circumstances. You knew him previously, so it's obvious you received a lot of signals I didn't."

"That's right," Ali replied simply. "When things get dicey, as Peter would put it, we can count on RIO."

"How?" I wanted to know. "They're un-armed."

"So were you on the Topawa Airport railway platform," Ali reminded me.

"Now you've got me worried, Ali," I admitted. "If you can suborn RIO, someone else can, too. Who else has gotten to them? My God, if they're that susceptible to violating world trust . . ."

"They're not capable of being suborned or even of violating their oaths," he replied. "But Peter has some discretion concerning whether or not to make a public announcement of detected military activities on a powersat. He knows that I know that he won't waffle. He'll yell. He may yell in my direction first. He'll do that even over the head of the RIO commander because Commandant Otasek will double-check and triple-evaluate the situation before making a public announcement. Otasek *detests* violence.''

"That's a good trait for the RIO Commandant to have," I interjected.

"That depends."

"On what?"

"A person who hates violence may be very reluctant to take action to prevent someone from being violent," Ali observed pensively. "Commandant Otasek is likely to wait and hope the provocation will go away. He could wait too long. Rutledge won't let him . . . I think. I hope."

"What about our own powersats? RIO will be watching those, too."

"They already are. But, Sandy, the Commonwealth doesn't have any hell-beamers in orbit. The Tripartite Coalition nations do." He watched the astrogation displays on the panel.

The computer was quietly working and reassuring us it was by continual status reports on peripheral displays. The space of the Earth-Moon system was full of moving objects. The ones of no concern to us were de-emphasized on the displays. There were military ships and stations and satellites among those targets, but nobody was shooting at one another. There was peace in space.

There wasn't peace on Earth. The comm/info net and the telenews broadcast a running stream of information on brushfire wars, guerrilla wars, terrorist raids, banditry, and piracy taking place all over the surface of the blue-and-white pie-in-the-sky in my left window.

Ali must have picked up something of what I was thinking because he suddenly went on, "Too bad, isn't it, that fights take place earthside where a lot of people get killed rather than out here where very few people would get hurt?"

I shook my head. "No, Ali, if our forefathers had been smart, warfare would have stopped at the stratosphere."

"You're right. War is such an uneconomical, inefficient, and temporary way of trying to get something."

"In the long run."

"There is no other."

"Convince the world of that."

"We will."

The display reminded me to get to work. "Time to earn our keep. We're ready to rendezvous with Ell-Five . . .''

There was a message waiting for Ali when we got into the ComSpat module. He scanned the hard copy, then told me, "Vershatets wants a telecon. Gather the group, please, Sandy."

Ursila was out-base on a run to Dianaport for a load of acceleration-sensitive blood fractions that couldn't be tossed by a mass driver.

Omer was about to land the *Toreva* at Vamori Free Space Port.

Tsaya told me by telecomm from the Clinic, "I can't release The General to the ComSpat module yet. Can you rig a conference circuit into the Clinic?"

Ali said no because there was no way to ensure a secure scramble with a remote through the Clinic's facilities.

I was able to round up only Jeri Hospah.

"It's just the three of us," I told Ali in the telecon compartment.

Ali shrugged. "I don't know what it's about, anyway."

"What did the hard copy say?" Jeri wanted to know.

"Didn't specify," Ali replied.

"How was it signed?" I asked.

"Just Vamori, LandlimoCorp."

"Which Vamori?"

"Could be any of them," Jeri guessed.

"So we'll be prepared for a full-dress Landlimo executive committee meeting, even though some of our group isn't here." Ali glanced at the time display. "Thirty seconds. Okay, Jeri, punch-up the net for us."

The only person on the net earthside was Ali's father, Rayo Vamori, who looked stern. "Sorry to have put you to the trouble of getting together," he said. "Ali, have you been having problems with comm links there?"

"Not that we know of. Jeri?"

Hospah shook his head. "Negative, chief. Space-to-space circuits are fine. Occasionally there's some delay on the earthside nets. Nothing out of the ordinary."

"We've had considerable difficulty getting earth-to-space circuits," Rayo Vamori told us. "We believe there's a reason for it. We've been able to get through only when we've identified as Landlimo Corporation, which is why I sent the hard copy message as I did. I need to speak to Ali. The rest of you may go, and my apologies if I took you away from something important."

Ali scribbled on a note pad which he slipped unobtrusively to me. His note told us to get out of video range and stay silent. We did.

When it appeared to Rayo Vamori that the conference room

was clear, he said to his son, "We need your grandfather back here immediately."

Ali shook his head. "Doctor Stoak won't let him travel yet, Father."

"Are you certain?"

"I am."

"How long?"

"A week. Perhaps longer."

"Too long."

"Why not Sandy Baldwin, Grandfather's military deputy?"

"No, Baldwin isn't fully committed and doesn't have a depth of knowledge of the Commonwealth."

"If you want military advice, why not call in the indunos of the impys?"

"They're too close to their own military problems to grasp the overall picture. On the other hand, we aren't military people and we don't have the necessary background to handle some of the problems facing us. We need your grandfather."

"Then you have no choice but to accept his deputy. I'll certainly vouch for Sandy," Ali told his father.

There was silence on the net for a moment. I couldn't see Rayo Vamori's face on the screen. Finally, Ali's father spoke up again, "Very well, but to supplement Baldwin's expertise, we'll need your background in our space operations as well. The two of you should therefore come to Vershatets on the next available ship leaving Ell-Five."

"Father! The RIO matter is critical at the moment! I *must* stay here!"

"Alichin, I am told the *Tonolia* is loading now at Ell-Five for departure to Vamori-Free."

"But . . ."

"I can't explain or give you reasons, Ali. You simply must do what I tell you."

"What if I don't comply, Father?"

"Alichin, requests can be discussed, but direct orders must be followed in any organization. This is a direct order. The *Tonolia* undocks in two hours, and you will be aboard her. There is no further discussion. I will see you after the *Tonolia* grounds."

And without another word, the circuit was cut from earthside.

Ali was livid. "I'm not going!" he exploded.

I moved to his side. "Ali, I think you'd better."

"Why?"

"Has your father ever given you such a direct order?" I asked.

"Yes, once, many years ago when both Vaivan and I were seven, we decided we had the right to run our own lives and refused to go to bed one night."

"That was a long time ago under different conditions," I pointed out. "We'd better see what your father wants that's so important he'd act as he did. Bump the *Tonolia's* co-pilot, I'll bump the pilot. We'll go down together."

"I'm not going."

"We must. I'm not totally familiar with your Commonwealth customs yet, and certainly not with your family ways, but if you've never been given such a direct order as an adult by your father, there's something going on that he can't tell you even on a scrambled link. Whatever it is, it's important. Stop being your usual stubborn self, Ali, and realize your father's at least as smart as you are. He wants you earthside," I told him, then added, "Don't forget: this is war."

CHAPTER 10

In the Heart
of Vershatets

Things had deteriorated in the few days since I'd been to Vamori Free Space Port.

There was no such thing as an overall Space Traffic Control authority in those days. Each space-faring nation had its own STC Center to handle ships that passed through the atmospheric interface over its national boundaries and entered its "official" national airspace at 100 kilometers altitude. International agreements had extended the individual authorities of these national STC's upward through the low-Earth orbit zone to 25,000 kilometers. Geosynchronous orbit was in turn controlled by other national STC's located in GEO, and their volumes of authority were determined by other international agreements because various nations had "preferred locations" where they had their metsats, comsats, and powersats. Beyond GEO, three other STCs controlled sectors 60-degrees in width centering at L-5, the Soviet-dominated L-4 sector, and the Lunar STC Center at Dianaport which was operated by Equadorians, West Irians, and Swiss, again as a result of international agreements hammered out on the anvil of green felt-covered tables in Geneva and Singapore.

Threading one's way through this maze made space flight a challenge even in times of calm because there's always some person/computer who doesn't get the word. The system works 99.9 percent of the time, but there isn't a space jock, military or civilian, who hasn't tangled with the "Tenth-Percent Law" at least once.

Given the situation with the Commonwealth and about twenty other small nations telling the rest to stuff it up their nozzles with a purge pipe, the system was suddenly very sporty.

We ran into no deliberate delays, but everybody operated exactly and precisely according to their version of the book.

No matter what the system or device is, if it's run by the book or the rules all the time, either it'll become so confused it's worse than no system at all, or it'll bend something.

Our undocking from L-5 went on schedule. Then we hung dead in space for forty-two minutes until the computer system found a slot for us down the right corridor. "Computer error." Our destination code showed as DP instead of VP and the computer had cleared us to Dianaport instead of Vamori-Free.

Eurosynch Center claimed our beacon was faulty when we entered their sector and made us change codes. But the temporary code wasn't the one anticipated for us when we entered StarBase One Center in LEO, and we were verbally challenged by AmSpace Command as an intruder. We got that straightened out. Wichita Center vectored us into a 200-kilometer inclined holding orbit because of outbound traffic from Guyana, but the orbit was phased so we had to either expend a lot of delta-vee to get into Vamori-Free or wait for six orbits. We elected to expend the propellant, which in turn put us in a non-standard approach.

This grand tour was topped by the fact that nobody told Vamori STC Center or Vamori Approach. Communications had been deteriorating since Alichin walked out of the Santa Fe Conference. Vamori Approach cleared the *Tonolia* for landing on Runway Nine-zero, Area Seven-three. We had to set up for an unusual approach from the southwest.

Our non-standard approach took us through the airspace of Malidok who didn't appreciate sonic booms or an unanticipated passage through their sovereign airspace. I think they shot an ASAT and missed, but I don't remember because Ali and I were busy flying the screwed-up approach.

I manually flew the ship into the landing system capture circle and had to take her the rest of the way manually and visually. Something was interfering with the landing beam.

After all we'd been through, landing the *Tonolia* on Runway Nine-zero was a piece of cake. Once the *Tonolia* squatted on the runway, we were out of the clutches of a non-caring STC complex that somehow didn't exactly seem to have our best interests at heart.

I was irritated by the general screw-up. "Dammit, Ali, is every ship coming and going from Vamori-Free having to put up with this crap?"

Ali shook his head. "I don't know, but I'm going to bitch to Vaya Delkot about it."

The area boss driving the pickup van reported, "There's an aerodyne waiting for you, Alichin. You're to go directly to Vicrik."

Ali looked at me. "You're right, Sandy. Something's afoot."

"Quite so, Watson," I replied, mimicking Peter Rutledge.

"Want to fly?" Ali asked as we debouched from the van at the waiting aerodyne.

"I've had all I can hack today. You fly. I'll cheer."

Ali settled in, powered up, and called traffic control. "Vamori Departure, Victor Mike Charlie Seven Zero Whiskey, Area Seven-three, ready for departure, request Victor Ten to Vicrik. And will you give me the latest Vicrik hourly sequence, please?"

"Victor Mike Charlie Seven Zero Whiskey, this is Vamori Departure. Vicrik reporting one thousand broken, ten thousand high thin scattered, wind zero eight zero at one five. Caution advised for moderate to severe icing on the eastern slopes of the Dilkons at three thousand and above. Lenticular clouds reported over the ridges. Mountain peaks may be obscured. Moderate to severe turbulence reported five hundred meters above terrain. Intermittent light rain in the Vicrik and Dekhar areas, scattered snow showers reported in Tewahk and Sedamu passes. Ready for clearance?"

"Typical March weather," Ali muttered and replied, "Seven Zero Whiskey, ready to copy."

The clearance appeared on the display. "Departure, Seven Zero Whiskey, query," Ali transmitted.

"Go."

"We show cleared Victor Ten, Oidak, Victor Fourteen, Dekhar, Victor Eight, Vicrik."

"That's affirmative."

"Why the deviation?"

Pause. "Oidak Center says security reasons and take it or leave it."

"Cancel! We'll go visual Victor Ten direct Vicrik!" Ali snapped, obviously angry. I was perplexed, too, because I'd *never* had any clearance offered take-it-or-leave-it.

"We don't advise that, sir. Aeronote Delta Seven restricts uncleared flight within twenty-five kilometers of the Oidak rectenna. Uncleared aircraft will be intercepted."

"Ali," I said, "take the clearance. Sounds like the Commonwealth's on alert status. We'll find out when we get to Vicrik. Let's get there and bitch later."

He sighed. "Departure, Seven Zero Whiskey confirms and accepts clearance."

"Roger. Seven Zero Whiskey cleared for lift, climb and maintain two thousand, heading two-one-zero to join Victor Ten, expect five thousand ten minutes after lift."

Earth has something that space does not: weather. It was a cruddy day in the Commonwealth. We popped in and out of scattered clouds at two thousand meters until we were cleared to five thousand. That put us above it but underneath a thin layer of cirrus.

"Typical spring weather," Ali remarked. "The intertropical convergence zone begins to shift north about March first and the South African thermal low breaks down. Our normal northerly winds aloft shift anticlockwise until they're southwesterly in June. This time of year we get a shear line with moisture pumped up the eastern slopes of the Dilkons. Our rainy season. Lasts about three Krick cycles until the summer pattern becomes established. Things will begin to get nice again in May. But we need the rain to keep our impoundment reservoirs full for the irrigation net. We get three growing seasons on the Toak Plains because of it."

The flat Toak Plains below us were partially hidden by a broken layer of low clouds. Our flight plan took us over the seemingly endless kilometers of lush farmland until I saw the broad, gleaming expanse of the Commonwealth's powersat rectenna glistening in the sun a few kilometers beyond the city of Oidak. The blue Dilkon Range became visible through the haze. Following flight plan, we swung north along Oidak Lake and up the valley of the Dekhar River, turned southward at Dekhar Nav, and made a bumpy let-down through the broken clouds into the high Vicrik Valley.

Even with the lousy weather, the Vicrik Valley was verdantly gorgeous. Some 2500 meters above sea level, it was surrounded on the east, south, and west by mountains soaring up to 3500 meters. Towering over Vicrik on the west were the jagged spires of Mount Doradun, its treeless summit poling through the cloud decks into the sunlight.

The town of Vicrik was on the southeast shore of a man-made lake that filled a large portion of the valley. I got the impression this was a major Commonwealth resource area because I spotted power lines, hydro plants, railways, mine tipples, saw mills, and paper mills. It was also one of the best winter sports areas in the world.

Ali took manual control over Vicrik Nav and flew to where a cluster of buildings was visible among the evergreens up against a granite massif.

"Vershatets," Ali pointed it out to me.

"Another family compound?" I wondered.

Ali shook his head. "Old word meaning 'mountain keep' or 'castle.' Emergency headquarters for every Commonwealth firm.

Portions are leased to Commonwealth Defense as a first-line command post.''

"Ali, there aren't enough buildings for that," I observed as he set the aerodyne down on a landing stage.

"See that granite cliff? They took three billion tallys of gold out of that mountain before the lode petered-out. A holo of the complex shows more than a hundred kilometers of tunnels under there."

Vaivan was waiting for us. She and Ali embraced. I would have liked to because in the two months we'd been gone, Vaivan hadn't lost a bit of her sensuality. I had to be satisfied with a friendly hand touch.

"Where's Father?" was Ali's first question. "I want to get this matter settled right now!"

"Ali," she said in a comforting tone as we quickly walked off the landing stage in the cold drizzle, "didn't you recognize that as an excuse to get you here?"

"Sandy had some suspicions along that line," Ali admitted as we reached the covered verandah of a wood-sheathed house.

We settled around a table in the warm front room. It seemed strange to sit at a table again. Vaivan produced hot cups of *chai* for us. It must have had some *supaku* in it because it warmed me as it went down, then sat in my belly radiating heat outward into the rest of my body.

As we sipped *chai*, Vaivan put up her hand to silence Ali and explained, "Ali, we had to get you and Sandy back here in spite of the urgency of the RIO operation."

"What's going on, Vaivan?" Ali asked his sister.

"We urgently needed a critical planning meeting."

"But why must we be here in person? We've got a scrambled telecon net."

"Not any more. The scramble code's been broken."

"Broken?" Ali sounded incredulous. "It's so complex that nothing's supposed to be able to crack it."

"It was cracked. Our telecon net is no longer secure."

"Even on lasercom?"

"Tell me, are you set up at Ell-Five for lasercom yet?"

"Uh, no. Jeri reports mid-June at the earliest. Something about equipment delays."

"We're getting a lot of delayed shipments and back orders," Vaivan observed. "In some cases, we're having to deal through secondaries to get equipment from Tripartite countries."

"Vaivan," I put in, "this was an inside job. A complex code

can be cracked only by compromise. Someone dump-copied or modemed the computer memory.''

"I think that's what happened.''

"Who?"

"I don't know.''

"All right, since we know the net's not secure, and since they don't know that we know, we can use it to provide some misdirection and false data.''

"Of course,'' Vaivan replied. "But, in the meantime, we have no secure comm until we get lasercom installed, and that means face-to-face meetings.''

"Anybody working on a new code program yet?'' Ali asked.

"That takes time we haven't got,'' his sister said.

"Look, what's the best code in the world?'' I put in.

"There's no unbreakable code,'' Vaivan reminded me.

"I know. That isn't what I asked. But I'll answer my own question: The best code in the world is one nobody believes is a code. If we come up with another scramble code, it'll get compromised the same way,'' I told them.

"Did you have something in mind, Sandy?'' Vaivan asked.

"How much commercial comm traffic goes on in the Commonwealth?''

Ali whistled. "I don't know the exact number, but there must be over ten thousand voice channels available along with at least a thousand wide-band video and video-holo channels. As for data exchange channels, I haven't got the foggiest idea of how many thousand there must be.''

"How many people would it take to monitor all the commercial communications of the Commonwealth?'' I persisted.

"Several thousand at least.''

"Co-ordinating that effort would be extremely difficult, wouldn't it?''

Vaivan nodded, her shoulder-length hair bouncing across the scarf pulled over her shoulders against the cool mountain air. "And every monitored channel would have to be screened to determine whether it contained any important information. Then that would have to be evaluated. It's a massive effort, almost too expensive and time-consuming to be considered.''

"There's our answer. We use ordinary, everyday commercial telecom in the clear. Each day, we'll use a different channel determined by a computer utilizing its random number generator. The information about the next channel will be passed along each day as a password,'' I explained.

"Password? That's ancient technology!'' Vaivan objected.

"It works."

"Not if the spy knows the password," Ali pointed out.

I held up my hand. "Aha! Ali, you've served in the AirImpy, right?"

Ali nodded.

"Did everybody on base know the password?"

"No, only those on guard and those with permission to leave or enter."

I shrugged. "My point is made. The password must be known only by a selected few. Vaivan, you're the one to select those few."

Vaivan was thinking out loud. "Ali, Sandy, Wahak, Shaiko Stoak, Kariander Dok . . ."

"Don't make the list too long," I reminded her, then suggested, "You might also set up a second list, and we'll use that to trap our spy."

"Nice move," Ali commented.

"In the meantime, we'll keep fake telecons going on the compromised net; we don't want to reveal we know they've broken our code. Teleconferencing in the clear need be known *only* to those with the password; let everyone else believe it's being scrambled."

"The new system won't work forever," Ali pointed out.

"What does? And it doesn't have to," I told him. "This situation is going to come to a head soon. Look, even if they discover we're teleconferencing in the clear, they'll have to monitor thousands of channels. They'll have to know the modulation characteristics. We can drive their monitors absolutely nuts!"

Ali looked at his sister, and she looked back at him. "Well," Ali said with finality, "now that that's settled, let's shag out of here back to Ell-Five!"

Vaivan shook her head. "Not yet. You just arrived. It would look strange if you and Sandy left immediately."

"Who knows we're here?"

"Most of the Landlimo Corporation officers and executive committee, plus President Nogal, Defense Commissioner Abiku, and the imply indunos. We took the precaution of getting Induno Dati of the AirImpy to issue flight restrictions and clear you in via the north approach. Anybody tracking your beacon with a hand-held unit at Vamori-Free would have seen you disappear up the Dekhar Valley in the direction of the Saddleback Recreational Area where we've established a dummy control post."

"Vaivan, they could have tracked us from orbit," I told her.

"Not into the Vicrik Valley," she replied adamantly. "There

are four mountain peaks around us with summits above four thousand meters. There are particle beam generators on those four peaks. We've got lots of hydro power to run them, and they create a layer of partly ionized air of higher dielectric constant that lays over us. This valley can't be seen clearly from orbit by any sensor operating below the infra red. That doesn't hide the mines and other facilities from infra red snoopers, but it certainly makes it very difficult for anybody in orbit to keep radar on anything flying in or out of here. Right, Sandy?''

She was. The United States Aerospace Force had a similar radar-smeared installation at Tincup in Colorado's Taylor Basin.

As it was, I was learning more and more that the Commonwealthers had already done an outstanding job of getting ready for what The General had known was coming for more than fifty years. Sometimes I wondered why they needed me.

Vaivan and Ali had told me. I offered them both modern military expertise as well as an objective critique of their activity. After all, critiques are an important tool in defense preparedness as well as military training.

Vershatets was a super-secure Commonwealth keep, but it was more than Cheyenne Mountain or Tincup. It was used by commercial firms as well as by the defense forces. If there was military action against the Commonwealth—outright invasions, terrorism, or blockade—business had to go on. The Commonwealth had to continue to function. If Topawa, Oidak, Manitu, Hitason, of any of the other commercial/industrial centers were damaged—it had been accepted for over a century that the Trenchard area-bombing doctrine combined with nuclear explosives made such centers prime targets—the commercial/industrial leadership had to be as secure and continuous in operation as the military leadership.

All but the most trusted customers of Commonwealth firms were met in Topawa and most business affairs were conducted there, albeit now under heavy but unobtrusive security because there'd been a definite increase in terrorism since the Santa Fe meeting. Trusted friends of Commonwealth businesses were wined, dined, entertained, and negotiated with in Vicrik or Saddleback. But no outlanders saw Vershatets.

About two hours after we arrived, Wahak informed us that our presence was requested at an emergency meeting of the Commonwealth Commerce Council about the powersat situation.

The weather had cleared, and it was the sort of bright, clear day that reminded me of springtime in the Rockies and the glorious breaking of winter's grip on the Rampart Range above

the Academy. I wanted to get out and utilize the walking muscles that had been so useless at L-5. But I didn't get the chance.
I found myself with hundreds of meters of rock above and
around me in the heart of Vershatets and seated in the conference
room of the Commonwealth Commerce Council, called "C-cubed"
in the vernacular.

This was the big-time in the Commonwealth. The top people
in the Commonwealth, all CEO's of their respective organizations,
were in that underground conference room. This time I recognized most of them because I'd met them at Karederu Center the
night it burned:

Shaiko Chuili Stoak, Tsaya's father and CEO of Commonwealth Glaser Space Power Corporation.

Ali's father, Rayo Sabinos Vamori, ComSpat.

Landlimo's CEO and Vaivan's husband, Wahak Gramo Teaq.

Marcu Sanostu Sabinos of Commonwealth Space Services
Corporation or ComServ.

The pudgy Kariander Alhanu Dok of the Topawa Finance and
Investment Company with his counterpart from the Commonwealth Bancorp, Komel Dok Kokat.

The beautiful Prime Manager of the Vamori Free Space Port,
Vaya Volakata Delkot.

Two other Commonwealth women graced the Directors'
meeting—Emika Vaspua Kom who ran the Pitoika Sea Port,
Drydock, and Ship Company, and Nanya Liputa Tahat, head of
Commonwealth Tourism, Inc. or ComTour, the biggest firm in
the huge Commonwealth tourist industry.

An obvious outlander was Donalo Jon Tomason, head of Rose
& Mariyama, Inc., the engineering and construction firm.

And there was Heinrich von Undine representing Chiawuli
International Factors and Underwriters, Limited.

"What's the General's role in this?" I asked Ali as we took
our seats around the huge circular table.

"He's Chairman of C-Cubed."

I lifted my hand. "Ali, I can't run this meeting as The
General's deputy! I don't even know what the agenda is."

"Don't worry. My father's going to run it for The General *in
absentia.*" He laid his hand on my arm. "Listen, take notes, and
comment if you wish. Father's getting the show on the road."

Rayo Vamori began, "The purpose of this meeting is to bring
us all up to date on what's transpired in the past twenty-four
hours and to make the necessary decisions required to proceed
with Phase Three of our long-range plan."

Kariander Dok raised his hand. "Rayo, it's rather unusual that our associate advisors from out-country aren't on the screens."

"We have some communications problems." Rayo Vamori didn't reveal that the scramble code had been broken.

"Tripartite interference?" Tonol Kokat of ComBank inferred.

"No. If we need to talk to Mukhalla, Phalonagri, Chung, or Sinclair, we'll get them on the line," Rayo replied gracefully. "But we probably won't have to, Kariander. Things are going as planned."

We'd decided we'd use teleconferencing in the clear if absolutely necessary; the passwords had been disseminated by courier. But Vaivan didn't want to do it extensively. Since we didn't know whether or not somebody in C-Cubed was leaking information, she was also doing other things. For example, unbeknownst to the participants, the meeting was being videotaped; later, Vaivan's experts would edit it carefully, insert false information, and squirt it out on the compromised, scrambled telecon net just to keep up the charade that we didn't know we'd been unscrambled.

"Shaiko, will you bring us up to date on the powersat situation, please?" Rayo said to the tall man on his right.

"InPowSat, InSolSat, and PowerSat intend to shut down the additional power beams as they've threatened," the Commonwealth Glaser CEO reported. "I've offered Hong Kong a split beam on a temporary basis provided they'd come up with the capital through the Chungs for R-and-M to build a dedicated powersat for the Hong Kong complex."

"Pardon me," Kariander Dok interrupted, "but I haven't been advised of this. Anything that's done out-country should by rights go through Chiawuli . . ."

"And ComBank," Tonol Kokat added.

"You'll get your usual percentage," Shaiko told them.

"Shaiko, let us handle this with Wen-ling Chung," Kariander pleaded. "We know the international financial scene. We can smooth the way for much of the international fund transfers, for example . . ."

"Sorry, but Chung insists. The capital sources who've come to him willing to finance their own powersats wish to deal through Chung directly with R-and-M."

"Isn't that rather unusual and contrary to practice?" Tonol Kokat asked.

Shaiko shook his head. "These are unusual times, Tonol. Let me finish my report because there's more." He held up sheets of hard copies. "Wen-ling just informed me that we got more than we bargained for. The government of Ch'ien has authorized the Chung bankers in Hong Kong to request bids on three powersats.''

He was talking about the government of mainland China. The Chinese were still fiddling around with their spelling. China was now officially called ''Ch'ien'' and most of their city and province names had changed, too. They were having a very hard time standardizing the spoken languages in the country. The prime benefit of the ancient writing was that an ideograph meant the same everywhere in the country, regardless of the local dialect. But an ideographic script with more than 50,000 characters is incompatible with the WSICI code and machine instructions with which the rest of the world communicated.

Part of the inscrutability of the Yellow Peril was due to their incompatible writing.

Their penchant for doing things in old and established ways was obvious in their preference for carrying out their large international dealings through the Hong Kong financial institutions. Although the British treaty with China had long lapsed and Hong Kong was therefore a Crown Colony in name only, it was an extremely convenient doorway. With their mass of people, the Chinese government wasn't yet able to establish a national policy of free enterprise and a free market; it would take several more decades of mass education through the comm/info network before the Chinese would be able to catch up to the rest of the world in the basic education it takes to make a free system work.

''How can they pay for them?'' von Undine wanted to know.

''They've got the up-front money from their petro reserves,'' Don Tomason of the engineering firm put in, referring to the fact that at that time China produced far more petroleum and natural gas than even the old OPEC nations at the height of their production. ''We can get started almost at once, Heinrich. Those three powersats can be on line in six months with ComServ supplying the lunar materials, ComSpat getting them from Luna to geosynch, R-and-M putting the powersats together, and Commonwealth Glaser operating them under contract. Sweet deal all around. Tonol, you're our banker. Heinrich, the critical high-tech components will come through Chiawuli International . . .''

''Are those the Chinese bid requests?'' von Undine asked Shaiko Stoak, indicating the hard copies.

''Yes.''

''Are we being sole-sourced?''

''As far as I know.''

''Shaiko, please find out. Get Sinclair on the line.''

''Our scrambler's out, Heinrich,'' Shaiko made up an excuse.

"Want to discuss this matter in the clear on an un-monitored channel?"

"How soon before we can use the scrambled channel?"

"Wahak?"

The chief of Landlimo Corporation replied carefully, "I'll check."

"Soon, please."

Wahak looked over at his wife. "Vaivan, telecon net status, please?"

There was a moment's hesitation while Vaivan consulted a VDT. "Vaka is up and available," she replied. She was using one of the Esperanto passwords, indicating to Wahak, Ali, and me that she didn't want to use the normal scrambled channel but had an in-the-clear channel ready.

"We'll use it," her husband told her and turned to Shaiko. "Coming up."

Skinner Sinclair looked like he'd just gotten out of bed, which he had. He was groggy but his usual well-controlled self. He didn't complain about the time differential.

"Did the courier bring you the hard copy?" Shaiko asked him.

Sinclair nodded. "Looks good, Shaiko. Why'd you call?"

"We think we're sole-source, but we wanted to check to see if you know anything else."

"The bid was sole-sourced to you, but I found out through the Old Boy Net at a Shelco-Phelps party tonight that there will be another bidder in spite of it."

"What? On a sole-sourced RFQ?"

"Yup."

"Who?"

"The Socialist Hegemony. More specifically, the Soviet Union."

CHAPTER 11

A Matter of Opinion

"Underbid them." Vaya Delkot of the Vamori Free Space Port broke the silence that followed Sinclair's announcement. "I'll cut revenues if I must."

"Trip," Wahak put in, "is that bid rumor or hard intelligence?"

"You know I don't like soft intelligence. As far as I'm concerned, it's no good unless it's hard."

Don Tomason piped up, "What's their bid?"

"Far below anything we can match," Sinclair reported, "but their terms may give us leverage."

"Let me guess," young Tonol Kokat of ComBank said. "The Soviets own the powersats and lease them to China."

"You're close," Trip replied. "Leaseback."

"Very interesting!" Kariander Dok mused. "The Soviets build the powersats and China pays for them. China then leases the powersats back to the Soviets and receives monthly rentals from the Soviets. But, in the meantime, China pays delivered power charges from powersats it already owns. Why? What advantages are there for both parties in that arrangement?"

"The only one I can see is that SovBank may loan China the up-front money at their usual percentage so China doesn't tie up capital it could use for other purposes," Tonal Kokat observed.

"There's also a military reason," I interrupted because I was the military advisor and felt I should. "China may own the powersats, but the Soviets will control them. This makes the powersats unavailable to China for military use. Soviet thinking *always* considers military implications. But don't worry; the Chinese won't take the Soviet offer. They distrust the Russians— not the Soviets, but the Russians. There's a difference. The Russians took the Amur Penninsula away from them and China hasn't forgotten; China wants it back. And China hasn't forgotten that the Soviets came out on top of Space War One."

"Space War One?" Kariander asked.

"The Sino-Soviet Incident," I corrected myself.

Trip Sinclair went on, "Ladies and gentlemen, the Soviet

122

offer is only one reaction to our powersat ploy. Rockland/Incomp/ Philips/Offenhauser ConsortCorp, resurfaced yesterday as the conglomerated Tripartite tool. Good old Rip-Off is back in business. The Word on the Street and in the Club indicates that Rip-Off intends to offer China a package of coal-fired plants.''

"China hasn't got easily-mined coal," Shaiko Stoak said.

"But the United States does," Trip reminded him. "Scrape it off the western desert, pump it as a slurry through a pipe to a tanker on the West Coast, then ship it across the Pacific. It's the modern version of the Orient trade that's obsessed Americans for two hundred years.''

"I'm not worried about American competition," Don Tomason scoffed. "We offer non-polluting solar power without stack residues or problems with foreign resource allocations.''

"Worry about it," Sinclair advised him. "What's the design life of a powersat?''

"Thirty years nominal; fifty years with up-dating.''

"I understand a coal plant has the same," the Houston attorney told him. "And in thirty years, the whole situation will change—politically, technologically, and economically. Rip-Off will offer a powersat follow-on option. Knowing them, it will be a refurbished powersat now on-line but life-cycled and uneconomical in hi-tech by twenty-seventy. Worry about the Rip-Off proposal, Don. The Tripartite has the financial clout to make it attractive to the Yellow Peril.''

"And the Tripartite would just love to get the Yellow Peril locked into an OPEC-style coal cartel, wouldn't it?'' Shaiko Stoak of Commonwealth Glaser muttered.

"So what are your plans?'' Trip wanted to know.

"Ladies and gentlemen, any suggested change resulting from this information?'' Rayo asked the convocation.

"No,'' Don Tomason put in quickly. "We've thought this through carefully. This is no time to make changes.''

"I don't like any financial arrangement that bypasses ComBank and Chiawuli International,'' Tonol Kokat objected.

Vaya Delkot snapped back, "Tonol, you're using scarcity-economics thinking again! Don't worry about your share. A dozen other low-tech countries will step up to get delivery positions on Commonwealth powersats when the word gets out, and you'll be involved.''

I stood up to get and hold attention, a trick I'd learned in conducting Aerospace Force briefings. "Maybe I'm too locked into scarcity-economics thinking, but so are our adversaries. So I don't understand why you've convinced yourselves that the Tripartite *or* the Hegemony, real or not, would come head-to-head with you and not try to win by any means at their disposal."

I started to walk around the table as I spoke, passing behind each of them and forcing them to turn in their chairs to follow me. "Thus far, we're doing very well fighting an energy war."

I stopped, put my hands on my hips, and stated, "But that doesn't mean we'll win. The Tripartite powersat companies can't continue to pull plugs on small countries to whip them into line. When they see what we're doing, they'll shift to other forms of warfare. Let's look at their possible responses and our vulnerabilities. How about economic warfare?"

"We're not vulnerable," Rayo Vamori countered. "We're self-sufficient. We may lose some foreign trade with Tripartite organizations, but we'll pick up others who've never liked being Tripartite underlings. We'll survive. South Africa did. So did Nicaragua, Chile, the Philippines, Pakistan, and a few more."

"The Tripartite knows that," I said. "Your adversaries *aren't* stupid. Don't fall into that trap. You're may be underestimating their next move. They discovered we won't knuckle under, so they'll start to play rough. Are we ready to play rough, too?"

Rayo Vamori coughed. "Sandy, we anticipate the possibility of military action against the Commonwealth. Defense plans and programs have considered all possible assaults that could be mounted against us from our four neighbors."

"Or from space," Ali added.

"There won't be any military activity for some time yet. The Tripartite hasn't exhausted its non-military options," Vaivan insisted.

"Suppose the Tripartite decides the options are invalid because of our response to date? Suppose they resort to armed conflict next?" I walked back around the table and resumed my seat, telling them as I did so, "They'll choose the time, place, and method, but they'll need a pretext. What do your plans say about where they'll create an incident?"

"They'll do it in space with powersats so it appears to be a military threat from the Commonwealth." Ali said firmly.

I shook my head. "No, that won't suit their purposes. It's remote from people. Forget any space incident. It will happen here on the ground where people will get killed and property damaged or destroyed, where telenews can cover it in all its gore. And they'll make it look like you started it."

Kariander Dok laughed. "That's incredible! Why would we attack any Tripartite interests? *How* could we attack them? We have an old folk story about a brave mouse and a lion . . ."

"Spare me," I told him. "All cultures have folk stories and most of them are misleading because they're intended to teach only the young. I know we wouldn't attack; it's contrary to the Commonwealth's basic principles. But the rest of the world doesn't know because the rest of the world doesn't understand abundancy-economics. The next move of the Tripartite will be armed conflict fought on our territory to occupy the time and effort of our leadership and drain our resources away from any competitive powersat programs."

There was again silence throughout the group in the under-ground conference room. Finally, Kariander Dok asked Shaiko, "What does General Vamori have to say about this?"

I was growing to dislike this big, fat man with his pudgy little face and supercilious manner. "The General's still recovering from his burns," I answered. "I'm his deputy."

"Why didn't The General deputize *you*, Alichin?" Tonol Kokat asked pointedly.

"Because Sandy's an educated professional military man whereas I've served only a three-year hitch in the AirImpy. Sandy's a pro; I'm not," Ali told him. "My expertise is in marketing and operating space activities, not war."

"Your grandfather was no military man when he beat Chase," Tonol pointed out.

"He had no alternative. He didn't have a man like Sandy Baldwin. I do."

"This man could be another Chase." Tonol Kokat kept the pressure on.

Alichin came to his feet, his hand on the hilt of his still-scabbarded iklawa.

I knew a bit more about Commonwealth customs. I was on my feet, too, my hand grasping my own iklawa. I didn't draw it. I reached out and laid my left hand on Ali's shoulder. "Please, Ali. He didn't refer to you."

Ali shook his head. "No!" he spat out. There was fire in his eyes and I barely detected him shaking slightly.

I was trembling too, but it was from adrenalin pumping through me. This was my first encounter in the Commonwealth, the first time someone had insulted me in public. It had been done at a very high level, so I had to follow through.

"Sandy, he implied that Landlimo Corporation—myself, in particular—brought you to the Commonwealth to lead a *coup*!" Alichin went on, breathing hard. "The privilege is mine!"

Kokat had risen slowly to his feet, but his hand didn't drop to his iklawa. He was older than I. He would have been easy to take, but I hoped I wouldn't be forced to fight. I had to maintain a front, so I growled at him, "Tonol Kokat, I came to the Commonwealth in response to a call for help."

"Chase came as a mercenary," Kokat reminded me.

"Chase was a looter, a man on horseback, a modern Atilla!! Alichin put in. "He came to help our forefathers put our own house in order. Sandy didn't. You don't know American military philosophy. Sandy's trained to take orders from civilians. He's doing the job we asked him to do. Retract your words, Kokat!"

Heinrich von Undine reached up and touched Kokat. "Tonol, my friend, the time isn't right. You have great responsibilities . . ."

"Yes, Tonol," Kariander Dok added. "And how long has it been since you've drawn? An apology wouldn't wound you as severely as Baldwin's iklawa. I believe you were reacting only to the possibility of someone repeating our great national trauma of fifty years past." Kariander Dok was a soothing arbitrator.

Ali was reluctant to disengage. "Kokat, you've also insinuated that my grandfather did wrong because he appointed Sandy as his deputy. Defend yourself or retract your words!"

The banker looked around. His hand still hadn't touched his iklawa which was primarily ornamental and decorative. Around the room, nobody moved. It was obvious he didn't have the support of those present, although the rules probably kept them from interfering. Kariander Dok may have acted on the very edge of propriety, but perhaps an attempt at arbitration was allowed.

It was Rayo Vamori who broke the impasse. "Tonol, we have more important things to attend to. Our families and our nation are at stake. They take precedence. Would you withdraw your remark?" Rayo Sabinos Vamori could well have taken issue himself. Everyone knew it was the Rayo's father and his son who were part of Kokat's insinuation.

Tonol Kokat looked directly at me and, with a total absence of emotion in his voice, said, "I withdraw my remark but reserve the right to hold a private opinion until events either prove me right or wrong. If right, I'll take action to protect our families and our nation. If wrong, I'll apologize then." And he sat down.

I sat down, too, as did Ali.

I was astounded at my own actions. I'd never believed what my father believed. I'd let it all hang out as far as possible in the air and in space, and I'd even burned a Soviet. I didn't like one-on-one hand-to-hand. Yet I'd reacted to a personal challenge, had almost drawn my iklawa, and was strangely happy that nothing had happened. At twenty-eight years of age, was I beginning to show the inevitable signs of an aging tiger?

"Ladies and gentlemen, we've received some new information here today and discussed some new possibilities," Rayo Vamori remarked. "Any comments?"

"Bid the Hong Kong deal," Vaya Delkot said.

"As low as possible," Wahak added.

"Underbid if we have to," Shaiko put in.

"Underbid it? We can't stay in business doing that!" Don Tomason objected. "We'll lose money, and it can't be made up in volume."

"Yes, it can," Wahak reminded him. "Our low bid will attract those who lose Tripartite space power. If we build twenty low-cost powersats to satisfy demand, that's cheaper than building five because we can spread fixed costs. Run the numbers."

"You may be right," Don admitted.

Emika Kom of the Pitoika Drydock and Ship Company looked at me. "Rayo, in view of what Sandy told us, I'd like to have him get together with Defense Commissioner Hannu Abiku and his staff."

"Yes," Kohatu Tatri of CommTrans agreed, "our depty military advisor has some points well taken."

I never got out of the mountain that day. Alichin made a call from the meeting room, and the next thing I knew he was guiding me through rock-lined corridors in an electric car to yet another excavated cavern.

This one bore a sign over its entrance, "Commonwealth Defense Commission, Vershatets Redoubt Headquarters."

"It's about time," I said to Ali.

"Why?"

"I should have come here earlier."

"When would that have been, Sandy?" Ali asked. "We took The General to Ell-Five the same day you arrived here, you've been on Earth once since on a down-and-back packet run, and we got here only hours ago."

Sometimes when things happen fast, I tend to forget simple sequences, to say nothing of time periods. It seemed that I'd been on Earth for days.

Again, another conference room, but this one with a decidedly military feel. There was no round table where everyone sat as equals. There were six console desks facing a wall which had situation display screens and another console desk in front of it.

"War room," Ali said curtly.

Six people followed us into the room. Five wore the first

Commonwealth military uniforms I'd seen, and these were obviously Type B Garrison or its equivalent because they were plain, working clothes with only small badges of rank. Each uniform was slightly different.

Alichin performed the introductions, and more names got thrown at me, some of which I didn't fully recall at the time although I knew Commonwealth people considered all three of their names important because it indicated family linkages and lines.

Hannu Chuili Abiku wasn't in uniform because he was the Defense Commissioner directly responsible to President Conobabi Nogal.

The others were the commanders of the five impys or military services:

AirImpy Induno Tanana Pinala Dati must have been a fighter pilot because of her small size.

LandImipy Induno Nenana Husila Pahtu's necklace medallion told me she was an armor weaponeer.

CoastImpy Induno Naco Yumi Shokutu with classical naval shoulder boards of rank framing his otherwise broad shoulders; his sword didn't look out of place with his white naval uniform.

The uniform of SpacImpy Induno Eloy Minto Chervit followed the old tradition that military dress derives from battle gear; his white drop suit was well-tailored.

Induno Kivalina Soldata Moti was an older woman in charge of something new to my military experience: the Commonwealth's citizen reserve, the CitImpy of more than a million people.

Alichin gave me a promotion in introducing me. "Deputy Induno Sandy Baldwin, formerly of the United States Aerospace Force Academy Class of Forty-One." I didn't know what my new rank was.

The introductory greetings of each were polite but curt. It was obvious they'd been called from their daily work for this impromptu meeting. Ali had undoubtedly used the considerable political clout of his grandfather.

They didn't waste any time but sat down behind their console desks. The Commissioner motioned Ali and I to the lectern in front of the wall display screens. "Alichin, this is your request. Please proceed."

Ali stepped to the lectern. "Thank you for taking the time from your schedules to meet with us. Induno Baldwin's vitae are available at your consoles. General Vamori has appointed him his deputy for the duration of the former's rehabilitation. We've just come from a meeting of the C-Cubed Directors, and here's the current situation.''

Without visual aids, Alichin outlined the powersat and commercial-financial situation. The people responsible for the defense of the Commonwealth listened carefully. Some took notes on their desk keypads. Others called up various items of data on their VDTs.

There was a VDT next to the offstage chair in which I sat. I queried the library computer. The rank of ''induno'' was that of a general officer, but there was only one General in the Commonwealth, the title now being the highest possible national honor. Ali had booted me up several ranks in one sentence. I hoped he had the authority, but I wasn't going to argue.

''Induno Baldwin has analyzed the economic and military situation. As a recently naturalized Commonwealth citizen, he brings us a fresh, objective viewpoint based on his expertise in military science,'' Ali went on following his situation briefing. ''He believes we're faced with military action sooner than anticipated and in a different manner than previously considered. The C-Cubed Directors believe this, too, which is why we're here. Sandy, take over and tell them what you told C-Cubed.''

Ali found a chair at one side of the room, leaving me the lectern.

I had no notes, no prepared briefing, and no visual aids.

One of my most valuable Academy courses had been a required three-credit seminar called ''Briefings 301.'' It was known to be a nut-buster, but I'd loved it! At each class session, one cadet was chosen at random and given a situation whose data he could call up on his VDT. He had ten minutes to acquaint himself with the situation. Then he had to present a thirty-minute briefing to the class. Following this, he had to open the briefing to questions. To the rest of the cadets in the classroom, it was a grand game of playing generals out to poke as many holes as possible in the briefing by asking questions. If the class wasn't rough on the briefer, the instructor would break in to make it rough. If the briefer bobbled it, or if the class could find critical data that hadn't been included in the verbal briefing, the briefer ''crashed and burned'' for the day but had the opportunity to try again later. The course taught me to think fast, talk convincingly, and *never* use the old advice, ''If you can't convince them, confuse them.''

I gave the Commonwealth's defense directorate the same basic pitch as I'd presented extemporaneously to the C-Cubed meeting. This time, I plugged some of the loopholes.

"I don't know your defense plans, although I've been told that some of my scenarios have come close to the mark," I concluded. "You undoubtedly know far more about the Commonwealth's vulnerabilities than I do. However, I would *strongly* urge you to study these vulnerabilities *very* carefully with an eye toward someone creating an incident for which the Commonwealth can be blamed."

"Sounds like something for your LandImpy, Nenana," Commissioner Abiku remarked to Induno Pahtu.

Induno Pahtu was one of those non-feminine women who're hard as nails and look it. She wore her greying hair close-cropped for a woman, and her attitude was one of total professionalism. In her gravelly alto voice with just a hint of coarseness to it, she replied, "Staff Study Ganto Oro. My staff made a thorough investigation of our vulnerabilities to land offensives. Call up the synopsis on your VDT."

"Put it on the screen, Nenana," the Commissioner told her.

A topo map of the Commonwealth formed on the screen behind me. I stepped to one side and looked.

"The classic historical avenues of attack are primarily along the coastal Toak Plains," Induno Pahtu explained as two arrows appeared on the map. "Easy to sweep into the Commonwealth this way. No great geographical barriers. Crossings of the Liupp River can be forced at several places. From the south, the Lipuputu River border is more difficult to cross because of its banks. The Dilkon Range offers several passes which could be penetrated . . ."

"Excuse me," I interrupted. I don't usually interrupt generals during their briefings, but I felt I could get away with it here. I did. "I wasn't speaking of overt invasions, Induno Pahtu. Nazi Germany started World War II with an invasion of Poland justified on the basis of a supposed Polish attack on a German border outpost. It was actually carried out with German soldiers in Polish uniforms fighting their own people. The Germans used it as a provocation to justify their invasion which followed within hours. That was the sort of thing I had in mind."

Induno Pahtu shook her head. "There's no way it can happen. All of my troop concentrations are well back from our borders except where the Lipuputu River borders the Chibka Socialistic Republic. Actually, I don't have many LandImpy troops stationed at either border because I could move them rapidly by road and rail to prepared positions on the rivers. At Outpost Eight up on the abandoned rail line into the Ilkan Empire, there's a minimum garrison just to send a message to the Ilkans that we're ready if they should try to sweep southward toward Liupp. But they don't have the capability. The country's in a sad state.''

"Induno, the terrorist who tried to kill me at Topawa Airport three months ago was Ilkan," Ali reminded her. "And Ilkans burned Karederu Center. They've apparently get the wherewithal to conduct terrorist operations in the Commonwealth.''

"Internal counter-terrorist activity isn't my responsibility," Pahtu said testily.

"Induno Pahtu, with all due respect for the abilities of your staff," I put in, "both of the potential trouble points you've mentioned suffer from two problems.''

"And they would be?" Induno Pahtu asked with a great deal of doubt in her voice.

"One: they're obvious. Two: they are not strategically important to anyone.''

"They are certainly strategically important to me!''

"I agree. You're charged with the land defense of the Commonwealth. They're important to you. *But not to the Ilkans or the Chibkas!* Why would we attack either of them? According to the map, there's nothing the Ilkans have that we want, and your forces would have to cross more than a hundred kilometers of desert to capture their capital city. Why fight for possession of that village of hovels? The same logic rules the Chibka front. South of the Lipuputa River, the Chibkas don't have any land or resources that would be useful, just coastal swampland and tropical jungle. They haven't converted it to farmland the way the Commonwealth did with the Toak Plains.'' I looked up at the display. "But there's a region that's bothered me ever since I first studied a Commonwealth map from a military viewpoint. What's up there in the northwest corner of the Commonwealth?''

"Lake Nyira and the provincial capital of Kulala," Induno Pahtu told me. "It's well garrisoned, and the Sayhuto Pass through the Dilkon Range is well defended, too.''

"I'm sorry, but you're missing my point," I replied. I was crashing and burning this session of Briefing 301 in the real world. But I was talking to people who'd been living with the maps and the plans for years. "A major transportation route cuts across the northwest corner of the Commonwealth and goes through Kulala: the Rhodes Cape-to-Cairo Railway. I'll bet the Ilkans and the Emirate of Kalihol don't like it.''

"You have a point, Sandy," Commissioner Abiku admitted. "That corner isn't ours by choice. It was part of the old Republic of Liupp that resulted from a Geneva conference when this part of the world came out from under colonial rule seventy years ago. But we don't detain any rail traffic through there and we don't make customs inspections or charge duties; it's an open railway. It's important to us because our railway through Sayhuto Pass to Kulala connects to it, making it our major rail link to the interior.''

"Do you think something will take place there, Induno Baldwin?" CitImpy Induno Moti asked me. She seemed to be interested in what I was saying.

"Seems logical."

"The map is not the territory," Pahtu remarked. "If you think the region's critically important, why don't you go for a look? I think you're wrong now, but I'll listen to your analysis of the Kulala situation once you've been there. You might see something we haven't.''

I hesitated. I should get back to L-5, I told myself. If the balloon went up, my best position was in space because that's where I knew how to fight best. "Ali?" I asked.

Ali shrugged. "They brought us down at a critical time, but I'm in touch with Peter. We can't return immediately, so two days won't make much difference. Go do it. Pahtu's right: you might discover something everyone else has missed."

"I'll take him by rail," Induno Moti offered. "The trip's spectacular.''

"I'm not here to sightsee, Induno.''

"True, but consider it part of your education in the military realities of the Commonwealth," she told me. "I believe you've spotted a weak point, Baldwin. But you need to see it to be certain. With your background, I think your analysis could even include a recommendation that might sway even Induno Pahtu. How about it, Nenana?''

Induno Pahtu merely said, "I told you I'd listen, Kivalina.''

"Good! May I use your railcar?''

CHAPTER 12

The Other Side
of the Mountain

There were only four of us aboard Induno Pahtu's Henschel rail car—myself; CitImpy Induno Kivalina Moti; her aide, ComExec Elwok Bylar Oraibu; and the white-turbaned, sport-shirted Sikh driver, Kirpal Sandhu Singh.

Singh was proud of his steed. The fittings had been polished and even the coal bunker was wetted down. The steam plant was compact, using fluid-bed dual combustion and a 20-atmosphere fire-tube boiler. A heat exchanger condensed the used steam to conserve feed water. There was no vibration from the opposed four-cylinder steam engine tucked underneath the front of the twenty-meter car. In accordance with custom, two metal plates above the shovel nose and another inside above the windscreen announced Engineman Singh had named it *Allakaket Mountain*.

"It's a fine machine," he explained proudly as we descended Dekhar Gorge. "It will take fifty tonnes over the pass to Kulala. But my normal run is Topawa-Oidak express passenger service."

"Isn't this Induno Pahtu's railcar?" I asked.

"The car's leased from ComTrans," Moti said from where she sat in the left seat, viewing the rails sweeping in front of us down the Gorge. "We also lease railway right-of-passage."

"I don't understand two things, Induno Moti," I remarked.

"Call me Kivalina. What are they, Sandy?"

It didn't bother me to be on first name basis; she was old enough to be my mother. "Why bother with rail? Aerodynes go anywhere and don't depend on right-of-way."

"It's a tactical mistake at any time to depend on one form of transportation." She pointed to the clouds scudding along the 3500-meter peaks alongside the Gorge. "We have two heavy weather seasons when air ops are difficult. Can't move troops or equipment by air or road in foul weather. Railways run in any weather."

"Provided you maintain security and repair damage quickly," I pointed out.

"That's always a problem and an advantage," Kivalina

admitted. "But railways can be easily and quickly repaired. And for hauling big loads of great weight, flanged wheels on rails can't be beat."

I knew the military role railways had played for two centuries in a world that never stopped fighting. "Sorry, I'm still using high-tech thinking."

"You're doing quite well, considering the length of time you've been here. Now, what's your second problem?"

"I can't figure out the Defense Commission."

"It's just a government subsidiary service corporation."

"How can the Commonwealth run the armed forces like a service corporation?" I wondered.

"We got the idea from your country."

"Come on, Kivalina! The Departmen of Defense is one of the most inefficient tax-supported government organizations in the world!"

"I wasn't referring to DoD," Kivalina replied. "The United States has excellent, efficient, low-cost security systems that protect people, facilities, shipments, all the things armed forces should do. You've heard of Pinkerton's or Brinks'? Our Defense Commission is patterned after them. It doesn't have to make a profit, but it must be cost-effective. After all, it's a government business."

"A business? A government exists to create business entities, not to be one itself."

"Sandy, have you read our Constitution?"

"No."

"Well, you've got it backwards. A government provides definite services to both individuals and corporations. Ours is a non-distributive corporation, and every citizen or domestic company is a stockholder/member. The annual membership charge for an individual is ridiculously low. That for a business is based on a small percentage of its capitalization. It's not costly enough for anybody to spend time and effort to avoid. One of the things the government handles is the common defense. It's the old protection racket, but we know it. And there's no other common way to do it."

I shook my head. "That doesn't make sense. A government performs social functions in addition to defense."

"Name ten 'government functions' that can't be done out better by a private operation," she challenged me. "If something's necessary and people are willing to pay for it, someone will risk capital and effort to do it."

"How about not-for-profit organizations?"

"Are there such things?"

"Sure. Service clubs and civic associations and the like."

"Oh, my, Sandy," Kivalina said with a frustrated tone in her voice. "An organization can't spend more than it gets. It must charge for value delivered. There has to be profit."

"The non-profit organizations I'm talking about don't distribute any monetary dividends to their members," I explained.

Kivalina brightened. "Those are non-distributive corporations. Singh's Engineman Sodality is one. He contributes regularly to it and it provides him with salary protection, medical care, and old-age benefits."

"That's a union."

"A sodality isn't a union. Individuals retain their own bargaining rights in a sodality."

"But that leads to worker exploitation!"

Kivalina advised me, "Stop thinking in scarcity-economics terms, Sandy. Any organization that mistreats its workers can't stay in business. A disgruntled employee can form another company to do the same thing and treat its workers properly. Soon the original firm won't be able to compete because it won't have good workers. The same holds true for our defense forces. The CitImpy would be an ineffectual back-up force if I depended on police action or other physical coercion. And we wouldn't have the sense of pride and tradition that's absolutely necessary to keep the CitImpy from becoming a revolutionary mob."

"We've tried to get a militarily-trained citizenry for almost three hundred years in the United States," I pointed out. "How'd you manage?"

Kivalina smiled. "Universal military training."

"Universal military service is something Americans won't buy."

"I said 'training,' not 'service.' At eighteen years of age, everyone undergoes nine months of the basic military *training* necessary to defend the Commonwealth. This includes the handicapped because there are lots of jobs they can do in the impys. Each new citizen receives a registered assault rifle and is expected to use it if required. That citizen is responsible for its maintenance, use, and *mis-use*. Defense of the social organization doesn't conflict with freedom. We believe it's the *duty* of all members of a free institution to defend it and the *duty* of the institution to compel it. If you don't like it, you're free to find another one."

"Suppose I'm a young Commonwealther who refuses to participate?"

"You'd never become a citizen. You couldn't do things reserved for citizens. You couldn't vote. You couldn't join a sodality. You couldn't become a director or officer of any Commonwealth corporation. You couldn't open and maintain a bank account. You'd be legally a child. In other words, you'd be treated as a non-responsible individual." She looked like a wistful grandmother for a moment, then went on, "We remember childhood as a beautiful, wonderful period in our lives and forget that the last part of it, adolescence, is miserable. A child is a young animal upon whom the thin veneer of civilization must be placed by parents. I have four grown offspring of my own." She looked directly at me. "You think you came from a free country? Sandy, you're going to find out what freedom really means! Can you accept total responsibility for yourself and your actions? Some outlanders can't."

Singh maintained 150 kilometers per hour down the winding Dekhar Gorge. We came through mountain forests of lianas and heaths and skirted the northern marge of a Lake Oidak past the SPS rectenna. Two hours out of Vicrik, we entered Oidak, the Queen City of the Toak Plains.

Oraibu brought aboard food and additional drinking water for the galley while Singh topped coal and water. "It is five-hundred-seventy kilometers to Kulala over steep grades," Singh explained, "I must re-water at Sayhuto Pass although the *Allakaket Mountain* reuses her feed water ten times."

We ate lunch as *Allakaket Mountain* sped northward along the Oidak River. The Toak Plains, once a savannah nutured only by twice-yearly rains, were a carpet of irrigated farmland. We raced past kilometers of hypergrain wheat, millet, soybean, and cotton fields. As we left the river valley and paralleled the Dilkon Range, the land became grassy steppe. The railway turned westward toward the Dilkons and we started to gain altitude.

Twice we took sidings on word from Singh's comm. Unit coal trains rumbled past southbound. We went "in the hole" for a tourist special returning from the Sayhuto Pass recreational areas.

It seemed impossible that a railway could breach the mountains ahead, their flanks dappled with green-blue vegetation and wispy clouds. The grade became steeper and *Allakaket Mountain* slowed from the 250 kilometers per hour Singh had maintained out of Oidak to a creeping 100 km/hr as the railway climbed the gorge and hung on the side of the cliffs over the churning white water of the Sayhuto River below. Into the clouds we went, then out into bright mountain sunlight. Tunnel, bridge, fill, cut—the Sayhuto Pass Railway had to be one of the great engineering feats on Earth, unrivalled since the days of the Colorado narrow-gauge. It would have been impractical, if not impossible, to put a standard 1.44-meter railway across these mountains; the gradients and curvatures taxed even the Commonwealth 1.07-meter gauge.

A narrow two-lane road paved with the Commonwealth's coal-slag ersatz macadam twisted through the gorge with the railway. It wouldn't be rated better than a tertiary road in high-tech America. Commonwealthers had put their capital and effort into the railway instead of a road at the mercy of weather.

And weather there was. At about 2500 meters, it began to snow lightly, coating the heaths and fern trees with a dusting of white. But *Allakaket Mountain* whined ahead, the rails guiding it through the snow.

It was below zero Celsius at the top of Sayhuto Pass, but there was no snow on the ground. The tops of the Dilkons poked out of the cloud deck, turning the peaks into islands in a sea of white. The trees looked like pines but weren't; some were stunted by the cold. The fern trees were also smaller with a dried, brown, dessicated look.

Singh stopped in a small railway yard with locomotive re-watering facilities near a cold-looking village of less than a hundred people. Kivalina stayed in the warmth of the railcar. I quickly got chilled in the high mountain air and went back inside, leaving Singh to oversee re-watering.

"This is one of four passes through the Dilkons," Kivalina remarked and pointed out the window toward the tree-covered mountainside. "It's heavily fortified."

I looked where she pointed but didn't see anything unusual. "A good camouflage job," I complimented her.

"Nothing I-R couldn't spot, but sometimes you have to get a visual to discriminate a target out of clutter. Rocket and artillery batteries sweep both the railway and the highway. You wouldn't believe the antipersonnel booby traps out there. The terrain's impassable except to mountain ranger troops—and neither the Ilkans or the Kalihols have them."

"They could hire mercenaries," I pointed out.

"Mercenaries often don't fight well when the going gets deadly."

As we talked, the sun disappeared behind clouds. Thunder reverberated over Sayhuto Pass. When we left ten minutes later, the visibility was nearly zero in freezing drizzle.

The western side of Sayhuto Pass was steeper, the curves tighter, the tunnels longer, and the bridged canyons deeper and more numerous. We went in and out of clouds, mist, snow showers, sleet, drizzle, fog, and warm sunlight.

The culmination of the dream of Cecil J. Rhodes, the Rhodes Cape-to-Cairo Railway had been routed along the eastern and southern shores of Lake Nyira a hundred and fifty years ago with dynamite and hand labor. Kulala was settled as a railway division point from which the Germans blasted the Sayhuto Pass Railway through to the coast.

Twenty klicks out of Kulala, Singh pulled into a passing track. A few minutes later, a goods train went by up Sayhuto Pass.

Singh came back from the cab with a concerned look on his face. "Induno Moti," he reported, "something's wrong. Those were not ComTrans locomotives; they were Rhodes Railways Diesels. The brake van was also Rhodes. The consist was reefers, grain gondolas, and livestock wagons. Down goods trains never carry food from Kulala." The Sikh was obviously disturbed at this unusual operation on the railways that were his life work.

"Strange," Kivalina remarked, then asked, "What does Kulala Despatch say?"

"I received orders from them to cross the train here and to proceed after crossing. I reported the crossing and everything appears to be normal."

"Proceed then, Mister Singh," Kivalina told him.

As the railcar moved off the siding, Kivalina and Oriabu opened a cabinet in the galley. She handed me a rifle and a bandolier of ammunition. "Know what it is?" she asked.

I looked it over. "Israeli copy of the Arisaka Type Twenty-one. No, it isn't! Never seen it before."

"Commonwealth A-R-Three, our version of the Israeli copy of the Arisaka," her aide Oraibu explained. "Same basic Arisaka action, almost impossible to jam, can be freed-up by spitting on it. Seven-point-six millimeter high-velocity directionally-solidified round, fifty to a clip. It'll take the head off a man at a hundred meters or blow his guts out."

At the Academy, I'd studied every known weapon except this one. When Elwok told me what it was, I knew how it worked and what it would do because of the weapons it had been derived from. Short of an anti-vehicle cannon, it would stop anything and at long range, too. It had hitting power designed to take an enemy permanently out of action. Its 2.5-kilogram weight came from extensive use of high-stress composites, and the recoil of the high-velocity round was absorbed by gas cushion and venting. The Israeli version could be dragged through sand, dunked in mud, used to hammer tent stakes, and never cleaned. It would work perfectly years after being so abused, and it would keep on working, It was the ultimate soldier's firearm.

Kivalina checked hers. "It's the CitImpy rifle and the ammunition is everywhere."

"How many murders are committed with these every year?" I asked.

"None. It's too much for a social purpose weapon. And the penalty for mis-use is the public gallows, leaving the murderer's family the burden and shame of paying the debts, obligations, and family support of the murdered." Kivalina slung her AR-3 over her left shoulder and the bandolier over her right. "Load and lock," she ordered. "We may have trouble at Kulala Despatch."

"Hi-jacked food train," I remarked, "with an Ilkan crew looking like Commonwealthers."

"No, probably Kalihol troops," Kivalina corrected me. "The food trains go northbound from the Emirate to the Ilkans who can't feed themselves."

This was the incident I'd forecast! It would be made to look like the Commonwealthers had diverted a food train passing through their territory destined to feed the starving people of the Ilkan Empire. "Kivalina, if this isn't the opening move in a brush-fire war, it's certainly a preliminary."

She nodded. "I'll bet there's trouble at Kulala Despatch." She stepped over to another cabinet that housed military comm gear. A few minutes later, she closed it. "Electronic countermeasures. But we'll beat that game . . ."

She had Singh stop the railcar about five kilometers from where Kulala lay sleepily on the edge of Lake Nyira. Oraibu and I went with her back along the track to what appeared to be a signal box. Lifting the cover of the box, revealed a mike and a speaker. "As I said, Sandy," Kivalina remarked as she pulled the equipment out, "any military organization that relies on a single technology is out of business in the opening minutes of any fracas. To satisfy your whetted curiousity, opticom cables buried under our railways. If they get cut, we have an I-R lasercom with relays on most of the Dilkon summits." Kivalina then spoke into the mike, "Tondro Six, this is Onklino One! Do you read?"

"Onklino One, this is Malmola Lead! Where are you? We've been trying to contact you for an hour!" I recognized Induno Pahtu's gravely voice. The circuit was all the way through to the Vershatets Headquarters.

"We're five from destination," Kivalina replied.

"There's a down goods train from Kulala. Stop it."

"Too late. It passed us ten minutes ago," my host reported back. "It can be stopped at Sayhuto Pass."

"We don't think it'll get there," Induno Pahtu's voice came through again. "We're on lasercom and opticom to Kulala garrison. Kulala Despatch was overrun by people with CitImpy brassards who diverted an up food train to Ilkan with a Kalihol crew aboard. Get to Kulala, assess the situation, and report."

"Will do. Put the CitImpy units in Kulala district on Alert Plan Domo, units report to assembly points. I'll call from Kulala."

By the time we got back to the railcar, the sun was obscured by heavy clouds and rain had started to fall.

Kivalina ordered Singh to proceed into the Kulala marshalling yard at reduced speed. She and Oraibu slipped bright orange brassards over their left arms. She handed me one. "Put it on so you won't get shot at. Under Plan Domo, CitImpy's identified by orange brassards."

The railcar shuddered to a stop.

We went up to the cab to find out what was going on. A bright red double signal light glared down the rain-slick track. Singh explained apologetically, "Induno, I cannot pass a double red."

Kivalina snapped, "Emergency over-ride! Proceed at cautious speed. The terrorists in Kulala Despatch probably set the signals against arrivals. Sandy, take the right cab door and cover. Elwok, take the left."

In the rain and deepening dusk, I couldn't see anything beyond a hundred meters. Kulala gave me the impression of being an old colonial village. Huts and fences clustered along the right of way. Domestic animals huddled under shelter or foraged about in door yards. Nobody was out in the rain which was now falling heavily. I spotted the yard limit sign. The single track became a network of crossovers. A cluster of railway sheds loomed ahead.

The railcar's headlamp went out with a pop and the unmistakable splat of a bullet's shock wave.

I was thrown hard against the forward edge of the door as Singh applied emergency brakes. Swinging the bottom half of the door inward, I dropped to the deck plates.

Almost immediately, automatic weapon fire raked the railcar. I heard the sound of a body falling to the deck.

There wasn't anything to shoot at in the gloom. I wished there was an I-R scope on my AR-3.

Over the sighing of the railcar, I heard sporadic rifle fire ahead.

A wet hand touched my leg. I looked back to see Kivalina

crawling into the doorway next to me. Her hand and arm weren't wet with rain but with blood.

"Despatch signals control tower is about two hundred meters ahead," she breathed. "They've got us ranged from there. We've got to get out of here."

"You're hit."

"Just cuts on my right arm from pieces of windscreen glass. I put up my arm to protect my face," the leader of the CitImpy explained curtly. "I've got my field pack. I can bandage my arm after we get out of this death trap. Let's go for that coaling bunker about twenty meters to the right. Give me covering fire. I'll go first. Then Sandy. Then Elwok."

"What about Singh?" I wanted to know.

"He died at his railcar controls," Kivalina said with no trace of emotion in her voice. "Cover me!" She dropped to the ground and ran hunched through the gloom toward a coal bunker. She drew no fire, so neither Elwok or I shot back.

Then it was my turn. I dropped the meter to the ground, alighting on the sharp ballast rocks. That was the easy part. The ground between the tracks was a morass of gluey mud that sucked at my feet. I drew fire. I *hate* mud and the sound of high-velocity rounds whiffling past. I heard covering fire from Kivalina and Elwok.

I didn't think I was ever going to get there. I made it to the bunker whose mass of coal was more than adequate protection against anything except mortar fire.

Kivalina was shooting around a corner near the ground. "Eleven o'clock, two hundred meters, about four meters up," she gasped, still out of breath. "Take this side of the bunker. It's easier for me to shoot left-handed on the other side."

We should have run for it together. Kivalina's break had identified a target. I gave them the range. Elwok didn't make it although I squeezed off a full clip to cover him.

The rainy dusk of the marshalling yard was suddenly lit by *Allakaket Mountain* blowing up. A round found her boiler. When 20 atmospheres of steam lets loose, it tears things up. The coal gas from the fluid-bed combustor mixed immediately with the air, creating a fire ball. Pieces of glowing coal were flung outward in the violent disintegration of the railcar.

In the flare of light from Engineman Kirpal Sandhu Singh's funeral pyre, I clearly saw the Kulala Despatch control tower.

And I could see how to get to it.

So I emptied a fifty-round clip toward what was left of the second floor windows, then yelled at Kivalina, "Keep shooting!

I'm going around to the right behind the sheds and clean out the tower building.''

Blood was running down her right side from her lacerated arm. "Don't do do it! We don't know where the garrison troops are and when they'll attack!"

"From the looks of things, they don't even have the building under fire," I pointed out. "One A-P rifle grenade will take care of that second floor."

"And disable all the railway control and switching circuitry! That'll will put the railway out of action for weeks!"

"Then how the hell can we flush those bastards out of there?"

"I don't know. Wait and see what the LandImpy does. Stay here. The area's full of CitImpy. You'll get shot."

I really didn't trust Kivalina's citizen irregulars who might shoot at anything. On the other hand, I didn't want to stay pinned down behind a coal bunker in the pouring rain with a wounded woman all night. Someone had to do something because the terrorists in the tower could wreck everything there anyway, and the Commonwealth would catch the blame regardless.

I'd been a passive participant in Commonwealth affairs long enough. "I'm going to clean out that tower."

"Be careful! Don't shoot at orange brassards!"

"I'll shoot anyone who shoots at me!" I told her and dashed across five meters of open area to a shed.

I slowly worked my way to within fifteen meters of the control tower in the growing darkness. As I was sizing up the stairway on the north side of the tower, a bullet smacked into the bricks above my head.

I reacted by swinging in a crouching turn, the butt of the AR-3 against my hip and the selector on full-auto. In the alley between two buildings, a form became a rag doll thrown violently backwards. Someone else stepped out, rifle at the ready. He got off two wild shots before I hit him, too.

"Cease fire, you trigger-happy CitImpys!" came a yell. "The enemy's in the tower, not down here!" A helmeted man stuck his head over a window sill. "Plan code password!"

"Plan Domo!" I called. "I'm from the railcar!"

"Domo it is!" A uniformed warrior stepped out of a doorway while someone else pinned me in the beam of a spot light. "Orange brassard!" he confirmed.

In a few seconds, I was surrounded by LandImpy warriors. These were the men I needed to do the job.

"Induno Baldwin from Vershatets," I identified myself and took command whether I was supposed to or not. "CitImpy

nduno Moti's wounded behind the coal bunker back there. You:
et a medic and help her. The rest of us are going to clean out
hat tower. You and you and you: up the ladder to the roof of
hat shed. When you see me start up the stairway, put covering
ire into those upper windows . . . *but don't hit me!* You and
ou I want at the base of the stairs and under the landing to shoot
nyone who steps out. Move out!''

I presumed they were trained professional troops who'd follow
rders, so I worked my way to the tower and laid myself against
he north wall by the stairway. I looked for the three warriors on
op of the building across the alley. I saw a gun barrel there and
tarted up the stairs.

And received no covering fire to pin down the tower occupants.

I went up four steps before having second thoughts. In my
moment of hesitation, a man stepped out on the landing and
opened up with a sub machine gun.

I got off four rounds which hit him, pitched him over the
railing, and dropped him to the ground.

I discovered I couldn't stand up. Something was wrong with
my legs. I fell backwards down the stairs.

Then I heard my covering fire! And two warriors trampled on
me where I lay in the mud.

There was a lot of rifle fire, but I didn't care. Rain fell in my
eyes and soaked me while nauseating waves of pain rippled up
from my legs.

There were bright lights in the sky. I'd always wanted to see a
flying saucer, and as my lights went out I saw one hovering over
me.

CHAPTER 13

History Books Do Lie

"Old comrade, you feel better now?"

I was warm and dry and floating on a cloud in a brightly lighted room. Nothing seemed to matter. I couldn't feel anything anywhere. Things were dreamlike.

"If I'm dead," I muttered, having a hard time getting the words out, "it's better than mud and rain."

A man grinned at me, the ends of his bushy black mustache pointing straight out. It had to be Omer. "Out of the mud, Sandy. You took a seven-point-six in left leg and two in right, above knees, missed bones. Old Pay-pay-shah Sixty good only for shooting flies off the wall."

"But shot my legs to hell . . . Still in Kulala?" I asked thickly.

"*Da*. Bad weather to fight in, but we don't get a choice. Tough to fly an aerodyne through it. Brought a MEST team. They patched you up. Rest easy. We lift from Kulala at sunrise. I won't fly Dilkons at night in *this* weather except in emergency."

I slipped back in the bliss of nothingness.

Bright sunlight hit my eyes. I heard a turbine whine and felt an aerodyne rocking as it broke ground and stabilized.

"Welcome back." Kivalina had her right arm covered with synflesh. "You should be dead because of what you did."

"Terrorist in the tower hit me with a sub machine gun. Didn't get covering fire. Luck of the draw. Your armed citizens almost got me first," I told her. "Those idiots shot at everyone."

"I told you they would. They're supposed to make it hazardous for everybody around. We expect they'll shoot a few of their own. LandImpy troops pull back when the CitImpy goes into action," she explained.

"Lose lots of citizens that way?"

"We've got almost two million in the CitImpy, only nine months to train each of them, and only one chance to do it. We can't expect them to be as good as professional warriors. Their duty is to make an invasion very difficult and costly."

144

For both sides, I thought.

I guess I'd lost a lot of blood before somebody found me at the bottom of the Kulala Despatch tower stairs. There were good medical facilities and people at Vershatets where I was taken, but I was sluggy the rest of the day.

The following day, a nurse gave me a glass of sweet glop and I could walk for a short distance without getting whoozy with pain. Must have been some of that Commonwealth folk medicine Tsaya told me was integrated into their medical procedures.

I wanted Tsaya to fix me, but she was still in L-5.

On the third day, I discovered an R&R ward outside on the mountain slopes. The doctors were reluctant to let me move there because of "bad weather." On the fourth day, I walked out of the mountain to the R&R ward during my required afternoon stroll and refused to go back. They let me stay where I could see the mountains, the valley, the sky, and the clouds.

They were right. The weather was lousy. And at 2400 meters even in the tropics, it was cold. But I didn't care. I grew up camping and hiking in mountains—the Santa Ynez range above Santa Barbara, the Bradshaws during pre-Academy prep in Prescott, and the Front Range of the Rockies.

Omer, Wahak, Kivalina, Defense Commissioner Abiku, and even Rayo Vamori visited me. Vaivan came the day after the ruckus caused by my voluntary relocation from the bowels of the mountain to the outside R&R ward. She was more beautiful than ever, and that made up for not being able to see Tsaya.

"I'm glad you survived," Vaivan told me. "When I learned you'd gone to Kulala, I was worried."

"On my account, Vaivan?"

"No, not totally on your account," she replied, taking some of the puff out of my ego. "I had information that something was brewing over there."

"Why didn't you let me know?"

"I didn't see you after you left the C-Cubed meeting with Ali, remember?" She sighed heavily and shook her head sadly. "Sandy, that was a risky thing you did, thinking you could clean out the terrorists in the tower. You got yourself shot up in the process. What ever possessed you?"

I thought about that for a moment and finally told her, "Somebody had to do something, Vaivan. And none of the LandImpy warriors were doing anything. I know why. Remember my confrontation with Tonol Kokat?"

She nodded.

"Nobody really wanted to fight," I observed. "The Commonwealth *code duello* has made you too polite. You act like you'll fight, but you won't.''

Vaivan's hand dropped to her iklawa. "Oh, really?"

"Yes, really. And get your hand away from your iklawa," I snapped with irritation. "That motion's almost automatic, but it doesn't make a fighter."

"We'll fight if we're pushed," Vaivan insisted. "We're closer to our savage ancestors than you."

"Matter of opinion. My forefathers in the last century engaged in sports that killed people while they were playing for fun. And they rode pell-mell across the English countryside to watch a pack of dogs tear a fox to bloody pieces." I stopped because I was getting angry. My legs hurt in spite of Commonwealth folk medicine.

I calmed down and went on, "Vaivan, I don't doubt you'll fight if attacked. But Commonwealth people aren't used to sticking their necks out as far as they can, then sticking them out a little more."

"What do you mean by that?"

"The French call it *élan*. American military manuals name it 'aggressive motivation.' In the Aerospace Force, it was 'letting it all hang out.' Not bravery. Not heroics. Seeing a challenge and taking it . . ."

"The sort of thing you did in Kulala?"

I nodded.

Vaivan sighed. "You're crazy. So's Omer."

"I know it. What brought him to mind?"

"He stole an aerodyne and flew it to Kulala to get you," Vaivan explained. "Nobody could stop him. The weather was impossibly dangerous—hundred kilometer winds through Sayhuto Pass, extreme turbulence and heavy icing over the Dilkons, and American and Soviet space cruisers orbiting at a hundred-fifty kilometers."

"I owe him one," I muttered, "and we need more like him."

"Why do you say that, Sandy? Our professional impys are well equipped and well trained."

"From what I saw at Kulala, they may not be well led," I observed, "Vaivan, I was told to stay put, keep down, play it safe, and don't try anything because it's dangerous or impossible. So I pulled an old military leadership trick: I stood up, moved forward, and hollered, 'Follow me, men!' And they did because nobody else was leading them."

"Have you mentioned this to Abiku and the indunos?"

"I will."

"Can we do anything about it?"

"No, it's too late. Takes four to ten years to develop leadership abilities. There's no time left," I said glumly. "We're about to be tested."

"For what? We've withstood the test of fifty years' . . ."

". . . During which all you did was keep your klutzy kalakak neighbors out of your backyard. That wasn't done well at Kulala, although we muddled through to victory anyway. Shouldn't have happened in the first place."

"Why not? What went wrong?"

"The indunos are enamored with their own staff studies. They may be competent—time will tell—but they're complacent."

"That's hard to believe. My commercial intelligence net and their military sources were waving red flags all over the place. There's nothing wrong with our system."

"Maybe, but you're going to find out how good it *really* is by going up against others."

"It's good. We'll win."

"Saying it doesn't make it so."

"You told me not to underestimate the enemy," Vaivan said. "Sandy, I'm telling you not to underestimate your colleagues and friends. The years since the Founders' War may have mellowed us and taught us to control our violent tendencies, but it's a pretty thin shell."

"I hope so."

"Plans can and will be changed, Sandy," Vaivan went on. "You're keeping our thinking from becoming inbred, something far more dangerous than getting physically soft or letting defenses grow lax. I'm reassigning you here to Vershatets to keep on doing . . ."

"Vaivan, I've got to get back to Ell-Five!" I objected. "We've got to head-off a modern version of Space War One. There's a ten-gigawatt powersat idle at one-zero-five East Longitude. We've got to support Rutledge and his RIO teams! They may need our muscle because they're unarmed."

"I don't believe you've got a case there, Sandy," she told me. "The major action is going to be here on the ground, and your job will be helping Abiku fight off our nasty neighbors."

If I could get the indunos to listen, she might be right, I told myself. But I knew she wasn't.

If I stayed in Vershatets, it would be a major change of plan. The worst military mistake any general can make is to change his carefully-made plans before the battle instead of letting the action take shape before moving opportunistically. A good general, which automatically means a winning general, knows when to throw out the prearranged plan and go with the flow.

Maybe Vaivan knew something I didn't, but I doubted it. Regardless of what her little black spies said, my military background told me there was no way any of our neighbors could handle the professional impys, to say nothing of the CitImpy. And I couldn't see the Tripartite becoming involved in a long and drawn-out war to break up the Commonwealth.

Military action against the Commonwealth would have to come from another source, if it came at all. I didn't know what it might be. There had to be something we hadn't considered, but I didn't know what it was.

I had time to think about it. I began to feel better as my body recovered from the shock of wounds and blood loss.

Although Vaivan's regular daily visits fed my libido, I also looked forward to seeing Omer who came daily bringing both the flowers of Tartar tradition and a half-liter of either strictly *verboten* vodka or *supaku*.

We swapped stories about the Good Times we'd both had in our respective former services. Aerospace jocks are the same everywhere, letting it all hang out as far as possible in the hottest machines available, then sticking it out a little more just to tell the world to go to hell because you're the best. It's still called "hangar flying." Omer and I flew a lot of hangars.

I tried to follow what was going on in the world through the telenews nets and got different slants depending on whether I watched the internatnet or the Commonwealth net. But Omer always brought me the piece of hot skinny that filled in the whole picture.

I still may not have the whole story of what happened and why, but I understand why Duc Francois de la Rochefoucauld said that "history never embraces more than a small part of reality." The history books *do* lie! The General was right.

Kivalina and I had been caught in a guerrilla operation at Kulala. A Kalihol group wearing CitImpy brassards took over the Kulala Despatch tower, killing the ComTrans people. Then they permitted their compatriots, also marked as CitImpy, to take the food train up Sayhuto Pass instead of continuing northbound to its supposed destination in the Ilkan Empire.

They wouldn't have gotten caught if the signals man at the Sayhuto Pass station hadn't noticed Singh's report of going in the hole to cross the unscheduled food train. Sayhuto Pass was the changeover point between the Oidak and Kulala divisions and normally got signals from both. Oidak Despatch had given

Singh a green board out of Sayhuto Pass because they knew of no train coming up the west side of the Pass. And Kulala Despatch hadn't told Sayhuto Pass of a southbound special. So the Sayhuto Pass signals man called Kulala for confirmation of the unscheduled train and couldn't get an answer. He called Oidak Despatch and reported it. They in turn told Vershatets where Pahtu ordered her garrison in Kulala to investigate.

Meanwhile, the Kalihol crew deliberately derailed the train in a tunnel on the west side of Sayhuto Pass, effectively blocking the line, after which they disappeared into the hills.

That's the way Omer and I pieced it together.

Omer added, "When we found out at Vershatets, they pushed panic buttons. They wouldn't let me fly. Bad weather they said. But *Frontovaia Aviatsiya* flies in worse. I stole an aerodyne from the Vicrik AirImpy Base."

"Risky, Russkie." I was the only one he allowed to use that nickname.

Omer shrugged and grinned. "I know how to steal aircraft. It was not difficult. Compared to the *Frontovaia Aviatsiya*, AirImpy security is nothing."

The world press thought it was despicable that the profit-mad Commonwealth, "already suffering hunger and privation from the trade embargo, would hijack a train carrying food to the starving natives of the Ilkan Empire." The Commonwealth got a lot of bad press which is just what somebody wanted.

The Kulala Incident also caused the Emir of Kalihol to send a warning note to Commonwealth President Conobabi Nogal through the legation in Topawa. The Emperor of Ilkan puffed himself up on telenews, his medals glittering, and demanded the release of the train and its contents within 24 hours.

ComTrans CEO Kohato Tatri himself was on the scene with the crews trying to get the Sayhuto Pass line open again. There was no way ComTrans could return the train immediately. President Nogal said as much in a telenews statement that wasn't seen outside the Commonwealth. The Commonwealth President's offer to permit both Kalihol and Ilkan observers on the scene was ignored.

ComTrans met the ultimatum by cutting the derailed Rhodes Railway Diesels off the front end of the train, coupling ComTrans units from Kulala on its rear end, backing it down to Kulala, and hauling it north to the Ilkan border.

Since Ilkans didn't know how to operate ComTrans' advanced technology coal-buring units and wouldn't permit ComTrans crews to take the train into the Ilkan Empire, the train sat at the border for two days. ComTrans ran ice from Kulala to keep the reefers cool, but almost half the food aboard either spoiled or was stolen by Ilkan looters.

The spoilage and theft were blamed on the Commonwealth by telenews, but not one word of ComTrans' gut-busting effort to keep the reefers iced was mentioned.

I'd been in sick bay for about 10 days and was getting restless when Omer burst into my room shortly after breakfast. He had a hard copy in his hand.

"Sort of early, isn't it, Russkie?" I asked.

"Not early. Almost too late. Look!" He thrust the hard copy in front of me.

120450> 0317Z> MESSAGE 12037> VERSHATETS DEFENSE HEADQUARTERS SIGNALS FROM TOPAWA SIGNALS MONITOR> URGENT> KALIHOL RADIO REPORTS COMMONWEALTH LANDIMPY ATTACKING RHODES RAILWAY KHIBYA STATION JUST INSIDE KALIHOL BORDER> MESSAGE 12037> 0318Z> END>

120450> 0320Z> MESSAGE 120311> KULALA SIGNALS FROM VDH SIGNALS> REPORT STATUS OF GARRISON AND CITIMPY> CONFIRM NO REPEAT NO CROSSING OF KALIHOL BORDER TO KHIBYA> CODE NEGO> MESSAGE 120411> 0321Z> END>

120450> 0330Z> MESSAGE 120312> VDH SIGNALS FROM KULALA SIGNALS> CONFIRMING GARRISON IN CASERN> CITIMPY ON STAND DOWN IN HOMES> CONFIRM CONFIRM NO NO CROSSING REPEAT CONFIRM NO CROSSING OF KALIHOL BORDER TO KHIBYA BY ANY LANDIMPY> CODE TRANCILETO> MESSAGE 120412> 0331Z> END>

120450> 0345Z> MESSAGE 120313> VDH SIGNALS TO ALL SIGNALS STATIONS> RED ALERT> RED ALERT> RED ALERT> THIS IS NO DRILL> STAND BY FOR ORDERS> CODE PASKO> MESSAGE 120413> 0346Z> END>

"Where'd this come from?" I wanted to know.

"Vaivan's teleprinter. What you think?" Omer asked.

"Terrorists," I replied. My hands were shaking slightly as they held the hard copy.

"*Da!* Ilkans in LandImpy uniforms paddled across Lake Nyira and hit Khibya station. Khibya is another Gleiwitz." He was referring to the German radio station on the Polish border that was attacked by German troops in Polish uniforms the night before the Germans invaded Poland in 1939.

I'd suspected something like this was going to happen ever

since the Kulala incident. The Khibya attack was a propaganda ploy. The one it was patterned after hadn't worked, but that didn't stop them. "We're about to be blamed for starting a war with our neighbors because we got caught stealing a food train . . . which nobody knows we don't need because everyone else around us is starving. We're embargoed, so we're supposedly starving, too."

"Sandy, it is time to act. We have our job to do."

"Vaivan thinks I can do a better job telling the indunos how to fight here."

"Your job is not here."

"I know. But I may not be allowed to leave."

Omer grinned broadly again. "I get out of Soviet Union. I show you how to get out of Commonwealth!"

I still had three holes in my legs, but I could walk. Once in space, I wouldn't need my legs anyway. And I knew a beautiful doctor in L-5 I wanted to see in the worst way because I had to tell her something I'd neglected to mention before.

And I was worried about ten billion watts available from Powersat One-Zero-Five-East.

"Got a spare pair of pants with you?"

He had a SpacImpy flight suit in a package under his arm.

We walked out of the medical R&R center together acting like we'd just visited a friend. Omer had "borrowed" a landcar somewhere. I let him drive . . . and was sorry. "I cannot steal another AirImpy aerodyne. They know me at the AirImpy Base. But I have Landlimo aerodyne borrowed from Vamori-Free. I almost did not get here, so we may have to bootleg back because there is a big political fight now between business and military because of Red Alert."

"I'll bet Abiku was pressured into drastic measures by the impy indunos," I guessed.

"*Da*. Captain Kevin Graham tells me they are arguing about it right now. Abiku wants to suspend all non-military transport operations."

"Omer, that's almost impossible! Abiku can't stop the system with a snap of his fingers; it's big and has too much inertia. Any suspension order would bring incredible pressure on President Nogal!"

Omer nodded. I just hung on. "Graham is fighting for freedom to move. It will make some delay for Abiku. We will use it. Politics are bad. I do not like politics. I am a warrior and I go where I must to do my job." He grinned. "But not as *Frontovaia*

Aviatsiya or *Kosmonautika* or AirImpy or SpacImpy now. As Landlimo pilot. It makes difference. Hah!"

"Uh, Omer, I know we've got to get to Ell-Five before they try to shut everything down, but this is too fast for this road!" I complained.

"This is good road! You must see roads around Magnitogorsk or Chimkent. Very bad."

I was in the hands of the Mad Russian Space Jockey, and there was nothing I could do. But it was impossible to relax and enjoy it. Omer was letting it hang way, way out.

He brought the car to a halt on the edge of a mountain meadow. A Mikasa Facel aerodyne was parked there.

My legs hurt as I got out, but I could fly. I'd rather fly than let Omer do it. "Russkie; you know the country. I'll drive."

"You know how to drive a Mikasa Facel?"

"I owned one once. Just right for this hop. It's fast at low altitudes." A Mikasa Facel had won the Madras-Colombo Classic two years in a row.

I scanned the sky before stepping in. There were scattered clouds about 1000 meters above us.

"We'll go visual in spite of the weather," I decided. "See and be seen. We'll have no hassle with traffic control and it'll save us trouble if Abiku tries to shut down everything." I strapped into the familiar seat, punched the start code—Commonwealth Founding Day—and felt the old surge of excitement as the big turbines came to speed. The Mikasa had gobs of Coanda-lift surface and big turbines to blow them.

"Go visual direct VIC direct DEK direct VOL direct VAM," Omer remarked, setting the nav station identifiers into the computer. "Course does not contain rocks if you do not descend below two-six-zero-zero meters to DEK nav station. Bust clouds. *Prodolzhate!*"

The flight was not for the faint-hearted. I used tacair procedures but without the benefit of tacair equipment. There were times when I bent rules and entered clouds. I wasn't worried about ATC waiting for us when we landed at Vamori-Free, but that the clouds might contain rocks because I'd always been taught they did. Omer assured me they didn't. He was right.

We monitored comm but heard nothing except routine traffic. We kept a silent radar profile, not using forward scan or radar altimeter, only the required radar transponder with a visual flight code.

I wanted to look like Bill Flannelmouth The Travelling Salesman starting to make his rounds for the day.

Once we'd cleared the rocks and crags of Vicrik and Dekhar Gorge, the weather broke into high thin clouds with visibility reduced only by haze.

I flew not more than a hundred meters above the savannah and the spring crop of hypergrains. There are detectors that can spot a target on the deck, but I was counting on the traffic overhead to mask us. I was also counting on (a) my absence from the hospital being yet undetected and therefore they weren't looking for me, and (b) nobody suspecting we were sneaking out of the Commonwealth.

"What happens at Vamori-Free?" I asked Omer as we sped eastward over the Toak Plains.

"I'm scheduled to lift the *Tomahok* to Ell-Five at noon local time," Omer explained. "You'll be aboard."

"Who does the manifest say I'm supposed to be?"

"Co-pilot with oversleep. You will be assigned instead. Is all arranged."

"By twelve-hundred hours, they'll be looking for me, Omer, and somebody on the pad will recognize me."

"You want to put on my mustache maybe? Sandy, I have many friends at Vamori-Free. And people there do not like the idea of stopping freedom of space. The League of Free Traders has members other than space pilots."

"Landlimo people?"

"*Da!* What does company name mean? Frontier is free and must stay free! What else we going to fight for?" The Mad Russian Space Jockey checked the nav computer. "In two minutes, bounce up to a thousand meters and get approach clearance to Area Seven-seven."

The launch area was identical to Area Seven-three but there was something different about the *Toreva* Class packet on the catapult. I mentioned it to Omer as we parked the aerodyne and sauntered across the pad, acting as couth as any pair of space jocks.

"Has been refitted with 'tracking enhancement' equipment. It is actually partial hell-beam hardening," Omer said quietly.

"Who instigated that?" I wanted to know.

"Ali."

Maybe all Commonwealth people weren't such polite non-fighters after all.

But when we got in the flight deck of the *Tomahok*, Omer told me, "Sandy, take the left seat. Fly it. I run nav and counter-measures."

"Is it that touchy out there now?"

"*Da*. Engagement zones are expanded," Omer explained. "United States, Europa, Bahia, all announce new requirements five days ago."

"Sounds like transition-to-war conditions."

"Maybe. Commonwealth ships have had some problems. Somebody soon maybe make a 'mistake' with a Commonwealth ship," Omer pointed out. "Or we get clearance that is wrong and takes us into engagement zone. So I got from Kevin Graham new data showing positions of all orbiting objects and load into computer. I will make sure clearance and trajectory do not lead us into danger."

Twenty minutes before noon, clearance came over the up-link. Omer checked it and gave me a thumbs-up. I accepted it. We made a straightforward departure with the catapult slinging the *Tomahok* into the air at a one-gee goose. I climbed out according to flight plan and watched while the air-breathers transitioned to scram-jet mode and finally lipped-over when the mains ignited at 60 kilometers. I wasn't particularly looking for anything to happen at that point because we were still in international airspace over the Indian Ocean.

The *Tomahok* was handed-off from Madras Center to LEO Orient Center as we ascended through a hundred kilometers. I expected something to happen then. It did.

"*Tomahok*, this is LEO Orient Center. Amended clearance."

It came on the up-link. Omer shook his head. "*Bojemoi*!" he exploded. "Reject it!"

"LEO Orient Center, this is *Tomahok*. Negative the amended clearance, sir."

"*Tomahok*, what's your reason for refusal?"

"What's your reason for issuing this amended clearance, sir?"

"AmSpace Command request through LEO Canambah Center."

"The amended clearance takes us into the engagement zone of Gran Bahia *estacao baixo doze*."

"*Tomahok*, stand by. . . . *Tomahok*, amended clearance: De-orbit for Woomera landing. We can't get you through."

I knew what to do, and I let it all hang out. "LEO Orient Center, *Tomahok*. Negative the amended clearance. We are initiating no-clearance flight under I-A-R Regulation ninety-one-point-eight. We'll take her up to Ell-Five as filed under our responsibility to detect and avoid."

Omer reached over and clapped me on the right shoulder.

There must have been consternation in LEO Orient Center because it took several seconds for the traffic coordinator to acknowledge. "Uh, *Tomahok*, Center, roger! Service is terminated. Proceed on your own responsibility. Retain your current beacon code."

I acknowledged and told Omer, "Get ready to thread the needle, Russkie! Let's see if we're good enough to make Ell-Five before somebody burns us with a hell-beamer!"

CHAPTER 14

Through LEO's Jaws and the Ball of Yarn

There I was, flat on my back at 30,000 meters, nothing between me and the ground but a thin regulation.

I'd invoked a seldom-used International Aerospace Regulation that harked back to Earth's oceans where a ship captain was an absolute monarch responsible for himself, his ship, and everything in it. It had been carried into the air by a rule that made the "pilot-in-command" solely responsible for the safety and operation of his aircraft and everything in it, regardless of what traffic coordinators on the ground told him.

In effect, I'd told the space traffic people I'd fly without their help. Avoiding an engagement zone isn't difficult *if* you know where it is. Space is mostly empty.

The various STC Centers would continue tracking our beacon to keep other spacecraft clear of us. Military trackers would do the same in case we broached their engagement zones, which would mean Trouble for the *Tomahok*.

I'd waived clearance while still under ascent thrust on our original trajectory to a 200-kilometer parking orbit. Our delta-vee margin was excellent even though the *Tomahok* was running with a full cargo bay of—would you believe it?—cotton underwear.

Clothing wears out, and we hadn't established any clothing industry in space yet. Spinning, weaving, dyeing, and tailoring are ancient technologies, but they were among the last to be adapted to the weightlessness of space. As for cotton, one of the Commonwealth's primary products, nobody has yet developed an artificial fiber quite as comfortable.

We had a lot of leeway in changing our flight path because the *Tomahok* had "bulked-out" before she "grossed-out"—the hold was filled long before maximum weight was attained.

"Russkie, I hope the League data's good," I told Omer. "Display our current flight path and the projected positions and engagement zones of other sky junk."

"Blinking blips aren't in League data," Omer reported. The Kazakh became laconic when he was under pressure, probably because he was thinking in Russian and mentally translating into aerospace English with adrenalin pumping.

I studied the display. A blinking blip indicated a polar orbiting satellite. In parking orbit, we'd broach its engagement zone.

"There's our problem," I pointed out. "AmSpace Command recon bird. That's why the amended clearance. We'll burn out of parking orbit to miss him. What are the options?"

Omer punched the keypad. A series of trajectories came on the display. "Take high delta-vee option. It will be obvious we're avoiding the reconsat."

"But we may run into trouble with this one, Omer," I said, indicating another target with my finger. "It's displaying no code. What is it?"

Omer queried the computer. "Not in League data. Unknown."

"It's got to be registered! I'll query Center for identification."

"Let it be for now. We handle when time comes," the Mad Russian Space Jockey suggested. "We take problems one at a time. Sandy, get us in parking orbit and watch engagement zones. I work on vector for transfer orbit to Ell-Five."

The mains shut down on schedule while I was punching up several special frequencies on the commscanner. "Omer, I'm going to monitor some Aerospace Force freqs in addition to unicom. Know any *Kosmonautika* frequencies?"

"*Da*, but they are special side-banded and will sound ducky."

Without special receivers, suppressed-carrier sideband transmissions sounded like a duck quacking, but I'd learned to make sense of them. Anyone who flew military aerospace ships knew how because the adjustments on the receivers were so critical for proper reception that almost half the transmissions were ducky.

Our burn out of parking orbit came as re-programmed. While we were under thrust, we got a sensor alarm. "Targeting lidar!" I snapped. "Aerospace Force has seen us closing on the reconsat."

"We go laser-hard," Omer said, reaching for the switch.

"Negative!" I snapped. "They'll see it, interpret it as a countermeasure, and try to burn us." I indicated another target on the display. "That's annotated as an unspecified military satellite; it's a ten megawatt hell-beamer."

"Hokay, so we do a little tsig-tsag! Give me controls!"

I did and continued to check displayed targets. Omer called out his actions. "Tsang plus-x ten meters per sec."

I got a surface temperature warning signal. "Warning shot without a call. That's not SOP!" The Aerospace Force tapped the data stream from the world STC net and they *knew* we were the unarmed *Tomahok* out of Vamori-Free.

"Maybe you got wrong freq. We did not broach engagement zone of reconsat, and now they see us burn into new trajectory. So we are out of hard place under rock for now. You fly now."

Low earth orbit zone is tricky to work in. Velocities and closing rates are high. There isn't much time to detect, track, make decisions, and maneuver. It's full of sensitive earth-oriented reconsats that are automated and passive. They can't defend themselves or maneuver. Even though such unmanned sky-apies are considered to be expendable scouts, my former colleagues were sensitive about them. Everyone knew where everyone else's were, and nobody bothered them for fear of retaliation. Fortunately, sensitive satellites advertised themselves with "no trespassing" signals.

Hell-beamers were another matter. They were unmanned with auto defenses. Unless they spotted the proper beacon password—which we didn't have—they'd shoot at anything that broached their engagement zones. We *had* to stay clear of those. We'd been lucky once.

Some that looked like hell-beamers weren't; they were decoys or legitimate R&D space telescopes. The sensor signatures were the same. If you wanted to find out if one was indeed a hell-beamer, you had to make a hands-on inspection which was *very* risky not only because of the auto-defenses but also because some of them were booby-trapped.

Nobody liked the hell-beamers, especially the League of Free Traders. But the low-powered ones in LEO were no threat to people on the ground. And nobody had been burned in space by them, so they were tolerated as a necessary evil.

I didn't like them right then.

Omer pointed to a moving target on the display. "Soviet Black Tiger deep space fighter."

The Soviet pilot was maintaining a low closure rate and a respectable range.

"He's watching us. But so are these unmanned Soviet facilities," Omer continued. "Russians do not trust equipment or people by themselves. Must always have dual data from machines and from people. If people data not match equipment data, people data discarded in favor of equipment data. Russians are strange."

"What do you think he's up to, Omer? We've got no beef with the Socialist Hegemony." Except the competing Soviet powersat proposal to China . . .

Omer shrugged. "I am Kazakh. I cannot always read crazy Russian mind."

One would think that an aerospace "defense" team could act on receipt of danger data. But it couldn't. It had to get approval from a general or political leader. The principle of "dual phenomenology" ruled. Like their Soviet counterparts sitting under Smolensk and Magnitorgorsk, the Americans under Cheyenne Mountain and Tincup required that two independent systems detect a situation. The weapons were too powerful to entrust to anything less.

I'd been cashiered because I'd made a flagrant violation of that policy and because "he's done it once so he's capable of doing it again if he stays in."

That operational philosophy saved our butts as we threaded our uncleared way through the maze of space weapons systems.

There was silence on the military freqs. Either all of the five military space powers were quietly observing us from their space watch centers or we'd selected now-unused channels. I suspected both.

If we didn't provoke them, they'd probably do nothing.

"How about that Black Tiger, Omer?"

"Changed orbit plane with us."

"New target?" I asked, indicating a blip.

Omer shrugged. "*Nyet*. Same no-code unidentified as before."

"What and who is it?"

"Not Soviet. All *Kosmonautika* ships use beacon codes. Soviets always follow rules to letter, get others to do dirty work for them."

"Not American, either. The Aerospace Force follows the rules, too."

"I watch it."

"You do that. Where's the data for the matching burn at L-5?"

Think of Earth as being at the bottom of a funnel-shaped well whose walls become less steep as you climb away from Earth.

Paint the walls of the funnel in zones of different colors to represent the various space traffic control center jurisdictions. The ones nearest Earth at the bottom of the funnel are controlled from national centers that are, you hope, in communication with one another and swapping data. The ones further out are watched by seven other centers located in GEO. And the ones in the nearly-flat upper part of the funnel are four in number centered on L-4, the Moon, L-5, and a huge "uncontrolled sector" stretching around lunar orbit from 30-degrees ahead of L-4 to 30-degrees behind L-5 where there wasn't anything then.

Now spin the funnel so the bottom part representing a distance up to 50,000 kilometers goes around once in 24 hours. Spin the top part from 50,000 kilometers altitude out to a half-million kilometers at the lunar rate of 29.5 days.

Located on the walls of this madly turning multi-colored funnel are marbles spinning around its surface fast enough so they don't fall down the funnel. Some of them are deadly marbles; come close and you'll burn. Others are big and fragile, but massive enough to destroy your ship if you hit one. Still others are ships like your own, plying space for fun, profit, or military purposes. An unknown number of the last are capable of whanging you with various and sundry weapons.

Your mission: without coming afoul of any of this, get to the flat tableland on top, then locate and dock to a group of fly-specks called L-5.

Try it on your computer. Good luck,.

The Black Tiger had a respectable range but sidled closer at a *very* low rate. Omer didn't lay radar or lidar on him for more than two pulses in sequence over a period of a minute. He said the Black Tiger sensors had difficulty discriminating those dual-pulse ranging blips from the howling storm of radar and lidar pulses bouncing around the Earth-Moon system.

The unknown target also stuck with us.

"*Tomahok*, this is Landlimo Prime Base. Anybody home?" the comm speaker barked.

I recognized the voice. "Landlimo Prime, this is *Tomahok*. Hi, Vaivan!"

"You're supposed to be in the hospital, Sandy. What are you doing up there?"

"Helping Omer fly the unfriendly skies of Earth."

"He doesn't need you. He had another co-pilot assigned for this flight."

"He said his co-pilot overslept or something."

"The co-pilot was found drugged in the RON shack."

"I don't know anything about it, Vaivan. But Omer really needs me. If I didn't know what and where the military stuff is out here, you'd have lost a ship. Thank me for that some day."

"What's going on, Sandy? Woomera Center reported you cancelled your clearance."

"Raise hell with Space Traffic Control for clearing us into the engagement zone of an American reconsat. And while you're at it, complain that the United States Aerospace Force shot at one of your ships."

"Sandy, you and Omer are going to have to answer some questions. We've got rules and procedures . . ."

"You hire two space jockeys, you think you get pussycats or tigers?" Omer broke in. "The General tells me if I think like slave I be treated like slave. If you want no-think order takers, hire real Russians!"

"Just get to Ell-Five, Sandy." She wasn't giving an order; she was expressing a wish.

I told her I would but that we were getting busy and had to cut the chatter.

We'd run a gauntlet of low-orbit facilities and were coming up on geosynchronous orbit. Although we were several degrees above equatorial GEO where most of the civilian facilities were, we had to get through the web of military satellites in inclined geosynchronous orbit, weaving paths around the planet like a ball of yarn.

Omer asked the computer to enhance the very weak returns from these stealthed facilities. We were going to come close to some Japanese and European targets, but not within their engagement zones unless they'd changed them and we didn't know it.

That possibility didn't bother me as much as the Soviet Black Tiger still nibbling at our track. Unlike a surface-to-space Black Bear, a Black Tiger had far more delta-vee than the *Tomahok*. He could make his move—whatever that might be—with a decreasing delta-vee requirement as we both climbed up the shallowing walls of the gravity well.

I didn't know his motive, but he made his move as we neared GEO and the ball of yarn.

"He think we too busy getting through to watch him too," Omer explained as we saw him make a delta-vee burn.

"Comrade Astrabadi, got any idea of his intentions?"

"Maybe he will have an accident with us."

"Our unidentified target has done something, too," I said, pointing to the display.

Omer studied it for a moment, then announced, "He will intercept the Black Tiger soon. A Black Tiger is sensor-blind in aft hemisphere except for attack warning radar. Unidentified is now operating with radar stealth. We see him only on lidar."

"Watch them. Report changes. I've got my hands full going through the ball of yarn," I told him.

But it happened before we got there.

The unidentified overhauled the Black Tiger. Suddenly, the Soviet space fighter zanged sideways as if engaged in evasive maneuvering but kept going. The computer erased the old projection of the Black Tiger track on the display and flashed a newly projected track into the lunar sector of high Earth orbit beyond GEO . . . if the Black Tiger made it unscathed through the ball of yarn and the engagement zones there.

"I think he got a missile up his main engine," Omer observed quietly.

And we were about to run another gauntlet with an unidentified armed space fighter on our tail!

There was no Mayday call on any frequency but the Black Tiger may have had its own emergency frequency. L-4 was too far away, so we never saw whether or not the Soviets sent out a rescue mission.

"Watch the unidentified, Omer. I've got to dive through our hole here." I spent the next few minutes trimming trajectory so our projected flight path went through an opening in the skein. If I nailed the center of our window dead-nuts, we'd be well outside any previously announced engagement zone.

We'd computed correctly, guessed right, and used the proper amount of Kentucky windage.

We sailed through unharmed.

I must have breathed a sigh of relief because Omer reminded me, "Sandy, is not all copasetic. Unidentified target came through same window two hundred kilometers behind us. Closing rate eighty meters per second. Intercept course."

Friend or foe? I didn't know. He'd gotten a Soviet space fighter off our track, but we hadn't seen how he did it. Now he was on our track.

Friend or foe? I had to know. And I wanted the rest of the world to know, too.

I wasn't going to sit there and be blown out of space quietly. I used the international ship-to-ship unicom frequency that everybody in space monitors. It's also monitored at every STC Center. I'd be heard by a lot of people, and that's what I wanted.

"This is the commercial packet *Tomahok* of Commonwealth registry out of Vamori Free Space Port for Ell-Five. Our beacon code one-two-seven-three. Hailing the unidentified space vehicle on an intercept two hundred kilometers behind us. Please identify yourself, sir."

A strange voice replied, "*Tomahok*, switch to frequency Echo Hotel."

Several frequencies had been assigned for use by ships registered under the Commonwealth flag, and these in turn had been assigned code names by ComSpat and ComServe.

Whoever was in that space vehicle knew the Commonwealth frequency codes.

"This is *Tomahok* on Echo Hotel," I broadcast on the Commonwealth channel.

"*Tomohok*, this is People's Space Navy cosmolorcha *Heavenly Lightning*. We are instructed upon request for contact and identification from you to transmit to you the kindest wishes of Wen-ling Chung for a peaceful and successful journey."

Of course! The People's Republic of China was not a signatory to the International Astronautic Conventions, the Singapore Treaties. They'd consistently boycotted international space treaty meetings, claiming the Soviet Union and its Socialist Hegemony were hostile. The Chinese had always been both wary and desirous of external relations, and they hadn't been helped by coming off on the short end of the Sino-Soviet Incident.

"*That's* why they do not show beacon I.D.!" Omer exclaimed.

"*Heavenly Lightning*, this is *Tomahok*," I replied slowly and carefully in Basic Aerospace English. "Thank you, sir. Please return the regards of Sandy Baldwin and Omer Astrabadi to Wen-ling Chung. What are your intentions, sir?"

"This is a training flight to trans-lunar space with landing at Dianaport. Request permission to pass within five kilometers of you."

"Training flight? Hah!" Omer exclaimed. "Chung has given us an escort!"

"Yes, but why?" I wanted to know. "What's going on dirtside that we should know about?"

Omer shrugged. "Let Chinese escort us. It will discourage more hassle."

If the Chinese cosmolorcha wanted to escort us, there was nothing we could do about it. It was armed. Cis-lunar space is no place to get whanged; it's a long time to anywhere.

"Permission granted, *Heavenly Lightning*," I replied. "Be advised you are within our zone of damage if we should have a catastrophic failure." The last was bluff, but nobody wanted to be near a space vehicle if it catoed, regardless whether it was due to an internal or external cause. I didn't think they'd shoot, but I wanted to give them every discouragement because anybody who takes on a Soviet Black Tiger is a very tigerish tiger indeed.

"*Heavenly Lightning*, do you have any information about the Soviet space vehicle that passed near you?" I added carefully, hoping to garner some data.

"*Tomohok*, the Soviet ship had an accident. We were not permitted to assist."

Period. That was all. We never got any more information.

The *Heavenly Lightning* crept up on us, decreased its closure rate, and was in visual range for almost 20 hours. We had a chance to look her over and get her visual, radar, and electromagnetic signatures on tape.

There wasn't much difference between the *Heavenly Lightning* and the old *Beikel* class. A hybrid like her namesake, the sailing lorcha, she'd been up-rated with more modern propulsion and other systems. She was a black-and-white dart in the sunlight, looking like the paper airplanes we used to make as kids. She was right out of the history tapes. She might have been considered obsolete in high-tech; she was an operable space vehicle and had managed to whang a far superior Soviet Black Tiger.

And she was on our side at the moment.

Sometimes old technology isn't obsolete. The seas of Earth are being plied even now by Chinese ships of a type known as the junk, a design so successful that it hasn't changed for centuries.

Because of the sensitive approach and engagement zones of L-5, I called long before it was necessary to do so. L-5 Center probably had the same data all the other centers had obtained on our squirrelly flight track through the maze, plus that of the *Heavenly Lightning*. But I wasn't taking chances. We of the Commonwealth were apparently the current pariahs, and I didn't know if that image had spread to L-5. No sense being stupid and getting burned after more than seventy hours of sneaky tricks and fantastic luck. No sense in pushing that luck, either.

L-5 Approach gave us a straightforward, no-nonsense clearance, but added, "*Tomohok*, we're painting you as two targets. Is that another ship with you?"

"Affirmative. She's the Chinese *Heavenly Lightning* on a training flight to cis-lunar space with landing at Dianaport. Are you experiencing difficulty communicating with her?"

"That's affirmative. Be advised we may issue an amended clearance into an inspection holding sector if she doesn't separate from you shortly."

As if on cue, the *Heavenly Lightning* executed a delta-vee burn into a new trajectory our computer showed as passing well clear of the L-5 sensitivity zone.

I called ComSpat and informed Jeri of our arrival clearance.

"Roger, *Tomohok*. Ali says to tell you everything is copasetic in spite of his sister. He claims he can handle her, but, if so, he's the only one! And we're monitoring and taping all Approach Control data as well as our own independent sensors jay-eye-cee. Your anatomy is covered.''

There was one more wrinkle. "*Tomahok*, this is Approach. United States Aerospace Force requests permission for a close approach to verify your configuration and markings.''

"Let them,'' Omer advised. "They must cover their anatomy, too. They know ComSpat is taping. And I know all Aerospace Force cutter pilots. They good drinking buddies!''

We watched a cutter swing out of a parking sector and set up an intercept. But we hardly had time to get a visual because it passed at a high rate, scanning as it did so, a procedure intended for minimum exposure to hostile action.

We passed inspection.

We were home at Lagrange.

Ali was waiting for us in the portlock with Jeri and Tsaya. He looked relieved. "You had us worried.''

It was like coming back from a hot hypersonic ground attack run where I'd let it hang very far out. It was my nature to play Bruce Couth under those circumstances. "Worried? Why? We're pretty damned hot stuff, you know.''

Jeri sighed. "Space pilots! Most modest people in the universe!''

Omer was obviously feeling the same way. He grinned and brushed his mustache with his hand. "Hah! You just want some clean new underwear, Jeri! Whole cargo hold full of it. We use none of it ourselves. Help yourself!''

I added fuel to the fire. "Must be pretty grim out here to ship a load of undies by packet. Or did they put you on short water rations so you couldn't use the laundry?''

"No, they started using too much starch in our shorts,'' Jeri put in.

"Seriously,'' Ali put in, "you had us in a sweat. To put it bluntly, Vaivan was very upset when she discovered you'd left, Sandy.''

"I presume you mollified her? After all, there isn't much she can do about it.''

"She's catching hell from the Defense Commissioner as well as from Wahak,'' Ali said. "I didn't accomplish much, but The General had a few well-chosen words with people dirtside.''

"How's The General?'' Both Omer and I asked the question in unison.

"Excellent,'' Tsaya reported. "He can go back any time.''

"Great!'' I observed. "But not right away. We've been jammed in that can for three days. I want a shine, shower, shave, and shampoo, among other things.''

''In good time,'' Tsaya told me, taking me by the arm. ''You left Vershatets without being released. Wahak and Vaivan want a full med check on you. Let's go to the infirmary.''

I didn't resist although I was tired, dirty, and hungry.

In ComSpat's infirmary, Tsaya checked me over. ''You're healing very well,'' she observed, inspecting my scars. ''Don't over-stress those leg muscles.''

''There's no stress on them in weightlessness,'' I pointed out.

''True. But you're not back to normal yet. Your blood pressure and heart rate are elevated.''

''I can't help that.''

''You've been through a stressful experience.''

''That's not the reason, Tsaya. You know why.''

''I won't speculate. A diagnosis should always be based on hard data.'' She was still acting very professional, but she took my chin in one hand and checked my eyes with the other. ''Just as I suspected. A hopeless case. Hyperexcitability caused by hypoaffection, a chronic malady affecting people who go down to the sea and up to the stars. Fortunately, it can be treated. Good thing, too, because it also affects those who wait, *moapa*.'' She spoke that word softly but with intense feeling. Cradling my face in her hands, she kissed me.

Tsaya went at something wholeheartedly once she'd decided to. Being both a medical doctor and a witch doctor, she knew precisely what to do and how to do it. I'd been shot at and hit, then chased all over the sky. Nothing makes a man more ready, willing, and able than being exposed to danger.

More than that, I wanted the love of this woman and to love her.

I wanted to tell her that, but I couldn't. Kissing Tsaya fully occupied me.

''You said I shouldn't overstress my legs,'' I reminded her when we came up for air. ''How about the rest of me?''

''You won't stress your legs; you won't need to use them. Sandy, *moapa*, next time please don't get hurt. Somebody cares about you, you know. Somebody cares a great deal,'' she said softly.

''How could I know? You're wearing an iklawa,'' I reminded her.

Her iklawa clanged as it hit the bulkhead. ''My love for you is now defenseless.''

She really wasn't defenseless.
Be careful when making love to medical-witch doctors.
But enjoy it.
I did.

CHAPTER 15

Of Love and War
and Guiding Lights

"What you did," General Vamori remarked, "was courageous."

"No, it just seemed the right thing to do at the time. On the other hand, what Omer did took a lot of bravery," I told him. We'd gotten some rest and were in The General's compartment for a social get together.

General Vamori had completely recovered from his burns. Tsaya had also done some reconstructive surgery he'd put off for years, so she said he was even better than before. He acted that way, too. "You confuse courage and bravery, Sandy," he observed.

"There's a difference?"

"Bravery is a defiant act against great odds; kittens are brave. But the word courage comes from the Latin word for 'heart' and describes a conscious act based upon the moral judgement that it's 'right.' You and Omer exhibited courage in both Kulala and the *Tomahok*."

Omer sipped *supaku* from the plastic bag and shook his head. *"La!"* he replied forcefully in Kazakh rather than in Russian. "Getting to Kulala and back was the only way to help Sandy. Coming out in the *Tomahok*, it was a big challenge to get from Vamori-Free to Ell-Five without STC. We're proud we can do it without help!" In the relaxed surroundings of The General's quarters, Omer's speech was less abbreviated.

"And with two military space ships following us," I added.

"How did you know who they were and what they might do?" The General asked.

"Our combined knowledge of both the American Aerospace Force and the Soviet *Kosmonautika* made us a team," I explained. "I knew what the Aerospace Force was up to. Omer knew the technology and tactics of the *Kosmonautika*."

"But you didn't know about the Chinese ship."

"The Chinese are inscrutible on purpose," Omer remarked, setting his empty *supaku* bag down on the adhesive table top. "They have a different kind of language and think differently than Russians or westerners. This serves their foreign policy well; nobody knows what they are doing. One does not approach the unknown without caution.''

"You told me you were just an old *Frontavaia Aviatsiya* tacair driver who was never taught history," I said.

Omer shrugged. "I can see. I can read. I can hear and listen. And I can make up my own mind, too.''

"We're not even sure what the *Heavenly Lightning* did to the Black Tiger," I told The General. "Omer thinks the Chinese put a missile up the Soviet's boattail. Whatever happened made the Soviet pilot change his mind about whatever he was going to do.''

The General sighed. "It made the situation worse.''

More than four days had passed since we'd left Vershatets. I hadn't paid any attention to the telenews. I'd been kept happily busy by Tsaya.

I hadn't considered all the twisty little international legal implications of the *Tomahok* Incident, as it was being called by the world press at the time. It involved a possible attack on a military vessel by the military vessel of another nation in which a third commercial vessel played no part whatsoever, although its name was hung on the incident. It took place in "non-national space." None of the ships had operational safety clearances from Space Traffic Control and were operating under the "detect-and-avoid" freedom of space rules. The *Tomahok* being a civil vessel registered under the Commonwealth flag wasn't open to attack by the Soviet ship because no provocation had been given. And there was no way to know whether or not the *Heavenly Lightning* had responded to a provocation from the Black Tiger or if the Soviet pilot simply got the hell out of there. Nobody knew anything. Therefore, the news media had a field day analyzing, editorializing, and playing "let's suppose." None of this reflected any familiarity with the law of armed conflict.

The law of armed conflict holds regardless of whether or not an actual state of declared "war" exists.

As a youngster, I'd had the typical layman's view: "All's fair in love and war," the 19th Century German *Kriegsraison* doctrine which asserted that military necessity justified anything; the world clearly rejected that during the Nuremberg Trials. At the Academy, it astounded me to discover there was a law of armed conflict. It isn't "law" as we ordinarily think of it. There's no central enforcement authority. The law of armed conflict is part of international law where nations are the subjects, not individual persons as in domestic law. It's called the law of armed conflict because there hadn't been a formal declaration of war since 11 December 1941. When the UN Charter was adopted in 1946, nations formally revoked their sovereign right to use war to achieve political aims.

But this didn't stop armed conflict. Nations continued to justify it as an exercise of their right of self-defense against aggression. The various brushfire wars and the Sino-Soviet Incident are examples. Nor did it stop terrorism or guerrilla warfare because it doesn't apply to "internal conflicts." But the law of armed conflict *works* because it actually diminishes the effects of confrontations. The Tomahok Incident didn't start a war because of the law of armed conflict and other aspects of international law relating to such activities.

The Soviet foreign minister presented a diplomatic note to the PRC Ambassador claiming an unprovoked hostile act by the *Heavenly Lightning* and demanding compensation for damage to a Soviet vessel engaged in deep space activities. He didn't say what those activities were.

The Chinese foreign minister replied that the *Heavenly Lightning* had been on a training mission and expressed regret that there had been an accident involving the Soviet ship. He didn't say what the accident was. The Chinese government paid a small token indemnity without admitting that *Heavenly Lightning* had struck.

"The real reason behind the Soviet action and the Chinese reply is the powersat situation," Vaivan reported during a telecon. "When you cancelled clearance, the Black Tiger was assigned to stalk you in hopes of learning about some of the military facilities. The Chinese ship had standing orders to cover any Commonwealth ship being stalked by the Soviets. The Soviet reaction to the incident tells me the Soviets are showing military restraint because they hope to conclude their powersat deal. The Chinese are saving face through inscrutability and protecting their options."

"Those two nations have had a love-hate relationship for well over a century," I observed. "The Soviets consider themselves oriental while the Chinese think of them as occidental. They're sparring with one another as usual."

"Not exactly," Ali put in. "The Chinese get about a hundred gigawatts of their electrical baseload from ten powersats whose output they've leased from the Nippon Taiyo Denki Kaisha . . ."

". . . Whose financing is handled by the Tokyo Foreign Investment Bank," The General finished, "whose President in turn is a member of the Tripartite Steering Council."

"Puts the Chinese in a tough spot, doesn't it?" I remarked.

"Will ComGlaser be able to divert enough output to pick up any of that baseload?" Ali wondered.

Vaivan shook her beautiful head. "No. Not even a significant percentage of it. We've picked up the primary baseloads of those rectennas that PowerSat and InSpaPow pulled the plug on. Now there's no reserve, only the five gigawatts coming into the Commonwealth's Oidak rectenna."

"That's a last ditch switch-over," Ali reminded her.

"We can pick up most of Oidak's power with additional capacity built into our coal plants," Vaivan added.

"I'm concerned about what the Chinese may do if their rectennas lose their power beams," I put in.

The General looked at me. "Sandy, what's your evaluation of that situation?"

I shrugged. "My guess is the Chinese Revanche. It's an American war college scenario. The Chinese have over two billion people to feed. To make maximum use of their resources, they use energy-intensive agriculture. Without space power, they can't harvest, transport, store, and distribute enough agricultural product. They'll have to resort to less energy-intensive agriculture which requires more land. They'll move to get it, even though they won't get a crop from it this year. They can pull through the coming winter with reserves on hand plus what they can purchase on the international market. To get agricultural land, they'll go into the Amur Region and through the Irtyush Gap to Semipalatinsk or along the Tien Shan to Alma Ata."

"A repeat of the Sino-Soviet Incident," Vaivan observed. "The Soviets will use the same space beam weapon response."

"No, Vaivan," I told her. "RIO's operating now. It wasn't during the Sino-Soviet Incident."

"What can RIO do? Otasek's crews are unarmed."

"Don't sell RIO short," I advised her. "Milan Otasek may be adverse to taking action, but Peter Rutledge has already gotten a strong message to PowerSat Corporation concerning One-Zero-Five-East. In any event, let me finish my scenario: The Chinese will buy time by armed conflict if they have to and if they can. We'll build new powersats for them. The Chinese may capture some Soviet rectennas. These will help their baseload needs and after they string power transmission lines from them. When the dust settles, there'll be a cease-fire, not a peace treaty, because there won't be a declaration of war from either side. The cease-fire terms will probably include some new political borders, perhaps some internationally-policed border areas. If the Chinese win, we'll see the emergence of a new power transmission network in east Asia."

"Vaivan, my dear," The General told his grand-daughter, "I believe you should bring this to the attention of the C-Cubed. We may find ourselves in the middle of a Sino-Soviet confrontation, and I'm not sure we want to be there."

"Do you recommend we withdraw our powersat offer, Grandfather?"

'No, that would reflect poorly upon our integrity. I think it's time for me to return to the Commonwealth. I'll book passage for myself and my doctor aboard the *Andoric* which is due to stop here the day after tomorrow on return from a lunar cruise."

"General, the *Andoric* isn't one of our ships," Vaivan observed. "Sandy and Omer can bring you back in the *Tomahok* or *Tonolia*."

"They're needed here," The General said.

"I don't like it, Tsaya," I confided privately to her afterward.

"I don't either," she admitted. "It means leaving you, *moapa*. I'd be much happier if you and Omer took us back. Then we might have some time together. I know a lovely place practically untouched and a long way from everyone on the slopes of the Amimontos."

"I'm not that familiar with Commonwealth geography yet," I admitted.

"They're the twin volcanic peaks on the south end of the Dilkons that were once called 'the breasts of the Earth.' "

"I prefer two other breasts far more lovely and another mountain near them which is more exciting yet."

In planning political, diplomatic, and military strategy, one must assume a "surpise-free" future. Such a thing doesn't exist.

The suprise came two hours before The General and Tsaya were scheduled to go to the main docks to board the *Andoric*. A stranger some four billion years old paid us a visit. It was an irregular nickle-iron object with a maximum dimension of about 25 millimeters. As meteors go, it was large. It punched through the Comspat module's double-wall meteor shield and produced an 18-centimeter hole in the transit corridor linking us to L-5. The auto-hatches slid shut when sensors detected a pressure drop. It isolated the ComSpat module from L-5 for three hours while repair crews plugged the hole.

General Vamori and Tsaya Stoak missed the ship. The captain of the *Andoric* declined to delay departure because he had more than two hundred passengers who expected to arrive at Woomera on schedule.

A lot of people waited in vain for loved ones and business

associates scheduled to arrive at Woomera. The *Andoric* never got there.

The international board of inquiry eventually issued a report that satisfied no one. It will never be known why the *Andoric* and the *Borgholm* collided. Space is three-dimensional and there's a *lot* of volume to maneuver in, even close to Earth and deep in its gravity well. None of the 314 passengers and crew of the two ships survived, and the post-collision velocity vectors put both in escape trajectories where they *might* be found some day in the future if they don't get ground to dust in the planetoid belt first. The STC traffic coordinators involved were useless in the inquiry. Two of them committed suicide before the inquiry convened, and three others including a supervisor suffered from shock or other psychiatric conditions because the guilt was far too much to live with. The tapes showed that separate clearances from Brisbane and Gran Bahia were not coordinated as they should have been. Apparently the ships were cleared right into one another at a closing rate in excess of 15 kilometers per second. The sensors in both ships probably rejected their data as being absurd. But we'll never know because the on-board recorders weren't recovered.

I suspected foul play.

But I dismissed it as paranoid. After all, who'd deliberately set up an "accident" that claimed 314 lives just to get General Vamori? I couldn't bring myself to believe the Tripartite or any other power group could possibly be that ruthless.

Tsaya permitted herself to appear only mildly shaken when we got the news. She trembled slightly, bit her lower lip, said nothing, and disappeared. I knew what had happened. I went to her compartment where she'd retreated.

It isn't a pleasant job to calm a hysterical person who won't otherwise permit her normal emotions to reveal themselves because of professional pride as well as fear of the world.

I discovered myself beginning to share Tsaya's joys and griefs, her hopes and fears. I'd known and made love to many women, but I discovered I'd loved none before Tsaya. I had to include my mother because it came as a stunning surprise to me to discover in my growing relationship with Tsaya that I'd never loved my mother nor had my mother shown any love toward me. With Tsaya, I began to discover that love can be limitless and boundless.

But it took time. It didn't happen overnight.

Within hours of receiving the news of the *Andoric/Borgholm* disaster, we held another council of war. The term was used deliberately because we knew this was a *de facto* state of war although there'd been only a series of disturbing, harassing, disconcerting, distracting, and apparently disconnected incidents against the Commonwealth, its facilities, and its people. We wanted to be ready for whatever happened next.

We met without benefit of video because it wasn't deemed necessary. An audio-only teleconference required less bandwidth and wouldn't be considered important by snoopers. We also restricted participation to a few people so it would sound like an unimportant commercial business call. Ali handled our end at L-5 while his sister spoke for those in Vershatets. A tape loop of room background sounds was paralleled into the link so that when either Ali or Vaivan lifted the talk switch in order to speak to any of us, the background noise on the line sounded normal in spite of a dead transmitter.

I'll report it here on the basis of who said what, not as what Ali or Vaivan relayed. Sometimes they had to paraphrase or re-word.

The major matter was the *Andoric/Borgholm* disaster and its consequences and potential.

"I must consider it an accident," The General said. "It's not necessary to destroy two ships and hundreds of lives to assassinate me. In any event, I'm not necessary in order for the Commonwealth to win."

"We'd have difficulty winning without you, Grandfather," was Vaivan's response. "You're still the guiding light of the Commonwealth."

"I will not permit myself the luxury of self-importance," General Vamori replied flatly. "An inflated belief in self importance has brought down far too many leaders throughout history. The combination of such a belief and continual fear for one's life is a sure and certain pathway to the paranoia that's plagued national leaders and turned them into irresponsible conquering despots since the Alexander The Great fell to its siren song."

The General put his finger on the reason I detested and refused to use my given first name, that of a warrior who was one of the greatest conquerors of all time, who left his mark across most of the known world, and who lives on in the names of dozens of cities in Asia and Africa.

"Believe what you want, General, but we're going to protect you," was the reply from his son, Rayo Vamori of ComSpat.

"Very well," General Vamori said stubbornly. "But my enemies know where I am. If I travel in obvious fashion in an independent vessel, it will act as a deterrent against 'accidents' because that ship will be well-marked on every control display. If anything happens, people can be sure they'll be called to task for it. The telenews has made a big story of the fact that I happened to miss boarding the *Andoric*. Even if someone had managed to plan the *Andoric* accident, they wouldn't resort to such a thing a second time. Book me in a free trader registered under the Commonwealth flag.''

"Don't you want Omer and me to pilot you home?" I asked.

The General looked pensive and replied to me, "No, Sandy, we need you and others here because what happens on the ground will depend upon what's done in space. That's our reserve of strength and power. It may well be that we're entering the last great world crisis in a period of great transition. And perhaps we alone embrace the new philosophy of a world of abundance gained by opening the skies above our planet. If so, we must marshal our strength to preserve that. Even if, which I do not for a moment believe, our Commonwealth were somehow subjugated and starving, as long as we have our people beyond the skies they will in good time with all their new power and might step forth to the rescue and liberation of the world itself.''

I'd heard something like that before in a very old recording in a history class. Regardless of whether or not General Vamori was consciously paraphrasing those powerful words of the past, they still held enormous motivational power.

Jeri Hospah had a tape running in the room. The General's words have been heard many times since. But I heard them there in L-5 when they were first uttered.

A person doesn't have to be a politician, a military commander, or a diplomat to change the course of the world. But a person does have to be a leader, and leaders come in all varieties, including those who continue to lead if only quietly from the sidelines.

The General left within hours on the Free Trader *Arthur M. Dula*. Tsaya went with him. I didn't have time for a private goodbye. As a result, it was a cool, calm, professional farewell because Doctor Tsaya Stoak still resolutely maintained her strong defenses against a world she understood well enough to fear.

I didn't have time to mope about it.

Three hours after the *Dula* undocked and broke orbit for the Commonwealth, I was with Ursila and Ali in his compartment where they were keeping me from drowning my sorrows alone. Omer had gone out to do some proficiency training in the skalavans, and I was feeling blue over Tsaya's departure and worried about Powersat One-Zero-Five-East.

We hadn't gotten any word on One-Zero-Five-East for a long time, and a ten gigawatt powersat off-line for anything other than maintenance or repair is something to worry about. We were counting on RIO to let us know if something changed.

Which they did.

A priority scramble telecom came through from GEO Base Zero.

It was RIO Inspector Peter Rutledge.

"Happy hour, eh?" Rutledge began. "I say, Ali, your scrambler is out of synch."

Ali shook his head. "Afraid not. Locked right in. Given the current state of affairs, somebody is tapping or jamming, or both."

"Won't make a bit of difference in the long haul," Rutledge went on. "But I hoped to pass the word to you on the Q-T. RIO has already notified InPowSat and PowerSat in scramble. We're proceeding according to operational priorities, and if InPowSat and PowerSat do not rectify matters bloody soon, we'll broadcast in the clear."

"Powersat One-Zero-Five-East?" I asked.

"More than that, old chap." The veddy British mannerisms of Rutledge were now clipped and almost emotionless. "PowerSat has apparently developed an advanced computer program capable of altering the phasing of their new transmitter arrays in very short order. The resident team on One-Zero-Five-East has reported tests of quick beam redirection. I have one of my spot check teams on the way over for a look right now. It doesn't appear that there's been any power redirected, but from the way the beam's slewing we suspect it may be tracking some satellite in an inclined geosynchronous orbit. Sandy, would they be pointing at one of those American laser stations out there?"

"Probably, and it scares me, Peter. Now I'm going to scare you, too. I've told you there are Arospace Force hell beamers in inclined geosynch. There are three big laser stations there in three 60-degree inclined geosynch three equatorial zero points around the world for full global coverage. Each has an output of five gigawatts."

"Five gigawatts! I say!" Rutledge breathed. "Rather powerful, what? Why didn't you tell me how big they were before this?"

"You implied you knew."

"Perhaps I'd better start being less implicit and more explicit," the RIO Inspector said *sotto voce* then observed, "Areospace Force must have some stealth measures I don't know about

because those must be rather large facilities for that energy level
. . . and we haven't spotted anything big.''

"They're small because they'll get their energy from ten-gig
powersats."

"We should be able to spot any satellite receiving antenna
large enough to accept ten gigawatts," Rutledge said.

"Not necessarily." It was Ursila Peri who replied. The Canadian knew what she was talking about; she had her Ph.D. in high
energy physics, a fact she kept hidden. "Powersat energy beams
are limited in energy density for space-to-earth uses because of
potential biological effects on the flora and fauna around the
rectennas. This restraint doesn't exist for unmanned hell-beamers
in space. So a powersat beam can have an energy density several
orders of magnitude greater than the maximum allowed for
space-to-earth power transmission. This permits the satellite receiving antenna to be small. I suspect a check would show that
the beam transmitting antenna phasing at One-Zero-Five-East not
only redirected the beam but narrowed it as well.''

"The big hell beamers mount small deployable receiving antennas that don't even show themselves until moments before the
hell beams are triggered," I added.

"So that's why all of them in inclined geosynch look like
innocuous recce or surveillance snoopers," Rutledge mused.
"But what anyone want with a hell beamer that powerful?''

"Selective targeting space-to-space and space-to-earth appli-
cations," I explained.

"But a hell beamer doesn't need *that* much power to be
effective!''

"In space-to-earth mode, it does.''

"Sandy, it won't work space-to-earth," Ursila pointed out.
"The beam is spread too much to use against ground targets
from geosynch.''

"You've heard of adaptive optics?''

"Yes.''

"And you already know the low I-R absorption qualities of
some of the special alloys we're making out here for domestic
use. Don't you think that the technology can be stretched for
military hell-beamer use?''

"Probably.''

"It has been. Don't ask me how; I wasn't privvy to that data.
I was just an Aerospace Force officer who had to know about the
presence of such hell beamers so I could stay out of their way if
things went toes-up. But those five-gig hell beamers can put a ten
meter diameter beam on the Earth's surface.''

"But five billion watts! That's an absurd power level! It goes far beyond anything that would be required . . ."

"And it's quite contrary to the application of the law of armed conflict requiring economy of force, too," I pointed out. "Nonetheless, three of them exist. They're the modern equivalents of columbiads, block busters, and hundred megaton thermonukes. They're blackmail weapons and considered as such."

"My God, why?" Ursila breathed.

"Because the Soviets have three big inclined-GEO hell beamers for the same purpose," I told him. "The Americans weren't about to be blackmailed if trumps were played in any future confrontation."

"I feel ashamed of Canada if it was involved," Ursila muttered.

"How about me? I used to work for the United States Aerospace Force!" I retorted. "It didn't bother me to know they were there to provide counterpieces in the American-Soviet chess game, but I never thought my former comrades-in-arms would stoop to using them against a nation like the Commonwealth."

"Or China," Ali observed. "Or any of the other low-tech nations who've refused to knuckle under to the Tripartite's economic or energy pressures."

"Or against space facilities. We're sitting ducks," Ursila observed.

"That's why The General believes the space segment of the Commonwealth is important. We've got to stop the potential use of those big hell beamers. And we're going to. Not tomorrow, but right now. Peter, we're coming down to see you, and we want to meet with Commandant Milan Otasek." I told him.

"Our hands are tied on this matter, old chap," Rutledge reminded me. "We can't engage in paramilitary police action under international treaty and agreement."

"Peter, this wouldn't be the first time in history that international agreements have been bent because they were unworkable when the balloon went up," I reminded him. "The three of us are coming to see you as quick as we can get there, whether the red carpet is out or not. Maybe you don't know what a five-gig hell beam with only a few picoradian spread can do, but I know!"

"But I do know, and I must say I don't precisely like it," Inspector Peter Rutledge admitted.

CHAPTER 16

A Change of Command

"I say, you Commonwealth chaps at Ell-Five must have propellant to burn!"

"That's what it's for," I replied to Inspector Peter Rutledge as we stepped through the portlock at GEO Base Zero and relinquished our iklawas to the guard. We'd come in the *Tomahok* which wasn't economical, but she was fast and time was short.

Ursila remarked to the guard, "Don't lose that iklawa; I have a sentimental attachment to it."

"I'll get you another one if he does," Ali promised.

"Wouldn't be the same, dear. That's the one you taught me to kill with," she reminded him.

"You heard the news as you came over?" Peter said.

Ali nodded. "We expected they'd cut power beams to Sri Lanka and Liberia, but not to Echebar, Selangor, and Sorat."

"As usual, telenews told the truth and nothing but the truth . . . but not the whole truth," Rutledge told us as he escorted us through the weightless halls of RIO Headquarters. "Ten minutes ago, we broadcast on all warning frequencies that our resident inspection teams reported operating crews on ten more powersats belonging to PowerSat, InSolSat, and InPowSat redirecting power beams for reasons unknown."

"Is the military is taking over the powersats?" Ursila wanted to know.

"No, but every nation has some sort of emergency alert plan to be activated as a precautionary measure when it appears some sort of conflict is in the wind," I explained.

"Sandy, what do you think is behind this?" Rutledge asked.

"I'll tell you in Otasek's office," I promised.

"I hope you understand the sort of bind we're in," Rutledge remarked. "The Commandant is under no small amount of pressure. This is the first alert broadcast RIO has ever had to make."

"It was bound to come sooner or later, Peter," I said. "With the amount of military hardware tearing around this planet just

179

waiting to be powered-up, peace couldn't be maintained out here forever."

"I suspect not. But it's causing a lot of soul-searching among my personnel. If the balloon does indeed go up, a lot of our chaps are going to be in the line of fire."

"That's what we've got to settle," Ali remarked.

Commandant Milan Otasek of the Resident Inspection Organization was a large, full-faced, greying Moravian with the pudginess that's part of the gene pool of Mittle Europa. He wore his RIO non-uniform with a strange combination of pride and offhanded disarray.

"Please, please, seat yourselves," he remarked to us with nervous hesitation once his Chief Inspector introduced us. Otasek was obviously under stress. He spoke as though he were not totally familiar with English and carefully selected every word and phrase. As he did this, he had a tendency to pinch his lower lip between the thumb and forefinger of his right hand. "Inspector Rutledge tells me you wish to speak privately about this problem we are having."

There was silence until I realized I was going to have to run the show.

"Yes, Commandant, we do. Has Inspector Rutledge reported what he's found and what I've told him?"

"Yes, I have been told about Powersat One-Zero-Five-East and the United States gigawatt lasers. A very bad situation. But we can do nothing about them. We can report only what we observe on the powersats."

"I'm a former officer in the United States Aerospace Force," I said, but there was no longer the the pride I used to feel when I said that. Knowing full well what I was doing, I went on, "I'll confirm the stations are real. It's classified information whose disclosure is a capital crime in the United States. There's a price on my head for what I'm doing."

"Then why do you do it, Induno Baldwin?" Otasek asked, using my Commonwealth rank. This alerted me to the fact that he and Peter knew what was going on at L-5 and Vershatets.

"The world needs to know, and you've got to tell it because it trusts RIO," I explained to him.

"The knowledge may make other nations react. It may start a war."

"Probably. But there's going to be an armed conflict unless you do. And it also means RIO will have to change to meet the new conditions. Otherwise, RIO will cease to exist because the reasons for its existence will no longer be valid."

"Induno Baldwin," Commandant Otasek told me with a sigh, "I have a great dislike for war. My homeland for many centuries has been a corridor for marching armies who made destruction as they went. We learned that if we were to survive, we must not resist but must trade freedom for survival."

"You're no longer a citizen of your homeland, Commandant. You can't think in those terms now. As the leader of RIO, you're a citizen of the world," I told him bluntly.

"You do not need to remind me of the oath I took twenty-five years ago. I have seen to it that the duties and responsibilities of RIO have been properly carried out. I have reported to the world that our teams have discovered that powersat beams are being redirected. That is the full extent of my responsibilities."

"That may be, based on the original agreement which established RIO," I tried to point out, "but those were simpler times when an independent international inspection organization was needed to assure national leaders, military commanders, and business investors that powersats were not being used for military purposes. Times have changed. RIO's original task is finished, completed. Powersats exist. All of the world's powersat companies and powersat-subsidizing nations have recovered their original investments."

I paused, then emphasized, "Commandant, I'm surprised you don't see and accept your new responsibility to keep powersats from being used to energize weapons."

"How would we do such a thing?" Otasek wanted to know.

"Take physical control of any powersat known to be redirecting its output to any space weapon device, then insure that its power output is beamed to its assigned rectennas."

Otasek shook his head sadly. "I cannot do that. It is an act of piracy. It is beyond the scope of authority and outside the tradition of RIO."

"Have you thought about what will happen if you *don't*?"

"Commandant Otasek," Ursila spoke up for the first time, "Induno Baldwin's a professional military officer, but conflict's the last thing a professional warrior wants because he's the first to be involved and probably killed. I, too, come from a nation that doesn't like armed conflict but has fought for principle when necessary. The battlefields of Earth have seen far too much Canadian blood, but it was shed not only for Canada but for the principles of freedom we hold dear along with our friends on our southern border."

"I know the fine history of Canada," Otasek put in. "I also

know Induno Baldwin's background. And I know that you have a different view of these affairs."

"Then please listen to it," Ursila pleaded. "This situation happened because others couldn't compete against the Commonwealth. Our free market policy threatened them because they want all of a pie they think is finite, but isn't. They've tried everything short of armed conflict, and they've tried to instigate that and failed. Now the situation has escalated to the point where a general war could begin. You may have the last opportunity to stop it. If you act, it will be not only in the highest tradition of RIO, but also of the decent human principles of civilization."

Otasek pinched his lower lip between his right thumb and forefinger and looked at Ursila. "Doctor Peri, you know something of high energy lasers, but on the other hand I am no expert. I have a question for you."

"I'll answer it if I can, Commandant," she replied levelly, the emotion of her last statement now gone from her voice and facial expression.

"I have been told that high energy lasers based in geosynchronous orbit pose no threat to targets on Earth. If this is so, why is there so much fear of a five gigawatt laser station in GEO?"

"I'll try to explain it in non-scientific terms, Commandant," Ursila began. "Part of a beam's energy is absorbed and part is diffracted and scattered by the atmosphere. But a beam with very high energy density will self-focus and overcome diffraction and scatter. If it has high energy and narrow focus to start with, it can burn ground targets. But high energy hell beamers of the power required to do this can't be placed in LEO; they'd be so big because of their energy supplies that they'd be extremely vulnerable. So the greater protection of GEO is necessary. However, a several hundred megawatt beam that works from LEO won't work from GEO because even a few picoradians of beam spread prevents it from self-focusing. A beam energy of more than a gigawatt is required. However, the lack of suitable materials has rendered gigawatt hell beamers infeasible until recently.

"With the optics that can be built from space materials, it becomes possible now to generate a five billion watt beam with such pencil-thin dispersion that it *will* get through with enough energy to be a weapon against a ground target.

"Such a self-contained GEO-based laser would still be an extremely large and vulnerable target because of its energy supply. *But*, remove the need for an integral energy source, and it becomes very small. There's only one source in space that can deliver the energy to power a small GEO hell-beamer: a powersat.

"I don't know where in inclined GEO the big bell-burners are, but they're technologically feasible. The redirection of the power beam from Powersat One-Zero-Five-East appears to confirm this. Now for the first time, the space laser is a threat to innocent people on the ground. The military use of powersats must be stopped! Otherwise, we'll be involved in Space War Two within days. That's why you must take control of any powersat whose beam is redirected from its known and assigned earth rectenna."

Ursila concluded her explanatory lecture and sat back. I think I was the only one who noticed that the color had drained from her face.

Commandant Milan Otasek seemed to be mulling over in his mind what he'd heard. Finally he said, "Alichin, Commonwealth Glaser powersats don't seem to be involved. Why do you feel threatened?"

"Because we or our customers may become the targets of these weapons," Ali admitted. "If we're not the prime target, we wouldn't be treating our friends and customers properly if we didn't attempt to protect them for dealing with us rather than with those who cut off their trade in retaliation for trading with us."

Again, Otasek didn't speak for a long moment. "This is a very complicated matter."

"All big problems seem that way," I told him. "The solution's simple. The alternatives aren't. Do what you must do, rules or no rules, or none of us will survive the first few minutes of Space War Two out here where we're vulnerable to even the common beam weapons all around us. Think what a five giga-watt hell beam would do in space!"

Again, a long pause. Otasek put his hands flatly on his desk. "I cannot do as you suggest."

"Why?" I wanted to know.

"I am the person who must maintain half a century of RIO tradition that has worked well. It has kept the world's major space energy source from being considered a military threat. Our unique existence has required everyone in RIO to take an oath relinquishing national ties and to abstain from physical involvement in the powersat system. The entire RIO structure of trust and believability rests on this. RIO cannot carry out its functions otherwise. We cannot become involved. I am truly sorry."

"Otasek, if you don't act, there won't be any functions left for RIO to carry out!" I warned.

"That is not in the jurisdiction or the responsibility of RIO."

"Did it ever occur to you that RIO's responsibility now is the welfare of the people of the entire planet?"

"I am bound by international agreements and treaties that established RIO in the first place." Obviously, Otasek could not conceive of permitting his organization to act beyond its original character.

Chief Inspector Peter Rutledge moved over to the office door and threw the privacy latch. Then he turned to his commander. "Milan, old chap, excuse me for discussing internal affairs in front of outsiders. But they're involved and they do indeed have a point. Several, in fact. And they're friends, not adversaries. Milan, we've been through some sticky times together as RIO inspectors, so I don't feel out of line being rather frank at this juncture. It seems we're rather in somewhat of a bloody bind here. I'm compelled to remind you of Operational Rule Twelve."

"I am aware of the requirement to protect our people. I intend to evacuate RIO crews from powersats whose beams are being redirected. Their job in those facilities is finished."

"Would you be kind enough to let me know *how* you intend to do this, Milan?"

"There is something wrong with our RIO transport system?"

Peter Rutledge shook his red head. "No, but in short order I think it unlikely our vehicles will be able approach *any* powersat. The RIO broadcast of the military utilization of Powersat One-Zero-Five-East has brought everyone to a state of pre-conflict alert. Not only will military forces move to protect the powersats of their national interests, but the powersat companies themselves will bring in commercial security firms previously contracted for. We've been monitoring the communications, and it seems Brinks' have chartered space transport. There's bloody little space here in GEO that won't be considered part of engagement zones. So I have a bit of trouble understanding how we'll get our people off the powersats before the balloon goes up. That's why I suggest you may be neglecting Operational Rule Twelve. Our people are in a sticky spot at the moment, Milan. If you don't act, RIO will take losses. Are you quite prepared to answer to the RIO Steering Committee for those casualties?" Rutledge spoke in the clipped, emotionless British manner with the usual British penchant for understatement.

Commandant Milan Otasek thought, then pinched his lower lip again and replied, "Hmm . . . If our RIO ships cannot approach powersats to take our people off, the responsibility for their welfare no longer rests with RIO. Those who prevented us from removing them will be responsible."

"I say, Milan, that may be somewhat of a moot point if and when those of us who survive have the chance to tot-up casualties and damages. And don't you think we'd have a bit of a problem collecting reparations from the winner?"

Commandant Milan Otasek replied slowly and carefully, "RIO is an unarmed inspection organization. Once we have carried out our responsibility to notify the world of the military utilization of powersats, we have no authority to do anything else. If we are not permitted to take our people off the endangered powersats, we shall have to appeal to world opinion."

"That stands a bloody slim chance of protecting our people, Milan."

"I will ask the International Red Cross for assistance."

Rutledge shook his head. "Where are they going to get the ships?"

"I believe you are not correct in your assessment of the danger our people are in," Otasek said, taking another tack. "They are noncomabants. They are under the protective provisions of the various Hague and Geneva conventions."

"If the powersats on which they're based become military targets, our people will become 'regrettable noncombatant casualties.' You've run out of rationales, Milan."

"We cannot fight, Peter."

"We have to. We must be more than expendable sentries now. Too much depends on it." Inspector Rutledge straightened and moved over to Otasek's desk.

"The RIO teams are unarmed," Otasek reminded him.

"Really? Milan, weapons can be made from *anything*. It takes the will to use one's faculties or objects around him that turns a harmless and peaceful device into a deadly weapon. How do you propose to keep RIO people from defending themselves?"

"They have taken the same oath as we have."

"I rather think the instinct for self-preservation may be a stronger imperative. How long do you think their RIO oaths will prevail against their instincts for self-defense and survival? We may lose some crews by mutiny. If the pieces ever get put back together again, it will be an entirely new game. RIO can become the key to stability following this crisis . . . *if* RIO acts."

"I have no authority to act."

"Then, Commandant, as your Chief Inspector and therefore the second in command of RIO, I respectfully request you voluntarily relinquish your command authority to me because of personal inability to carry out Operational Rule Twelve and protect RIO personnel in a hazardous and dangerous situation.''

"I cannot . . ."

"Then it seems I'll have to take it under Operational Rule Three. I hereby relieve you of command, sir!''

"This is mutiny, Peter.''

"The RIO Steering Committee will be the judge of that, Milan . . . if I succeed. If I don't, it won't make any difference.''

Rutledge was right. He was the one who had everything to gain by action and everything to lose by doing nothing. So did we.

The history books say one thing about the Rutledge assumption of RIO command. However, we three who were present were rarely asked about it. It was quite emotionless and certainly non-violent because that reflected the personalities involved. Otasek was an imposing man with a dislike of violence and a reluctance to engage in self protection, traits that had survived generations of Mittle Europa's history of violence and conquest. On the other hand, Rutledge was cultured, friendly, and polite with an inner core that could be ruthless if the need arose.

Otasek reached out, pulled the keypad out of his desk, and typed his resignation of command. Without a word, he transferred it into the RIO data bank, noting time and date, then requested a hard copy print-out which he signed and handed to Rutledge. "I can only wish for you good luck," Otasek said with hesitation, his emotion showing only in his slight lapse into more of a slavic accent than he normally exhibited. "I must of course bring the matter to the attention of the Steering Committee.''

"I trust we'll both survive to be present at the meeting which deals with this,'' Rutledge replied. "As it is, it'll be touch-and-go for a bit whilst I try to muddle through to victory.'' He turned to us and went on, "I'm dreadfully sorry you were forced to witness this somewhat sticky situation, my friends. Usually, we don't air our internal disagreements in the presence of others. However, I can hardly apologize without pointing out that you were the ones who brought it to a head. I'll see to it you're accompanied back to your ship, and I'll certainly keep you apprised of developments.''

"What about Powersat One-Zero-Five-East?'' I wanted to know.

"I think we can take care of the matter,'' the new RIO Commandant remarked in his offhanded manner. "Our teams don't carry weapons, but neither do the powersat operating crews. I suspect the crews would rather go along with a situation that keeps them from becoming military targets. They're quite vulnerable, as you pointed out. After all, the choice between being killed or, if they survive, being fired . . . Well, it's not much of a choice, is it?''

"Peter, do you need any help? Any equipment?'' I wanted to know.

He shook his head as he showed us to the door of Otasek's office. "Thank, you, Sandy, but I don't believe that will be necessary right now. But shall we see how things develop, eh? Actually, I'm not going to seize the powersat network, you know. I'm going to take temporary control, not possession. The RIO resident teams will be instructed to see to it that power continues to flow to ground rectennas. We don't want to close the world down; that would cause more trouble than a war.''

"How do you intend to do it?'' Ursila wondered.

"Ursila, my dear, Milan Otasek was not totally aware of *everything* that went on in RIO. Although we're an unarmed parmilitary organization, that doesn't preclude us from having such organizational trappings of pure military groups as study staffs working on contingency plans and the like . . .''

It seemed too easy, too pat, too quickly done. But perhaps I'd overestimated the problem by assuming that only those of us in Landlimo Corporation and the Commonwealth had spent time thinking about the scenarios and options. After all, now-Commandant Peter Rutledge had turned out to be a rare combination of a thoughtful person and a man of action. He knew how to let it all hang out—with tassles on it. He would have been one hell of a good space jockey.

A RIO administrative officer guided us through the maze of corridors to the portlock where our ship was docked. We retrieved our iklawas, slipped into our ship, and closed hatches.

It was only then that Ursila grabbed Ali and embraced. Then Ali grasped my hand and arm. "Good work, Sandy!''

"I didn't think it could happen!'' Ursila was saying.

"We've won! *We've won!*'' Ali's relief at the lifting of the threat from Powersat One-Zero-Five-East was evident in his voice.

I held up my hand. "Keep a cool couth, folks. We haven't won yet. It looks like we're on the way to winning, but Rutledge has to bring it off. I don't know how he's going to do it, but he's apparently got plans. I just hope they work.''

We boosted for L-5 and the RIO order came on our unicom printer:

"RESIDENT INSPECTION ORGANIZATION HEADQUAR-

TERS SPECIAL MESSAGE 200450 2130Z> RIO RESIDENT
POWERSAT TEAMS HAVE BEEN INSTRUCTED TO RE-
QUEST POWERSAT OPERATING CREWS DO NOT RE-
DIRECT POWERSAT BEAMS FROM PREVIOUSLY ENER-
GIZED RECTENNAS AND TO RETURN ANY REDIRECTED
BEAMS TO ORIGINAL TARGET RECTENNAS WITHIN ONE
HOUR> POWERSAT OWNER ORGANIZATIONS ARE RE-
QUESTED TO ISSUE THIS SAME INSTRUCTION TO OPER-
ATING CREWS AND TO INFORM RIO HEADQUARTERS
UPON HAVING DONE SO> THIS SPECIAL REQUEST IS
BEING MADE TO ENSURE THAT POWERSAT BEAMS ARE
NOT REDIRECTED TO ENERGIZE WEAPON DEVICES
KNOWN TO BE EMPLACED IN EARTH ORBITS AND CA-
PABLE OF DESTROYING BOTH SPACE AND EARTH
TARGETS> NORMAL SERVICE FROM POWERSATS WILL
NOT BE AFFECTED> NORMAL SERVICE INTERRUPTIONS
FOR ROUTINE MAINTENANCE OR REPAIR WILL NOT BE
AFFECTED> HOWEVER POWERSATS WILL BE REMOVED
FROM SERVICE BY RIO ACTION IF POWERSAT BEAMS
ARE REDIRECTED OR ARE NOT RETURNED TO TARGET
RECTENNAS AS REQUESTED> SIGNED AND AUTHO-
RIZED P RUTLEDGE COMMANDANT PRO TEM> END MES-
SAGE> END MESSAGE> END MESSAGE> 200450 2133Z>''

"Nicely done, nicely done," Ali commented as he read the
hard copy. "Very carefully worded."

I had to agree. "Peter was careful not to say how he'd react if
he didn't get compliance," I pointed out. "It's a very astute
move not to reveal in advance what his intentions are."

"The big question," Ursila put in, "is whether or not the
people of the Tripartite will believe RIO can or will do anything."

"They'll test him," Ali guessed. "They'll pressure him first.
Then they'll conduct an experiment through some small and innocuous group. If the experiment fails—as I think it will—not much
will be lost. That's the way power groups operate."

"So do military commanders," I told him.

"Question," Ursila said. "The Tripartite and anyone else
with their fingers on this situation knows we went to GEO Base
Zero before the Rutledge message and are returning afterward.
We're running with an STC clearance."

"So what's got you worried?" Ali wanted to know.

"Aerospace Force has a lot of things at Ell-Five they don't
talk about and don't think anybody knows about . . . but we do.
My question: Will we be allowed to get back to Ell-Five or will
we have an accident first?"

"Have we got enough delta-vee left to divert to Criswell Base on Luna instead?" Ali asked.

Ursila, who was co-pilot, punched the on-board computer's keypad. "Yes, *but* . . ."

"But what?"

"Have we got adequate life support consumables to last for three more weeks in this ship? Yes, we can make it, but it would have to be done using aopgee kick in lunar orbit, which we intend to do anyway to match with Ell-Five, then drifting orbital repositioning thrust because that's all the delta-vee capability we'll have after apogee kick. Remember, we left Ell-Five running light with only enough delta-vee for the down-and-back flight plus normal contingency reserve."

I had to interrupt this searching for impossible alternatives. "We're already headed toward Ell-Five. We can't afford to divert to Luna. It'll take too long. So we'll muddle through, as Peter put it. We won't have any trouble. As The General observed, one *Aldoric* can be passed off as an accident, but two incidents in a row would be very embarrassing."

The commscanner sweeping through the Commonwealth commercial frequencies stopped blinking and beeped.

I punched up the freq and called, "This is *Tomahok* replying on Hotel Quebec. Go ahead."

"Sandy?"

"This is Sandy Baldwin."

"Thank God! At last! This is Jeri at Ell-Five. I've been trying to reach you for the last four hours."

"We've been in GEO Base Zero with the RIO commanders, Jeri. Why didn't you call us there?"

"Couldn't get through! All channels were tied up."

"I can understand why. RIO's . . ."

"Sandy, smoke it back here fast! All hell's broken loose down below," the ex-Aussie manager of the Commonwealth's Ell-Five facility told us, his voice strained with excitement. "There's been a revolution in Topawa! Kariander Dok and two others have taken over the Commonwealth government in a *coup de etat*!"

CHAPTER 17

Confrontation
and Conference

The images of the three men loomed on the screen. They looked like a victorious triumvirate—Kariander Dok, Tonol Kokat, and Heinrich von Undine.

"You really have no choice, Alichin," Dok said with a smile. "Our Freedom Army holds Topawa and Oidak. We control the highways, the railways, the primary seaport, and the Oidak rectenna. It's only a matter of time before we secure the rest of the country."

"Still fighting, eh?" Ali observed. "There's a lot of country out there you haven't touched yet, Dok. And 'Freedom Army?' Hah!"

"Our Freedom Army will take the Vamori Free Space Port before the day is out," Tonol Kokat bragged.

"You'll need outside help," I was trying to draw them out.

"We have it. Fresh contingent of the Freedom Army will be pouring into Pitoika soon. While you and Abiku's tin soldiers were fretting over your neighbors and powersats, we had time to make arrangements with our friends and move unmolested to make a long-needed change in the Commonwealth."

"You sold out to the Tripartite!" Ali exploded.

"You use terminology loosely," Dok said. "It's unfortunate you were the Commonwealth's representative in Santa Fe. A reasonable person would have seen the opportunity offered there. Your intransigence and that of the rest of the Vamori family and its stooges has cost us dearly in terms of lost business. The three of us set about to rectify the situation. It took time, but we have friends in America, Japan, and Europe. But enough of that. Now that the change has occurred, we must all pull together to get the Commonwealth operating properly."

"Having a bit of trouble, Dok?" I asked. "Some people resisting your new order? Your 'Freedom Army' is probably having fun fighting the CitImpy."

It was Heinrich von Undine who spoke up with agitation, "They will not resist forever. Members of the CitImpy who turn in their rifles and ammunition are being given full amnesty. Those who do not will be severely dealt with. I have brought in people to establish internal security police, and they know how to do this sort of thing very well.''

"'*Ve haf vays!*' I don't doubt that." I snapped. "They've had a couple of centuries of experience. Too bad they haven't learned yet."

"I said enough of this," Kariander Dok interjected. "We were forced to move quickly and didn't manage to establish the proper people in our Commonwealth space operations. Therefore, we're extending to you the general amnesty offered to other citizens . . . with the exception of the Vamori, Stoak, Tatri, Teaq, and other ruling families who've held this country in their grip for so long."

"Dok, if this weren't such a serious matter, I'd laugh at you," I told him. "You're spouting your own propaganda like you believed it! You're right out of a mid-twentieth-century war movie!"

"For that remark, Baldwin," Dok sputtered. "you'll be stripped of your rank and power just like your boss, Alichin Vamori!"

"Kariander Dok, someday I'll eat you!" Alichin Vamori vented the oldest and strongest Commonwealth curse.

I scribbled on a scrap of paper, "Stall. Promise nothing. Get back to him. Let me evaluate the situation."

"Ah, school boys passing secret notes to one another," Dok observed. "It's as childish as your anger. Lest we be misunderstood with regard to your family and others, we're not as barbaric as your curse. I came from one of the oldest civilized cultures where, in fact, civilization itself began. My colleague von Undine comes from an old European culture. We'd never consider murdering the the leaders of the old regime. Arrangements will be made to to free them without the means to regain the power they once used so badly."

Ali started to explode again, but I laid my hand on his arm and took over. "Dok, I've got to admit this is a surprise. We're tired and hungry. Give us a few hours to get some rest. You owe us that much for preventing a space war that would have cost the Tripartite dearly."

I was stalling and trying to pile it high and dry without it being obvious. I needed time to find out what was really happening down in the Commonwealth. Time to grasp the whole situation. Time to find out if Rutledge was succeeding. Time to organize the forces we had in space. Time to coordinate actions with the indunos. Time to plan what we could do.

I hadn't forgotten what The General said before he left for the Commonwealth with Tsaya.

Tsaya! She was down there.

So was Vaivan.

And The General.

And other Commonwealthers I'd grown to love and admire, people who'd had the guts to tell the world to quit playing its old games because they'd discovered a world of plenty if others would only see what they'd seen.

Where were they?

Wherever they were, I knew they'd be fighting like hell if they were still alive.

Time. I desperately needed time, and I'd lick boots and kiss ass to get those three to give it to me. If I got it, I wouldn't waste a second of it.

On the screen, there was a hushed conversation between the triumvirate. Kariander Dok finally replied smoothly, "We owe you nothing, Baldwin. However, a short delay is harmless since our Freedom Army will have most of our objectives secured soon. You have eight hours to convince the citizens there of the wisdom of accepting the new government. I'll call you on this channel at eleven hundred hours, Zulu time."

When the circuit was cut, I thought Ali would go berserk. "My father! My mother! My sister! My whole family! Grandfather, and everything he's given his years to achieve! All because of those greedy monsters who were bought by the Tripartite!"

I put both hands on him to keep him quiet. But he had his iklawa out of its scabbard and held in his right hand. Like all iklawas, it was sharp.

"Ali, sit down and shut up!" I shouted at him. "We don't know anything for sure yet! Keep your couth until we talk to someone other than Kariander's bunch."

"Get Omer! Get the skalavan squadron moving! Don't just sit there, Sandy! Do something! Move!"

The man was in shock. I put my life on the line and struck him across his face with the back of my hand. The impact threw the two of us apart. I rebounded off the bulkhead a fraction of a second before Ali collided with the opposite one. I moved sideways because I saw Ali's hand come down.

His iklawa rattled off the bulkhead where I'd been.

I grabbed a stool, ripped it loose from its velcro floor fittings, and held it in front of me. Then I pushed off toward him, driving hard with my legs against the bulkhead. Ali acted very surprised when I pinned him to the bulkhead with the legs of the stool.

This time I had my iklawa out with its point at his throat.

He acted as if he'd just come out of a trance. "Take your iklawa away from my throat. What do you think you're doing?"

"Trying to keep you from killing me, Ali," I snapped, not moving my iklawa. "Get hold of yourself, or I'll zero you right now and haul you down to sick bay where we'll tranquilize you."

Alichin sighed. "I'm sorry, Sandy. I don't know what happened to me."

"I do. You've got to learn to control it when you let it all hang out like that," I told him. "Let's hope the rest of the people in the Commonwealth can let it hang out, too. There might be some hope for us." I slipped my iklawa into its scabbard and moved the stool aside. I was still prepared to break his neck if I had to.

Ali was breathing hard but had calmed down. "My apologies, Sandy."

"You've got 'em."

"Let's get busy. We've got to mount a space rescue mission to Vamori-Free. You and Omer can cover me; I'll pilot one of the packets. . . ."

"No."

"What do you mean? Are you backing out?"

"Ali, you're in no condition to do anything like that, even if it would work—which it wouldn't because we don't know what's happening there," I said. "In fact, you're in no condition to lead anything right now because you're emotionally involved and you've never fought a war before."

"I flew AirImpy tacair against the last Kangatu king in the Commonwealth Southwest."

"That was a police action. This is a civil war," I countered, "Wars aren't won by emotional generals *or* emotional civilians. For months I've been trying to figure out how and where I really fit into the picture. The General tried to tell me but I couldn't grasp it because I didn't know what this was all about. Now I do. I know my role. I'll run this fight and win it. This is my show from now on. So follow me or get out of my way! Or I'll take off this iklawa. Peter Rutledge may need me if you don't."

Ali stared at me strangely, then took both my hands in his. "Sandy, it's yours. You're the warrior. I'm just a merchant manager. You're one of us even though you haven't taken a Commonwealth name yet. So I'll give you one. I'm pleased you're with us all the way, Induno Sendi Boldwon."

"Sendi Boldwon?"

"When a person becomes a Commonwealth citizen, he usually takes the Commonwealth derivative of his name. My family name generations ago was Van Mora. The family names Stoak, Tatri, Teaq, and even Hospah derived from other names in other hands and cultures. Our forebears infused the best of their heritage into a common wealth of social background. But in a free society there can be no minorities. To become free and equal citizens rather than a mob of hybridized outlanders, they took new identities behind new names altered to a common pattern. You were an American, but now you're a Commonwealth citizen all the way, Sendi."

I didn't feel any different, and I wasn't certain I wanted to be Sendi Boldwon. But if the rules required it in order to play the game, I'd go along. When in Rome . . .

"Okay, make a public announcement that I'm in charge," I told him.

"Why? You are."

"You ought to know why from your management experience that assumption of command is impossible without an authoritative announcement from a person known to have the power to delegate the responsibility. People must be told who's in charge." That was straight out of the Aerospace Force leadership manuals. I didn't want to waste time and energy convincing the Commonwealth space forces that I was in command. Time was of the essence.

Ali made the announcement.

While he did, I tried to organize my thinking and lay out a plan of action. I took over the comm console and punched-up Jeri Hospah. "This is Induno Boldwon," I told him.

"Congrats, sir! Who do we kill first?"

"We're going to find out. Get me a circuit to Vershatets."

"Uh, fearless leader, the blasted freqs are jammed," Jeri reported.

"Is the lasercom installed yet?"

"It is, but we haven't checked it out yet. It may be useful only as an expensive flashlight."

"Try it. If the r-f spectrum's unusable, Vershatets knows enough to monitor lasercom."

Lasercom was practically jam-proof. A low-power lasercom beam would be less than 3 meters in diameter at a distance of 386,000 kilometers. Outside the beam it would be undetectable. If it was undetectable, it couldn't be jammed.

It was working well enough for military use. I got through to Induno Kivalina Moti. She looked haggard but brightened when

Ali told her he'd put me in charge at L-5. "Good! We've got somebody running the SpacImpy! Eloy Chervit was caught in the Karederu Center round-up."

"Explain, please," I asked.

Karederu Center had been rebuilt following the fire, and a rededication party had been scheduled. Kariander Dok and his gang used the gathering as an occasion to launch the *coup* because it was an easy way to round up the Commonwealth leaders. But one of the last heavy storms of the season prevented some from getting there from Vicrik and Kulala. A *coup d' état* is like any other large operation: once the go-ahead is given, it's practically impossible to delay it for 48 hours. This is is particularly true if there's no contingency plan for a delay, and the Kariander triumvirate apparently didn't have one.

That told me their strategy was shallow and therefore vulnerable.

When the *coup* happened, Kivalina reported, a large number of people had been captured at Karederu Center. But the triumvirate hadn't gotten all the key people.

"Things are still confused," Kivalina admitted, "but it looks like they got the two Chairs of the legislature, Justice Silut of the Jurisprudence Board, Commissioner Abiku, AirImpy Induno Dati, SpacImpy Induno Chervit, Shaiko Stoak of Commonwealth Glaser, and Wahak and Vaivan Teaq of Landlimo."

"How about The General and Tsaya Stoak?" I asked anxiously.

"They're here in Vershatets," Kivalina replied. "We don't know yet where President Nogal is, so The General's acting as *pro tem* chief executive until we find the President."

I was partly relieved. "We have a good chance of winning this thing, Kivalina! The Commonwealth leadership's been truncated, but it's basically intact and functional."

"Right! And without The General, the triumvirate can't take over the country. In fact, they're trapped in Topawa." The leader of the citizen army went on, "I never issued a call-up to the CitImpy. They came out in a *levee en masse* after Dok announced the takeover."

"What's the current tactical situation, Kivalina?"

"Vicrik and Vershatets are secure. The rebels tried to send an armed force up Dekhar Gorge in marginal weather without tacair. Our tacair flew anyway. The river ran red," she told me with understatement. "We'll retake Oidak and the rectenna tomorrow. Pahtu's pouring LandImpy troops up the Manitu-Oidak road and down Dekhar Gorge. I might add that she's doing it over my objections because it's softening the defense points at Morosabi,

Tewahk Pass, and Sidamu Pass. We're leaving ourselves wide open to the Malidoks."

"Don't worry about them," I advised her, "or about the Kulala region, either. The Kulala operations were diversionary feints to distract us from Kariander Dok's activities right under our noses. Kivalina, we *never* considered a scenario where the strike comes from within! Everyone was so sure of our internal integrity that we forgot there were some citizens who could still be tempted by greed."

"I just don't understand it. I don't understand it at all," Kavilina admitted. "After three generations educated under abundance economics . . ."

"Von Undine wasn't," I pointed out. "He's an outlander. He never adopted a Commonwealth name, did he? Incidentally, I think we'll discover Kariander Dok's an outlander."

"Didn't you know that?" Ali asked. "He came from Basrah and married into my family through my aunt on my mother's side, Tanyo Nogal."

"The SpacImpy and our Ell-Five facility here is secure," I reported. "We can mount a mission to Vamori-Free."

"We've probably lost Vamori-Free temporarily," Kivalina announced. "The mercenaries went after the major input facilities—the Oidak rectenna, Pitoika harbor, Topawa International Airport, and Vamori-Free. Nobody enjoys air superiority right now, so Topawa International's unusable. We'll get the rectenna back, and we can operate without the rest *except* Vamori-Free."

"If you and Pahtu take Oidak and the rectenna," I pointed out, "that will cut off power to Vamori-Free. I can take it back with a space envelopment if you and Pahtu keep them busy on the ground. If Dati's AirImpy can control the skies over Topawa International Airport and Shokutu's CoastImpy can bottle-up Pitoika harbor, that prevents mercenary reinforcements from coming in. Then we'll go after Topawa. Does the strategy sound reasonable?"

"Yes, but let me get Pahtu, Shokutu, and The General in here. This has to be a closely coordinated operation, and there's a lot of staff work to do."

"Have the staff sit in," I advised, "then turn them loose to do their thing against whatever deadlines we set. We don't have much time."

I pulled together Ali, Ursila, Omer, and Jeri.

I was greatly relieved to see The General on the conference screen. I wish Tsaya had been there, too, but she was busy with the wounded from the Dehkar Gorge Massacre, as Pahtu called the engagement.

"I was worried about you, General," I told him with obvious relief. "Too bad we still have to fight our own greedy people to keep them from looting what your teachings built."

"Sendi," he replied with the vowel shift that indicated he'd seen Ali's announcement, "I never maintained we wouldn't have to defend our belief or our Commonwealth. Even after everyone understands there's plenty for all, it's going to take time for people to realize all the consequences. It'll take even more time to achieve the commonwealth of humanity because that doesn't mean the existing wealth's spread commonly, but that everyone is commonly wealthy. But right now we have to save ourselves."

We went over the strategy Kivalina and I had discussed.

"How're your internal communications?" I wanted to know.

"As long as we hold the Dilkons and space, we've got the high ground," LandImpy Induno Pahtu pointed out. "We control communications, not the triumvirate. As long as we do, we'll beat them."

"We couldn't get through on r-f spectrum because of jamming," Jeri pointed out.

"We're doing it," The General told us. "We've deliberately left holes in the jamming so the mercenaries will be forced to use them. That saves us a great deal of time monitoring a broad spectrum."

"That's the only thing standing against us," I pointed out. "Time. The triumvirate used time in the form of surprise. We have to use time against them by acting faster than they think we can. What are we missing or neglecting? Anybody got a critique? Can anybody shoot holes in this?"

"Yes." The General did. "We don't know where the triumvirate is holding our people, and we don't know if they'll use them as hostages."

"They will," Pahtu growled. "Dok comes from a culture that's utilized hostages often in the past century. As for Von Undine, I've got to believe he believes in *Kriegsraison*. I'm sure Dok has had a strong influence on his nephew, Kokat. If they don't hold hostages, the Freedom Army probably will because these mercenaries they brought in through our open ports of entry seem to be the dregs of most of the underdog cultures of the planet. No offense intended, Sendi, but some soldiers of fortune are pretty brutal."

"No offense taken. I'm no longer a soldier of fortune," I pointed out.

"They're holding my twin sister," Ali said darkly. "I know her as well as I know myself. I want to find her. I just *feel* she's in deep trouble."

"Ali, that's your job. You work on that," I told him. That would keep him busy and out from underfoot. For some time, Ali would be ineffectual because he had personal matters at stake which warped his judgement. I wasn't letting myself do that, although I had personal matters at stake, too.

We got our various responsibilities and duties settled and established a schedule based on the speed with which Omer could get our skalavans from Luna. I'd then have to be in the right place at the time with the five packets we could pull from various Commonwealth space facilities. The retaking of Vamori Free Space Port would be a combined ground, air, and space operation, and everything hinged on the timing of the space armada coming in from L-5.

"As for the triumvirate's prisoners, the rescue will have to be a commando mission once we find out where they're being held and what's being done with them," I pointed out.

The General was considering all of this pensively. He looked around at his people in the Vershatets redoubt, then at the rest of us on the lasercom link. "We must be prepared to deal with another unknown. Kariander Dok and his cohorts aren't acting alone. I'm certain they have covert backing. In Santa Fe, the Tripartite and the PetroFed were unsuccessful in bringing us into a controlled-market, and they've been unsuccessful in their try to squeeze us out of space commerce by economic pressures and military space threats. We've countered and won at every turn. So they attack us in a blind spot: internally through the financial contacts they control. I want to keep my eye on those external factors. Sendi, when did Dok say he'd talk with you again?"

"We've got five hours."

"They'll offer to parley," The General said, "because in five hours they'll know they're going to lose the Oidak rectenna. They may offer to negotiate. They'll try to do it through you since they have communications with you and not with us. They'll want to bargain. I think they'll offer the prisoners as part of the deal."

"Do you want me to parley with them?" I asked.

The General nodded. "Yes, please."

"I won't negotiate with human lives, General," I snapped.

"I don't ask you to. But I must remind you this is an internal armed conflict in which the various Hague, Geneva, and Manila conventions don't apply. There are no rules, Sendi. Do what you feel you must. Promise them anything but deliver them nothing, anything to stall for time and information about where they're holding our people. We'll be monitoring. In the meantime, let's proceed with the strategy we've developed, keeping in mind we must be extremely flexible. Many, many lives are at stake. If we make a wrong move, this civil war can still escalate into a worldwide general war. The Chinese have told me they're waiting to see what happens before they do what they feel they must.''

I was apprehensive and anxious in anticipation of Dok's return call. I worked hard to overcome this and fear as well because I felt was balancing the whole world on the honed edge of my iklawa. To keep cool, I worked on the planning of our Vamori-Free recapture mission.

I also delved deep into my memory, recalling what I'd been taught about wars and the causes of wars—the great miscalculations and mistakes as well as the high-risk chances that had become victories or defeats.

I had to keep reminding myself that this war—and that's what it was, not a euphemistic ''armed conflict''—would be totally different from any war fought to date. In recalling the lessons of history, I had to be careful I didn't fight it like any war in history. Analogies from the past wouldn't have a one-to-one relationship to the realities of this very different time.

Kariander Dok, Tonol Kokat, and Heinrich von Undine contracted me right on the dot at 1100 hours Universal Time. They weren't in the same place they'd been before. Wherever it was, there was a stone wall behind them. The lighting was bad, and the audio echoed as though they were in a very large, acoustically-hard room.

''Well, Alichin, have you decided to relinquish your people and facilities?'' Dok asked at once.

I took over. ''Since you've precipitated an internal confict, Dok, this is out of Ali's hands now. As the senior Commonwealth military officer here, I'm in command until this war is over.''

''So you're the hired mercenary who's taken over? Another Colonel Chase, eh? Well, we can deal with you . . .''

''Induno Boldwon is no Colonel Chase,'' Ali snapped.

''It makes no difference. Boldwon, what is your answer?''

''No surrender, Dok,'' I said vehemently. ''By the way, how's your 'Freedom Army' doing at Vamori Free Space Port?''

''I told they'd have it in their hands by this time. And they do.''

"And Oidak?"

"The Freedom Army already holds the rectenna. They'll cut the circuit on my order. That will leave a lot of people in the dark."

"Including you," I pointed out.

"This is wasting time," von Undine put in hastily. "Since you won't surrender, we're forced to use other methods. We hold a number of people of importance whose welfare is of concern to others including yourself. Do you know where we're transmitting from?"

"Not yet."

"It will become obvious, because this is where we're holding our prisoners."

"Hostages, you mean!" Alichin snapped before I could stop him.

"Call them what you will," von Undine said with a smirk. "But we have something to negotiate with. In exchange for your surrender, Alichin, no further harm will come to our prisoners."

I looked at Ali and scribbed him a quick note: "Stay out of this!"

And I replied to Dok's screen image, "You make threats and allegations, Dok. Who have you got and where are they?"

Kariander Dok replied. "We're prepared to show you what we have to negotiate with."

The video pickup left the three of them and panned to the left.

As if on cue, someone screamed.

It was a scream of pain and terror.

What we saw on the screen was something ten centuries out of the past.

Ali gave vent to an incoherent curse of rage.

Until that moment, I didn't know of the existence in the Commonwealth of dungeons and torture chambers.

CHAPTER 18

Honor and Revenge
at GEO Base One

"As you can see for yourselves," Kariander Dok's voice said over the muffled moans and painful screams of that grisly scene, "your friends and family are still alive."

This was a type of terrorism widely practiced in the Middle East and the Orient. It hadn't been common in Mittel Europa since World War II although people there were capable of it. The purpose has always been brutal and subtle: coerce by threatening friends and loved ones. It was worse than barbaric; it was inhuman. This was the middle of the twenty-first century, and people shouldn't be doing this sort of thing!

But there it was on the screen.

As the camera panned from person to person, I amost got sick to my stomach.

I forced myself not to look at what they were doing to Vaivan.

Ali was almost incoherent. "I'll wash my iklawa in your blood for this! I will slit your dead body open for the jackals to feast upon! I would not poison myself by eating you!" The old curses tumbled out of him.

"I believe we have something to negotiate with," Dok's voice came smoothly through.

I deliberately took a very hard line. "Dok, you can't keep those people in that condition very long. If they die, you'll have nothing to negotiate with. All I have to do is delay, and you'll lose your leverage and any popular support you may have. All I have to do is broadcast the tape of this to the world, Dok, and you're finished!"

"This is an internal affair. There have been things of this sort in other places; no one bothered to react. The world is full of pain and death. The verdict of world opinion means nothing; we'll be feared and respected instead. This is nothing new. Commonwealth law itself requires violent punishment."

"Law shows justice and mercy. You don't."

"You're prolonging the agony of these people," von Undine's voice broke in. "Surrender your space forces."

"Not without negotiation," I told him. I wanted to draw them out of Topawa into a meeting on neutral ground. "I want assurances you'll release these people if I surrender and assurances I won't end up in your dungeon, too. But I'll talk only if you start treating your prisoners humanely. Otherwise, I won't be able to control what the Commonwealth people will do to you."

"You're in no position to threaten," Dok's voice replied. The video panned back onto the triumvirate, ending the horror show.

"Neither are you. By rights, I shouldn't agree to negotiate, but I'll compromise if you'll give a little, too."

I hated to play with words when my friends were hurting. If this was war, it wasn't the sort this warrior liked to fight. I *had* to submerge emotions and feelings; there was no other choice except to give in to these bastards. And I wasn't about to do that.

I knew The General and others were watching in Vershatets. They wouldn't let this atrocity go unpunished.

"It will have to be done through intermediaries," Dok remarked. "We cannot leave now."

He was probably right. None of them could leave Topawa because they were directing operations of their *coup*. Their situation wouldn't improve. Their treatment of prisoners would motivate the impys to fight without quarter.

"I'll talk with an intermediary, but only on neutral ground."

"Zurich?"

That was one of the bastions of world power groups. Switzerland, Bahrain, and other places had interesting banking rules that made it possible to stash the loot.

"I want truly neutral ground, Dok," I was relying on the fact that people still thought of space in terms of distances rather than energies. "I'll meet you halfway: GEO Base Zero."

"Sorry. You have Rutledge and RIO in your pocket."

"All right, then GEO Base One."

"Why that one?"

"It's the old powersat construction base. Hasn't been used for twenty years," I explained. "It's parked at GEO Spot One-Eighty over mid-Pacific. It was last visited by a RIO Spot Inspection Team about a year ago, and the portlock module had pressure. I'll meet your intermediary there in twenty-four hours, unarmed. There'll be two of us, myself with Omer Astrabadi as my pilot. Who will you send?"

"I'll call you in an hour."

"In the meantime, start treating your prisoners according to the the Hague and Geneva conventions."

"We won't kill them."

That left a lot of leeway, but I knew he wouldn't kill them . . . yet.

Ali had calmed down a bit by the time I broke the circuit. He was still breathing hard. "Let me go with you," he pleaded.

"Not only no, but hell no! I couldn't keep you under control, Ali. Their intermediary wouldn't be safe. You'd try to kill him."

"But I've got to do *something*!"

"You can find out where they're holding the prisoners."

"It's obvious. That dungeon is under the old fortress on the plaza of Topawa Centrum. The building's our natural museum. We restored the dungeons to remind people of the horror of our past and warn them of what could happen with a breakdown of civilized behavior. Dok and von Undine took the old prison museum and put it back to use!"

The lasercom to Vershatets demanded our attention. It was The General.

"We saw. We know. The LandImpy and the CitImpy indunos are taking what action they can," the old man said with obvious sadness and grief on his face and in his voice. "It's worse than the atrocities of Colonel Chase . . . but we won't let this trio escape. Sendi, I can't provide effective leadership now. I'm much too disturbed by what's happened to my family. Will you take over, please?"

"Yes, I will, General." Suddenly with those four words, the whole future of the Commonwealth depended on me.

"Grandfather, I want to wash my iklawa in the blood of Kariander Dok," Alichin broke in with a firm, resolute voice.

"No, Alichin. We will not revert to savagery to avenge savagery," The General told him. "Their case will be handled under the law."

"But our family's being harmed! Our family honor requires revenge!"

"Alichin, you're behaving like your ancestors. We no longer live in a world of want, and we must *never* go back to its principles, regardless of the behavior of others. And don't confuse the custom of going about armed with an iklawa with the principle of defending honor. A family doesn't demand honor or revenge; a family exists with and because of love and mercy. And our nation doesn't demand honor or revenge; it requires respect and therefore justice . . . and gives both."

"Grandfather, don't tell me that my strength is as the strength of ten because my heart is pure!"

"But it is, Ali. Now call upon that strength. I've had to. How do you think I felt watching more than fifty years of my life shattered by outlander barbarians with a credo of greed *which is no longer necessary?*''

When your friends and loved ones are being tortured, it's hard to be logical and rational. It took all of my professional training to put down the emotions that surged inside me, a mere outlander who'd been a citizen of this new thing in human affairs, the United Mitanni Commonwealth, for less than half a year.

But Ali couldn't control his emotions. This made him ineffectual as a negotiator or military leader. The same was true of The General, but he knew it. In fact, the rest of the truncated Defense Commission—LandImpy Induno Pahtu, CoastImpy Induno Shokutu, and CitImpy Induno Moti—were probably also running on considerable emotional charge right then. I *had* to play the role of the cool, rational leader.

It was now my show, and I couldn't blow it.

Nor could I become another Colonel Chase.

I had to be General Anegam Vamori standing before Oidak on that long-ago Christmas Day leading 20,000 untrained warriors bearing only assault rifles, grenades, mortars, assegai, and iklawas facing a mercenary horde of 50,000 trained, experienced soldiers of fortune and professional looters armed with rockets, tacair, heavy machine guns, and artillery firing vapor explosives and seeker ammunition.

I wanted the *other side* to get emotional and to make mistakes because of biased or poor judgement.

And I wasn't just a mercenary hireling; I was a former outlander who was now a citizen warrior for the new prophet of plenty.

What a hell of an unsuspected spot for a former space jockey to find himself!

And the twisty way I got there was a subject for much personal reflection for years afterward.

While I was waiting for the triumvirate's reply, I conferred by lasercom with Indunos Pahtu, Shokutu, and Moti in Vershatets, further refining the plans and working out the details.

For the GEO Base One mission, I'd wear a full elastic pressure suit under my flight suit and a bubble helmet with an open microphone. If there was foul play or I bought the farm, the strategic plans would move ahead without me. But I'd be ready for foul play.

I'd go unarmed as promised—that is to say, I wouldn't be carrying anything that was obviously a weapon. It didn't mean I'd be defenseless.

The message from the triumvirate came was hard copy. "They're doing a good job down there," Jeri reported as he handed it to me. "The countermeasures and jamming from Vershatets are blocking almost everything. This came through on low-frequency narrow-band digital pulse code from Topawa."

"250450 1435Z> BALDWIN L5 FROM COMMONWEALTH PROVISIONAL GOVERNMENT TOPAWA> CONFIRMED MEETING GEO BASE ONE 1200Z 260450> GOVERNMENT AMBASSADOR PLENIPOTENTIARY PHILIP DUBOIS WOLF IS AUTHORIZED FULL POWER OF NEGOTIATION> ARRIVING YACHT PROXINOS GREEK REGISTRY BEACON CODE 6067> VON UNDINE FOREIGN MINISTER COMMONWEALTH PROVISIONAL GOVERNMENT TOPAWA> END MESSAGE END MESSAGE END MESSAGE> 250450 1437Z>"

"Who's this guy Wolf?" I asked Jeri.

"He's listed in the 'Who's Who' data bank as Vice President of the Bahrain Eurasian Investment Bank," Jeri said. "Guess you'll be rubbing shoulders with a micro-part of the Tripartite, sort of a Grand Exhalted Big Dipper of the Persian Gulf Lodge."

"I won't even be meeting with someone from the Commonwealth, just an outlander! Okay, let's get this over with," I told Omer and started toward the portlock hatch.

"Not yet, Yankee," the Mad Russian Space Jockey brought me up short. "You still look like typical space jockey."

"So?"

"You are now Induno Sendi Boldwon, Marshall of All Commonwealth Impys."

"If you put it that way, I guess I must be."

"So you must look like it."

"Why bother?"

"Is old Kazakh saying: a circus must have elephants."

"Okay, I get it. Is old Yankee saying: don't do a vast thing in a half-vast way."

"You got it now. So you get these. Stand still." Omer pinned the three golden triangles of a full Commonwealth induna on my collar tabs and added the crossed iklawa-and-assegai badge of the Impy forces on my left breast pocket. Then he embraced me Kazahk style.

"By rights, Tsaya or Vaivan ought to do that. Why couldn't you have been born a beautiful woman?" I asked him.

We had no trouble with STC. We filed for a full diplomatic priority clearance and got it . . . along with the best service we ever had. STC even kept us informed of the progress of the

Proxinos as the Greek-registry yacht bearing Philip DuBois Wolf also closed on GEO Base One simultaneously. It was as though STC had choreographed a ballet for two ships approaching an abandoned space facility in unison.

They opened communication with us first. "*Tomahok*, this is *Proxinos*. Do not—repeat, do not—dock with GEO Base One. Rendezvous and station-keep one hundred meters outside the station orbit. We will station-keep one hundred meters inside the orbit. Send your representative to the Base on a scoot or by eeveeay. Acknowledge."

"*Proxinos*, this is *Tomahok*. This is hardly diplomatic protocol," I objected.

"This meeting relates to an internal Commonwealth matter and has no diplomatic status."

"But I'm meeting with a representative who's not a citizen of the Commonwealth," I told them.

"I take it I'm talking to Captain Baldwin? This is Philip DuBois Wolf, and I'm a citizen by proclamation of the Provisional Government. If you want the parley you demanded, get over to the portlock now." Philip Dubois Wolf had an accent that said he'd grown up in the prep schools of the American Northeast. It was slowly paced and he used broadened vowel sounds, a far cry from the Good Old Boy Down Home Folksy Drawl of an aerospace pilot and certainly considerably different from the highly inflected Commonwealth English with its shifted vowel sounds that my ears had grown accustomed to.

I told Omer, "Hide in the structure of the Base with the sky junk in case someone decides to take a shot at you while I'm gone. You're my ticket home, Russkie."

"You are a distrustful, sneaky person, Yankee. So are they. Keep your mike open," Omer reminded me needlessly. "If you get into trouble, I will attack the *Proxinos*."

"Did you bring an AR-3?"

"No, I will ram him."

I knew the Mad Russian Space Jockey would.

I hadn't been EVA for over a year, but it's like riding a bicycle: Once you learn, you never forget. Omer had stopped a hundred meters from the end of the hexagonal inspection module. I didn't need a line for that short distance, so I pushed off. There was plenty of Base structure around to grab if my push was misdirected. But I didn't need it. Less than a minute later my boot soles smacked the old metallic plates of the hex module.

Wolf came over on a scoot.

Neither of us said a word to the other. I reached down and opened the portlock hatch. Once inside and sealed, I discovered enough residual pressure on the Base side of the lock to repressurize and let us use the module for a helmets-off conference. Although the photovoltaic cells on the module's external panels were about fifty years old, they had enough poop left to give us internal lighting and fans. I opened my face plate but I didn't turn off my transmitter.

Wolf did and didn't comment that I hadn't. I knew then he wasn't a spaceman. He'd probably learned how to handle a scoot and a pressure suit for sport or recreation in space as had many wealthy people in high-tech countries.

We were surrounded by metal walls that didn't block radio transmissions because they'd been designed and built with plastic-filled slots in every external wall. These acted as slot antennas to retransmit UHF signals in and out, eliminating the need to put an external antenna on every module.

Omer in the *Tomahok* only a few hundred meters away could pick up my suit radio easily. He'd relay it to L-5 and Vershatets.

When Wolf removed the helmet from his old style full-pressure suit and strapped it around a nearby conduit to keep it from floating away, I saw the features of a man who had the bland, undistinguished, forgettable visage of a bank clerk, advertising executive, insurance salesman, or telenewscast actor. To this day, I really don't remember what Philip DuBois Wolf looked like. He wasn't an individual; he was an automatic piece in a bigger game.

I suspected he'd cultivated his unnoteworthy appearance because, as a minor member of the Tripartite, it was to his advantage to be obscure and forgettable. He was one of the faceless people who ran the world.

Wolf didn't bother to be civil and introduce himself. He merely opened a sealed cannister—a space briefcase, as it were—and extracted some hard copies. "Captain Baldwin," he began, deliberately using my former Aerospace Force rank rather than my appointed Commonwealth rank, "do you have the authority to surrender the Commonwealth space facilities and personnel to the Provisional Government?"

"Would I be here if I didn't?" I snapped.

"A procedural question. Are you prepared to surrender them?"

"I'm prepared to discuss it."

"There's nothing to discuss, only the formalities to complete."

"That's not why I'm here," I reminded him. "There's a

question of assurances concerning the treatment and release of Commonwealth citizens now being held hostage in Topawa.''

"Oh, yes, the enemies of the Provisional Government seized at Karederu,'' Wolf muttered absently. "There can be no question of their release. They'd jeopardize the security of the new regime if they had the freedom they enjoyed when they ruled the Commonwealth.''

"I was assured that the hostages would be released unharmed and remain unharmed.'' I bluffed.

"Replay the tape of that conversation. No such assurances were given.'' Wolf called my bluff.

"Then there's nothing further to discuss, and you can return to report the failure of your mission.''

"Then we both will have failed because the Provisional Government will still hold the prisoners. And the price may go up.''

"I don't believe there's a question of price, Wolf, unless you admit to bargaining for power with human lives.''

"This is getting nowhere. I can assure you of the identity and condition of the prisoners and of their proposed disposition under the new regime. In exchange for the solemn promises and high agreements of the Provisional Government, you are to surrender all of the space stations, space factories, space vehicles, and powersats controlled and operated by corporations and other business entities chartered by the former Commonwealth government, and all personnel involved therewith.'' It sounded like he was reading it from the hard copy.

"And I came to find out if there was any basis for trust in your principals. At the moment, I have none, and you've certainly not created any. Furthermore, I'd expected to meet with a high level official, not a lackey called in and given rump authority so Dok and his cohorts wouldn't be exposed to equal risk with me.''

"You've received my bona fides. I hardly think your insulting attitude is justified.'' Wolf was a rude snob. I knew his type. I'd tangled with his buddies, some of whom had found positions in the American government as civilians in charge of military men. Raised by a nanny, sent off to a prep school, graduated from an ivy-covered university with a degree in literature or communications, and working with an investment or publishing firm even though the trust fund meant they didn't need to work at all, I understood now that they were the storm troopers of the power groups The General had taught me about.

"Your Tripartite bosses need the Commonwealth's space wealth and I believe I believe they'll do anything to get it. So how do I know I won't be signing death warrants not only for myself, but also for the hostages?" I asked.

"Sir, you have my word!" Wolf exclaimed.

I snorted a rude expletive. "Every time I've had to deal with a banker like you, it's never been a matter of a man's word, only the hard realities of legal tender and collateral. As far as I'm concerned, I'm returning the favor. *Trust you?* Hell no! You represent Dok, von Undine, and Kokat who've proved they can't be trusted. We'll deal either in the hard realities of agreements with teeth in them or in the equally hard realities of war. Take your choice."

Wolf shrugged noncomittally. "Surrender, or these people die. If you didn't believe the video transmissions, here are hard-copy full-color insta-photos that are impossible to fake." He held out a sheaf of photos.

I looked and wished I hadn't. The photos showed bruises, welts, cuts, and other external injuries. Wolf knew this would raise emotions within me that were useful for his purposes. I couldn't afford to let it warp my judgement in this critical encounter.

"You'll have to account for the injuries these people suffered," I did manage to say.

"There was a struggle when they resisted at Karederu."

That didn't explain every injury I saw.

"What are your terms, Wolf?"

"Total surrender of all Commonwealth people and property off-planet."

"And . . . ?"

"You will be treated well."

I shook my head. "Not good enough, Wolf."

"What more do you want?"

"A written guarantee published worldwide giving assurances that your provisional government and any other government that may grow out of it, if you should win, will observe the strictest adharance to the 1949 Geneva Conventions and the 2001 Manila Agreements relating to the treatment of the wounded and sick, the protection of civilians, and the treatment of prisoners of war. Furthermore, the Helsinki and Bombay human and civil rights standards and provisions must be strictly observed and applied to *all* Commonwealth citizens, past, present and future. Everyone who surrenders, including those you've already taken prisoner, must be treated according to those international standards and accords."

"This is an internal matter. International agreements don't apply."

"They must, or I won't surrender anything."

Wolf sighed and drew a hard copy out of his case. "We've prepared an instrument that spells out in detail every concession my government is ready to make. I suggest you read it because it represents our position in the matter." He started to hand it to me.

I just got it between the fingers of my elastic pressure glove when there was a shuddering jolt and the module started to come apart.

I didn't know what had caused it.

When a module five meters across and thirty meters long with a half-atmosphere internal pressure splits, it goes fast. There's several tons of total pressure on every module panel. When I saw the seam behind Wolf open, instinct made me immediately reach up and close my face plate. Then I concentrated on turning on my backpack.

When I looked about two seconds later, Wolf was gone.

He'd been blown through the opened seam.

But his pressure helmet was still strapped to the conduit.

Suddenly, I was in vacuum with nothing around me. The module had scattered itself in pieces.

The expanding globe of a diffuse flame front washed over me and dissipated in space. Pieces of space ship were tumbling outward from where the *Proxinos* had been parked.

"Sandy! You there?" Omer's voice came through my helmet comm.

"Yo! Omer, you all right? Where are you? Is the *Tomahok* hit?"

"Everything copasetic! The mass of GEO Base One was between me and the explosion. Keep talking. I home on you and pick you up."

"What blew?" I wanted to know.

"Somebody hit *Proxinos* with a hell beam. Explosion blew the module apart, too."

"Where did it come from?"

"North of us in GEO."

"Mark it. Track it. Report it to Ell-Five. Then . . ."

"Easy, Yankee! I got my hands full sneaking through GEO Base structure to get you. I don't want to be a target for that hell beamer. You get aboard, then we do other things."

I saw him coming through the clutter of old GEO Base One modules. A few minutes later I was back in the *Tomahok*.

I still had Wolf's agreement clutched in my hand. I put it away. I never got around to reading it.

Leaving my faceplace closed, I slid into the co-pilot's seat, strapped in, and connected my hoses to the ship supply. "Depressurize!" I told him. "Less damage if we're hit. And I owe you another one, Russkie."

"*Da*, but what now, Yankee?"

"I don't know who shot at us or why, but it'll be probably be explained away as a 'regrettable accident.' "

"*Tomahok*, Vershatets Command relaying through Ell-Five. You read?" my headphones came alive with a new voice.

I keyed my helmet mike. "Roger, Vershatets, *Tomahok* reads you loud and clear."

"Sendi, this is Kivalina. Jeri monitored that hell beam shot from Ell-Five and reports it came from a Janzus Pact facility in inclined geosynch. No single member of that four nation treaty group will ever accept responsibility for the shot because control is spread too thinly between them."

Which meant that hell-beamer was controlled by Tripartite interests.

They'd wanted to hit the *Tomahok*, but it had been too hard to spot. They'd shot at the obvious open target and gotten the *Proxinos* by mistake. Or they'd deliberately wasted the *Proxinos* in order to get the *Tomahok* which they couldn't see.

I took a deep breath and said, "Okay, Russkie, we're going to sit tight and hide in this old structure until we can get a skalavan escort. Then let's quit wasting time. Vaivan's being tortured in Topawa."

"Ah, *Tomahok*, this is the Free Trader *Star Viking*, Captain Kevin Graham commanding," another voice cut in. "Sorry to eavesdrop, but we've been monitoring your meeting with Wolf. Don't waste time calling in your warships. An unarmed escort of ten free traders is converging on GEO Base One. We'll see to it you get back to Ell-Five unharmed. It's impossible to hide a hell beamer shot or space fighter attack on such a large unarmed convoy, and somebody would have to do a lot of explaining when the damage suits came before various courts, to say nothing of the insurance adjusters . . ."

I reached over and punched Omer, then replied, "Hey there, Kevin! Forgot about you!"

"A lot of people have, and we're damned sick of it. There hasn't been much the League of Free Traders could do until now. But they've taken Vamori Free Space Port out of action and otherwise started to raise hell out here. It's cut our livelihood to pieces and damned-near ruined some League members. So we're taking sides. *This has got to stop, and we're going to help you stop it!*''

CHAPTER 19

Return to Topawa

"042950 0800Z> FOR GENERAL RELEASE THIS TIME AND DATE FROM UNITED MITANNI COMMONWEALTH SPACIMPY COMMAND L-5> UNITED MITANNI COMMONWEALTH SPACE VESSELS IN COMPANY WITH LEAGUE OF FREE TRADERS VESSELS IDENTIFIED IN APPENDED MESSAGE WILL MANEUVER IN ORBITAL SPACE COMMENCING IMMEDIATELY TO ASSIST COMMONWEALTH MILITARY FORCES WITH AN INTERNAL REBELLION> THE MOVEMENTS AND ACTIONS OF COMMONWEALTH AND ALLIED VESSELS ARE NOT INTENDED TO THREATEN NONCOMMONWEALTH PROPERTY OR PEOPLE IN SPACE OR ON EARTH> RESPONSIBILITY FOR COST OF DAMAGES INADVERTANTLY CAUSED BY THESE NON HOSTILE ACTIVITIES WILL BE ASSUMED BY THE GOVERNMENT OF THE COMMONWEALTH UPON PRESENTATION THROUGH NORMAL DIPLOMATIC CHANNELS OF DUE PROOF OF CAUSE WHICH IS SUSTAINED BY ARBITRATION UNDER PROVISIONS OF THE 2026 TREATY OF LUXEMBOURG> THE COMMONWEALTH GOVERNMENT RESPECTFULLY REQUESTS THAT THE ACTIONS AND MOVEMENTS OF ITS VESSELS AND THOSE OF ITS ALLIES BE VIEWED WITHOUT PREJUDICE OR FEAR> THE COMMONWEALTH GOVERNMENT FURTHER STATES THAT ANY REPEAT ANY HOSTILE ACTION TAKEN BY ANY REPEAT ANY PERSON FACILITY VESSEL OR NATION AGAINST ITS VESSELS AND PERSONNEL IN SPACE OR ON EARTH WILL BE MET WITH IMMEDIATE RETALIATION> THE GOVERNMENT OF THE COMMONWEALTH HAS NO INTENT OF HARMING OTHERS IN PURSUIT OF ITS OWN INTERNAL DEFENSE AND SELF DETERMINATION> SPACIMPY INDUNA SENDI BOLDWON COMMANDING BY ORDER OF THE EXECUTIVE DEFENSE COUNCIL OF THE GOVERNMENT OF THE UNITED MITANNI COMMON-

WEALTH> END MESSAGE END MESSAGE END MES-
SAGE> 042950 0805Z>''

I sent Kariander Dok my version of Grant's famous message.
"In view of your attack upon me at GEO Base One, no terms
except an unconditional and immediate surrender from you
can be acceptable now. You and your subordinates must
answer fully for the harsh and inhuman treatment of the
Karederu prisoners who must be freed at once. I propose to
move immediately upon your forces."

I never got an answer, but it didn't make any difference
anyway.

"Onward to Richmond!" became "Onward to Topawa!"

Battle cries, shibboleths, and heroic statements serve a
definite purpose in winning a war and are even more important when citizen warriors from a *levee en masse* fight side by
side with professionals.

The battles of Second Oidak, Pitoika Gate, and Topawa are
seldom described in detail in history books because of the revul-
sion most people feel for the violent human activity called war.
But they're still studied at West Point, the U.S. Naval Academy,
Sandhurst, St.Cyr, and the U.S. Aerospace Force Academy.

The Second Battle of Oidak pitted LandImpy and CitImpy
against the so-called Freedom Army. The CitImpy overwhelmed
the enemy by sheer ferocity and the LandImpy reduced strong
points with dogged professionalism. Then the Commonwealth
forces split.

Induno Kivalina Moti commanded the Northern Impy composed of CitImpy troops with LandImpy regiments in reserve.
They quickly regrouped after Oidak and surged along the power
transmission lines toward Vamori Free Space Port.

The Southern Impy was composed of the pride of the LandImpy
reinforced with CitImpy. Induno Pahtu led her troops in the
field, seizing the advantage gained at Oidak to ram columns
along opposite banks of the Topawa River toward the capital,
maintaining contact with the routed Freedom Army.

CoastImpy Flotilla Eight under Induno Shokutu fought a naval
battle as classic as Salamis. Shokutu's small, fast hydrodynes
mined Pitoika Gate under the Sunrise Bridge, then withdrew.
When the Freedom Army's reinforcement convoy approached,
Shokutu's hydrodyne force trapped them between the mined
harbor mouth and the open sea, outmaneuvered the convoy
screen, brought the convoy under attack, and sent all but three
ships either to the bottom or aground on the Sun Coast south of

Pitoika where the CitImpy slaughtered the shipwrecked mercenaries who came ashore.

I shouldn't have doubted the fighting capabilities of Commonwealth people, professional or amateur. The *coup's* biggest mistake was failure to gain control of communications and movement. Without these, they couldn't prevent the buildup or coordination of the impys.

The failure to control communications also meant that the pictures of the Karederu hostages were seen everywhere.

It doesn't help a military leader to be emotional, but emotion can motivate warriors.

The General's philosophy of the world of plenty and its success in the Commonwealth *had* been successfully communicated to three generations of people who were also kept reminded about the brutal life of times gone by. No one had the slightest desire to even sample that. Every citizen knew he'd been armed and trained because only he could prevent it from returning some day.

Man and woman, they fought.

They fought with a fury, gallantry, and *élan* comparable to when the Mahdi's *Jehad* forces overwhelmed Gordon's garrison in Khartoum or Cetewayo's kwaZulu forces broke the British square at Isandhlwana. Or when the Suomis stood firm then pushed the Russian Bear back into its own territory. They reminded me of the United States Marines at Guadalcanal or Wolmi, and the 101st Airborne at Bastogne. Their leaders weren't hesitant or fearful in the haze of battle and didn't use obsolete tactics.

The Commonwealth malcontents and outlander mercenaries who made up the Freedom Army had neither the legacy nor the will to withstand such an onslaught. They were worthy adversaries but couldn't match people who even in peacetime carried iklawas at their waists.

As CIC and SpacImpy commander, my missions were the recapture of Vamori-Free followed by the Topawa assault. I planned to move fast and alter plans in the face of new situations. That's the classic formula for winning a battle or a war. Like General Nathan Bedford Forrest, I wanted to git thar fustest with the mostest men.

Holding and defending a space port had never been done before, and the Freedom Army consisted of land warriors whose only experience with vertical envelopment had been with armored aerodynes. They planned to defend Vamori-Free on the ground and moved in a few shoulder-launched SAMs to defend against low-level tacair. They didn't know how anyone could attack and invade a space port from space.

I did.

A space port is mostly space.

Vamori Free Space Port covered more than 7,500 square kilometers and stretched more than 150 kilometers along the seacoast. It was larger than some nations. During normal operations, 25,000 people lived and worked there.

We mounted a two-pronged effort against the Vamori-Topawa objectives. Pahtu's river offensive would pin down Freedom Army forces at Topawa. Moti's Northern Impy would to hit the western edge of Vamori-Free by following the power transmission lines from Oidak.

Then my space contingent would strike Vamori-Free and land

It sounds easier than it was.

I first had to sanitize the threat of a couple hundred SAMs at Vamori-Free, then force the Freedom Army to keep their heads down. Omer would command our eight skalavans on low level passes at high mach numbers too fast for SAM reaction. The ear-busting shock waves would spread confusion among warriors who'd never experienced anything like it before—and at that time, nobody had because Omer had developed it while he was having "fun" letting it all hang out on high-Mach low-level tree-breaking flights.

Omer's skalavan sweeps would be followed immediately by tacair strikes to reduce the SAM threat. This operation was critical and had to be coordinated carefully with Moti's AirImpy squadrons because skalavans and tacair aerodynes moved at vastly different speeds.

Military C-cubed—command, control, and communications—was our biggest headache, as it always is in any battle. Our comm frequencies would be spotted quickly. But a number of different forces would be operating on this mission—Pahtu's Southern LandImpy sweeping toward Topawa, Moti's Northern LandImpy racing toward Vamori, Dati's AirImpy tacair squadrons supporting them, and my SpacImpy dropping from the sky in two elements: Omer's skalavan squadron, and Ursila's landing assault group. We used multiplex communications: each group working its own frequency and monitoring the other four. It would be difficult for the enemy to monitor all five channels simultaneously and sort out intragroup and intergroup messages and commands. It didn't buy us secrecy, but it did buy us time.

The tacair strikes were to be followed by a second pass of Omer's skalavans to cover the landing of Ursila's packets and free trader ships manned by as many swat teams as we could put together from CitImpy people in space. Some had to be flown by a single pilot because we were short of pilots. There was no ground power for landing aids at Vamori-Free and shipborne radars don't have the precision necessary for landing, so Omer had the crucial task of dropping a landing beacon on his second pass.

With Ali's family in danger, it would have wrong to have kept him in L-5 in spite of his emotional condition. I didn't want him in a command capacity, but he could fight. We were short of pilots, so Ali flew the *Tomi*.

When the landing assault force hit dirt, most of the enemy SAMs should have been out of action and most enemy troops in confusion or pinned down by Moti's land attack on Vamori-Free's western edge. We'd then operate from behind.

Once the Vamori Free Space Port was consolidated, our combined forces would turn southwesterly and pincer the final objective, Topawa.

A rescue mission involving vertical envelopment of Topawa Centrum was my responsibility after the landing.

It looked good in the computer. But Murphy's Law always has the last word. People suffer from failure of judgement, fail to seize opportunities, or fail to be where they're supposed to be when they're supposed to be there. That makes ball games and battles.

Everything went beautifully from L-5 down. STC was co-operative and got other ships out of our way. Or perhaps it was the other way around: other ships, fearful we'd strike anyone who got in our way, deliberately saved STC the trouble by scheduling around our armada's flight. No one wanted openly to start a war.

RIO Commandant Peter Rutledge gave me call as we left lunar orbit: "I say, Sandy, I do hope you won't spot the carpet, old chap. If this internal affair among you Commonwealth types were to blossom into something else, RIO would its level best to keep it confined to the ground. Rather new RIO policy, old boy. As you jolly well know, vacuum is somewhat thin and lonely stuff, and nobody out here really wants to get involved. If the balloon were to go up, I rather suspect from talking with the military commanders above LEO that most of them would turn out to be rather devout cowards, although none of them would ever admit it. Space is already far too dangerous without having others shooting at one's pressure hull. So we'll bloody well manage to keep anyone from shooting at anyone else. But be a sport, Sendi: don't ask how. You know full well what's out here . . ."

Was I glad to hear that! Maybe we wouldn't have Space War II after all. "Thank you, Commander Rutledge of the Space Patrol," I replied because, like it or not, that's exactly what he was.

We operated under STC clearance to prevent anything or anybody from getting in our way. Although this compromised secrecy and surprise, we gained the respect of others because, even in the midst of our great internal upheaval, we played by the rules. There may have been some tense fingers poised over buttons because we broached the engagement zones of several facilities, but nobody shot at us. Anybody who wanted to know where we were at any given instant could find out. And we damaged nothing.

But once Omer got his skalavans in the atmosphere, he let it all hang out. I wished I'd been with him, but I couldn't have gotten to the necessary level of competence. Hard as it was to accept, at physical age 28 I was already an over-the-hill space jock when it came to one-man hot vehicles like skalavans, Space Hawks, or Black Tigers.

I could hear Omer: "Hokay, Blue Boomers commence east pass. Blue Two and Blue Three formate on me. Down to angels one. Keep your canards retracted. Yo ho! Getting very hot! Mach fifteen! Hokay, Blue Boomers, close on me, commence nine gee loop . . . now. Uh . . . Red Boomers, commence your south pass, angels one. Hokay, I see you in my canopy. Yellow Boomers, start your run now! Green Boomers, you are out of position, but start east run now!"

The passes of eight ten-ton black skalavans at Mach 15 a kilometer above Vamori Free Space Port were enough to cause considerable damage from shock wave overpressures alone. The hypersonic carpets laid back and forth across the huge expanse of Vamori-Free not only caused the sort of confusion and consternation we'd hoped for, but also damaged fragile structures. It was a good thing one of the Commonwealth's primary industries is glassmaking because there wasn't a window left in any building in the immense vastness of the port.

Low-level tacair aerodyne gun ships were standing by. "Stomper Leader, this is Boomer Leader," Omer's voice continued. "You are clear to clobber. Quick look shows joy for you near Areas One-zero, One-seven, Three-two and Niner-zero. You have five minutes—mark!—before we start our second pass."

"Boomer Leader, Stomper Leader, tally ho! Recon confirms

quick look, and we are engaging. Blue Stomper to Ten, Red Stomper to Seventeen, Yellow Stomper to Thirty-two, and Green Stomper to Ninety. Purple Stomper, stand by to cover.''

"Boomers all, this is Boomer Leader, formate on me for second pass, line abeam, present co-ordinates are on computer down-link from Boomer Leader. Formation join-up location is on your display. Press for join-up now.''

"Purple Stomper, this is Stomper Leader. Join Yellow Stomper at Thirty-two for SAM suppression.''

Our ships went into blackout. When we came out of it, I heard the tacair mission commander call, "Red Stomper, join Yellow Stomper to cover for Purple Stomper. Never mind the comments. The tape replay will show what happened.''

We were over Vamori-Free's western horizon now, but I couldn't pick up Omer's implanted landing beacon. "Slugger Leader, this is Bold One. Do you receive signals from Prong Alpha?''

Ursila's voice came back, "Bold One, this is Slugger Leader. Negative on Prong Alpha. Something's gone wrong, Sendi!''

"Boomer Leader, this is Bold One coming out of blackout with Slugger. We are negative on Prong Alpha. Repeat, negative on Prong Alpha. Any problem?''

"Uh, Bold One, this is Stomper Leader. Purple Stomper was too high, and Boomer Leader made his second pass low to deploy Prong Alpha. They had a mid-air.''

Ohmygawd! Omer! Omer! The Mad Russian Space Jockey had let it all hang out . . . and some damned fool was where he shouldn't have been and cut it off. At a closure rate of Mach fifteen, neither had seen each other. The aerodyne may have been on Omer's screen, but he probably didn't have time to look at it.

It was my fault for mixing Mach zero aerodynes with Mach fifteen space ships!

There was no time to grieve then. We were less than five minutes from landing with no landing beacon to steer us in. If I didn't do something instantly, there would be a lot of pranged space ships.

"Slugger Leader, this is Bold One. Did you monitor that?''

"Affirmative! Sendi, I'll get down using calibrated eyeballs, but some of my pilots can't do it without help,'' Ursila reported.

"Get a beacon down there. *Any* beacon!''

"Stomper Leader, this is Bold One. Can you put your aerodyne in Area Twenty-four with its beacon squawking four-zeroes?''

"I'll draw fire if I do!"

"If you don't, you'll have real fire all around you from burning space ships! Or we'll overfly and leave you up the crick. Take your choice. We need your beacon in four minutes."

"I can't risk my . . ."

"Stomper Leader, this is CitImpy Prime One." It was Kivalina who cut in. "Comply with Bold One's request *now*! Everyone's risking everything here. *Topawa or the Dilkons!*"

That was The General's last call to his warriors before the First Battle of Oidak.

The reaction and reply were immediate: "Topawa or the Dilkons! Stomper Leader is cushioning in Area Twenty-four *now*, beacon squawking four zeroes. But please don't land on me!"

"Don't worry. And thank you," I told him. "Sluggers all from Bold One, critical instructions. Tape for replay. No time to repeat. Landing beacon is squawking four zeroes at Area Two-four. Repeat: Area Two-four. Have your computer offset for your specific landing coordinates. No need to acknowledge. Comply and execute . . . or you'll have a damned rough landing unless you put it in the ocean which isn't much softer. Break, break! Moti, what's the ground situation? Are they going to shoot at us?"

"Bold One, recon reports almost all enemy troops at Vamori-Free are involved with my units. Hey, Sendi, don't get your legs shot up, okay?"

"Give me covering fire this time, Kivalina."

With a momentary surge of grief, I recalled what Omer had taught me about working without the assistance of modern technology. I had two eyes and a functioning brain behind them. The *Tomahok* was a machine, a tool, and it was up to me to make it do what I wanted it to do. Omer had also been right in telling me that some day my life would depend on my ability to make a machine perform in spite of itself.

I had a load of swats, young Commonwealth space facility technicians and mechanics who'd gone through only CitImpy training. I told them to strap down, secure weapons, and stand by to land.

Tomahok swung around the alignment circle and the Area 73 runway was ahead. At 350 kilometers per hour, there isn't much time for making and correcting mistakes. I had it knocked until someone started shooting at me. A small SAM zipped past my nose and missed because I'd just deployed the forward canards

which decelerated *Tomahok* with their drag. Then tracers laced
the sky in front of me.

*Forget the shooting! If I get distracted now, I'll buy the farm
anyway!* If *Tomahok* took some hits, I didn't notice them. I got
on the runway and the hook caught the third decelerator cable,
which wasn't bad considering I'd landed with no help other than
a pair of experienced eyeballs while being shot at in the process.

The two-gee stop was designed for cargo payloads. My harness
held because it was designed to. But three of my seven swats
were injured.

It took all five of us to get the three unconscious young men
out of the ship and into the ops shack. I left it to two Vamori-
Free technicians there to patch up the busted legs and broken
arms.

I went back aboard to get my AR-3 rifle and bandolier of
clips, grenades, plastic explosive wads, and initiators. As I left
the cabin, I looked back over the tail of the *Tomahok* and saw
another space ship lined up for landing! Some green pilot got
confused about his assigned landing strip. Once committed to a
landing, there was no way on God's little blue Earth that the
pilot could abort and land elsewhere. I ran like hell because two
space ships were going to hit.

The explosion blew me off my feet head first into the mud
alongside the runway. One look at the pile of burning junk told
me nobody had survived.

My swats were nowhere to be seen or found. They'd melted
into the landscape to harass the enemy's rear as instructed.

I heard the distant popping sound of gunfire accompanied by
the occasional thump of a grenade or tube rocket doing its job.
But there was no action around Area 73.

In the propellant loading area next to the launch complex, I
found an emergency shower and washed the mud and grime off
me and my AR-3. A quick inspection revealed the assault rifle
hadn't been harmed. The old stories about its rugged constitution
were right.

Where were Ursila and Ali? They were supposed to land in
Areas 72 and 74. But no ships were in either area or in the sky.
Everyone was down somewhere on Vamori-Free . . . I hoped.

I had to move without them. Getting to Topawa for the rescue
was far more important than searching for my support. Vamori-
Free was too big to search alone. *If* everybody else involved in
the rescue mission followed instructions, they'd grab the nearest
aerodyne or other transport to Topawa and get there as fast as
possible. I had to hope Ali was in condition to do so, but I

couldn't worry about him any more than I could afford then to grieve over Omer.

A ComSpat aerodyne was parked near the ops shack. I got in, kept the window open with the black snout of my AR-3 sticking out, and punched the universal emergency start code: 11-20-01. I went up to ten meters in hover then headed southwest at full slot. I managed to see power lines and towers in time to go under or around them. I was hard to see coming because of my speed, and impossible to see after I'd gone by because of the sand, dirt, and other junk thrown up by the aerodyne's exhaust. A couple of tube rockets did catch me but went harmlessly past, their aerodynamic stabilization joggled by the aerodyne's blast.

I swiveled the aerodyne into a left slip with the muzzle of the AR-3 pointing along the line of flight because I saw a prime target I couldn't ignore: about fifty men in grey uniforms getting into an armored aerodyne. The AR-3's directionally-solidified bullets would penetrate that vehicle if they missed the men. I opened up on full auto at maximum range. By the time I'd used up the clip of fifty rounds I was over and past them.

There were a lot of aerodynes in the air, but none of them came close enough to shoot or be shot at. It looked like a hell of a fight going on to the west; there was a lot of dust and smoke, and the air was thick with tacair aerodynes.

When I zipped over a railway line, everything changed. I was suddenly over open country on a beautiful "blue" day with the railway line running straight toward the far white buildings of Topawa. I stayed at ten meters; I didn't want to hit a train.

As I grew closer to Topawa, I discovered we'd goofed by not being briefed on Topawa's layout and where the national museum was. Ali had said it was in the Centrum where the old colonial buildings still stood, some in use by the unusually small Commonwealth government, others left as exhibits and museums. I remembered from my first auto trip from the railway station to Karederu that there was a central plaza where the public gallows were located. That had to be the Centrum.

I roared down Chiawuli Street between the taller buildings and found the Centrum at the end of it.

It was deadly quiet and there wasn't a soul in sight. *They've moved the prisoners!* I told myself. But it wouldn't hurt to look anyway. So I cushioned the aerodyne in the Centrum plaza and got out, AR-3 at the ready.

Which building was the national museum? I had to go to each in turn to read the sign in front or look at what was cut into the sandstone above the entrance. The fourth one I came to was the National Museum.

The front doors were open. I dropped to my belly and peered around the bottom corner of the huge entrance. Two armed men in grey uniforms were talking about twenty meters down the hallway. One wore a crew-cut under his grey beret, but the other wore a kaftan. I caught part of the conversation:

"How long are we stuck here, Fritz?"

"They'll bring 'em out now, Ben. The aerodyne just arrived for the meat."

I didn't intend to wait. I stuck the barrel of the AR-3 around the corner and squeezed off two shots.

Both soldiers were thrown about four meters down the hall by the impacts. Almost before they hit the floor, I was on my feet and moving.

The sign was still there:

ENTRANCE
OLD COLONIAL SECURITY POLICE
INTERROGATION CHAMBERS AND DUNGEONS
Children Must Be Accompanied By Adults

Someone was in the spiral stone staircase that led down into the bowels of the building. He was wearing the grey uniform of Kariander Dok's Freedom Army, so I shot him through the chest. I followed his body down. Then someone else yelled in Arabic and shot from below. The bullet hit the stone walls and exploded, sending shards of chips into the stairway. I didn't bother to shoot back. I pulled the pin on a grenade and dropped it. Most of the shock wave was attenuated by the spiraling walls, and as it slapped over me I started down again.

Apparently, there'd been only two sentries by the heavy iron door at the bottom. I'd gotten them both.

But the door was latched from the inside. I couldn't swing it open.

When I put my ear to the door's surface, I heard the sounds of a scuffle beyond. I couldn't tell what was going on.

But the door hung to swing outward on massive iron hinges at the top and bottom. I molded plastic explosive around both hinges, set the initiators for ten seconds, and ran back up the spiral stairway.

I hadn't used much explosive, but it was enough to blow the hinges off.

The doorway was filled with dust when I got to it. I stepped through, ready to shoot down whoever was beyond the pall.

I got one of the biggest surprises of my life.

Heinrich von Undine lay on the floor, his belly slit open from chest to crotch. Standing over him holding an iklawa dripping blood was Conobabi Chukut Nogal, the President of the United Mitanni Commonwealth.

There were other bloody forms laying on the floor. I recognized one of them as Wahak Teaq who had apparently died with iklawa in hand.

A totally unbelieveable sight was Vaivan Teaq, clothes in tatters, the bruises of shackles on her wrists, neck, and ankles. She held Kariander Dok against the wall with one hand while she plunged an iklawa into his heart with the other.

Tsaya had been right. The word "iklawa" does resemble the sound the weapon makes when it's withdrawn from the body of an enemy.

CHAPTER 20

Manna

"Nobody's hurt beyond repair or disfigured permanently," Tsaya explained. "With the expertise here in Vershatets and at Ell-Five, we can rehabilitate everyone, even those who were given psychodrugs and allopeptides. And thanks to biocosmetics, there won't be any physical scars."

"But there are psychological scars, Tsaya," I added, "even among those who weren't in that torture chamber."

"Those scars may not be as deep as your cultural background may lead you to believe, *moapa*."

"I didn't like what I saw, and I don't have to like it. Dammit, Tsaya, I don't even like to think about the mercenaries I shot!"

"Sendi, you're a professional military man. You should know that wars can't be fought without casualties."

I looked over at the AR-3 that now hung muzzle-down on the wall. "I thought I was a fighting man, but fighting in the air and space is sanitary. It's something else to fire that AR-3 and watch a man weighing a hundred kilos get tossed four meters through the air by the impact of a bullet that also tears his guts out. I never before saw what happens to a man when he dies. Death turns out to be grisly . . . and real." I snorted with distaste and looked away from the weapon. "I never want to touch that thing again."

"Sendi, you may have to and you will when the time comes." Tsaya sat in my lap and tried to comfort me. "Until everyone knows The General's truth about the world of plenty, we'll have to fight to protect ourselves from those who try to take things away and make us slaves. It'll take time to conquer greed and power lust."

"That can't happen too soon for me." I shook my head. "But why does it have to cost so much to get people to see the obvious?"

"People have never seen it before, Sendi."

"The costs are enormous! Omer alone makes it too costly for my likes. but there was also Wahak . . ."

"You must go to Vaivan, *moapa*," Tsaya told me.

"Dearest, you know the risks a man takes consoling a widow."

"Of course, but we're known for taking risks. You took a risk tackling me at Karederu that far ago night. And we both took risks in marrying each other yesterday."

Why had I wed this cool, professional witch doctor? Do I have to have a reason? No one else needs one! It was far more than the heightened sexual drive that results from being shot at. I didn't have to get married to bed Tsaya.

Some psychotechnicians claim a man marries a woman who reminds him of his mother. There may be something to that. Tsaya did with one exception: she showed her love. I hadn't been celebate during my years in the Aerospace Force where succulent young people were always eager for those who'd assumed the heroic mantles of the sailors, railway men, aviators, and astronauts who'd preceeded them. But I'd never *loved* a woman before or had her love me. It's a fortunate man who marries his first love.

But the marriage ceremony had disappointed me because I'm a romantic; most Americans are. In the hybrid Commonwealth culture, the wedding bore the greatest resemblance to the Muslim practice.

I never informed my parents in Santa Barbara because they existed only as a dim memory. I was now a different person with a different name and a different way of life half a world away.

I was very happy except for one nagging thing that nibbled at me and wouldn't turn loose: Vaivan.

"Sendi, I know you better than you think. You must go to Vaivan. *Please* do so, *moapa*!" Tsaya insisted.

Tsaya's a strong-willed person, and I couldn't reason with her. Actually, my excuses weren't based on reason at all, but emotion. The images of that video transmission and those color photographs wouldn't vanish from my memory over night.

I decided to treat it as the duty of visiting recently-widowed wives of pilot comrades who'd bought the farm by plowing it.

To my relief, I found General Vamori sitting with Vaivan on a porch of the R&R center overlooking the green, watered Vicrik valley and the towering white bulk of Mount Doradun and the Dilkons. Synflesh covered most of her reconstruction, but the mere presence of those dressings reminded me of her ordeal.

"Sit down, sit down," The General offered, swinging a chair around. "A spaceman is never used to standing or walking on Earth."

"Yes, please sit down, Sendi," Vaivan repeated, her voice

and words thick because of the reconstructive surgery on her face and the lingering effects of psychodrugs. "I'm very glad to see you again."

I took the chair and told her, "So am I. There were times when I wondered if we ever would, Vaivan."

"It's over," she said.

"Not really," I said. "It may never be over in our lifetimes. But this one's over for now."

"Do you foresee an end to it, Sendi?" The General asked.

"I don't know. It's too soon for me to straighten out my thinking," I admitted. "The Tripartite still exists. We didn't hurt them much."

"But we survived the very worst they could do to us, Sendi," Vaivan pointed out quietly. "They can't ignore us. We won't go away. And they can't destroy us. We have too many friends now."

"And you changed the game, Sendi," The General added.

"Me?"

"You," The General said with a nod. "It's no longer the same system. RIO is now a non-national space patrol that commands the respect of everyone. You made that transition happen with your willingness to throw away provincial loyalties in favor of broader ones—an *extremely* difficult thing to do because one loses old friends and can only hope to keep the new ones."

I had to nod in agreement, too, but I did so sadly. "But because of what I did I can never go home again."

"It was never 'home' in the first place," The General observed, and he was right as usual.

"Sendi, the Santa Fe agreement collapsed yesterday," Vaivan said.

"I didn't know that. I've been . . . uh . . . busy."

Vaivan smiled knowingly. "Yes. The League of Free Traders refused to operate to space ports that imposed the Santa Fe Tariffs. League captains simply diverted to Vamori-Free. The League action didn't last eighteen hours because it disrupted commerce so badly that the various governments involved had to give in. You were the one who called the Tripartite's bluff in Geo Base One, Sendi."

"I don't care for the credit line," I remarked after a moment, "because tomorrow the world will ask me what I've done for it lately. *Sic transit gloria mundi*. It's nice to know, but that and a tally will buy me a shot of *supaku*. And if it's a new game, we'd better get busy figuring out the rules."

"This time," The General promised, "we'll help make the rules."

"Maybe, maybe." And maybe the last few weeks had made me cynical, or perhaps I was suffering from too much tension, not enough sleep, meals on the run, and trying to juggle seventeen balls in the air at once.

It was time stop stalling and do my duty while The General was still present. "I . . . I'm sorry about Wahak," I tried to express my sympathy, but it came out in trite and halting words.

She smiled in spite of the fact that it probably hurt her to do so. "We all are. But Wahak died fighting. He didn't stand there and wait to be killed. Do you know what happened in the museum, Sendi?"

"No, I haven't really wanted to talk about it with anyone."

"I *want* to talk about it because I'm *proud* of what happened! When we heard you shoot in the stairs, Kariander Dok gave the order to use us as human shields for the triumvirate's escape. Kokat was scared and got reckless when he unchained Wahak. My husband killed him and released Chervit who released me . . ."

"Uh, look, it's difficult to talk . . ." I began. I was the one who was finding it difficult.

"Difficult? Why?" Vaivan said with her eyes suddenly sparkling. "You had the difficult job, Sendi. You didn't know what was happening but you tried to save us anyway. You did. You made Dok panic. That made it possible for us to free ourselves and fight."

I couldn't imagine it. "Vaivan, you'd been physically and mentally tortured for over a week. How'd you have the strength to do *anything*?"

"What's preferable? To wait to be killed as cattle strung up for slaughter in an abattoir? Or to fight and die like human beings?"

"If one acts like a slave, one will be treated like a slave," The General said.

"It was a fair fight." Vaivan slowly worked the fingers of her hands under their synflesh to exercise the healing tendons.

"Fair?" I wasn't sure what her concept of "fair" was.

"Fair. Dok and I were both armed. It began equally and ended humanely," Vaivan said, then explained, "If Dok had survived, Stoa Silut and the Board of Jurisprudence might have sentenced him to public hanging or dismemberment and beheading."

"But I thought the only capital punishment here was hanging."

The General remarked, "Based on the nature of the crime, the Board of Jurisprudence may sentence an outlander to be pun-shed under Commonwealth law or the law of the offender's native land. It gives them latitude."

"As for Heinrich von Undine, Wahak was merciful, too," Vaivan went on, the brightness gone from her eyes and replaced with a rather grim look. "Von Undine was from the German enclave that remains at Dar-es-Salaam. The Board of Jurisprudence would've had the option of using his nation-of-origin's punishment for sexual offenses. In spite of all he did to me, that punishment is more than any man should face. That's why I wanted to get him first, but President Nogal was closer."

The General stood up. Perhaps he wanted Vaivan and me to be alone. I wasn't sure that's what I wanted. His presence made this far more comfortable for me. "Please excuse me. There is work to do. We don't have to rebuild our Commonwealth, but we do have to repair it. Sendi, you're no longer my deputy. You have your own distinguished career and the family ties to cement it. SpacImpy Induna Chervit served to the end and died with honor, iklawa in hand. You're his logical successor with a recent combat record to justify your permanent promotion and appointment. They'll be announced tomorrow."

I sighed. "General, I'm sick of fighting. I'm resigning for the second time this year. I think I'd be a better historian."

"And I'm the archaeologist who was a better warrior," General Anegam Vamori pointed out. "Sendi, don't resist the profession in which you're outstanding. I resisted once when I became a leader rather than the scientist I wanted to be. I was an unhappy man. Then I discovered it was possible to be what I'm good at *and* what I wanted to be. Sendi, the ability to do *anything* well is a prize beyond price that many people long to possess."

He started to walk away, then turned to add, "Sendi, I won't always be here. Long ago I exhausted my right to live. Someday I must get out of the way of young people such as yourself. It may be the best thing left for me to do. However, you'll carry on. For that knowledge, an old man is very, very happy."

I watched him descend the steps from the porch and walk in a surprisingly spry manner down the graveled drive to disappear into the conifers.

Neither Vaivan nor I said anything for minutes.

"I'm glad you came to see me, Sendi," Vaivan repeated.

"Well, I wanted to make sure you were okay. Losing Wahak is a difficult thing. I know."

"How can you know, Sendi?"

I sighed and told her, "Because I've done this before when a fellow pilot bought it. The waiting wife had to be told . . . and she'd been waiting for it and hoping against hope maybe for years. Vaivan, these 'widow calls' don't get any easier. I've made too many and I don't want to make any more.''

"This is different, Sendi."

"How?"

"Wahak didn't die far away from everyone he loved and who loved him. He died with me, fighting for me and for everyone else there. It wasn't pleasant. But, oh, am I proud of that man!''

Wahak had been such a quiet, peaceful, almost pliant person. He'd also been a highly civilized man because he controlled the basic savage that's in all of us. "I'm sorry."

"Why?"

"I understand him."

"Many people did."

"I also underestimated the Commonwealth and its people . . .''

"Some people did that, too." Vaivan looked squarely at me and told me, "And I underestimated you, Sendi. If you hadn't convinced Rutledge with your honesty, the powersats would be pumping hell beams now. If you hadn't gone to GEO Base One to gain some time, the Tripartite wouldn't have seen that they were up against people of principle which made the cost of winning greater than the price of co-existence. And without your assault from space, this civil war could have dragged on in killing and misery for years . . .''

"I had lots of help. And our people really won this one at Dehkar Gorge, Oidak, Vamori-Free, and Topawa Centrum. I can't take credit for a bit of it.''

"Oh, there were great acts of gallantry and courage in all the impys," Vaivan admitted. "But when you took Vamori Free Space Port you made it appear to the enemy that you could bring down infinite reserves and materiel from space. It was almost supernatural . . . magic . . . god-like.''

"Exodus Sixteen," I told her. "And several others.''

"Yes, but you did it.''

"With the help of others, including your idealistic, emotional twin brother . . . but he's exactly the sort of man we need on our frontier. There's a lot to be done out there, and he's the best man for it. He leads people well although he's no military man. He thought he was until the Vamori-Free mission. There's a lot of his grandfather in him.''

"That's where he gets his idealism, Sendi.''

"And lots of your grandfather in you, too.''

"Probably, but it's the other side of him that's my genetic

nheritance, I think.'' Vaivan suddenly looked intensely at me with those beautiful dark eyes of hers. ''And you're the mirror image of my grandfather.''

''I don't agree with him or with you on that.''

''It doesn't make any difference whether you do or not. You re who you are. We'll need the mirror image of The General now that we're in a new game.''

''Don't you think we should wait to see what history has to say?''

Vaivan managed to shake her head in spite of the synflesh around her throat. ''Sendi, you know history, but General Vamori *understands* it. If I may quote our prophet, 'History doesn't repeat itself; historians merely repeat each other.' ''

''You may be right.'' It was a phrase I used when I didn't want to argue pending a further study. ''But, Vaivan, you used the term, 'our prophet.' This part of the world has produced some of the world's leaders, but no prophets until now. Isn't it rather ironic it produced General Anegam Vamori?''

Vaivan smiled. It was a strained smile, and I knew it bothered her although accu-blocks were eliminating pain. ''To repeat what our prophet says about that, 'The times encourage the man of the times to change the times.' ''

''Who's going to write the holy book?'' I asked.

''What holy book?''

''Well, if history is a guide, somebody will write down the sayings of The General as the prophet of plenty,'' I explained, ''and it will become dogma for the new religion.''

''Sendi, all we have to do is take the words of other prophets and synthesize them into the new holy book . . .''

''So what else is new? How did all the other holy books of the world come to be?''

Vaivan was quiet for a moment, then asked, ''When are you going to start writing it?''

''That's up to someone else. There are other things for me to do.''

''Are you so sure?''

''About what?''

''Military men usually write their memoirs. What are those other than history? You told The General you'd make a better historian. Perhaps *you're* the one who should document this year of twenty-fifty A.D. in the Commonwealth.''

''I might, but not for that reason. We stopped Space War Two, but the hell beams are still there. The mass drivers and catapults didn't play a role, but they could throw rocks in future wars. We'll be moving planetoids soon, and a planetoid's the ultimate planet-busting terror weapon. Until The General's philosophy of plenty becomes fully understood and followed *somebody* will try to twist these technologies for military use.''

"Sendi, you use the word 'military' as an evil qualifier, word with negative semantic charge. It doesn't have to be."

"That's bothered me for years" I unloaded on her. It was paradox that haunted my professional life. Tsaya with her scientific outlook wouldn't understand it, but Vaivan might because she had a working knowledge of the real world. "We need technology desperately, but how can we keep it from being used for destructive military purposes? *How?*"

"I don't know why it bothers you," she replied without hesitation. "We've managed to do it. You do it yourself, Sendi. The destructive aspects of military activities can be kept in check and eventually overcome only by military professionalism itself. We honor the warrior because we're all warriors unafraid to fight if we really have to . . . although you didn't think we would. You didn't know that one of the principles we're taught came from your first president who was a prophet in his own right. We had to learn his words by heart, and it's the basis for our custom of carrying iklawas: *If we desire to avoid insult we must be ready to repel it; if we desire to secure peace, one of the most powerful institutions of our rising prosperity, it must be known that we are at all times ready for war.*"

"It's a different world in America today," I observed.

"Not really. It still produces people like you, Sendi. It just lost its momentum, and we were swept into the vacuum that was created. So were you."

"Be that as it may, Vaivan, my job now is to use the knowledge and experience I've got to keep all hell from breaking loose."

"Don't you believe Peter Rutledge feels the same way?"

I nodded.

"We aren't alone."

"But we've got very powerful adversaries. The Tripartite and the other power groups aren't going to go away."

"But they respect us now." She thought a moment, then added, "We've changed the world power balance, and it'll take time for the new system to stop ringing from the sudden change. We'll exploit that because we know it's happening. We'll also exploit the most valuable resource we've got: brainpower. We're the first to know the system's open. And we're the first to make use of it. Sendi, it won't be easy, but do you have a better picture of how you fit into the scheme of things now?''

''Yes.'' Then I asked, ''But what about you, Vaivan? You've helped me. How can I help you? *Can* I help you?''

''I've spent the long hours of the past day or so bringing myself up to date on what happened. It made it easier for me. I know what you did. I know what everybody did. But we've got to go on from here. Life goes on. I'll survive, Sendi.''

I'd seen it before: the squaring of the shoulders, the head held proudly high, the announcement to the world of the intention to forge bravely onward in spite of everything while the inner grief gnawed. At least, I thought this was the same. That's why when Vaivan reached out her bandaged hand to me, I took it even though I abhor the feeling of cool, synthetic synflesh.

''If you mean to provide solace and sympathy to the widow of a valorous man,'' she told me levelly, ''don't neglect the fact that our family ties are very strong. In fact, you're a family member.'' She sat back and looked out at the lovely mountains. ''I know you're 'family' because every member of my family has been to see me to share grief. But I think you came for other reasons, Sendi.''

I said nothing. I couldn't.

The beauty of this incredible woman was more than what was hidden by surgical dressings and synflesh coverings, and it radiated from her as she went on, ''You're the product of a puritanical culture, Sendi. There's nothing wrong with that. But you Americans are frustrated romantics because of it. On the other hand, we're logical people trapped in a romantic culture. I don't know which is worse, but all people have their problems.''

Her radiance was too much for me. I couldn't contain myself, so I blurted out, ''Dammit, I'm a newly and happily married man with a lovely, beautiful, talented wife! But I've also been deeply in love with you, Vaivan, since the first moment I saw you! And I've grown to love you more and more as I've gotten to know you! I held back because you were a married woman. Now I've got to continue to hold back because I'm the married one! But I had to tell you! I wanted to tell you but I couldn't. I was afraid to tell you, and I forced myself to come here today on the pretext of duty.''

''Oh, I'm glad you did, Sendi. It's been a time of war, and we haven't had time to talk of love . . . but I love you, too.''

I got up. ''I'd better go now . . .''

I was at the edge of the porch before she called out to me, "Sendi, you're being provincial."

I turned to face her. I didn't say anything. I couldn't say anything.

"My dearest Sendi," she went on, "we're a free people because we have a philosophy of abundance for everyone. Within the bounds of civil behavior, freedom also means there are few moral restrictions outside one's religion, if you have one. A free person's morality is based on what's right without harming others. What do *you* think is right for you, for Tsaya, and for me?"

"I don't know. The more I learn about this place, the more confused I get."

"Let me see if I can help. Tsaya told you to come and knows you're here, correct?"

"Yes."

"And all three of us realize we live in a world that has plenty of everything for everyone, correct?"

"I'm not sure I can grasp all of the implications of The General's philosophy yet, especially when it's applied to what you're leading up to."

"It's close to Muslim beliefs concerning the relationships between men and women: chivalry and its derivative, romantic love, but without the limits imposed by philosophies of scarcity. If a person, man or woman, can do justice to more than one mate, what's immoral about it?

"This is a world of abundance, Sendi, and that includes love . . . ."

Vaivan held out both her bandaged hands to me. "Sendi Boldwon, Tsaya and I know you're capable of providing unlimited love and respect. You're a free person in a universe of abundance. Something may still be rare, but it no longer has to be scarce, *moapa*."

I should end these memoirs as they began: in Topawa with flags flying, soldiers marching in the streets, and shops and schools closed. A year from the day I set foot in the United Mitanni Commonwealth, it was again a holiday, but things had changed.

Oh, how they'd changed! We'd survived our first great challenge and ordeal.

And I'd come through my own as well.

Celebrations, holidays, and other social functions are the glue that holds people together in their social institutions. I used to dislike ceremonies and celebrations until I went through the culture shock of the Commonwealth. Now their meanings are more clear to me.

The Sunday parade at the Academy in which the cadets march in ancient uniforms and obsolete military formations reminds them and the spectators of the thread of history that's never really broken.

Although Christmas and New Years' are now almost universally celebrated as altered versions of ancient ceremonial holy days, the Commonwealth celebrates them for new reasons as well.

But I wasn't in the Commonwealth that day to be part of the celebration there.

I insisted on participating in a special celebration.

We unveiled a plaque of Kulala gold on the outside of the Commonwealth L-5 module so that it faced the entire Universe.

ASTRABAD
named for
OMER KOLIL ASTRABADI
2025 - 2050
in honor of
all those who performed
to their limits
to free the human race
from the bondage of limits.

Trite. Schmaltzy. Melodramatic.

But history's full of such things. So is life. People's lives everywhere are full of little melodramas when they strive for high ideals. People's lives are full of heroisms regardless of the cultures they live in.

Culture, civilization, and humanity grow and progress because prople try to better themselves and their children. All great civilizations have depended upon this. The Commonwealth's an example of what can be accomplished when people decided to try by freeing themselves, decided that the future could be better if they worked to make it so, and discovered there's such a thing as hope to carry them through the difficult times.

As for myself, I find it impossible to label as "trite" the concepts of freedom—of choice, of trade, of type of social institution, or of anything else.

Whether we'll make it or not remains to be seen. But I think we will. We'll try. I think we'll finish the job my forefathers started in 1776.

It's too early yet to tell.

Ask my children three hundred years from now if you can find them among the stars.

APPENDIX 1

The United Mitanni Commonwealth

PEOPLE: *Population* (2050) 3,597,628. *Age distri* 0-14: 21.3%, 15-59: 61.4%, 60+: 17.3%. *Ethnic groups* not applicable; data not available. *Languages* English (official); Arabic, Galla. *Religious* Catholics: 11%; Protestants: 22%; Muslim: 32%; Hindu: 21%; other: 14%.

GEOGRAPHY: *Area* 567,300 sq.km., slightly larger than California. *Location* on Indian Ocean coast of Africa. *Neighbors* Ilkan Empire on N, Chibka Socialistic Republic on S, Kingdom of Malidok and Emirate of Kalahol on W. *Topography* Toak Plains rise sharply to altitude of 500-2000 meters (1640-6560 feet) from sandy coastal area and extend inland for 350 km. to meet the Dilkon Range of mountains rising as high as 4328 meters (14,200 feet) (Mount Doradun) through which 5 main passes at elevations of at least 3500 meters (11,500 feet) breach the Dilkon Range to the continental interior. *Capital city* Topawa. *Cities* Topawa (423,000), Pitoika (130,000), Chukut (53,000), Liupp (32,000), Oidak (55,000), and Vicrik (31,000) ar largest. Vamori Free Space Port and its Vamori City metro area have estimated population of 25,000 including transients.

GOVERNMENT: President Conobabi Chukut Nogal b. 14 July 2002, in office 20 July 2048. *Local divisions (countries)* Topawa, Liupp, Chukut, Vicrik, Oidak, Vamori Free Space Port, Maralha, Morosabe, and Kulala. *Armed forces (impys)* LandImpy 200,000; CoastImpy 10,000; AirImpy 50,000; SpacImpy 20,000; total regulars 280,000; reserves (CitImpy) approximately 1,500,000 additional.

ECONOMY: *Industries* space craft, astronautic equipment, primary metals, plastics, ceramics, light high-technology industries, tourism. *Chief crops* feed grains (wheat, millet), legumes, soy beans, cotton. *Minerals* iron, coal and coke, bauxite, molybdenum, manganese, chromium, titanium, gold silver, sapphires, granite. *Other resources* timber, fish, salt *Per capita arable land* 6.69 hectares. *Meat prod* beef 428,000 tons, lamb 30,000 tons, fish 52,500 tons. *Electric prod* 48,880.8 gWh (includes 5 gW SPS rectenna). *Labor force* 43.6% industrial, 31.3% agricultural, 20.7% services & professional.

FINANCE: *Currency* tally and score (100 score = 1 tally (approx. 0.936 tally = $1.00 US). *Gross domestic product* $8.8 billion. *Per capita income* $2446.70. *Imports* $2.75 billion. *Exports* $2.76 billion. *Tourists* 1,200,000, revenues $632.4 million. *National budget* $4.425 billion expenditures. $5.535 billion revenues; international reserves $3.25 billion. *Change in consumer prices* +1.05%.

TRANSPORT: *Motor vehicles* 703,300 in use. *Airports* 22; 3 international. *Airline service* 14 international carriers including 2 Commonwealth internationals; 4 internals. *Railroads* 8,100 track km. *Roads* 22,086 km. surfaced. *Seaports* Pitoika, Vamori, Liupp, Maralha.

COMMUNICATIONS: Telephones 1,760,000; TV sets 985,000; radios 2,500,000 (est). Int. & ext. networks are satellite-based.

HEALTH: *Life expectancy at birth* 97.6 years male, 98.7 years female. *Population increase* 1.87% annual. *Pop. per physician* 933. *Pop. per hospital bed* 175. *Infant mortality per 1000 live births* 7.3.

EDUCATION: *Literacy* 97.6%. *Pop. 5-19 in school* 98.3%. *Students per teacher* 38.

PHYSICAL QUALITY OF LIFE INDEX: 94.5

COMMENTS: "The Japan of the Tropics," the Commonwealth has risen in 50 years to a position of leadership in the developing world and one of the bridging nations to the Post-Industrial World of the remainder of the planet. By virtue of its Vamori Free Space Port, it has become a leading spacefaring nation with more space craft registered in the UMC than any other country. The nation is characterized by long-range planning, embracement of high-technology, adoption of selected parts of import cultures, high personal and industrial productivity, high sense of personal responsibility among citizens, the work ethic of the successful industrial nations of the past two centuries, and a strong base of free enterprise coupled with national pride and a compassion for other developing nations. The Commonwealth has developed strong international friendships because it has chosen a low-key competitive economic policy in the world markets. The Commonwealth is also respected because of its latent military strength which depends upon universal military training and, hence, a very large trained reserve. The strong military posture has been necessary because the nation's success has created envy among some nations, especially among its neighbors.

rom *The Terrestrial Almanac and Book of Facts, 2050,* Telenews Enterprises, Inc., Houston, USA. Used with permission.)